UNSIRED

Lawrence Hardin

This book is dedicated to my loving wife Laura and our amazing children
Andrew, Connor and Wesley. Without your belief in me,
I would never have been able to complete this work.

Chapter 1

"Please stop!"

A woman's quavering voice cried from the shadows of the first-floor apartment as Ashton hurried by, late for work. Then came the distinct sound of someone getting slapped, followed by a gasp and the sound of crying.

Ashton stopped in his tracks and looked towards the shadowed patio. He couldn't see anything, but he heard the woman's sobs and the man when he hissed at her.

"I told you, don't you ever tell me what to do. Now, shut your mouth and get inside. It'll be dawn soon."

"Are you OK ma'am?" Ashton asked, purposefully making his voice deep and strong. He took a step towards the patio.

"Mind your own fucking business," a seething voice warned from the shadows.

"I was talking to the other lady. Are you OK, ma'am?" he contemptuously replied.

Without warning, a man jumped out from the shadows and over the waist-high concrete wall of the patio. Before the man could even land, he heard the woman's voice, filled with fear as she pleaded, "no, no, no!"

The man straightened to his full height, which wasn't much, only feet away from Ashton. Ashton guessed the man was no taller than five-six and had a rail-thin body. He knew not to dismiss the guy as a threat. The man might have a knife or a gun but was only wearing boxers and had almost nowhere to hide one.

"You just had to mouth off, didn't you? Not enough that you don't mind your own business, but you think you can talk to me like that?"

"Hey, I call them like I see them. Why don't you get out of here and never come back?" Ashton took another step towards the patio, from where he could hear the woman pleading. To her, he said, "It will be OK, ma'am. Just get his stuff and throw it out to him. He's leaving."

"I'm going to love draining you, juice box," the short man said in a flippant and overly confident voice. Ashton turned towards him, the odd threat leaving him puzzled.

If the threat confused Ashton, the follow-through completely shocked him. Instead of punching or kicking, the man leaped onto Ashton with the alacrity of a cheetah. As fast as lightning, the man grabbed his left shoulder in an iron grip. His strength did not match his slight frame. Searing pain shot through Ashton's shoulder as the man mercilessly bore down. The man's other hand pushed Ashton's head back and to the right, exposing his neck. His feet rested on Ashton's thighs like he was climbing a tree.

"No! Please, stop it, leave him alone!" the weak voice of the woman croaked. Ashton did not know who she wanted to be left alone.

As Ashton forced his hands between himself and the crazy man, searing hot lightning blasted into his neck as teeth pierced his flesh. Ashton felt his blood squirt out. He panicked at the thought of the man ripping his jugular vein. He tried to push the man off, but that only made his body lift in the air. His teeth and hands acted as a pivot, creating a macabre image of a trunk opening. The pressure and pain on his neck didn't change. Finally, Ashton tried punching the man, but the blows didn't seem to have any effect.

Warmth radiated into Ashton's neck and spread throughout his body. He heard a slurping sound coming from the man's mouth, and the phrase juice box echoed in his mind.

"Is he...drinking my blood?"

Ashton's panic mounted. The man lifted his head and covered the wound with his hand as blood gushed out. His hand deflected the blood, and some sprayed back onto Ashton's face.

Dark, hate-filled eyes sat atop the blood-stained mouth of the small man. He gasped for air like a drowning man erupting through the water's surface or after chugging a beer. The latter idea caused Ashton

2

to shiver involuntarily. The man waited for Ashton's gaze to meet his. When it did, Ashton panicked.

"Sh, sh," the man tried to calm Ashton. "It's OK. Relax. I don't like my meat to taste gamy."

To Ashton's amazement, the words had their desired effect on Ashton. He immediately felt relaxed. Confusion and fear still showed in his eyes, but his body relaxed, and he slowly fell to his knees, arms limp at his sides. The man pushed him back until he lay flat. He lifted the hand that stopped the wound and put his mouth back onto his neck as if he were drinking from a pierced water balloon.

The warm feeling returned. As it grew, a euphoric feeling spread. Ashton could feel the blood drawn from his body. The man gulped it down, using each heartbeat to amplify the draw and the time between beats to swallow the precious blood. Ashton drifted into the most pleasant slumber he had ever known. The slurping and sucking sounds faded, and Ashton fought to keep his eyes open.

Without warning, the man on top of Ashton straightened at the waist and arched his back, arms trying to reach behind himself. As he did so, his head tilted back, and his mouth flew open, showing long white fangs protruding from the top of his mouth. A chunk of Ashton's neck pierced between the bony spears like meat on the tines of a fork. The euphoric and warm feeling left Ashton, and he bucked at his waist, trying to push the man off of him. He covered his neck with his hand. But he knew that wouldn't stop the bleeding. He just wanted the man off of him. Then he noticed the woman standing behind the man, holding onto something that looked like a short broom or mop handle. He followed the direction of the handle and then noticed that it wasn't short at all. Half of it was sticking out through the man's chest, under his rib cage and solar plexus. The other half protruded from his back. Blood was gushing out of the man's chest, running down the handle and splashing across Ashton's chest and neck. Ashton's bleeding had slowed as there wasn't much blood left in his body. Instead of squirting out with each slowing heartbeat, it seemed like the water level of a rocky beach, filling up a pocket here or there and then slowly draining out with the ebbing tide. Pools of blood gathered around the wounds on Ashton's neck. They filled with a mixture of his and the man's blood as it splashed onto his body.

"You missed my heart, you stupid bitch!" The man seethed at her, his hand almost on the make-shift stake protruding from his back.

She smiled back at him and pushed down on the handle, using his ribs to snap the wooden protrusion like kindling for a fire.

"Maybe I did, but this won't."

She spat at him and then plunged the broken stub into his heart. Ashton pushed the man over his head and towards the sidewalk.

Ashton knew he was dying and that nothing could save him. He didn't see how the man flew over his head, hit the ground, and rolled into a swath of sunlight bathing the ground. Nor did Ashton see the man burst into flames as his nearly naked body came to rest. By the time the battered woman dragged him by the arms into her apartment through the patio, he was already dead and couldn't have seen her come out later to disperse the ashes and pick up the charred boxers. Neither of them noticed the young man hiding near the trees in the parking lot across from the apartment.

Chapter 2

A few minutes after Ashton left his apartment, a lanky nineteen-year-old named Jacob Spence left his apartment in the building just south of where the violent confrontation would occur.

Jacob was out on the prowl, trying to catch a glimpse of any poor, unsuspecting woman who would have the misfortune of walking by a window in the early morning hours. Jacob had become obsessed with the perversion of being a peeping Tom since an accidental encounter a few years ago. For a variety of reasons, Jacob had to take a city bus to school early that day. He was still groggy from sleep and on his way to the bus stop when he looked up and saw a woman standing completely naked in front of her bathroom mirror. He stared through the second-floor window as she danced playfully while putting on make-up and singing into the mirror. She was in great shape, and her breasts swayed and bounced with her movements. He was captivated as if by magic, transfixed on the woman and excited by knowing what he was doing was wrong. From that day, he couldn't get enough of the perverse pleasure the experience offered.

He remembered it fondly and was still pissed that it would always be just a memory. From then on, whenever he went on his rounds, as he liked to call it, he always had his phone recording video. He wanted to amass a collection of as many different women as possible. He had even imagined what it would be like if one of his girls became famous. With some luck, he could get rich.

Jacob got up early every day and did his rounds, hoping for a score. It didn't take long for him to get a video of the woman who inadvertently started him down the dark path. In fact, he ended up with so much footage of her that he worried he was missing other opportunities by focusing on her. So he stopped going to her window. He didn't find out she had moved until almost three months after she had already gone.

It also didn't take him long to find which apartments had the best chance of paying off and where the best-looking women lived. He learned the hard way he needed to pay attention to what was going on around him while he was enjoying the view. While he watched a woman getting dressed one morning, another woman walking by noticed what he was doing and started yelling at him. He begged and pleaded with her not to call the police and promised never to do it again. He didn't keep his promise. Instead, he avoided that section of the sprawling complex for a few weeks and stayed more alert. Between constantly refining his methods, finding the best hiding places, and being extra vigilant, he continued his degenerate practice without detection.

It would be the sounds from what soon happened that morning that brought Jacob and his phone, video already recording, to the scene. He had started his day off, as usual, by scanning the apartments to the east of his building. Nothing was happening there, as usual. So, he hurried to the D building, where he had an eye out for the new beauty in 207D. To his joy, a light in her bedroom had just turned as he crouched next to a tree. She was close to his mother's age but still had a great body. The blind in the room was not down all the way. The gap at the bottom allowed him to zoom into the room, giving him a perfect shot of the bedroom and straight through to the bathroom. The woman in 207D got up and walked to the bathroom wearing a see-through nightgown. He could see that she had no bra or panties on as she walked to the bathroom. He could not wait for her to walk back to the bedroom as he would be able to see her from the front. He was getting more excited and impatient when an unexpected sound caught his attention.

Jacob couldn't tell what was said, but he could tell it sounded like there would be trouble. He couldn't decide between getting a video of a fight or the woman in 207D. When he looked at his phone again, he only saw a door. Jacob checked the room itself and realized that she must have closed the bathroom door. He decided to work his way towards the sounds.

Jacob had just crossed the parking lot and was making his way towards where he figured things were happening when he heard the man's deep voice say he was talking to the other woman. A step later and Jacob was able to see a tall man. He centered the camera on him right before someone jumped out of the shadows of the patio. Jacob nearly dropped his phone from the shock and crouched lower to stay out of sight.

"Wow," he whispered, adding commentary to the video.

Jacob kept both men in the frame and pointed out that the guy on the left was much shorter than the guy on the right.

"Little man better be careful." Before he could finish, the shorter man jumped on the taller man.

"What the...he crazy?" Jacob mused to his would-be audience. "I'm gonna try to get closer."

The camera jerked, and sounds of feet softly crunching gravel could be heard as he slunk out of the tree line and behind the corner of a parked SUV.

Then he saw the short guy pull his head away from the other guy's neck. He saw the blood and the evil look on the short guy's face, then the gulp for air before he buried his face back into the big guy's neck.

"Did you see that? He's biting that big guy." Then the big guy fell to the ground.

"He's down! He's down!" Jacob added in an excited whisper. Jacob watched the big guy get laid out on the ground. The other man kept doing whatever he was doing. It looked to Jacob like the man was eating the other guy's neck. He thought of zombies and giggled to himself.

Then the woman came out of the patio the short guy sprang from, holding a long stick, sharpened at one end. "Oh no, here comes crazy lady," Jacob whispered with shock in his voice. "She's got a spear." He tried to make a free Britney Spears joke. What happened next ended his desire to make a joke.

She plunged the make-shift spear into the little man's back. He snapped up with huge fangs that showed a chunk of meat hanging from them. Blood ringed his mouth and covered his neck and chest in drops. The woman pushed the wooden handle through the little man's back and out through his chest. A geyser of blood erupted from the wound and poured onto the man on the ground.

"No fucking way!"

Jacob couldn't believe what had just happened. His heart pounded and his legs, already tired from crouching behind the truck, began to tremble. He went to one knee to steady himself.

"She just...she...she..."

The amount of blood Jacob could see was unsettling. He thought he had heard the impaled man say something but wasn't sure what it was. Then came the loud snap, then the woman shifted the angle of the pole and shoved it back into the man's body. It did not come out the other side.

The big man on the ground managed to push the small man off. He flipped the small man over his head and into the sunlight as the dawn finally broke. Jacob felt pity for the small man and a sense of pride for the bigger man. He heard a muffled whooshing sound and then swung his camera to the guy in the sun a short distance from where things had just occurred. The small man burst into flames! He didn't scream, and he didn't move. He turned into a blackened outline of the man he was, with red glowing lines cracking the surface like firewood changing to embers. With a crackling and popping sound, the small man's form held for a moment and then crumbled to ashes.

"Holy shit, holy shit, holy shit....that guy just...poof...what the fuck? Oh, man. Oh, man."

Jacob was horrified and in terror over what he had just witnessed. The woman grabbed the bigger guy's feet and dragged him to the gate by her patio. He watched her reach over the gate to undo the latch and open the wooden door outwards. Using her hip, she propped it open and pulled the motionless man onto her patio. Darkness still enshrouded the patio preventing Jacob from seeing what she did. He heard her patio door slide open and assumed she was dragging the man into her apartment. A moment later, she came out to the spot where the man had burst into flames and used the head of a broom to disperse the ashes. Then she picked up a pair of scorched boxers and went back into her apartment. He heard the sound of her door sliding closed. Just like that, it was over. Jacob stood there, slack-jawed, trying to figure out what to do.

Chapter 3

Julia looked down at the mess of a man on her living room floor. She had seen him around the complex a few times. He seemed like a nice enough person and was always polite to her. She liked that he was tall and good-looking despite the bloodstains all over his face, neck, and chest. The terrible divot that Trevor had torn from his neck didn't help his looks much. That he had tried to help her was all that mattered to Julia.

What was his reward for such a brave deed? Death. If not completely dead yet, he would be soon. Once she got him inside and closed the patio door, she had checked his vitals. No pulse - no breathing - no chance. Part of her wanted to call 911 for help, but she had no way to explain what had happened without sounding like a schizophrenic basket case. Plus, she had a feeling that the big guy was down but not out. She was reasonably sure that the man on her floor would rise again as a vampire. Just thinking such thoughts reminded her how far down the rabbit hole she had gone in just nine short months. Back then, her life was going great. She was doing great at her new job and making good money. There wasn't anything happening in the romance department, and she was fine with that. She wanted to avoid any serious relationships until she was completely capable of being independent. Her cousin Robin had made the mistake of relying on someone from an early age, and now, at 45, she was on her own, rebuilding her life. Despite her best efforts, she realized she was in a similar mess, but not one of her own doing.

She could imagine how it would sound in a therapy session: "It wasn't my fault, honest! I had no control." Then the therapist would scribble notes and struggle not to smirk. "He's not even my boyfriend. He's an actual vampire!" she would protest, trying to keep her dignity intact. Then the eyebrows would go up, and they would talk about that. Julia never considered getting therapy an option.

Her mind clouded with a dark tempest of memories from her recent past. The rape, torture, control, and manipulation - all of that together - didn't compare to the humiliation she felt for what she had chosen to do to avoid more and more pain. Now, she faced a new chance for freedom. Trevor was dead. No doubt about that. She looked at the man on her floor again.

"What about you?" she asked the dead man.

"Are you going to be like him? Are you going to be worse?".

Julia had no idea what those answers were. Instead of wasting more time standing there and thinking, she wanted to be ready when he came back to life or unlife - or whatever she should call it. She walked to her bedroom and returned a few moments later, carrying a small rectangular jewelry case. She cradled it under her arm and then grabbed a chair from the dining room. She put the chair to the right side of the patio door and sat down. Then she set the jewelry box on the floor next to her.

Now she waited and watched the man stretched out on the floor. The gouge on his neck didn't look as deep or wide as it had minutes ago. She expected his wounds to heal quickly. After long nights of torment, Trevor would smear his blood over her before leaving to clear up all of the cuts and bruises he had inflicted on her. He told her that he wanted her to look her best the next time he saw her. One time, she had asked how the blood could heal her like that, and he said he didn't know.

"If it can bring a dead person back to life as a vampire, it isn't shocking that our blood can heal your wounds. It heals our wounds too."

He must have seen the horror on her face because he knew what she was thinking.

"Relax, when you die, you won't come back. You haven't drunk my blood."

Then he looked at her with that gleeful look he always had when he would say or do something to mess with her head.

"Or have you?"

After that, he regularly threatened to turn her and taunted her with how he would do it. He told her that once she drank his blood, all he needed to do was kill her, and she would come back as a vampire and be his toy forever. She would be under his control for all eternity. He told her that her death would be as painful as he wanted it to be. As long as her head didn't get completely severed from her body, she would rise again after dying. He seemed to glow when he talked of such things. It disgusted her how happy he became when planning to or was inflicting pain on others.

She shuddered, thinking of his cruel face and sinister smile. At the same time, she felt such relief that he was gone forever. Would the other vampires he had mentioned look for him? What about the man on the floor? How would he react to being transformed?

She was so tired at that moment. She opened the drapes enough to bathe herself in the sun's morning light then she took a small box from a compartment in the jewelry box. From with it she removed a golden crucifix and grasped it in her hand. Resting her head against the cool patio glass, she closed her eyes to rest before the man woke. Her mind began to wonder over the months since she met Trevor.

She drifted back to a time, about six months ago, when she had met Trevor for dinner with the hope of putting an end to his interest in her. She had driven out of the way to meet him for dinner. With her heels click-clacking on the pavement as she walked towards the entrance, she tucked her purse tight against her side with her elbow and built up her resolve. As she opened the door to go in, she hoped that maybe Trevor wouldn't show. He had stood her up a few times before and had never apologized or explained himself. Still, Trevor would call and set up another meeting, and she would agree. No matter what she planned to tell him when he called, she always agreed to see him again. Nothing about him appealed to her. She wasn't attracted to him, didn't find him to be charming, funny, or otherwise engaging. Yet, here she was, meeting him for dinner. Again, she held out hope that he wouldn't show. To her disappointment, he was already there. As Julia approached the hostess, Trevor came out of the men's room and nonchalantly walked to Julia. He greeted her with a nod and walked back to the seating area. Julia had come to expect this rude treatment from Trevor. It added to her confusion over why she gave him the time of day. Julia shook her head and followed him. This time, she was going to end whatever was between them.

After he placed his order of a few different rolls from the sushi menu, the waitress had turned to Julia and asked, "And what can I get for you?". Julia began to speak when Trevor told her to be quiet. She was stunned that he would be that rude and began to protest. Nothing came out - she couldn't speak. She was more confused by this, and she sought the waitress for help.

By then, the waitress had looked at Trevor with disgust.

"She'll have the same, thank you." He informed her.

He took Julia's menu, put it with his, handed them to the waitress with a warm smile as if nothing had happened. The waitress looked at Julia, who looked at Trevor with disbelief written on her face. The waitress was about to say something when Trevor turned to her and said, "now run along and take care of our order - everything is fine here." The waitress smiled, took the proffered menus, and went about her business. Julia couldn't believe it.

Once they had eaten, the waitress offered them the dessert menu. Trevor refused for the both of them and informed the waitress - and Julia - that they would be taking the air and were ready to leave. When the waitress brought the check, Trevor handed it to Julia.

"Be a dear and take care of that. It's the least you can do." He smiled as Julia, against her screaming mind to do otherwise, removed her wallet from her purse and placed cash on the table, enough to leave a very generous tip.

"Come now, don't be stingy." He looked at the remaining money in her hand she was about to put back into her wallet.

"Leave the rest of it. After all, you did make such a scene."

He smiled such a contemptuous and condescending smirk that she immediately wanted to smack him and tell him just what he could do with the bill. Instead, she watched herself set the money on the table.

A few minutes later, they entered the park - which was just down the block from the restaurant. They walked side by side, the silence growing uncomfortable as they moved. As Trevor led the way along the sidewalk, he casually reached back to take her hand. She noticed what he was trying to do and pulled her arm away.

Sensing her need to speak, Trevor released her from his command of silence.

"If you have something to say, please do."

"I'm sorry, Trevor, I don't feel that way about you." She explained to him. "I don't think it's a good idea to keep seeing each other. I hope you understand." She made sure to project kindness and concern into her voice.

While she waited for a reply, his shoulders began to shake. Immediately, she felt sorry and began to reach out to put her hand on his shoulder to comfort him. Before her hand had touched his shoulder, she heard laughter coming from him. He wasn't crying as she had thought. He was laughing! As the reaction was so unexpected, Julia grew concerned. She had been in similar situations in her life where the guy didn't react as she expected. Once, the guy had gotten so angry that she thought he might hit her.

"Oh, man, that's rich," he chuckled. Taking a deep breath, he briefly stopped laughing and then burst out laughing more intensely than before. Julia began to wonder if she was safe. She looked back over her shoulder to see if her car was close enough to run to and to see if there were other people around. Julia hadn't seen anyone in the park ahead of them. She began walking back towards her car.

At the sound of her heels hitting the sidewalk, Trevor turned to her. He wiped tears of mirth from his eyes. If the laughter had concerned her, the look on his face frightened her. She feared his cruel visage as he stared lustfully at her.

"You think that you can decide? Do you think that you have a say? You? Really?" his eyes narrowed as his lustful smile turned into a baleful smirk. Julia slowed but did continue her backward movement towards the car.

"Trevor, let's be adults about this, OK? I don't feel that way about you - I don't. I didn't mean to lead you on. I don't even know why..." her voice trailed off. She didn't even know how to explain herself. She also didn't want to be hurtful to him or make him more unstable.

He just stood there watching her with his beady, narrowed eyes as she continued to put distance between the two of them. He waited until she turned her back to him as she began to walk more quickly towards her car before he spoke.

"Stop!" he commanded in a voice that was only slightly louder than usual.

Her mind scoffed at the idea, but her body immediately halted. She tried to keep walking but remained rooted to the spot. Her heart began to pound, and her breathing quickened. She didn't know what was going on and felt trapped.

"What is happening?" she wondered aloud as the panic built inside her.

"Turn around and face me," he said in the same voice.

She turned to face him, fists clenched, eyes wide, and panic written on her face.

"Now, walk over to me and stand before me." He had a smirk on his face that she wanted to wipe off. She didn't want to move, but her traitorous body walked straight over to him, stopping about one foot before him. She was taller than he, especially in the heels she was wearing. She had no choice but to tilt her head down at him when she looked him in his eyes.

"You like that, don't you, Julia? You like looking down at men, at me. " His words seethed hatred at her, which she didn't understand.

"No, I don't. " Julia stammered, unsure of what to say.

"I wonder if I would like looking down at you?" he smirked at her.

Julia didn't know what to say or think. She remained silent.

"Get on your knees, Julia. Kneel before your man." His smile turned into a snicker as she began to obey.

Her mind screamed at her to refuse and run out of there. Despite her best efforts, her body betrayed her mind, and she quickly knelt before Trevor, paying no regard to her hose or her shoes as she did so.

"What is going on? How are you doing this?" Panic filled her voice.

Trevor straightened a bit as he looked down at her. "Yes, I rather prefer things this way, Julia. I am your superior, not the other way around as you think. I am your master, and you will do whatever I say. I know you don't understand it, but you don't have to."

She shook her head, and her panic and anger welled up inside her. Through clenched teeth, she muttered, "Never!". She looked up at him defiantly and then started to look around the park again.

"Look at me, Julia, look me in the eyes." He said in a calm yet powerful voice. Using every ounce of her willpower, digging her nails into the palms of her hands to use pain to break whatever spell he had cast on her, and praying didn't stop her eyes from seeking his out.

"No, no, no," she whimpered.

Trevor's smile widened.

His smile slowly vanished and changed to an almost tender appraisal.

"You are much more beautiful this way."

He reached down to caress her face with the palm of his hand. She turned her head away, but her eyes remained locked onto his. She thought she noticed a brief flash of pain pass through his eyes before they flared into a rage. He raised his hand to strike her. He held it menacingly in the air, seemed to think better of hit, and patted the top of her head instead.

"Stay there," he said and took five measured paces away from her. Her eyes remained locked on his. "Now crawl to me, Julia. Come to me on your hands and knees."

Immediately, she clambered towards him, fighting each movement futilely.

"Stop it! Stop it!" she began to shout at him.

He smiled, put his finger to his mouth, and hushed her. "Shhh, be a quiet little girl."

She couldn't speak. She couldn't close her eyes or change her course. Her knees hurt from several small pebbles she knelt on during her shameful journey to Trevor. Along the way, her purse slipped from her shoulder onto the ground. Once she was before him, her head craned back to see his eyes as she came to rest.

He smiled and put his hands on his hips. "Do you understand yet?"

Eyes remaining fixed on his, she shook her head.

"I am your master, Julia. I have been since we first met. You don't remember all of the details. Perhaps someday I will allow you to. Right now, I need to remind you of your place. On your knees, crawling to me is a good start. You don't like how I can control you. Who would? Using that ability makes this boring to me. What fun is there if only I am playing? Plus, you need a lesson. You need to know that I can make you do anything without this control." He looked around the park. "Ah, here we go - this will be fun."

Julia tried to follow his eyes, but she couldn't tear her eyes away from Trevor's. Realizing that she couldn't see, he released her from his command. "Look at the lovely couple coming into the park, dear." His voice had taken on a sing-song quality - he was enjoying himself.

As soon as he spoke the words, she followed his eyes back the way they had entered the park. An elderly couple, one she recognized from the restaurant, was walking along the same sidewalk Trevor and Julia were on. Julia tried but couldn't stand or speak. She began to fear for the couple and became embarrassed of her predicament.

As the couple approached, they showed their confusion at the scene before them. The woman was whispering something that Julia couldn't quite make out. Julia thought that the woman was telling the man to do something or maybe it was to ignore it. She couldn't tell which it was.

"Good evening," Trevor said in a bright, enthusiastic voice. He even tipped an imaginary hat at them. "Lovely night for a walk, wouldn't you agree?".

"Um, yes. It's a fine night for it." The man stumbled over the words. He was perturbed by what he saw. "Is there something we can help the young lady with?" He continued after the woman - who was clutching the man's bicep with both of her hands - shook him gently into action.

"Her? Oh yes, yes indeed. You can most certainly help her if you wish. Do you wish to help her?" Trevor asked, looking from Julia to the man. Now that they were close, she did notice them from the restaurant and remembered thinking how cute they were, holding hands during their meal.

"Yes, of course, if I can, I will." The man strode toward Julia, shaking his arm free and telling his wife to "Just relax!".

Trevor stepped between the man and Julia. "If you want to help her, please give her a nice smack on the ass. She has been naughty and needs a spank." Trevor looked over his shoulder at her, a devilish gleam in his eye.

Julia implored Trevor to stop, using only her eyes. She shook her head no.

Trevor shrugged.

"W-w-w-what did you say, young man? You want me to what?" the man was bewildered. Trevor shifted to stand next to him, both looking down on Julia. The woman made her way to the other side of the man, "Henry, we should get going."

Ignoring the lady, Trevor repeated his instructions. This time he compelled his obedience. The man strode forward, and Julia could see the confusion in his eyes. He even looked around to see if someone was pushing him.

"Now wait a minute!" the man objected but continued to walk towards Julia.

His wife moved to intercept him, and Trevor told her to stand still and be quiet. She immediately did so.

Henry stood next to Julia and bent slightly forward. His hand reared back.

"Make it a good one!" Trevor added at the last moment.

Henry's arm cocked back further, and once it reached its full measure, he swung it forward, landing his hand firmly on Julia's rump. A loud smack rang out over the grounds. She rocked forward on her hands and knees, closing her eyes to hide the pain and humiliation.

"I'm sorry...I don't know what - how - I.." The man walked back towards his wife. "Come on, Pat, let's get out of here." Pat couldn't budge or say anything. The man tugged on her, and she nearly fell over.

"Be sure to thank the good man for giving you what you deserved, Julia."

"Thank..y-y-you for giving...me...what...I deserved." As she spoke, tears of shame and impotence spilled from her eyes. Henry looked to his equally terrorized wife for comfort.

"Just a moment, good sir." Trevor stepped towards the couple and whispered a few things. A moment later, the couple walked back the way they came. Trevor was beaming - Julia was not. Her shame was complete.

He said, "I may have outdone myself with that one. Wouldn't you agree, darling? Come now, answer me."

"You're a monster. What is wrong with you?" She gasped, finally able to say what she was thinking. "You need to leave them alone. They did nothing to you, and neither did I - for that matter. However you are doing this, I will find a way to stop it."

"Oh dear, you still don't get it, do you. Well, be sure to check the news for the next few days for anything about this couple. When you find it, you'll know." He laughed aloud.

"What did you say to them?" she was sure she didn't want to

know.

"That? I just told them to go home and make love to each other. Genius!" he clapped his hands together and rocked forward on his feet.

Julia didn't understand. What was wrong with that? Sure they were elderly, but they seemed healthy enough. Then it dawned on her. She recalled how she obeyed whatever he told her to do or not do. Trevor was watching her closely while trying to seem that he wasn't. When she realized that he hadn't told them to stop and that they would keep at it, the look of pity and disgust told Trevor she had figured it out.

"I know, right?" he taunted her. "I wonder who will last the longest."

She couldn't believe how sick Trevor was. When she eventually saw the news and found out that the man outlived the woman for at least two days before he succumbed to exhaustion, she began to have an idea.

"Now, don't you think it is a good time to learn how to be a good girl without my needing to take charge? As I said, it gets boring playing the game all alone. I like a willing participant."

He stood next to her, putting his hand on her head like a dog. She watched as he started scanning the park again, looking for someone else to include in his twisted games.

Maybe she could get him to stop.

"You don't need to show me anything else, Trevor. I see you are in..." she swallowed loudly and then whispered, "...in charge."

"Really? You think so?" He squatted down next to her, raised an eyebrow, and looked into her eyes. He shook his head.

"I'm not convinced." They both knew he could do whatever it was and make her tell the truth. Instead, he wanted to torment her further.

"I do, Trevor. I think you are in charge. Please, don't hurt anyone else." She also looked around, hoping that no one was coming to the park.

"OK, you can convince me." He took several steps away from her, looked from her to his feet several times like he was measuring something, tilted his head, took one more step back, and then looked her in the eyes.

"Crawl over here, kiss my feet and tell me I am your master. Do that, and I will believe you. You can also have this back." He dropped her purse next to his right foot.

She tried to move forward and was dismayed to find she could. As she slowly moved forward, she was vaguely aware of a car pulling into the parking lot at the other end of the park. She heard a few doors open, and a woman called out, "Now wait for us boys, I need to get your sister in the stroller, and your dad is getting the football."

"Is it the glow-in-the-dark one?" One of the boys asked.

"It sure is," the deeper voice of a man replied.

She stopped crawling and looked over her shoulder at the family. Then she looked back at Trevor, expecting him to be staring at the family. Instead, he was looking sympathetically at her. He smiled and slightly turned his head to say, "Well?".

She hurried her efforts and tried to shut her mind to the humiliation she was putting herself through. She was so tired from the emotional roller coaster, and she just wanted it to end. As she drew closer to Trevor, she fought against subjecting herself to this humiliation. Once she did, it would never stop. She crawled slower and slower as she approached Trevor.

"Oh, that is such a happy family. A mommy, a daddy, and three little piggies. Aren't they just adorable? Maybe they'll let us play with them?" he looked down at her. "Should I ask?"

She shook her head and closed the gap that was between them. She stopped above his feet.

"Please, don't make me do this! Please, just go and leave me alone," she looked up at him with such pain and desperation that any decent man would have been unable to resist her earnest pleas.

Trevor was anything but ordinary. "I thought that you understood Julia. I am not making you do anything. It's up to you. You can convince me or..." he looked off in the direction of the family. Their voices grew louder as they approached the swings and the open field area, which wasn't far away.

She hung there, supported by her hands and knees, looking at his black tennis shoes. They weren't filthy, but they were not clean either. Far from it, to be precise.

"Oh, it looks like mommy noticed you on your hands and knees. She's pointing you out to her hubby." He extended his hand high over his head and waved.

He looked down at her. "She looks pretty. Maybe I'll save her for last. So many options. I know, how about a game of eeny meeny miny moe".

She quickly closed her eyes and kissed his feet.

Her mouth was dry, and she was shaking with humiliation and rage. She looked up at Trevor.

"And?" he smirked down at her in satisfaction.

As she said the words, something inside of her broke. "You are my master."

He saw what was going on inside of her. He had played this game many, many times before. "Now grab your purse, and let's go." He turned and walked towards his car. Julia grabbed her purse and followed. Inside she flooded with relief at having been able to spare the family from this monster's games.

They went to her apartment for the first time that night. One thing that never crossed her mind as Trevor followed her was that she was about to learn that vampires were real. That she would be fed upon for the first time never crossed her mind. Trevor's only first for the night was that he tasted Julia's blood. For Julia, it was the beginning of a long and painful nightmare.

Before leaving that morning, he looked at the battered and broken woman on the bathroom floor. "I'll be back in a few days, darling. Please be a peach and clean yourself up for me. Oh, you can tell anyone you like that I am a vampire." Two protruding fangs now punctuated his wicked smile. They didn't hang down over his lip as she had seen in movies. They fit neatly in his mouth, resting over the teeth below.

He bent down, grabbed her chin in his hand, and roughly tilted her head so that he could look her in the eyes. "I just wanted you to know that you need to clean your diet up. I could barely taste the misery in your blood."

Just like that, he left her alone on the cold tile floor of her bathroom. She lay there naked, except for the welts and bruises along her front and back. The scene would repeat itself over the next several months. She always suspected other things had happened, but no matter how hard she tried, she could not remember them. Now that Trevor was dead, more memories surfaced, and Trevor's methods of control and manipulation were much easier to identify. She shivered as she recalled one of the last memories he had wiped from her mind.

After a seemingly endless night of torture at the hands of the despicable monster, Julia was on the verge of dying. He had taken too much blood from her and had inflicted too much pain. Julia could now recall how eager she was for death as it would end the nightmare existence she now endured. As she slipped into oblivion, she saw a look of sorrow on Trevor's face. As he called to her to hold on, he had grabbed a knife from the kitchen. He knelt over her and cut a deep line across the outside of his wrist, opening an artery. He held it up to her, and his tainted blood filled her mouth. She was too weak to force it out and refused to swallow. She lost consciousness, and her body betrayed her, taking the in blood to clear her throat. She awoke with no memory of the incident and felt better than she had for months. Her internal soreness was gone, as were the many slow-healing cuts and bruises on her body. Trevor had saved her from death but also contaminated her with his disease. Whenever she did die, she would rise again as a vampire.

She never heard the words he spoke as his blood healed her body. "You have no idea what I must do next to protect you," as he stood to leave her, he added as an afterthought, "and me."

The sounds of gasping and deep breathing pulled Julia back from her walk down memory lane. Quickly, she put the crucifix back into the jewelry box and pulled the drapes over the glass patio door, leaving it pulled away from the door so that sunlight bathed her where she sat. She kept her hand on the drapes so she could pull them open if things started to get worse, and if that didn't work, she could open the door and run into the safety of the light.

Chapter 4

Ashton awoke from the most bizarre and vivid dream of his life. It was filled with strange people and places, floating around his mind like a discordant montage of inherited memories. They seemed somehow familiar, yet the connection to him was lacking. At some points in the dream, he heard languages he knew little of, like French or Spanish, and others he suspected of being German and Russian. Others were unrecognizable. The unusual tones and inflections served to disorient and confuse him. Some distant part of himself seemed to understand the words, but their meaning remained hidden. The dream ended with a choppy replay of the fight he was just in, but it was from the perspective of his attacker. He saw himself through the eyes of the guy who had bitten and tried to kill him. Ashton had never seen himself look so large before. It was very unsettling to him. When he woke, his mind wanted to drift back into the fantasy realm of his dreams. When he thought of a specific part of the dream, his mind jumped back to it and replayed it from that sequence. If his mind focused on other thoughts, it would fade into ripples of memories like echoes from the past. Then, if he refocused his mind on something from the dream, he was pulled back into it.

Slowly, he drifted to the present.

As his eyes opened, he found himself in strange surroundings. He realized that he lay on the floor in someone's living room. To his left was a cream-colored sofa with several pillows on its cushions and a decorative blanket draped over the back. To his right sat a metal-framed coffee table with a glass top and a few unlit candles on its surface.

As he became acclimated to his surroundings, a dull thudding spread throughout his head, pounding in slow and steady waves. As he looked around the rest of the room, he noticed an intense and bright light coming from what he knew to be the patio area. Then he saw a figure sitting in a chair next to the patio door. He could tell it was a woman and that it was probably the woman from the patio, but the intensity of the light washed out her features, making identification impossible.

He propped himself up on his right elbow and held his left hand in front of his face, shielding his eyes from the light. Squinting his eyes almost shut, he found that he did recognize the woman.

"Hello?" his voice was raspy and dry. He didn't know whether or not the woman heard him. He swallowed and tried again.

"Hello? Are you OK?"

Holding himself up was getting difficult. Ashton felt very shaky, and the light was drilling into his pounding head. Drawing his legs up, he pushed his back against the couch and rested his head on his knees. Then he remembered his neck.

He reached his hand to the wound, and it was gone! He started patting around the area on his neck to see if he could find it. Nothing was there except dried blood on his skin and shirt. He pulled the shirt away from his neck and chest to look at it. There was a bloodstain running down its side. The right side of his body appeared covered with blood. Yet, no matter where he checked, there was no trace of an injury.

He was trying to figure out what was going on when a trembling voice startled him with her answer.

"I'm OK, thanks. You are in my apartment. I dragged you in here after he, after Trevor attacked you."

Ashton wanted to see her expression. But, between his headache and the bright light washing over her, he couldn't look at her long without involuntarily looking away.

"Uh, thanks...would you mind closing the blinds a little bit? I have a terrible headache, and the light..., it really hurts my eyes."

The sound of the drapes dropping to cover the sliding door and the immediate relief from the brightness served as her answer. He raised his head slowly, looked at her, and started to say thanks. His voice trailed off into his shock at the sight of her.

She had bruises all over her face. Ashton could tell that most of the bruises were a few days old. They were in what he and his friends used to call the mustard stage when bruises turned that faded yellowish color around traces of deeper bruising. Her bottom lip was swollen and split. There were numerous cuts on her cheekbones, surrounded by still other bruises. Around her neck was a wicked collar of deep purple. When he looked at choke marks, a vision of hands squeezing her neck flashed in his mind. A disturbingly sexual jolt accompanied the images. His stomach turned. His eyes continued to inspect her, and he noticed how thin the woman was. It was too much for him.

He tried his best to smile as he looked into her eyes.

"Thanks for dragging me in here."

He noticed the defiance in her eyes, realizing she had observed him looking at the catalog of abuse written on her very being. He felt smaller for it, somehow diminished by the fact that not only had a fellow human being done this to her, but it was also a man. Unwanted memories from his childhood threatened to break free of the protective shell he learned to keep them in. Then came the familiar anger, almost rage, as he struggled to contain his childhood demons.

The woman must have noticed the change in him. She shrank back in her chair and reopened the drapes, allowing the bright light to flood the room. The pounding in his eyes returned, throbbing with each beat of his heart.

"I am so sorry for what has happened to you. I wish I had known sooner. Maybe then I could have stopped it." He could sense her fear of him, and it unsettled him.

He quickly added in a defensive tone, "I was just trying to help you."

She stiffened in her chair and kept her hand on the drape, holding it out from the window, bathing herself in the light.

"I never asked you to get involved. It would have been better if you didn't."

Her words were like a smack to his face. Was she going to blame him now? Was she going to defend the guy who beat her, if not worse? He shook his head and closed his eyes, trying to calm himself. He decided that getting out of there and heading to work would be his best option. He thought of his appearance and amended his plan to go home, call work, shower, change and then get to work - maybe. Then he realized that he didn't know what time it was. He started patting his pockets, looking for his phone. The sudden movement made the woman gasp and stand up next to the patio door. She turned slightly and gripped the drape with both hands, preparing to open it entirely. She looked over her shoulder at him with terror etched on her battered face.

Ashton held his hands up, palms out in a placating gesture. "Easy! I need to find my phone to call my boss and tell him why I am running late. Then, I'll get out of your hair. I need to get home and get cleaned up. I don't want to bother you any more than I already have." Even though he tried not to, he crammed a ton of sarcasm into the part about bothering her, making it clear she was overreacting.

He saw her features sag a little as she must have realized that she was being less than cordial to someone who just tried to help her from being abused. She turned towards him but instead of sitting, she put her left foot against the wall, knee jutting out, and straightened her right leg. She rested her left hand on her left knee. She seemed to debate whether or not to let the drape close and eventually did so. She kept hold of it with her right hand.

She took a long, steadying breath and spoke in an even and measured tone. "My name is Julia. I appreciate the help, but you don't understand what was happening. I said it would have been better if you didn't get involved. I meant it would have been better for you. That bastard is dead, and he is going to stay that way. For your help in that, I will be forever grateful. It's just that..." she had such an endearing and pained expression on her face that Ashton didn't know what to think. Maybe if he just tried restarting the conversation, that would help. Taking his queue from her introduction, he tried to do just that.

"Hello Julia, my name is Ashton. It's nice to meet you." He tipped his head towards her and smiled ironically.

She made no move to come toward him for a handshake, and he didn't want to try getting up and going to her. He figured she would be wary of such action. She only nodded slightly in reply.

"You don't need to thank me for trying to help. I don't know the history of what was going on. But what that guy did, talking to you like that and hitting you. That was wrong."

He wandered his eyes over the atlas of abuse printed across her body.

"It doesn't seem like it was the first time either. If I didn't step in, I wouldn't have been able to live with myself. I thought about calling the cops, but we both know that they wouldn't have shown up soon enough to stop what he was doing."

When Ashton mentioned calling the cops, he patted his pockets, making it clear he was looking for something as she hadn't responded the last time he asked.

"Do you know where my phone is?"

He tried to lighten his expression to ease her fears. She shook her head.

"Your phone is broken. It fell out of your pocket when I drug you in here. So I put it on the counter, over there. The screen's cracked, and it doesn't turn on. Sorry."

She nodded towards the kitchen, and then he saw it on the counter. He stood up slowly and had to steady himself. His head was pounding, and he felt odd. He felt out of place or something similar to that - he couldn't exactly put his finger on the feeling. After holding his hand out to steady himself, he slowly walked to the counter and picked it up. Even though she had just told him it didn't work, he still tried. Nothing happened.

"Damn it!" he shook his head and dropped the hand holding the phone to his side. Then he slid it into his front pocket and turned toward Julia. The light was still bothering his eyes.

"Well, if you're OK, I need to get to my apartment. Do you want me to go out the front door or use the patio?"

He jerked his thumb over his shoulder in the direction of the small foyer off of the living room where her front door was.

"Before you go, we do need to talk about something important. It has to do with you." She remained still against the wall, eying him closely.

He looked at her, waiting for her to continue. She just stared at him. He decided to do the same and held her eyes. He hoped that she would tell him.

Several moments passed, and she had said nothing.

"Just tell me already, say something." He shouted the words at her in his mind. She flinched and looked terrified.

"No! Don't!" she shouted and closed her eyes and turned her head away.

Her outburst took him by surprise, and he staggered back a few steps, suddenly feeling very lightheaded and dizzy. He put his hand up to his head, rested his arms on the counter, and then shifted his weight to them. He wasn't sure if that would be enough to keep on his feet. From the corner of his eyes, he saw the dining room table and chairs. Carefully, he hooked the rear leg of one of the chairs behind his heel and dragged it next to him.

His legs gave out as he sat down, and he hit the chair with a grunt.

"Don't what?" he asked weakly, "I can barely stand, let alone do anything. Plus, I already told you I'm not going to do anything to you."

He was getting irritated, and then he remembered how jumpy his mother would be after his father came home between runs. He wouldn't find out for years that she always wore pants and long sleeves because of the bruises on her body. He felt like an asshole for getting upset with her for being scared. After all, she was the victim here. Then his thoughts turned to his injury, which somehow was gone. He began to feel very uneasy.

"I know, I know Ashton. I don't want to upset you either, but I'm afraid that there is no real way around it. Trevor, that man you, I mean, we fought. He was a monster. You have no idea how evil he was. I don't know if you are going to be like him now. He said not all of them are like him - that some are worse and some are not. He even said some even scared him."

Her eyes implored him for forgiveness.

"I'm so sorry, Ashton."

"Why would I be like him or them or whoever? Why are you sorry? I already told you it was my decision, not yours."

His confusion mixed with impatience. He was getting more uneasy the more Julia spoke.

"You just, you just don't understand." She almost whimpered. He could see tears starting to run down her cheeks. She began to shake her head.

She said, "I'm so, so sorry."

Ashton was starting to get very worried. He had a vague sense of her meaning. Something in his mind had walled the idea away to protect him from its implications and absurdity.

"Maybe I don't want to know."

His voice shook almost as much as his hands as he rested them on his knees. His sense of foreboding grew into a pulsating klaxon, shrieking warning and danger in his mind.

"Trevor was a vampire, Ashton. When he bit you, you died."

She licked her lips, unable to speak for a moment.

"His blood got all over you. He told me how one vampire makes another, and everything he said was there. He drank your blood, he shared his blood with you, and then you died. Now, you are back."

She hesitated, then said, "Now you're a vampire, Ashton."

Chapter 5

Jacob was barely able to catch the bus that morning. After the lady got the guy into her apartment and he was able to gather his senses, he stopped the recording and noticed the time.

If he had not sprinted to the stop, he would have missed the bus. The bus driver would not wait even thirty seconds longer. The driver had to stop at every bus stop on his route. If no one got on or off, he would pull away. Jacob had asked him about this the day after he missed the bus last year, wanting to know why the man would not wait a minute or two as he knew Jacob was always there. The driver reluctantly explained that he wasn't required to remember every person at every stop or their schedules. Plus, he had to be at every stop on time, or he would have to explain why he was not. Valid excuses for being late on a route did not include waiting for a rider. Jacob knew he could not argue with that, so he never brought it up again.

There he sat, desperately trying to catch his breath. He wanted to watch the video. He still had a hard time believing what he saw, even though he was there and recorded it. He knew that it had value. As he watched and rewatched it, he fantasized about becoming rich and famous. He would be the person who had revealed to the world that vampires existed. Jacob took a screenshot from the video where the woman stabbed the vampire, forcing his head back and fangs out. It took him a few tries to get the picture he needed. Then, he switched to the photo app and zoomed in on the face of the vampire.

"Smash! That's the cheddar!"

He sounded like a punk on Christmas. He glanced around the bus after that outburst. There were only two other passengers on the bus at that time. One was an elderly lady who was always there, and the other was a thirty-something who was there occasionally. Jacob did not know either of them.

At the next stop, his friend and coworker Evan would get on. He couldn't wait to show the video to him. Jacob had a sinking feeling. The video started with him doing his rounds, as he called it. Jacob did not know how to edit the video on his phone. Until he could delete the beginning, Jacob could not share it. He knew Evan would want a copy or tell him to post it on social media.

Jacob looked out the front window and realized that Evan's stop was coming up fast. He didn't have time to download an app to edit the video or look for a tutorial. Jacob needed to think of why not to share the video. Perhaps he had to keep it secret for now - until he could talk to a lawyer. That might be believable, providing that Evan would believe him about wanting to see a lawyer. Then there was the fact Jacob could not afford an attorney, and they both knew that. Jacob seemed to remember hearing something about getting a free legal consultation as part of their benefits package. He would have to check on that.

By the time Evan was on the bus, Jacob was already fantasizing about becoming famous. He was nervously bouncing his knees when the bus stopped, and Evan got on. Evan slowly walked to his spot across from Jacob while playing a game on his phone.

"Dude, you ain't playing? What up with that?"

Evan asked in his best imitation of a gang banger, one hand grabbing his crotch as he sat down across the aisle from Jacob.

"You missin' out on this raid! We strippin' these fools blind, dog."

Evan hadn't even bothered to look at Jacob. No sound was coming from his phone as his thumbs frantically raced around the bottom area of the screen as he controlled his character in the game.

"Yo E, some whack shit just dropped at my complex." Jacob's tone dropped the fake accent and grew worrisome at the end. Evan raised an eyebrow and shot him a quick look. He held up the index finger of his left hand.

Evan continued playing his game, sucked some air through his teeth, looked pissed, and looked at Jacob.

"What?" was all he said.

Jacob looked at the driver and then shot over to sit next to Evan.

"You gotta see this, bro. It's off the hook Cray Cray."

"Man, I don't want to see any of your pervy shit, bro." Evan looked disgusted.

Jacob remembered showing him one of his apartment videos last year. He said he didn't like it, but Jacob knew better. Evan didn't tell anyone at work about it either, so Jacob figured he could count on him to keep this secret too.

Jacob held his phone sideways and leaned in to get closer to Evan. Evan reached for the phone, but Jacob pulled it back and said, "No, watch it. You'll understand."

As Evan watched the video, Jacob looked at him to gauge his reaction. Jacob couldn't believe that Evan didn't react to the video. It ended without comment. Evan turned his attention back to his game.

"Not bad, bro. You made that this morning? How did you get them to be in it?" Evan asked disinterestedly.

"What?" Jacob asked, confused by the question.

Then he realized what Evan was thinking. He covered Evan's phone before he could protest, then he added, "no, this isn't a prank. That shit is real. That just happened about fifteen minutes ago. That guy was a real-life vampire!"

Evan stared at Jacob, his initial anger over having his game interrupted faded as he took on a more quizzical look.

"Man, how stupid you think I am?"

He started to return to the game, but Jacob's hand still held his phone. He gave Jacob a "What the fuck you doing?" look that would usually lead to Jacob moving his hand.

"Nah, bruh. I'm serious." Jacob dropped his street act. "It's real. Watch it again. You can tell I didn't edit it."

"Message it to me. I'll check it out later." He pulled his phone away from Jacob and cursed, "damn it, you made me miss the raid. You better hope I don't get kicked from the clan."

Evan put his phone in his pocket and glared at Jacob.

"I can't. I have to keep this private so that no one can share it." Jacob hoped that would end the debate.

"You don't trust me? What am I going to do with it?" Evan seemed a little offended.

"It's not that. I want to see a lawyer first. I want to make sure that I am the only one who will get credit for this. That's why I'm not going to post it anywhere until I can copyright it or whatever I have to do."

"Right, you're going to go to a lawyer? You broke like me, fool!"

They felt the bus slowing and realized they were at the stop by their work. Evan led the way off the bus as Jacob followed behind, keeping his voice as low as possible.

"I'm going to check with Rodger about the lawyer thing. I think we get a free session, or whatever it is called, through our benefits. If not, I might ask my dad about getting a free visit with a lawyer. He should know."

"Damn right! He's on, like, his twentieth DUI, right?" Evan chided him.

"More like his third." Jacob hated that his dad had a drinking problem and had terrible luck. He was a nice enough guy, but since he and Jacob's mother started having problems, he started drinking - really drinking. It ended up being one of the reasons he and his mother divorced. Until then, Jacob had only seen his father drunk once. It was after a New Year's party when Jacob was eleven. Now, he rarely saw his father sober.

"Third, thirtieth, he'll know," Evan teased.

While they walked the rest of the way to their building, Jacob verbally recounted what he had seen. By the time they got to their job, Evan was already tuning him out. Jacob took his silence for contemplation or maybe even fear. In reality, Evan believed that it was nothing more than a hoax.

They only had a few minutes before their shift started, and they hurried to their separate areas. When their first break at 10:30 rolled around, Jacob rushed to the break room to talk with his other friends, Mika and Carlos. When he walked into the break room, Mika and Carlos were sitting in their usual spot at one of the four tables.

Mika saw him first and nudged Carlos.

Pointing at Jacob, she said, "Look out, Carlos! It's Jacob Van Helsing, the vampire hunter!" They laughed.

"No, it's Cunt Dracula!" Carlos said in a thick Mexican accent.

Jacob was pissed. "So, Evan told you guys? What did he say?"

"He said you tried to get him to buy some b.s., Holmes...and you'd probably try to get us to buy it next." Carlos looked challengingly at him, daring him to try it, to tell him about the vampires.

Jacob turned to Mika. She nodded.

Jacob had planned to show them the video. Now, he knew it was pointless. By the time lunch rolled around, he would be the laughing stock of the entire company.

"Fucking Evan..." he muttered.

"Is that what the video is? You and Evan?" another voice called out from the other side of the break room. Their manager, Rodger, was standing in the doorway, a wry smile on his face. Although he was pushing forty, he still cracked jokes with his team.

"Isn't it against company policy for coworkers to be romantically involved?" Mika asked Rodger, barely able to stop laughing.

"That's right, Mika. Do I need to call HR on you and Evan, Jacob?" Rodger gave Jacob his best "you're in trouble" face. Then he chuckled. Mika and Carlos joined in.

"Ha, ha," Jacob replied sarcastically. Then he remembered he had a question for Rodger.

"Hey Rodger, do we get a free visit with a lawyer? I remember hearing something about that at one of our benefits meetings. You know anything about that?"

Rodger took on a more formal air after Jacob mentioned a lawyer. Mika and Carlos picked up on the change. Carlos put his hand on Jacob's shoulder and gently shook him.

"Dude, we just playin'. No need to get like that!" Carlos half-joked with him.

Mika stopped with her spoon of yogurt halfway to her mouth.

Jacob realized what they were thinking. "No, no, nothing like that. I want to make sure I get the credit for the video and get paid when it is on the news and stuff. I gotta look out for me."

The laughing started again, a little louder this time. Jacob waited for Rodger to make his way to the table next to them and open up the paper as he did every day.

"Seriously, Rodger, do you know about that?" Jacob asked him, trying to ignore Mika's and Carlos' giggles.

Rodger realized that Jacob was being sincere. "Yes, we get a free consultation once a calendar year. You can find out about it on the employee benefits portal."

Jacob was afraid of that. The portal was slow, and it took forever to find anything normal like payslips or benefits information. He didn't want to have to find it on his own. He knew Rodger would find it in two seconds.

"Can you send me the link Rodger? I want to look at it during lunch. I doubt I could find it by the time my lunch is over. Everyone knows how good you are at finding stuff on the portal." He hoped he didn't go too far by adding the compliment. It always worked for Mika.

She smiled at him and mouthed, "Bravo!" to him before Rodger made a show of snapping his paper and pulling one of the pages back with his finger to look at Jacob. It seemed as if he was evaluating his seriousness.

"Please?" Jacob even put his hands together in a pleading gesture.

"Fine." Rodger went back to his paper.

By the end of the day, Jacob had learned a few things. Evan told everyone about the video, and everyone thought that Jacob was nuts. He also found out that he had to wait two weeks for a free appointment. He could get in sooner, but it would cost more than he was willing or able to pay.

On the bus ride home, Evan tried to apologize to him, but Jacob didn't even care by then. He had realized that his road to fame and fortune would be a lonely one. Jacob would take it alone because the world had to know about vampires. Out of nowhere, inspiration hit.

"Maybe I could become a vampire?"

He smiled at the thought and lost himself in dreams of being immortal and having mind control powers over women. He didn't even hear or acknowledge Evan as he apologized again before getting off at his stop. He almost missed his bus stop.

After getting off the bus, Jacob initially thought to go to the apartment where everything had happened. Instead, he went home and searched for a way to edit his video. When Jacob watched it, it finally registered from where the idea of his becoming a vampire had come. He realized that not only did he have the only proof of the existence of vampires, but he might also have the only video showing their creation.

Jacob spent the rest of his night on research. He needed to know how to get safety deposit boxes and create a death plan. And, of course, how to vampire-proof an apartment. He finally fell asleep. A small bowl with freshly grated garlic sat on his window sill, a pop sickle crucifix pinned to his wall, and another in his hand. He had a list of to-do items on the nightstand next to his bed, where his phone lay charging. Last on the list - "blackmail tall man to become a vampire."

Jacob slept the best he had in years. He dreamed a series of dreams where he was an all-powerful vampire lord, with minions of sexy cheerleader vampire vixens awaiting his beck and call.

Chapter 6

Ashton wanted to laugh, make a joke, or even deny it, but something stopped him. The nagging feeling he had since waking up now lay exposed like a terrible secret thrust into the light of day. That is why she was camping out by the patio window. She was protecting herself. She was afraid of what he was, not who he was. Did it matter who he was any longer? Would he become a vile and evil creature of the night, driven by the lust for blood? Would he need to sleep in his grave? He didn't even have a grave, did he? Maybe he would be one of the types of vampires that went back to high school. He closed his eyes and shook his head. He didn't want to consider all of the possibilities.

More mundane concerns began to trouble him. What about his job? How would he support himself? Must he drink blood every day, several times a day, or once a day? His mind raced through the plethora of vampire books, stories, and movies. He was going to need help figuring some things out, and the only person that might be able to help - Julia - was terrified of him.

He rubbed his face with his hands and ran his fingers back through his hair, ending the motion by squeezing his head and then slapping his hands down on his knees.

"Damn!" he spat the word out like he wanted to spit out the curse on him.

"What am I going to do?"

He jumped to his feet, oblivious of Julia's startled reaction. He began to pace between the couch and the kitchen. To her credit, she jerked in her chair when he jumped up but did not react otherwise. She watched him closely and stayed ready to open the blinds and run into the light if she needed to.

As he paced, a tsunami of concerns crashed into the core of his being, threatening to pull him back into the dark depths of an ocean of despair. He had to deal with it. He had to make it right. Could he make it right? The torrent of worries and what-if scenarios created a storm of fear and panic inside him. His breathing began to quicken, and his steps came faster and faster.

"Ashton!" Julia had to yell to get his attention.

He shook his head as if to shrug off the words.

"Ashton, calm yourself down. Ashton?" fear began to creep into her voice as she watched the spectacle of Ashton pacing like a madman, back and forth, back and forth. She decided to try once more. If that didn't work, she would need to use the light to get his attention.

She drew a deep breath and yelled, "ASHTON!" Her voice seemed to echo off the walls of the otherwise silent apartment.

He stopped his pacing, midway between the couch and the kitchen counter. As he turned to Julia, his mind came back to the present. He left the flurry of thoughts behind and looked at her as if for the first time. Her eyes held a mixture of fear and sorrow. Tears ran down her cheeks, collected on her chin, and dripped onto the floor between her legs. She was beaten, broken, and God knew what else - yet she still cared enough about a stranger to have shed tears for him.

He was reminded of his sister and her last days in the hospital years ago as he tried to comfort her in those dark times. Ashton wanted to comfort Julia as well. Each time he had tried to go to her, she reflexively pulled away and used the sunlight as a wedge to drive him back. He assured her that he wouldn't hurt her. She must not believe him. He tried to consider things from her perspective in the hopes that he could form a connection with her. He tried to imagine the ordeal she had endured. A terrible ordeal wrought against her at the hands of not just a man but a monster. He started to get a vague sense of the suffering she must have gone through. Images of them together blasted through his consciousness with enough force that he winced and put his hand to his head. He steadied himself by putting his other hand on the arm of the couch.

As quickly as the images started, they ended, but impressions lingered in his mind of what occurred in those images. Somehow the flash of scenes had transferred the knowledge of the entire event to him, bringing with it hints of feelings. He knew that the feelings he experienced belonged to the dead vampire. Trevor's perverse pleasure from twisting Julia to his will and his sadistic delights from violating her echoed in his mind. Wave after wave of the vile scenes had crashed into his brain. The power of these images hit Ashton harder than any physical blow ever had. Part of him wished he could somehow unsee these macabre interludes and erase them forever from his mind. Yet there remained something inside of him, something separate or somehow detached from his ego that yearned for more and more of them. The raging war between who he is and this dark presence inside him was nearly unbearable. He collapsed onto the couch and began to rock himself back and forth like an injured child. He was aware of Julia watching him. When he looked up, she saw the turmoil he was going through and thought it was over the news of what had happened to him.

"My God, what is wrong with me?" Ashton wailed. The violence of what he had just encountered left him feeling battered and ashamed. He turned to Julia, images of her suffering, torture, and rape pulsating through his mind.

"I'm so, so very sorry, Julia. Oh my God, am I so sorry."

He held his head in his hands, palms clasped over his ears as if trying to block something out. He had been hurt, both physically and mentally, in his life. He had endured much. Nothing had ever made him feel so wretched and unworthy of love. He had never despaired over his actions, which is what it felt like he was doing. Part of him knew Trevor had done these deeds, but part of him was Trevor. He lost himself in his anguish.

Many long minutes slowly passed as Julia watched Ashton break down. She imagined that being a vampire was not the best thing, but she hadn't expected despair to be his reaction. Maybe rage or an instant transformation into a monster like Trevor, but not this. He seemed like he wanted to repent for some terrible deed, but he hadn't done anything - yet. She began to panic as she considered if he was apologizing for something he was about to do like he was trying to resist the urge to attack or bite her. When she saw the look in his eyes, she understood. He was apologizing to her for what Trevor had done. She remembered some of the few times Trevor had mentioned to her that not only would he relive their encounter, but others would as well and that they would enjoy experiencing her as he had. The thought of Ashton seeing through his eyes embarrassed her. She cringed as she wondered if he saw the things Trevor had done to her. She lowered her eyes and gripped the drape tighter in her hand.

"I know you have gone through a terrible and unimaginable time, Julia. You can trust me on that, I know. I think I am about to go through some very dark times too. I can't begin to accept what we both know is true, what I am now. I am something different - I can feel it. It's so much for me to get my head around. I'm kinda freaking out, you know?"

He turned his head towards her and smiled a sad but hopeful smile. She felt for him. He seemed like one of the good guys, which made what had happened to him more difficult to accept. She decided that until he said or did something to threaten her, she would trust him and do what she could to help.

She returned his smile and let go of the drape. She walked over to the couch and sat next to him. His smile grew, and he nodded his head a few times in appreciation. With just a hint of hesitation, she clasped his left shoulder with her right hand, squeezed it, and then let it rest there. His skin felt very cool to her touch.

"I'm sorry too, Ashton. You're right. My life has been one long nightmare for months now. I've never been through anything like this before either. When you were, um, asleep, I saw your wound heal. That's when I figured you were going to turn. I didn't know what to expect, but I didn't want to turn you away into the sunlight because you helped me."

He had clasped his hands in front of him, elbows resting on his knees. He turned his head slightly to look at her and said, "well, you killed him."

"But you helped me," she repeated and shook his should gently to emphasize her point.

"I couldn't have done it without your help. You pushed Trevor into the light, so maybe you killed him?" She considered this momentarily and added, "it doesn't matter, as long as he's dead."

She saw his jaw clench a few times. When he spoke, he sounded tentative and measured, "How much do you know about vampires? Do you know if he had rules? Did he ever talk about that stuff, or did you figure any of it out?"

"You mean like crosses and daylight, that kind of thing?" she replied.

"Yeah, like, can I turn into a bat or a fog? Can I control wolves?" when he said control, he noticed that she flinched.

"I don't know if he could turn into a bat or fog. I do know that Trevor had mind control. Just by speaking, he could make you say or do anything, and I mean anything! I know dogs would bark non-stop whenever Trevor was around them. Once, he said he preferred wolves to dogs. I don't know what he meant, but considering he was so controlling, I bet Trevor would have preferred an animal he could control over one he couldn't."

She thought for a few moments, then added, "Trevor did turn into ash in the sunlight, but sunlight seems to be more of a nuisance for you than a lethal threat."

"Listen," she dropped her hand from his shoulder and used it to shift her position, angling herself more towards him, "I was saying that I didn't know what to expect, and I still don't. I am willing to try to help you, but I need you to agree to something first."

"Sure, what is it?" when she shifted herself around, he scooted to his right and leaned back into the couch. Then he extended his left arm along the back. She noticed how long his arm was and how tall and powerful he was. She hurried to make her request.

"If you feel like you will lose control and attack me because you need blood or something, please let me know. I won't make you leave the apartment. I can at least get out of here if you can't control it."

He said nothing because he was shocked into silence. He couldn't believe what Julia had just said. The silence grew, and she felt awkward.

"You know, just, it's just that I don't want..." she began to fumble her words and hoped she hadn't upset him.

"No, I get it, Julia. I'll let you know, I promise." He kept staring ahead.

"One more thing." Her voice was barely louder than a whisper. "Can you also promise not to make me say or do anything?"

He thought about that. He had no idea how it worked. What if he just asked a question - would Julia have a choice but to answer? Or did he have to look her in the eyes in dim lighting? He decided that asking her would be the best way to know.

"I'm not sure. I don't know how it works. Do I ask you something or tell you to do something, and you do it? Or do I have to do something while doing it, like have you look into my eyes?"

"I think you have to do something. Sometimes, Trevor would ask me or tell me to do things, and I could choose whether I did. Other times, I had no choice. It didn't matter if I was looking at him or not."

As she explained this, his mind flooded with images and scenes of Trevor doing what Julia described. Then he knew. He only needed to mean it as a command. Then she had to obey.

"I promise, I won't do that, Julia. All I want is to figure out what's going on with me. I need to know what I have to do to stay alive. If I'm even alive anymore." He shook his head and rolled his wrists back so that his hands made a "what else can I say" gesture.

"You mind if I use your bathroom?"

"No, it's just down the hall to the left." He knew where it was. His apartment used the same floor plan.

He stepped into the bathroom and closed the door with the lights still off. He wondered what he would see when he looked into the mirror. Would he be invisible, or would his clothes be standing there without his skin or hair showing? He turned to face the wall where the mirror was sure to be. He looked straight ahead, reached out, and flicked the light switch up. He was staring at his reflection, right at his own piercing blue eyes. Something seemed different about the color, but he wasn't exactly sure what it was. Then he noticed the bloodstains on his shirt and his face. He saw a red crust around his ear lobe and ran his finger over his outer ear. Small pieces of a reddish-brown crust stuck to his finger. He pushed his outer ear forward and turned his head to the side. The same reddish-brown residue seemed to coat it, and he saw some more of it in his hair. He would need to wash that. He returned his attention to his eyes. Maybe his eyes were brighter, or perhaps his pupils were larger? Then he realized that he had no red in his eyes at all. Usually, his eyes had those red squiggly lines, as if they were a little bloodshot. Were they veins or capillaries? He didn't know what to call them, but he did know they were gone. All traces of red were gone. He thought to check his right wrist for a scar he got from fishing when he was twelve. It

41

was gone. No scar at all.

"That's awesome!" he exclaimed and began thinking of other scars he had.

Under his chin, there was a small scar from a dog bite that happened when he was six. That one was gone too. He had a tattoo on his left shoulder from when he was drunk at nineteen at a friend's house. It was of Perseus riding Pegasus, brandishing a sword. He lifted his sleeve and turned his shoulder to face the mirror. That was still there, completely unchanged. "Weird," he thought. He wondered why that was still there, but the scars were gone.

A gentle knock at the door, "Ashton, you OK in there? You need anything?" Julia asked. Without thinking, he quickly turned the handle and opened the door. Julia gave a startled gasp and jumped back, arms defensively raised in front of her. She cowered reflexively. She recovered her composure and quickly asked, "What is it?" She could tell he wanted to say something.

"My scars are gone. Isn't that a cool side effect?"

She nodded to his reflection, "You can see your reflection in modern mirrors. The ones made of silver don't cast your reflection. Trevor mentioned that to me."

His mind began to replay his saying that to her as if he was Trevor. When he tried to push the thoughts away, they faded.

Julia asked him, "What is it?" He must have shown something in his expression.

He thought about explaining it to her, and then he remembered what happened last time he mentioned having those types of memories. He didn't want to make her feel uncomfortable as she tried to help him, so he shrugged and said, "It's nothing."

"So, no reflections in silver mirrors. What about silver itself. Does it hurt," he hesitated before adding, "us?"

"I think it does, but I am not sure. Trevor asked me if I had any silver, but I didn't. He didn't ask about gold or diamonds, just silver. He used his mind thingy on me. He wanted to make sure I wasn't lying."

"Compelled," Ashton suggested.

"What?" Julia asked, not sure what he meant.

"I think it's called compelled. Trevor compelled you to tell the truth.

Even if that isn't what he called it, I think that's what I'm gonna call it."

"Makes sense to me," Julia said. "I felt compelled to tell the truth, that is for sure. Sometimes I wanted to lie. I just couldn't."

Julia walked back to the living room, and Ashton followed, turning the bathroom light off. As he passed the kitchen, he had an idea.

"Do you have any garlic?"

She laughed, "Nope, none - not a trace, no garlic salt, garlic butter, garlic sauce, or anything with garlic. He hated the smell. He said it overpowered everything." Her face went a little pale, and she trailed off. "He wouldn't even let me eat it." She whispered in a haunted voice.

She took on a defiant demeanor, "after I first learned what he was and that I couldn't get rid of him, I ate tons of Italian and Mediterranean food. I ate anything with lots and lots of garlic. Trevor showed up a few days later and had to leave because he couldn't stand the smell. He had to compel me to stop eating garlic too."

She blanched and said in a barely audible voice, "That night, he didn't feed on me, the evil bastard."

Ashton used the mental push to make sure no such images came to mind. He did not want to see Trevor feeding on Julia. Even so, the thought of it excited him, and he hated that.

"Well, we also know that wood and sunlight are harmful."

He thought about it more and then asked, "what about crucifixes or religious stuff?"

Part of him didn't want to know the answer to that question. Its implications were staggering.

"That one is tricky," she said and turned towards her chair.

She walked over to her original spot next to the patio door and sat down. She picked up a small rectangular jewelry box. She opened it and took out a small golden crucifix. She held it up so that Ashton could see it.

"Do you see or feel anything from this?" she shook the hand holding the crucifix. It made a plastic sound as it shook against the necklace.

"Nothing. I mean, I see the crucifix. It just looks like a crucifix. I don't feel anything unusual or scary."

She got up, set the jewelry box on her chair, walked over to him, and held it out. Hesitantly, he reached out to take it. Bracing himself, he held his palm out instead. He waited for her to set the crucifix in his hand. He expected something to happen when she dropped it into his hand, but nothing did. He let out a sigh of relief.

"Hold on." She turned around and went back to her chair. Next, she lifted a red velvet lid from a compartment of the small jewelry box. She removed a small velvet-covered box from inside. This time, she turned to face Ashton. She carefully lifted the lid off the small box and kept an eye on Ashton as she did. As the top of it separated from the bottom, a warm glow shone out from whatever was inside. When Ashton saw the light, he had a vague sense of foreboding. Julia studied him closely.

"Anything?" she asked expectantly.

Ashton replied in a subdued tone, "I see a warm, glowing light. What is in it? Some motion-triggered light?"

Julia answered by asking him a question, "Do you feel anything? Does the light bother you?"

He shook his head slowly, his eyes transfixed on the glow. "No...it doesn't bother me, but I feel like I need to be careful. You know?" he asked, raising his eyes at the end.

Instead of speaking, she lifted the lid completely off the box and the room filled with the warm light. It gave everything that it touched more definition and detail, like looking through a magnifying glass. The experience was very odd, and the feeling of foreboding grew.

Still watching him, she reached her hand into the box and pulled out another crucifix. She held it up before Ashton.

He sat up straighter in his seat and leaned forward. "Wow. What is it?" he asked.

She moved it about a foot to the right, back to the center, a foot to the left, and then back to the original spot in the center. Ashton tracked the movement with his head, keeping his eyes locked on the crucifix.

"You don't know what it is?" she seemed a little puzzled by his question.

"I can tell it's a crucifix. I don't know how you get it to glow like that. I've never seen anything like it."

"I'm going to set it on the coffee table in front of you, OK?" she asked cautiously. If Ashton noticed the look of concern on her face, he didn't let on.

"That's fine." He answered in that same restrained tone of voice. She thought he sounded subdued or pacified, almost like he was drugged. As she thought about it more, he seemed hypnotized or in a trance. Whatever it was, she hadn't heard Trevor sound like that.

She slowly walked towards him. She kept the smaller box in her left hand, leaving the lid in the jewelry box. As she approached, Ashton felt the warmth of the light get stronger. It didn't get hotter, yet the heat seemed to have more force - as if it could penetrate deeper. The foreboding took on a more ominous feel as if something was imminent. In the back of his mind, he began to worry. He tried to read her expression, but he couldn't take his eyes off it.

Julia set it on the coffee table. Once the crucifix no longer had her hand below it, the light emanated from every surface, casting its glow in all directions.

"This belonged to my grandmother. She had it since she was a little girl. She was a devout Catholic and almost became a nun. She joked with us that if she hadn't met my grandfather, she would have married Jesus instead. She would tell us that God put my grandfather in her life to be her husband. She said she just knew. Her grandmother never had any regrets about not becoming a nun. She always wore that crucifix. The only time I know of when she didn't wear it was when she had surgery."

"I've never seen anything like it. It's beautiful, and it's something else." When he said that, Julia's attention snapped to him.

"It's what?" she pressed.

"Terrible," he droned, "it has terrible beauty. I've heard those words before, but now, I truly know what they mean."

"You want to try to touch it? If you do, be careful. I don't know what would happen," she cautioned him.

She also wanted to know what would happen.

He didn't look up when he answered her.

"I'll try."

Eyes wide and transfixed on the crucifix, which he now noticed had a small metal hoop on it to let it put on a necklace, he reached out. He pointed his index finger and tucked the other fingers under his thumb. As his hand got closer to the object, he hesitated. Once it was a few inches away, Ashton began to second guess touching it. The foreboding was gone. Now it was a sense of impending doom. Warnings flowed through his mind, telling him not to put his hands on it.

By now, his finger was little more than an inch away. He felt hair standing upon his arm, and he also could vaguely see the hair on his index finger standing up. He stopped his hand and considered what he was doing. Part of him wanted to stop, but a different part wanted to know what would happen. He took a deep breath and thrust his hand forward, making contact with the crucifix. A crackling sound immediately preceded the jolt of lighting that slammed into his finger and spread throughout his body. Ashton was pushed back into the couch so forcefully that his head smacked into the wall behind. After the shock wore off, he held his hand before his face, inspecting it for damage. As he drew it near his face, the smell of ozone mixed with burnt hair and flesh nauseated him. His fingertip was charred to the second knuckle. A stream of smoke wafted from the center of the tip of his finger, right where it made contact with the crucifix. The implications of this reaction added to the weight of everything else that had happened that day. Not only was his life in ruins, he now had a major issue on his hands. Was he turned to evil? Did his soul depart his body when he died earlier that day - or was it now condemned?

He looked down at the table where the crucifix lay. The light it had been emitting was almost completely gone. At the heart of the crucified Jesus, a dull light pulsated. He looked up to Julia, who was staring open-mouthed at him.

"Wow, I didn't expect that!" he said, looking from the crucifix to his finger. His injury was already much improved. The pain was nearly gone, and the burned skin almost healed. Just the area around his fingernail remained black.

"Wow," he said slowly. Before his eyes, the blackness disappeared from the bottom up. He shook his head in wonder.

"That's awesome!" he smiled broadly and added, "I guess it isn't all bad."

"It's in your blood. It can heal normal people's wounds too."

When Ashton turned to her, trying to register what she said, Julia put her hand over her mouth and looked mortified.

"I didn't mean that you aren't..." she tried to explain.

"Normal?" Ashton asked, still smiling at her.

"I guess I'm not."

His mind was racing, still trying to get around everything. His thoughts returned to the crucifix.

"Did you ever show that to Trevor?" he wondered what Trevor's reaction to it would have been.

"Nope. He commanded me not to wear or display silver or crosses or crucifixes. I suppose something about those things bothered him, or he wouldn't have gone through the trouble to command me. My gut tells me that it would have affected him much worse than it did you. It's funny the one thing he let me keep around was the broken broom handle. He told me that a wooden stake through the heart could kill him and that I would never be able to use it on him. He probably figured I wouldn't have the courage to try knowing what he would do if I failed."

"I guess he was wrong." Ashton offered.

"Yeah, I guess so." Julia caught Ashton's attention as she reached for the crucifix on the table. He noticed that the light it emanated had grown, and the foreboding feeling returned. He wanted to know more about it, but he began to feel very tired. His head throbbed, each heartbeat radiating pain from the back of his head straight through his brain into his eyes.

"Julia, do you mind if I lay here until after dark? I want to go home, but my head is hurting, and I feel exhausted." He put his hands on either temple and began rubbing them in circles, trying to relieve the pressure in his head. He would have to wait until he got home to deal with his work situation. Right now, he needed to rest. Since touching the crucifix, he felt drained.

"Sure, you need a pillow or anything?" she asked, walking towards the bedroom with the jewelry box. If she needed to get Ashton a pillow, she could do that when she put the box back on her dresser. When he didn't answer, she turned to him. He lay on the couch, feet up on one of the arms and head upon the other, fast asleep.

"I guess not." She shrugged and went about her task.

Chapter 7

Raven stood on the balcony of her room, looking out over the vast estate in the fading dusk, the cool mountain air chilling further as the sun's warmth left the sky. A warm breeze from across the plain danced across her skin as the land itself surrendered its vestiges of comforting warmth. She took a long drink of her piping hot coffee, sighing as its heat spread throughout her body. She closed her eyes and faced the oncoming breeze, allowing it to renew her. It brought forgotten feelings, suggestions of change, and promises of hope. She let it enter her body and soul as she offered those feelings any purchase to cling to. Deep in her mind, neglected needs and desires stirred, churning in their dormancy, seeking momentum to break free of their subdued state. Her heart raced, and she raised her empty hand to lay across her chest. She could not remember the last time she had such passionate impulses.

"Perhaps Trevor's absence is a sign that things will change?" She thought, taking a steadying drink of the hot brew. She hoped she would never see him again, let alone tonight.

A soft knock at her door drew her attention from such revelry as she turned to answer it.

As the door opened, the syrupy voice of Isabeau called out in exaggerated excitement.

"Oh! You're up already! I was sure you still slept."

She stepped into the room and kissed Raven on either cheek, giving her a quick hug before stepping past and picking up the mug Raven had just set down. She lifted it to her nose and inhaled the bitter aroma. She curled her nose and sat it back in its place in disgust.

"How can you drink coffee without cream and sugar, lots and lots of sugar?"

Raven had just closed the door and turned to face her when Isabeau had set the mug back down. She nodded her head towards a porcelain tea set on the sideboard.

"Would you like a cup, Isa? There is fresh cream and sugar as well." Raven much preferred Isa to the odd-sounding Isabeau. So did Isa, but only after she had permitted one to use the familiar form of her name.

"Oh, no, thanks. I don't want to put you out." She turned and walked to the balcony.

Raven poured a cup for Isa and added a generous amount of cream and several spoons of sugar. Then she carried it with her as she joined Isa on the balcony. Raven set the cup on the iron-wrought table near Isa's chair.

"You shouldn't have!" She exclaimed, picking the cup up and sipping the steaming beverage.

"Perfect!" She set the cup back down. Raven knew she wouldn't drink any more of the coffee and that she would have made a fuss with the others if Raven hadn't made it for her.

Raven took up the same spot on the balcony she occupied before Isa's arrival, leaning the curve of her back against one side of the railing, looking out across the landscape.

"It is pretty here." Isa offered, taking in the view. "Your room has a nicer view than mine," Isa pouted.

Raven stifled a laugh, "your room is right next to mine. You could jump from my balcony to yours with no effort!"

"True, but you aren't in the middle like I am." Raven knew she was referring to having Claud next to her room. She wouldn't like that either.

Isa rose and stood next to Raven.

"Have you heard from Trevor?" She asked in a low voice.

"No, and to be honest, I hope I never do," Raven replied without emotion.

"You're terrible!" Isa squeaked and elbowed Raven.

"Would you be sad if you never had to deal with him again?" Raven asked, a subtle smile curling her lip.

Isa didn't speak, but she smiled like a cherub and shook her entire body back and forth instead of just her head.

"I asked Marius last night, and while some of us have missed the first night of the gathering, no one has ever missed tonight's ceremony."

At the mention of the ceremony, Raven's back stiffened. She disliked the ritual but understood its importance.

"Who knows," Raven offered, "Maybe he'll go two for two?"

Isa's devilish smile broadened. "Now you're just being mean!"

"No, I'm being me." Raven countered with a nod and a wink.

"True, it's not like we can hide how we feel."

"Blood is life and truth." They said in unison and then laughed.

"Let me know if you hear anything about Trevor, and I will do the same, OK?"

"I am sure you will know something long before I do, but I will let you know if I hear anything."

With that, Isa left, leaving Raven alone again. Raven returned to her languid perusal of the grounds. The well-trimmed lawn was expansive and hedged by shrubbery. An elaborate fountain sat centered behind the estate. The view reminded her of Paris and her journeys with Isa almost two hundred and fifty years ago. Their coven formed only a few years earlier, along with it came the creation of the Blood Communion. At the thought of this adventure, her mind with her memories from that time. It was the happiest time of her vampiric life and the only time she gave in to her hedonistic side. It was also the last time she had allowed herself to love. Pushing away from the painful memories, Raven focused her attention on preparing herself for the night.

At a quarter of an hour before midnight, a single gong rang and could be heard throughout the estate, signaling the imminent start of the annual ceremony. Raven left her room and joined Isa in the hallway. They hurried along, hoping to avoid Claud on their way.

A few moments later, they entered a chamber in the basement of the grand estate of their host, Gitlam, the eldest vampire in their coven. The sparse room reflected his spartan views on function over form. A triangular table stood in each corner of the room. Warm light radiated from pillar candles that sat atop those tables, standing in stark contrast to the cold stone of the walls. Thick rugs covered the floor where they would walk. A round table and chairs filled the center of the room. A plain, wrought iron chandelier hung above the stone table with ten arms extending out from its center, creating a line from the center of the table to each chair. On the chandelier, a candle illuminated the chair below it. Another candle sat along the iron beams at the center between the chairs and the table. Overall, it appeared like the spokes of a large wagon wheel, minus the rim or the metallic rim that would join the spokes together.

A round table is used for the ceremony, as its layout did not suggest a leadership position. However, all looked first to Gitlam and then to Marius for guidance. Yet each of their votes had the same value as their peers. Once the Blood Communion was devised and adopted by the coven, they all agreed they had the purest form of democracy ever existed. The Blood Communion shared their memories amongst them, making deception and intrigue impossible. They could not deceive one another as the blood contained the truth. As they would die without blood, their mantra was soon born.

"Blood is life and truth."

The vampires took their seats by their age. Gitlam took the first unoccupied chair. He is the oldest known vampire and could trace his roots to ancient Sumer. His terse nature was often confused for rudeness. Living his life in quiet isolation and contemplation, he was more of an observer in life than a participant. His dark shiny skin maintained an almost bronze glow. Like most men of his era, he was small in stature and thickly muscled. He was the shortest in the coven at just over five feet. His hair and beard are tightly braided, reflecting his station before becoming a vampire. Some have suggested that he may have known the Gilgamesh of ancient legend and that some mutual adventure they undertook led to his becoming the first vampire.

His wife, Zana, sat to his left. They nodded in a formal acknowledgment of each other. While just a little taller than Gitlam, her ivory skin and fiery red locks betrayed her European origins. Captured at an early age, she had been a slave who had risen to prominence in her era, several hundred years after Gitlam had become a vampire. Using her cunning, wile, and beauty, she quickly became an invaluable asset to her owner, a minor political figure of his time. He capitalized on her many skills. He gained political influence and began his ascent. She caught Gitlam's attention during one of her many behind-the-scenes political negotiations. They eventually fell in love, and he purchased her for an unbelievable amount. He immediately granted her freedom and asked her to marry him. Gitlam gave her control of his estates, and under her stewardship, his fortunes and reputation prospered. Gitlam had never used his vampiric powers on Zana. The love they shared was genuine and deep. It was strong enough to endure the revelation of his true nature. Her love of Gitlam led Zana to agree to become a vampire.

The next to be seated, to Zana's left, was Marius. Gitlam had turned the Roman legate for his ability to hide and protect him and Zana. During one of many waves of vampire panic, many of the remaining ancient vampires were discovered and destroyed. Marius was a statuesque legate who had served his empire well. In customary Ancient Roman fashion, betrayal was the reward for his successes. Marius' political enemies assassinated him, but not before Marius had consumed Gitlam's blood. Marius had known about the plot against his life and prepared for its inevitable success. All of his wealth, Gitlam and Zana, had been transported away well before the assassins got to him. Marius served the coven well, if not better than he had the empire.

To Marius' left sat Tamjen, the other surviving vampire created by Gitlam. He received the gift of eternal life after developing an unparalleled reputation for being an engineer and administrator. Gitlam turned them for his benefit, not as a benevolent act. For eons, to succeed, one required a mighty and disciplined military and an efficient logistical operation. Both Marius and Tamjen were crucial cogs in his plans.

Isabeau was next to be seated at the table. Zana was her dam as she had turned Isabeau. Everyone who got to know the remarkable woman loved her. Her light-hearted and carefree personality hid a deep intelligence and passionate devotion to all who considered her a friend. Her whimsical nature, without exception, led to her dismissal as a threat. She was the only one in the coven that Raven considered a genuine friend.

Then came Beatrice. She was by far the most abrasive and standoffish among them. She served Zana and worked on her behalf.

Her efforts grew to include protecting Zana's secret. After years of such faithful service, Zana offered her blood to Beatrice. If accepted, Beatrice would rise again after her death. At first, she refused. Over time, however, Beatrice fell in love with Zana and feared losing her. She risked her soul instead of losing Zana forever and accepted the offer. To her misfortune, Beatrice lacked the nerve to confess her love before deciding, which would have saved her the pain of finding out later that her love was unrequited. She agreed to turn Claud, in part to spite Zana and in part because of a blind and misplaced feeling of love for him.

Claud was by far the most manipulative and base member of the coven. His ability to manipulate Beatrice into turning him was what he considered to be his masterstroke. He relished witnessing the pain he caused her by rejecting her afterward. His sadistic side was well established before becoming a vampire, and once turned, he exploited his ability to compel others mercilessly. The slow and painful downfall of his enemies was legendary during his time. While unable to directly compel his peers in the coven, he worked tirelessly and shamelessly on any agenda he undertook. Among what many in the coven considered his personality defects was his utter lack of decorum. He had no shame and would engage in any activity that offered him even the slightest hint of pleasure. And at every Blood Communion, the others bore witness to his depravity while he sadistically relished in their discomfiture.

Claud turned Raven and eventually Trevor. Raven, or Coronis in her native tongue, was a nickname her mother gave her one day in the wild fields near their seaside town. She was running among the wildflowers and shrubs when her mother said that all she could see of her beautiful daughter was her jet-black hair flying like a raven through the field. Raven was clever and strategic throughout her childhood. Once her mother thought of the nickname, it stuck. Soon after, she made everyone call her by Coronis. After her mother's death, Raven no longer answered her given name. She kept her name secret. Not even Claud would dare to call her by it.

Other unnamed vampires had perished throughout the history of the coven. Most died in the centuries before Gitlam had sired Claud. Living amongst humans grew more dangerous for vampires as remaining undetected became more difficult. They had discussed coming out of the shadows and taking a more active role in society, but doing so would risk the ire of people and the churches. The coven rejected the option each time they voted on it.

To Raven's left is where the sullen Sasha sat. She was once Isabeau's lover, while she and Raven had spent time together in Paris almost two and a half centuries ago. Sasha was a young noblewoman who had married a tyrannical, old, and fat nobleman through her father's arrangements. Isa became acquainted with Sasha, and the two had an immediate attraction. Isa helped free Sasha from the marriage, and then Sasha became Isa's muse. For years, they loved each other, and the death of one of the forgotten vampires allowed Sasha to become part of the coven. Raven had warned Sasha that Isa would eventually lose interest in her. It happened quicker than Raven had predicted, and Sasha never seemed to recover from this rejection.

The unoccupied chair belonged to Trevor, the youngest among them a little over two hundred years. The empty chair screamed the implications of his absence. It was the first time a seat remained vacant during the Blood Communion. Being a superstitious lot, they all shared the belief that this was an omen. Has another hunter emerged to threaten their coven?

Gitlam stood, his gaunt figure draped in the flickering shadows that danced around the chamber. His austere bearing alone was enough to command their attention.

"Before we get started with why we are here today, it is important that we recognize that one member of our coven is not here with us tonight." Following his lead, all heads turned to the empty chair. "We will find out why this is." He looked at Marius, who nodded his understanding.

He swept his commanding gaze around the table, looking each member in their eyes.

"We formed this coven to assure the survival of our kind in the face of relentless persecution. We also want to protect humans from the out-of-control growth of our numbers, as we witnessed so long ago. To assure that we keep this coven, we agreed to use the truth contained within the Blood Memories to show that none of us act in any way that would endanger the others. This decision protected us over the years. Now, we may be the last coven to exist. Blood is life and truth."

All present repeated, "Blood is life and truth."

"Now, let us share our life and our truth." Gitlam lay his left forearm onto a channel carved into the stone. With their enhanced senses, they could hear faint clicking sounds followed by the turning of well-oiled gears as the mechanism built into the table sprang into action. On the outside of Gitlam's wrist, a small metallic tower emerged from the table, a thin layer of stone covering its top. A spring within it released, and a needle appeared, jutting out towards Gitlam's wrist. A split second later, the tower snapped forward, and the metallic thorn pierced the radial artery on Gitlam's wrist. For a few moments, nothing appeared to happen. At the center of the table, two half circles of the stone surface separated and retracted into the table, leaving a circular hole in their place. While retracting, a platform rose from the recess created by the disappearing sections of stone. It spun in a counter-clockwise direction, revealing more of itself with each revolution. In the center, ten pairs of arms held a glass sphere aloft. The arms belonged to the five male and five female figurines, each representing one of the ten vampires that would occupy the chairs. These figures stood atop a stone slab supported by what appeared to be ten pewter columns. Intricate carvings decorated the surfaces of the columns. Soon, the spiraling contraption came to rest. The figures holding up the sphere stood before the vampire they represented. A soft whirring sound started. The hands of Gitlam's figurine streamed blood into the vessel as the mouth of a cherub replenishes water in a fountain. When the blood level reached a spot below the hands, the device stuck into Gitlam's arm lifted, and the needle disappeared. Moments later, the metallic tower returned to its hiding place in the stone.

The whirring sound grew louder, and the blood drained from the glass ball. Once the blood drained, the pewter columns slid forward, coming to rest next to the left hand of every member, except for Gitlam and the empty chair. Each of the eight glasses held equal amounts of blood withdrawn from Gitlam's artery. The vampire who provides the blood does not need to consume their offering.

"I give you my blood. It is my life and my truth." He spoke these words emphatically to impart their importance.

"We accept your truth and your life," the group replied in unison as they lifted the goblets to drink the blood. Once they replaced the goblets atop the small conical shapes which brought them forward, they returned to their original position under the platform.

Tamjen broke out into a huge grin. His vulpine face stretched tight with his satisfaction and pride. It was the first time the device he had designed needed to function with an absent member.

Sasha smiled at him. "I bet you worried if it would perform correctly this time, didn't you?" She asked, not because she didn't know the answer, but because she wanted to recognize his magnificent accomplishment.

"Indeed, indeed." He was beaming his pleasure and satisfaction. "We tested it many times during its creation, but I didn't know if the paths would function as expected." He turned to Claud, lifting his chin in triumph. "I told you! We didn't need to use new technology." He waved his hands to dismiss what he considered a preposterous suggestion. Isa covered her mouth to hide her grin.

Claud shrugged and replied, "Let's hope it stays that way. There are still eight of us left."

A look of alarm flashed across Tamjen's face, then disappeared as quickly as it had come.

"I am sure it will go fine." He declared.

Isabeau agreed. "I am sure it will too, Tam."

He cringed at the use of the shortened version of his name. Regardless, the slight irritation wasn't enough to alter his good mood.

Beatrice laid a hand on his shoulder. "We know it will work fine. You are the master tinkerer after all." She gave him a warm smile as she added to his unease. On any other day, Tamjen would be incensed at being referred to as a tinkerer - master or not. He thought of himself as a master artisan, at the very least.

Everyone held their breath, waiting to see if he would explode. He was thinking about the mechanism's functioning and retraced the paths in his mind, searching for anything he may have missed when he serviced the machine after the last ceremony. Tamjen noticed the delay. He looked around the table, trying to discern the cause. Realizing what they thought, he shooed them on.

"Well, get on with it then!" He looked at Zana's elegant guise and blushed a bit, and hurriedly added, "Please," as she raised her left eyebrow at him in surprise. Suppressing a chuckle, she lay her arm on the table and repeated the words spoken by Gitlam.

The process repeated until all members of the coven had offered their blood. Each member provided eight goblets of blood and consumed as much, one from each peer. The Blood Communion was complete.

Gitlam rose again, and they set aside all other considerations.

"Now that we have shared our life and our truth, it is time for us to reflect." He returned to his seat and rested his elbows on the armrests. He steepled his fingers and closed his eyes. The others closed their eyes and focused their minds on the new blood memories.

They determined that about one ounce of blood would contain the memories of a vampire. This excluded memories from before they became a vampire. The accepted theory being those memories are recessive to the stronger and more ordered memories of their vampiric lives. Through repeated practice, they honed their abilities to drift through the memories of one another and scan them for any alarming incidents, much like one would fast forward through a video for a specific type of scene. Doing so resulted in a profound lack of privacy that had unexpected consequences. The modest members of the coven forwent the pleasures of the flesh while more base members, like Claud and, after some time, Trevor, once he became a member, seemed to enjoy the unease caused by their many perverse escapades. Sharing the atrocities the two had committed at an orphanage in the mid-nineteenth century didn't embarrass them, nor did the outrage of the others. They seemed to revel in the emotions they created in the others.

All were grateful that the Blood Memories did not contain the thought or emotion.

Chapter 8

When Ashton woke, the apartment was still. No light filtered in through the edges of the drapes, and Julia was no longer sitting in the chair. He knew instinctively that the sun had set. The darkness called him like a new lover, caressing his mind as hands would caress his body. Its ethereal fingers probed his mind, exploring all of its hidden places, seductively pulling his consciousness out into the shadows of the world around him. It promised something new, something exciting. His mind, no longer contained by his physical form, expanded into the world around him, revealing a primordial and predatory nature within himself. He did not know if it was from the tainted blood or was there his entire life, waiting until called on. It was both a part of and separate from himself, like the voice of his moral consciousness, yet with a coldly calculating intelligence that would serve to keep him alive and on the trail of prey. With each breath he took, his mind drifted further and further outward from his body, expanding the realm of his awareness. He became aware that the air from the ceiling fan wasn't blowing in a constant stream but at a regular pulsing interval. He heard voices reverberating through walls. His mind continued to reach out into the unknown around him, searching for something - searching for prey.

Suddenly, he was aware of Julia, in her bed just down the hall from where he lay, sleeping peacefully under the covers. All else, every tendril in every other corner his mind had crept, immediately receded. The energy used to have been in those places now reinforced his disembodied exploration of Julia and her surroundings. Her slow and rhythmic breathing soothed and excited him. Here was prey - waiting helplessly to fulfill its purpose in the great circle of life. He remained where he lay on the couch in the other room as he marveled at this transcendental experience. His mind descended upon her body, working its way down her head towards her feet. Her brown hair was slightly damp, and the air in the room was redolent with fragrances of shampoo, body soap, deodorant, and perfume. The delicate feminine balance of these aromas belied the subtle addition of another, far more intoxicating scent. It clung to her soft, supple skin, acting as a pheromone of lust and hunger. It pulled him to her. It was blood - it was life. Still, it was so much more, and it was there, waiting for him, wanting him to take it. His mind crept its way down her face. The bitter traces of salve covered some of her wounds with its medicinal odor. Her eyes fluttered as she breathed a deep and sensual breath, finishing in a barely audible moan as her head slid to the side. Her damp hair clung to her exposed cheek. He could feel her warm and vital breath as she slumbered. A drop of water freed itself from her hair as it stretched to remain taut against her skin. It ran down her cheek, over fading bruises, under the curve of her jaw, and disappeared, lost in the subtle curves of her neck and throat. At the thought of her throat, the tendrils of his mind surged forward and wrapped around her delicate neck. It throbbed in passionate response to the sweet blood pulsating through her veins and arteries. She shifted back and forth in her bed, pulling the covers down with her restless feet. She lifted her hand and laid it on her flat and warm belly. Her fingers spread out and traced circles on the cotton on top of her silky skin beneath. Her hand rose with her breathing, and her cheeks and chest flushed with color. Her feet rubbed against one another and then against the instep of her legs. Her slow undulation rose to an expectant writhing, her body making itself ready for something more. Her mouth parted, and the single word that dripped from it acted as a lightning strike of lust in his soul.

"Yes!"

The word lasted for a second and an eternity, reverberating inside of him, granting access to her, inviting, begging Ashton to claim what was his. She licked her full lips and opened her mouth, awaiting his lips or tongue. Perhaps, something more.

Suddenly, he gasped and sat up on the couch. Chagrinned at the thoughts he was about to have and the erotic stirrings he had. He froze, wondering if it was just a dream. He felt a sick sense of perversion as if he had somehow trespassed. Not only where he was uninvited, but upon hospitality and kindness as well. Julia was the woman who saved his life. He thought of her injuries and all that she must have endured. Then he felt small and despicable. Closing his eyes and shaking his head, he chased away the vision of her lying there and the fading memory of his lustful thoughts.

He heard her voice from the other room but did not understand her meaning. Whatever had heightened his senses seemed to have faded and returned to normal.

He heard the door open and briefly caught her outline as she walked to the bathroom. She was wearing a tee-shirt and sweat pants, but he could still see the lithe body they covered. He averted his eyes, hoping that she would not look his way. Once he heard the door close, he walked to the kitchen. The digital clock on the stove indicated that it was 08:23. He thought of his appearance in the mirror and remembered he needed to wash his face before walking outside. Looking at his shirt, he saw the large bloodstain. He needed to change clothes too.

Julia avoided eye contact with Ashton as she made her way to the living room. Glancing at her, he could see that she was flushed and unsettled. She noticed Ashton in the small dining room and walked by without looking at him. She sat on the couch, at the end farthest from where he had been sitting.

"How are you feeling?" She asked.

He turned around and leaned his hip against the counter. Julia sat with her feet resting on the edge of the coffee table, arms crossed over her breasts. She kept her knees bent up towards her chest. Ashton recognized this defensive posture and felt ashamed. He also wondered if she knew what he had done.

"Uh...I'm feeling much better, more normal again. Are you OK? You seem upset or something." He asked, hoping to ease the tension or address it if it needed to be.

"Mm-hmm," she sounded a bit distracted. With her left hand, she reached down to pull up the right hem of her sweat pants, and then she pulled down her shirt. It was an effort to preserve her modesty. Unfortunately, her shirt grew tighter around her breasts, outlining their fullness.

"I had a... um, disturbing dream." She flushed and quickly pulled her hand back up and placed it on her right arm again.

"Me too." He hastily uttered before he thought better of it.

"Oh?" she looked up at him questioningly.

"Yeah." He ran his hands down his pant legs and felt for the keys in his pockets. He thought about his duffel bag in his car. He kept some clean workout clothes in his trunk.

"Would you mind doing me a favor? I mean, another favor? Would you mind getting my duffel bag out of my car so that I can change? I don't want to walk home looking like this." He waved his hand over the bloodstains and made a circle around his neck and face, turning his head from side to side to show the caked-on dried blood.

"Sure, I can do that." She answered, thankful for something to distract herself from the dream.

She looked up at Ashton, hoping that he couldn't see her embarrassment. She couldn't believe that she had that sort of dream about him. Sure, he was attractive and seemed to be a nice person, but he was a vampire. Just the thought of the word made her shudder.

"You can wash up while I get it for you."

As Ashton dug in his pocket for the keys, Julia walked back to her room. A moment later, she came back, wearing slippers. She held out her hand, and he put his key fob in it.

"It's the black 300C, just down the lot a little way, in the guest area. If you press the unlock button, the lights will flash." He pointed to a button showing an opened lock.

"Pressing this one twice will open the trunk." He pointed to a slightly larger button showing a trunk popped open.

"Fancy!" She jested.

"You should either take a shower or at least wash-up. You still have a lot of blood on your face."

He thumbed his hand over his shoulder in the direction of the bathroom.

"You have a washrag and a hand towel I can use? I can get cleaned up a bit and then out of your hair."

She was already walking towards the patio door. "Yep, you can find both in the linen closet." She pulled the drapes back, slid the door open, and walked into the night. The outside of the apartment was well lit. He felt a bit of apprehension for her as if it were his job to protect her. He shrugged to himself and walked to the bathroom. Once there, he quickly found a maroon washcloth and hand towel. He took his shirt off and turned on the hot water. He filled the sink about halfway and then leaned over and cupped water into his hands. He lifted the water to his face and spread the water on each side, keeping his eyes closed while the water dripped back into the basin. After doing this a few times, he used his fingers to push the water away from his eyes. When he opened them, he saw the water in the basin had turned pink. He stopped, with cupped hands halfway to his face, and just stared at the water. He knew that his and Trevor's blood diluted in that water. He pushed the plunger down, allowing the water to drain without filling the basin. He repeated the process, now keeping the water running and letting it drain out. He finished using the washrag, cleaning himself enough to get to his apartment and not arouse the suspicions of anyone he passed along the way.

He heard Julia come in through the patio door.

"Got it!" She announced, closing the door and then walking to the bathroom.

"Nice car," she said.

She handed him his key and the duffel bag.

"Thanks. I really like it." As he engaged her in small talk, he tried to wring all of the blood out of the washrag. She looked down at what he was doing, and he followed her eyes with his. He was relieved to see the water running clear from the washrag as he wrenched it one last time. He watched as her eyes slowly ran up from his waist. One of her eyes lifted slightly. She bit down on her bottom lip. As her eyes continued to make their way upwards, over his massive chest and broad shoulders, she must have realized what she was doing because she blushed and averted her eyes.

"I'll leave you to it then. I'll be in the kitchen if you need anything."

She seemed upset and shocked at what she had done when she smiled and turned towards the kitchen.

After a few minutes, he came to the kitchen wearing his spare clothes. A plain black tee-shirt, dark gray sweats, and an older pair of sneakers couldn't hide his sculpted physique. He held up the duffel bag and smiled. He noticed Julia's eyes linger below his waist for a few seconds when a hint of hunger flashed over them. He had to resist covering himself.

"Thanks."

She looked up at him in shock and embarrassment.

"Thanks for grabbing my stuff."

He watched relief spread over her face.

"I am gonna get home. I have to deal with a lot of stuff. You going to be OK?"

"Me? Oh, yeah, I'll be fine. She picked up her cell phone from the charger in the kitchen. Then it seemed like she thought of something.

"I'll call you so that you will have my number. When you get your phone working, give me a callback, OK?"

He told her his number, and she placed the call. It immediately went to voice mail, and she left her number on the message.

"There! That should do it." She ended the call and set her phone back on the counter.

Ashton walked to the front door, opened it then pushed open the metal privacy door on the outside. He half-turned to her, indecision causing him to pause. His voice took on a serious tone as he looked into her eyes.

"I do appreciate all you have done, Julia."

As he looked at her, vivid memories of her in bed came to mind. He sensed that she wanted to say something more, but he wanted to get out of there as soon as he could. He stepped through the door and let the security door close. Stretching his stride, he made haste for his apartment, hoping that he didn't run into anyone - especially anyone who wanted to chat. He was in luck, and a few minutes later, he was inside and leaning against the closed and locked door to his apartment.

His apartment had never felt so empty. It seemed like he was returning from a long journey, and in some ways, he supposed that he was. The familiar surroundings offered him little comfort, nor did he feel welcomed. In some respects, he felt like an intruder in his own home.

He walked to the kitchen counter and set his keys down. Before he could start thinking about all that had happened, he hurried to the bathroom for a nice hot shower. He hoped that would help to calm his nerves and make him more relaxed.

He stood in the shower, hot water pouring over his scalp. He looked down to his feet and watched as the water ran from a dark pink to clear. Occasionally, it was highlighted by light pink streaks as his scrubbing fingers loosened more of the dried blood from his skin. When the water ran clear, he started his customary ritual of cleansing himself. He washed his hair, goatee, the hair on his chest, and, finally, his manhood with the fragrant shampoo. As the lather spread over him, the aroma nearly overpowered his senses. He had never noticed how strong the perfumes in the shampoo were. His stomach began to rumble from hunger at that point too. Detaching the showerhead from the stand, he furtively rinsed the suds from his body and returned the nozzle. Using a washrag, he lathered it up with body soap and scrubbed every inch of his body that he could reach until his skin was bright pink. He sat down in the shower and used a long-handled scrub brush to scrub his back and the soles of his feet. He finished his feet using the washrag to get in between his toes, changing sides between feet. Feeling that he had sufficiently cleaned all traces of the terrible encounter from his body, he turned off the water and began to dry himself off.

He began to dry his near shoulder-length wavy dark blond hair and muscular body. His lightly tanned skin shone and rippled as he wiped the wetness away. As he did so, a question he had avoided began to press him for an answer. He focused his mind on drying himself and tried to push the questions from his mind, but the nagging sensation would not leave him alone. The back and forth agitated him more and more. After he dried himself, he wiped a small circle in the steamy mirror and looked at himself. He wanted to see his eyes. After all, they are the mirror to the soul, the gateway to the depths of one's being. Were his eyes still the same? At Julia's place, he noticed there was no trace of red anywhere, but he wasn't looking at them then as he did now.

His pupils contracted from the bright light in the bathroom. A light circle of blue, the color of an overcast sky, surrounded his pupil. Darker blues intermingled with randomly placed black shapes, and then the iris met the whites of his eyes. As he stared into his own eyes, Ashton realized the last time he had done so was when he was a child. He would have no way of comparing how his eyes looked now to before. Nothing alarmed him, such as the distinct lack of a soul or any feature that would mark him as a vampire.

"At least those seem normal." He shrugged. Then he had another idea. He opened his mouth wide and looked at the eye or canine teeth. That is where he had seen fangs in Trevor's mouth. Ashton had none. He turned his head left and right and then tilted his head as far back as he could while still being able to see his teeth in the mirror. He saw no fangs.

Tentatively, he prodded around his teeth and mouth, trying to find some pressure point to force his fangs to extend. Nothing he did would make them show. He wondered if Julia was tricking him and if the whole thing was some elaborate prank. He dismissed the idea as he knew that something was different - that he was different. He knew that he was now a vampire.

He took a moment to put the towel on the towel rack, grabbed his clothes, and went to his bedroom to get dressed.

He didn't bother to turn the lights on while getting fresh clothes from his drawers. While dressing, he noticed how the lights outside of his apartment dimly lit his room. Since living there, he had never lowered the valance blinds as he relied on the curtains to provide privacy. Now though, he had much graver concerns than privacy. He lowered the blinds, and dust billowed around them. Waving the dust away, he used the rod on the side of the blinds to turn the valances until they closed. He stepped back to see if the light was still getting in and was disappointed to see that it was. He was going to have to do something about that. He wondered what else he needed to do to make his apartment safe from sunlight.

Ashton laughed when he remembered the times he had read or seen vampire stories and wondered what it would be like to be a vampire. He had never invested any time thinking about the mundane aspects of that existence. Now Ashton had no choice and admitted that it was overwhelming. He had to struggle not to lose himself in despair as he once again realized that his entire life had changed.

His stomach reminded him again that he had yet to eat that day. He figured he could make a mental list of things needed while cooking something to eat. That thought pierced the barrier he had erected around the topics that worried him.

"Can I even eat food? Or can I only drink..."

He pulled his mind from the thought, not wanting to even think of the word. Instead, he grabbed a few small boxes of leftover Chinese food out of the fridge. He smelled the food to make sure that it was good. He dumped one container of beef and broccoli into a skillet and added another container of chicken and mushrooms. Then he realized how strong the food smelled. It didn't smell bad, just strong. Plus, he could discern various scents mingling together. He failed to tell which spice matched which smell, but he could distinguish the layers of odor. As the pan slowly heated the food, aromas grew stronger and more pronounced. His stomach grumbled constantly now, teased by the bouquet wafting into the stale air of the apartment. He didn't even bother getting a plate. He turned the burner off, stirred the lukewarm food, and feasted.

Never had he tasted such delicious food. He could taste so many individual flavors that his mind was overloaded. Saliva poured onto the food as he chewed, forcing him to swallow before too much of it subdued the explosion of flavors. He rolled his eyes in joy, blissfully unaware that an eight-dollar dish had risen to the best culinary experience of his lifetime. After polishing off all of the food, he looked in his fridge for something more to eat. His fridge was usually barren as he seldom cooked, opting for take-out or delivery. Cooking reminded him of Sam, and thinking of her always made him sad. For the briefest of moments, he considered what she would make of his situation and had a vision of her looking up at him in such a way that always made him feel like a child. He shook his head and scolded himself. He did not have time for such thoughts.

"Stay focused, man!" He said in an exasperated whisper.

He figured he would also need to get some food as well. He added food to his mental checklist. Then he remembered his phone and added that to the list.

This busy work helped keep his mind from more significant issues of his new existence. Staying active was a fallback defense from his childhood, dealing with his abusive father while trying to help his mother and little sister. After his father had died, he stayed busy helping his mother deal with that grief. Then came the news of his sister's illness. Since then, it seemed, he tried to keep busy. Now would be no different. He would make a plan and deal with the challenges as they came.

He realized he would pass Julia's apartment on the way to his car and thought about stopping by to see if she wanted to go with him but decided against it. He figured keeping his distance from her and giving her space would be best. They both had been through a lot, and he knew from experience that the timing was wrong to get involved, especially not in that way. A few minutes later, he was in his car driving to a nearby Walmart with the hope of getting the things he needed.

It was relatively early, just after 9:45 pm, when he arrived at the Walmart Supercenter near Chaparral and the 101. He double-checked the hours as he walked into the store. It closed at 11:00 pm, giving him plenty of time.

He grabbed a cart and headed into the meandering aisles of the store. As he passed a section that sold paperbacks, he noticed a well-heeled woman dressed to the nines addressing an employee wearing the ubiquitous blue vest. He kept his eyes forward and quickened his pace, not wanting to stare. He focused on the hunger to distract his mind from unwanted thoughts. He couldn't help overhearing the woman as he continued on his way.

"Excuse me. I need a replacement for my toiletry bag and a few other things. Can you tell me where I might find a travel kit?" he noticed that she seemed to have a European accent, maybe Italian. The employee told her where to find them. Her sincerity in how she thanked him piqued his curiosity enough that he looked over his shoulder to get a look at her.

She was stunning. Her wide smile projected her appreciation and kindness. Ashton seldom saw this sincerity in such attractive women. Their eyes met, locking with a jolt. Out of reflex, he smiled at her. The connection formed between them in this brief encounter stirred his desire and stoked his hunger. He noticed her raise her hand to her chest, near her throat. She had a puzzled look but made no effort to break the connection. His pulse quickened, and his hunger urged him forward - to her. He must either break the contact or give in - he was running out of time to choose. He struggled to pull his gaze from hers and walked towards where he hoped he could find the curtains.

"What was that?" he asked himself, the sensual energy subsiding, leaving him feeling embarrassed and dissatisfied.

He walked towards where he guessed the drapes were - somewhere by the light bulbs and paint. He wanted to turn around and seek the woman out. He pushed all thoughts of her and the encounter from his mind.

Ashton found the curtains a minute later. As he was looking at the various offerings, hoping to find something that claimed to keep light out, he noticed the same woman enter the aisle from the opposite end. When she saw him, she seemed relieved and slightly embarrassed. She pretended to look at the items on the shelf in a foolish attempt to hide why she was there in the first place. She concluded there was no point in the pretext and began to walk up the aisle towards him.

He picked up a square plastic pouch that listed UV protection. He held it up in a position where he could look at the woman while pretending to read the package. Sure enough, she was staring at him as she continued to close the distance between them. As she neared, he lifted his head to meet her eyes. They reconnected, and again, seductive energy coursed between them. She let out an "oh" and nearly stumbled as she came to a stop, putting her hand onto his cart to steady herself.

"Um, excuse me," her voice was very soft, and it seemed to Ashton that she had to force herself to speak.

"Yes?" he asked.

Now that the woman was standing before him, he could see how attractive and overdressed she was for a store like Walmart. She smiled meekly, showing her gleaming white teeth. Her olive skin did not hide her blushing. Neither did the curly locks of black hair that fell along the sides of her face. She wore a shiny black choker around her long and elegant neck. A silky golden blouse fit loosely on her frame, and the neckline showed just enough of her ample cleavage to remain modest while enticingly revealing. She was tall, and the modest knee-length skirt she wore did little to disguise the shapeliness of her long legs. Her golden patent leather heels finished her outfit. Her natural beauty and well-dressed presentation tugged at his self-control. He returned his gaze to her eyes, and her breath caught. His blue eyes were alight with deep and sensual passion. His height and muscular build scared and soothed her. She could sense the massive power in his broad shoulders. She felt small as she stood before him. She knew he was dangerous, and it excited her. For the first time in her life, she wanted to surrender to a man. He sensed her willingness as his eyes bored into her, his predatory side exploring her for any sign of danger or deception. Neither spoke. The silence between them grew expectant. He detected the first notes of her scent and his nostrils flared as he inhaled her, breathing her in to become part of him. It was intoxicating. His pulse quickened, and his nostrils flared. He resisted the urge to paw at the ground with his feet, like a bull before it charged.

"I usually don't do this, but I just…I was wondering…" She trailed off and began to tug at her hair with one of her hands.

"I couldn't help but notice you here by yourself and that you don't have a ring on" she tilted her head towards his left hand "are you involved with anyone right now?"

He was stunned. He continued to look deeply into the lady's eyes while thinking of what to say. He felt something more than simply a connection when looking at her. It was also more than a simple attraction. It was animalistic, and it was real. He noticed that she breathed faster as his eyes fell to her neck. He saw her pulse throbbing with the rhythm of her heart. He imagined the blood flowing throughout her body, warming her soft center, giving heat to its depths. Then, that same blood would return to her heart and be pushed throughout her body again. He could sense her desire as it mirrored his own. She stepped forward and put her warm hand on his chest.

"I've never been so forward, never. I'm usually quite shy about this sort of thing." She breathed in through her nose, her nostrils flared as she exhaled and moved her hand up his chest to his shoulder, tilting her head back to look at him.

He couldn't take his eyes from her neck, and the throbbing, gushing ecstasy he knew waited for him. It called to him. It wanted mouth, his kiss, and it wanted him to penetrate its walls and free it from its fleshy confines so that it could flow into him - to feed and nourish him.

She tilted her head back farther, her wet lips parted, and her tongue flicked across their moist tenderness.

"Please," she whispered in the most sultry and desperate voice he had ever heard. Her hand tightened on his shoulder. Her other hand went to his waist as she pulled herself to him, pressing her full breasts against his body. He could feel their excitement pressing into his flesh. Her left foot raised out behind her, and her knees opened, hugging his left leg between them.

He wanted nothing more than to take her right there. Ashton recalled the desire he had felt for Julia and how he had felt that he had violated her with similar thoughts. These feelings helped pull him out of the grips of passion and restore him to his senses.

It took every ounce of his strength to disentangle himself from the woman's embrace. He heard a quiet and pitiful whimper squeak from her as he did.

"I'm sorry. I am, um, in a relationship." He hoped that would be enough to deter her. He was wrong.

"I don't care. I don't. I can't explain it, but I want to be yours. No, I have to be - I must be yours. I want you to take me." She had such a pleading look in her eyes that he felt sick telling her no. She looked as if she were about to weep at the rejection. His mind screamed for him to take her and her hot blood. The thought of drinking her blood flooded his body with sexual energy. Somehow picking up on this renewed deluge of desire washing over him, the woman stepped back into him. She bit her lip so hard that a drop of blood ran down her chin. He reached out and cupped her face with his hand and rubbed the blood off with his thumb. She closed her eyes and nuzzled her cheek into his hand. Ashton had the idea that if she could purr, she would have.

"I...I can't. I can't. Not right now. I want to - more than you know - but this is not a good time."

She persisted. Ashton felt her hand touch his outer thigh and continue to rise up and over towards his inner thigh. The touch was like lightning, and his passion throbbed. He knew he could not resist either desire for much longer. He grabbed her wrist with his hand and pulled it back to her side.

"No!" he said in a stern, quiet voice.

She immediately stopped. Her abruptness in doing so made Ashton need to steady his balance as she shifted her weight back, no longer pushing against him.

The look of disappointment was palpable. Ashton wanted to soothe the woman and be gentle in his rejection of her. He put his hands on her shoulders and looked into her tear-filled eyes. It was a struggle for him not to kiss her.

"I need you to go about your business here. Just get what you need and go. That is what I am going to do. I don't think what is happening between us is normal. Please, go now."

She turned around and walked down the aisle, back the way she came. He let out a long sigh of both relief and disappointment. He stood there for a few minutes, thinking about the encounter with the woman. He had mixed feelings. He felt good about not crossing any lines but felt like he had done something wrong - as if resisting the urges was unnatural. These competing emotions only served to confuse him more.

He refocused his attention on the tasks at hand.

"Stay focused," he reminded himself. After selecting curtains and drapes for the two bedrooms and the patio, he headed towards the grocery section. Before he could see it, he smelled the meat. No, that wasn't right. He smelled the blood in the meat section, and the other hunger welled up inside him.

He picked up a package of rib-eye steaks and sniffed them. He was surprised that it did not emanate the intriguing smell. It was close but not exactly what had grabbed his attention. He continued searching for the origin of the alluring aroma until he finally came to a section that had several round containers labeled beef liver. He fought the urge to rip open the package and drink the blood. The thought of it disgusted him. Yet he wanted nothing more than to do just that. He put two of the containers into his cart. He noticed an elderly man in the produce section looking at him, shaking his head.

Ashton hurried to the check-out section and stopped by a carousel of sunglasses. He quickly grabbed a pair of aviators and dropped them into his cart. The urge to drink the blood from the liver was strong, and Ashton was unsure if he could resist much longer. He was feeling like he was going to get sick. While ringing up the beef livers, the cashier gave him a look of disgust. Ashton said nothing, wanting to get out of there as quickly as possible. He paid and hurried to his car and deposited the bags into his trunk. Ashton didn't bother putting the cart in the return area. He just hopped in his car and drove off to his apartment.

He drove far too fast in the parking lot at his complex, drawing a warning yell to "slow down!" as he braked hard and jerked his car into his parking spot. He jumped out of the car, popped the trunk open, grabbed all of the bags, and closed the trunk with an elbow. He turned and ran to his apartment, unlocking the door while bags hung around his wrist. He double pressed the lock button and heard the corresponding horn blast from his car. He entered the apartment, closed the doors, and searched for the bag with the blood in it.

"No, no, not blood, liver." He corrected himself, hoping to get his mind off of the topic of blood.

Since finding the liver in the store, he remembered how much he hated the food. Everything about it disgusted him. Why had he picked that of all of the meat? Then he remembered reading something the previous year that the red liquid in meat packages or rare steaks wasn't blood. It was something else. It sounded like hemoglobin - myoglobin. So why the liver? He just assumed that it must have blood in it.

Now, he stood over the two containers of beef livers. He stared at them with fascination. The new hunger he was experiencing was powerful, but it wasn't strong enough that he was willing to drink the blood from the containers.

"Leave it," he said as he put the containers in the fridge. "In case of emergency," he added.

Chapter 9

Raven stood looking out over her porch at the darkening sky as the sun faded on the distant horizon. She had been uneasy since the Blood Communion and the mysterious absence of Trevor. It had only been a few days since the gathering had dispersed, yet the uneasiness remained and grew stronger each day. Now, it felt like an ominous foreboding. Her calm exterior would never betray the feeling of panic she was trying to sort through. Her centuries of being a vampire had forged her composure into impenetrable armor. Yet, upon occasion, an emotional torrent would rage beneath her icy exterior, testing her strength of will to suppress unwanted thoughts. She knew this feeling had nothing to do with any concern for Trevor or his well-being. She secretly hoped he was dead. He was a vile and hateful monster whose desire to inflict pain and suffering on women fed his lecherous self-aggrandizing ego. No, it wasn't Trevor that concerned her. It was a foreboding of something to come, something just out of sight and looming around the next corner. Like the distant rumblings of a deadly storm, unnamed ideas and portents swirled in her mind and threatened to prevent her from having peace. Her disciplined mind was strong enough to isolate this turmoil. She was doing so while standing naked in the first moments of the night, sipping hot coffee, and preparing for a swim. She had always found peace in the water.

She drank the coffee and allowed its bitter warmth to spread into her body. Holding the cup near her mouth before setting it down, she slowly and deeply inhaled the steaming aroma as it rose from the cup. Her mind settled, and she set the cup on the flat handrail and walked down the steps of her porch and towards the dock a few hundred yards away. Languidly, she sauntered through the warm grass and began to hum. Her mind wandered back through oceans of time to a fine summer's day - the last time the sun's caress covered her body in its heating pleasure. Rarely would she allow her mind to wander back to that day as doing so brought such a terrible sense of profound loss that she could feel her soul weep tears of blood.

Soon, her bare feet touched the wooden planks as she stepped onto the dock and walked towards the water. She stretched her arms wide, allowing the warm air blowing over the lake and towards the shore to caress every inch of her lithe body. Her pace slightly quickened as she rose to the tips of her toes. Her arms swung back and then forward, adding to her momentum. Raven bent her knees slightly before her arms swang in front of her body. She pushed off of the edge of the dock and extended her arms over the top of her head. As her feet left the last plank of wood, she softly closed her legs. Her knees and ankles touched, and her toes reached back towards the pier. She dove gracefully through the night air, her body rising and falling with delicate purpose. Just as she pierced the surface of the now cooling water, the last traces of the sun's light faded from the sky. Her body slid into the dark depths. As she sank into the waiting darkness, the sense of impending catastrophe receded from her mind. She stopped humming and lost herself in the peace of her stilled mind as her momentum slowed. Then, she swam with powerful strokes, angling her body to carry her deeper into the lake and farther from the shore. After each stroke and kick, she undulated her body with her arms pressed to her sides and her legs. She penetrated deeper into the murky depths of the lake.

Once she had reached the point in the water where the warmer and more shallow section of the lake gave way to the deeper, colder water, she rolled onto her back and held her arms wide. It felt as if she was flying. The cooler water became cooler air in the night sky as she soared amongst the clouds. She only ever felt such peace in the water like this. Usually, she would drift for minutes, wrapped in this cocoon of solitude and grace, untouched by the cares of her world. This time was different. She let her mind drift and hoped that something would help her make sense of the feelings she had been having. Her mind drifted back to that day so long ago when she had last swum in the sun's light. For a few blessed moments, Raven existed in both times. Her body and soul drifted through both perfect moments. Then she was outside of herself, observing the two times, yet somehow also existing in the two separate realities while remaining apart from either one. The ancient scene changed as the sunny sky darkened. A giant shadowy hand plucked her from the ocean and pulled her to the nightmare maul of a withered demon. Her present body gently rose towards the lake's surface and the darkness of the night. Her other body was pierced by what felt like a thousand bony spears, draining her of life's precious blood. The third her - the one observing both scenes - felt such deep sorrow and helplessness from the terrible and unchangeable act that she knew in her core the only chance for healing to occur was if she found revenge against the monster that had done this to her so many long years ago. She must find a way to avenge herself against Claud for forcing her to become an immortal monster, living on the blood of others. While caught up in the tide of emotions, as the divergent scenes coalesced into the present, Raven's body silently broke the surface of the placid lake. Using her legs to tread water, she ran her hands over her head, pulling her hair into a glistening sheen of jet black silk. She opened her eyes and blew air from her lips to keep the lake's water from entering her mouth. The first thing she saw was her lonely home, sitting near the shore of this isolated lake. She slowly began to smile as she contained the despair inside herself. She now knew why she had felt such ominous feelings of late. The suspected death of Trevor was much more than an unexpected, even if welcomed, change. The juxtaposition of her current existence over the nightmare events of her distant past was new to her. How they were both real and separate intrigued her. To Raven's thinking, this meant that she had an opportunity to heal the wound of her turning and still be able to exist as she was currently doing. By the time she had swum back to the shore, the smile was no longer on her face. If an observer knew Raven and looked long into her dark yet warm eyes, they might be able to tell that the smile left her lips to hide in her eyes.

She reached the pier and effortlessly lifted herself out of the water. She stood for a moment and looked towards her house. The warm water flowed off her naked body running in rivulets over her taught skin and shapely curves. As she walked to her home, she wasn't surprised to see Claud standing on her porch, staring at her. When she drew near enough, she saw him gawking at her body as she made her way to the front porch. When Raven neared the top of the steps, he stepped in front of her, blocking her way. She watched as his eyes completed the lustful inspection of her body. As he did, he took a long drink from her coffee cup, smacked his lips, and set the cup down.

"Mm, good coffee Raven." He smiled his familiar, arrogant, and contemptuous smile. Raven had seen this so frequently that she wanted to wipe it off his face.

"Are you just going to stand there staring at me, or are you going to get out of my way?" she asked in measured tones, maintaining her calm and icy demeanor. She raised her eyebrows as if to say, "well?"

He stepped aside and lifted her cup out for her to take. "There's still some in there." He offered, swaying the cup back and forth. The coffee made a faint sloshing sound.

She looked at the cup and then back up at him. "Too bad, I liked that cup. Just finish it and throw the cup in the garbage." She smiled and opened the screen door. "I'll be right back."

She let the door close without asking him to come in. He noticed her step into some sandals once she entered the house and stared at her naked backside. After so long, she continued to stir his desire every time he saw her. Naked as she was, it was nearly intoxicating as his indulgent thoughts danced through his perverted mind. She walked through the kitchen and turned down the hall. He turned his gaze back to the serene landscape around him. He didn't enjoy the countryside, he was a city man. He vastly preferred the hustle and bustle of the city to the intolerably slow pace of country life. He liked how the size of a large city could swallow someone up in its labyrinthine landscapes.

A few minutes later, Raven emerged onto the porch, wearing a thick terry cloth robe and carrying a fresh cup of steaming coffee in her hand. His disappointment showed as he noted she did not bring him a fresh cup and that she was no longer naked.

"We have a problem, Raven." He met her eyes and took on a more serious air.

"Yes, we do," Raven replied coldly. Her few words communicated clearly to Claud what wasn't said. She hated him and would never forgive him for turning her. She didn't need to remind him of it. The fact that she did in this passive-aggressive way got under his skin. That she knew it did, made it worse.

Rolling his eyes, he continued, "Trevor is still missing. No one has heard anything from him. We need to figure out what has happened."

This fact had crossed her mind as well. The amount of damage Trevor could do was alarming. All they needed was an outbreak of vampirism in this day and age. It would spread like wildfire in a drought-ridden forest. She also knew that Trevor wasn't her problem.

"What do you mean we? Do you have a mouse in your pocket? I know the customs as well as you. He is your creation. You turned him. He is your responsibility, not mine." Even as she said it, his presence made sense now. He wouldn't have traveled the long distance to her house to ask. Somehow, he got one of the elders to agree to her figuring things out. He could have called to tell her, but he wanted to see her face when he informed her that she had no choice.

"That is very true, Raven. As I am his sire, the task would normally fall to me. However, Marius and I are working on a project requiring both of our attention."

She could see the satisfaction in his eyes.

"I don't recall anything from the Blood Communion about a project. Nothing was shared with me in the memories nor in person while I was there." She tried to refuse but knew it was pointless.

"Yes, and again, that is true. It is a new project. Marius discussed it with me after the ceremony. I suppose we should have waited to get started on it until after Trevor turned up, but it is somewhat time-sensitive, and we need to focus on it now. Thus, you are being, shall we say, requested by Marius to handle this." His smile oozed self-satisfaction.

She said nothing. What she wanted to say would reveal her anger, and she refused to show any emotion to Claud. Over the years, she had learned that not showing any emotion was the best way to hurt him as he fed on emotions, perhaps more so than blood.

"Plus, everyone knows you are the best at this." His attempt at flattery was useless, and they both knew it. He couldn't help being himself, though.

"Fine," she smiled and tilted her head questioningly, "is there something else?".

"I need you to report to me on this as soon as you know something.

If you fail to find anything within a few days, let me know. You can call me. We can send..."

She interrupted him, holding her hand out in front of herself to quiet him.

"I will send my reports to you and Marius." He started to object. She slightly waved her hand and continued, "you said this is coming from Marius. I will copy you on the report out of courtesy. I'd be surprised if I can't find something within a few days. Trevor leaves his stain wherever he goes, and he won't be hard to track down. My only question is, what do I do when I find him?"

"Contact us with the details, and we'll let you know."

"We're done then?" she asked.

"For now, yes," he tried to hand her the coffee mug again.

"Keep it if you like. I'd just throw it away. I won't be able to get the stink off of it now."

Immediately the rage flared in his eyes, and he stepped next to her, so close that she could feel the heat coming out of his eyes.

"You better watch it, Raven. One of these days, you're going to push too hard and..."

"And what? You're going to do something terrible to me?" she laughed in his face. They both knew turning her into a vampire was the worst thing he could ever do to her.

Fighting his rage and humiliation as Raven had once again provoked him into losing his cool, he squeezed the mug so hard that it shattered in his hand. He looked at the mess in disgust and noticed a porcelain shard was sticking into the ball of his hand. He pulled it out, threw it down, and stormed off towards his car.

She looked at the bloody shard and chuckled again. She liked that mug even more now. She went into the kitchen for a broom and a dustpan to clean it up. She whistled the entire time.

Chapter 10

As planned, Ashton picked Julia up a little after 8:00 pm. He knocked on the metal security door and took a few steps back. He didn't want her to feel crowded when she opened the door to let him in. Instead of inviting him in, she came out and locked her doors. She surprised him by doing this. He brushed it off, thinking she just wanted the trip to be over.

"Hi," she said as she stepped towards him. "Are you parked over here or in your normal spot?"

"I parked out front." He jerked his thumb in the direction of the parking lot.

As they left the recessed common area in the front of the building, they could see his car parked at the end of the walkway, lights on, and the engine quietly idling. He moved to get the door for her, but she waved him off.

"I got it. It's not like we are on a date." She seemed to regret the words as soon as she spoke them. Her face reddening, she stammered, "it's not like I wouldn't go on a date with you. I mean, it's not that we are dating."

Ashton chuckled at her growing consternation. "It's fine, Julia. I know what you mean."

While they drove to Trevor's house, Ashton shared his various discoveries about being a vampire. He didn't mention the beef liver to her, wanting to keep that private. When he told her about the woman who had made a pass at him at the store, she seemed almost jealous when she said she couldn't believe that had happened.

They drove on in silence as the road meandered its way to Trevor's street. Once through the twists and turns, the road straightened out. The neighborhood changed as well. The homes were more modern, much bigger, and more tightly packed together. And much more expensive.

"That never happened with Trevor. I never agreed to go on a date with him. I was never attracted to him, and I never saw anyone, male or female, who paid him more than a passing notice. But, he could make people do anything, just with his words." She looked down at her hands.

"What a piece of shit he was." He mumbled through clenched teeth and tight lips.

Ashton realized she must have been thinking about Trevor as they neared his house. Ashton knew she referred to his ability to compel people. He gripped the steering wheel tight. His knuckles turned white from the force. The sound of flesh creaking on leather caught her attention. She saw muscles in his jaw flex as he ground his teeth. His eyes glared straight ahead.

"And a rich one at that." He nodded towards the homes on the right.

A large nature preserve ran along the left side of the street. It was bordered by a stucco-covered concrete retaining wall. The dim glow of several lights, dispersed throughout the area towards the mountains, marked the various points of interest to the residents and gave an eerie glow to the landscape. No parking signs lined either side of the street, nor could he see a public parking lot.

"That's for sure."

"Yeah, he was. You can get a lot of wealth as a vampire."

"I'll bet. The bastard probably had tons of antiques, old art, precious metals."

As he thought of Trevor and his wealth, images of the safe came to his mind again. They played out like mini-movies of Trevor putting things into or taking them out of the safe. He tried exploring these images, eventually recalling the combination used to unlock the safe. It was easy to remember, even if it was a little puerile.

"He would tell people to give him money. And they did it. Jesus, I gave him so much money," Julia recalled.

With this revelation, Ashton saw it as if he was there. Trevor held his hand out to Julia, and she wrote him a check and then told him how lucky she was to have such a gracious master who allowed her to give him such small gifts. Ashton's anger rose again, and he had no choice but to push the images from his mind.

Julia pointed, "there it is, the second to last house."

Lights lit nearly every square inch of the exterior of the house.

Despite the warm lighting, Ashton felt unwelcome here. Even on the outside, the house had a lonely feeling.

He parked and continued to look around the estate. Ashton met Julia on the walk to the front door. He was surprised when she pulled a key out of her purse as they stepped up to towering front doors. She slid the key into the lock and turned it to the left. She looked quizzically at Ashton.

"What?" He asked.

"The door is unlocked. It's always locked."

"Let me."

He reached for the door handle and pressed down on the lever. Julia stepped slightly to the right to allow Ashton to enter the home first. Ashton wondered if he could walk in or if he needed an invitation. When he stepped into the house, nothing seemed different than any other time he had entered a home.

Julia put a hand on his arm before Ashton let go of the door handle and whispered to him.

"The alarm isn't beeping either. Trevor always keeps his doors and windows locked and the alarm system armed."

"Where is the alarm panel?" He whispered in reply as he didn't see one around the entrance.

She pointed, "it's in the kitchen."

He led the way, and she followed, still keeping her hand on his arm. As he walked through the home, it struck him again how uninviting it was. It was cold and hollow. He saw the kitchen through an arched doorway. Once they entered the kitchen, Julia pointed to the alarm panel on the wall near the French doors that led outside to the pool. The alarm panel was open, the plastic door hanging straight down, exposing the illuminated keypad.

"Someone disarmed it." Julia seemed frightened. She began to look around furtively.

"Do you want to wait in the car?" Ashton asked her as he reached into his sweatpants pocket to get the key. He turned to walk with her to the front door, but she pulled his arm and whispered to him.

"No! I don't want to be alone."

Just then, they heard a click, like a door being closed.

"Hello?" A female voice echoed down to them from the second floor, "is someone here?"

Julia's face drained of color, and she slid behind Ashton. Ahead lay the stairs. She put her palms against his back as his presence comforted her. Still, he could feel her tremble.

He turned around and put his mouth to her ear. "You're his ex-girlfriend, and you're here to get your things. I'm your new boyfriend and am here to protect you, just in case Trevor made a scene. OK?"

When he turned around, her hands ended up on his chest. He realized how close they were. She gazed at him expectantly with a look of longing mingled with fear and excitement. He moved his hands to her elbows and gently pulled them away from his chest. He gave them a subtle shake to get her attention.

"OK, Julia?"

She snapped out of her distraction and said, "yes, getting my stuff, boyfriend, in case... got it."

"Hello?" The voice called out again. This time, it was closer, probably at the top of the stairs.

"Uh, hello, we're in the kitchen," Ashton called out in a loud speaking voice, putting effort into projecting it power and deep bass.

"Oh? Who are we?" The voice sounded cautious.

Ashton led Julia by her hand towards the stairs.

"My name is Ashton, and this is..." he stopped speaking when he saw the woman standing on the stairs. Julia took this as a cue. Ashton was stunned for another reason - he recognized her from the strange dreams.

"Julia, my name is Julia. Is Trevor up there with you?" She looked scared, which helped to sell their story. "I don't know if he mentioned it to you, but I am here to pick up some of my things."

"No, he didn't mention anything." The lady, who Ashton now recalled was named Raven, gracefully finished walking down the stairs and stood at arm's length before them.

"You have things in the kitchen?" The woman asked, briefly looking in the direction they had come.

"What? No. I was checking the alarm, it is usually on, and the door is usually locked." Julia explained. She held up her key to prove her right to be there.

"I see, but this is my brother's home. I didn't receive word that he was expecting anyone."

"You're Trevor's sister?" Julia asked, clearly not believing it as there was no resemblance between the two, not to mention that he was a vampire and had no sister.

"Nice to meet you, Julia. My name is Raven." She held her hand out to Julia, who shook it briefly.

Raven turned to Ashton, and her expression changed ever so slightly. She held her hand out to him with a questioning look. Ashton was stunned by her elegance and beauty. Her comportment indicated that she was a refined lady. Her effortless grace and practiced movements left no doubt of this. Her high, angular cheekbones, jet black hair, and lithe figure belied the power he knew she commanded. His attraction to her was immediate and intense. So much so that he struggled to think of what to do next.

Raven sensed the hesitation and withdrew her hand as indignation spread across her face.

"I'm sorry, please, forgive me."

He blushed as he realized how oafish he must seem to such a lady. In an attempt to salvage his dwindling dignity, he delicately took her hand in his. In a sudden movement, she slipped her hand around his and bore down hard, her expression not changing in the slightest. At first, he thought his hand was going to break. Then, a reflex kicked in, and he met her strength with his own. Without thinking, he then added more power to his grip. She gave him a knowing look and shook his hand.

"Nice to meet you, Ashton." She flashed a broad and warm smile.

"Yes, nice to meet you as well, Raven." He returned her smile. Did he see a flash of playfulness dance across her eyes? If his dreams had informed him correctly, she certainly did not get along with Trevor. Then why was she here in his house? It couldn't be a coincidence that Raven would turn up at the home of Trevor the same day he and Julia had. Ashton and Julia had come there with a purpose. They hoped to get Julia's money back, and perhaps Ashton would be able to get some for himself. He thought of it as compensation for what Trevor did to him.

He suddenly realized that he was still staring into Raven's almost glowing brown eyes. Growing embarrassed and feeling like a schoolboy, he slid his hands into his pocket and turned his attention to Julia, who was paying close attention to the interchange and seemed annoyed.

"Oh, I can go up and get my things if you two wish to talk." Julia offered, turning to the stairway.

"Just a moment, please." Raven's lofty voice froze Julia in her tracks. Her tone was not one to be questioned.

She waited for Julia to turn and face her before she continued. "I think you should wait for Trevor to return. I have no way of knowing what is or what is not yours, and I wouldn't want any problems between the two," she turned to include Ashton, "or three of you."

Julia looked at Ashton, imploring him to help.

"Well, when do you expect him to return?" he asked.

"I don't know when he is due home. I have been unable to reach him. Which reminds me, when did you see him last?" She didn't change her focus to Julia. Ashton turned to Julia for help this time.

"A few days ago, when we decided to end our," she swallowed loudly, "relationship."

"Oh no, that's tragic! I do know that Trevor can be such a beast at times." She guffawed and somehow made even that sound charming.

"More like a monster," Ashton thought, unconsciously making a fist with his right hand.

Julia had turned white at the outburst.

"Oh dear, are you OK? I didn't mean to upset you," she rushed to Julia and gently led her to the sofa, "please, sit down. I'll be right back."

Before either of them could object, Raven disappeared into the kitchen. They heard a cabinet open and clinking of what sounded like a delicate crystal. In a few moments, she returned to the living room with a decanter of what looked like brandy and two cognac glasses. Lifting the bottle, she skillfully meted out the proper pour of the brandy into one of the glasses and handed it to Julia. She looked at Ashton to see if he wanted one, which he declined.

Julia, unaccustomed to such attention, quickly sipped the brandy, cupping the glass in both hands.

While Julia sat and recovered, Raven turned to Ashton. "I am sorry to have upset the poor thing."

Ashton didn't like Julia referred to as a thing. "Your brother," the accusatory tone in his words came out unbidden, "put her through a great deal, much more than anyone should ever endure." He reached his hand out and set it on Julia's shoulder, taking a protective posture over her. Raven smiled at this, realizing that Julia could be leverage. She also liked that he was protective of her. The disparate nature of the two thoughts did not phase her.

Ashton, on the other hand, was growing weary of the game. He knew that Raven was a vampire. He was pretty sure that she knew that he was as well. Why then keep up the pretense?

"Come on, Julia, let's get out of here." He stepped back to let her stand up. She did so and set the glass on the table and muttered her gratitude. Ashton began to lead her to the door. As they approached the door, Ashton took his key out of his pocket and handed it to Julia.

"I'll be there in a minute," he told her.

Julia looked at him questioningly.

"I need to get her contact info," he explained.

She looked like she had more to say, but Ashton shook his head and put a finger to his lips. Then he pointed to his ears. She took the keys and hurried to the car as Ashton turned and walked back to Raven, who stood waiting in the doorway. As he approached, she stiffened. Ashton noticed a flash of something in her eyes. He wondered if it was fear. As he reached into his pocket for his phone, he could tell that Raven closely watched him.

"If you give me your number, I'll call you if we see Trevor." He held his phone out before him, ready to dial her number. She stepped closer to him and gently took his phone from his hand. When her hand touched his, he didn't pull away. He liked the way her skin felt against his.

She dialed her number, and before calling it, she looked up at Ashton.

"We both know that Trevor is dead." Her matter-of-fact tone and disinterested delivery of the assertion stunned Ashton. He didn't say anything. She pressed the send button to initiate the call.

"You have no idea what you have gotten into, Ashton." She handed his phone back. A moment later, they could hear the faint sound of a phone ringing. Presumably, it was her phone.

"Come back tonight at around midnight. We can talk then. We need privacy to discuss the situation, and Julia doesn't need to be involved."

"Why can't we just talk on the phone?" He asked her, doing his best to maintain his calm.

"I prefer to discuss these things in person. You never know who could be listening in on a phone call."

Ashton heard his car start and looked over his shoulder. He was surprised to see Julia behind the wheel.

"Go on, get her home. We can talk later." She noticed that he was hesitant. "If you don't trust me, we can talk a little over the phone, but there are some things that I refuse to discuss unless it is in person. I can assure you that you have nothing to fear from me."

"Yet?" He asked.

She shrugged. "I hope that it stays that way."

She stepped back into the house and started to close the door. He put his hand on the door and looked her in the eyes. He realized that it wasn't fear he saw in her eyes. He saw concern - for him.

"OK," was his only response. He walked to the car and sat on the passenger side.

"What was all of that about?" Julia asked as she backed out of the driveway and headed towards their complex.

"I don't know," he watched the house as they drove away. Part of him wanted to catch a glimpse of Raven before they left.

Raven leaned against the closed door. Her heart was pounding for more reasons than she cared to admit. How the coven would interpret her actions always concerned her. She was confident that she hadn't said anything compromising in nature. Her attraction to the man was what really bothered her.

On their way home, Ashton explained that Raven wanted to meet again. He hadn't told her that Raven was a vampire or her warning.

"You don't think she's his sister, do you?" She glanced over at him.

"No."

"She could be one of his other, you know, victims, like me," her voice quavered.

"No, she's..., " he didn't want to get into it as she was driving. Traffic ahead slowed as they came to a stop at a light.

"She's what?" Julia asked.

"Let's talk when we get back, OK?" he asked, hoping that she would agree. The light changed, and the cars ahead pulled away. She didn't drive forward. He looked at her, and he could tell that she knew. The car behind them beeped. She quickly pulled ahead while glancing at Ashton with concern on her face. When they arrived at the complex, instead of pulling into Ashton's spot, she drove to her side of the lot and parked close to the one he had used a few days earlier. She turned off the engine but didn't get out of the car. She unbuckled her seatbelt and turned to face Ashton.

"She's a vampire too, isn't she?"

Ashton could tell that she was doing her best to seem stoic.

"Yes, but she doesn't seem to be like the others." He offered, hoping it would soothe her. It didn't. She put her hands to her head, raked her fingers back through her hair, and then clenched them into fists. She squinted her eyes and grunted in frustration.

"I want to be done with them!" He didn't know if she included himself in that statement. He wouldn't blame her if she did.

"I am so sick of this shit. I want my life back. I want things to be normal again."

"No kidding." He agreed.

Julia gasped and covered her mouth when she realized how that must have sounded. She put her other hand on Ashton's arm. He glanced down at the contact.

"Oh, my God. I am so sorry, Ashton, I wasn't thinking. I didn't mean anything. Please, can you forgive me?" Her hand slid down his arm to his hand and held it between hers.

"Oh, don't worry. I know what you meant. I do agree with you too. I want normal back as well. Well, at least I want the old normal back. As far as Raven goes, I don't think she is anything we should be worried about." He explained that he had seen her in the strange dreams he had been having. He also told her that he thinks that the blood has something to do with those dreams, and somehow the blood contained memories or some inherited knowledge.

"Why do you think that she wants to meet you tonight?" Julia asked, wanting to change the subject from blood or vampire-specific topics.

"To be honest, I'm not sure, but I want to find out."

"She *is* hot, isn't *she?*" Julia teased him.

She could tell he was embarrassed.

"That's not why I am going. You know why I want to go. Maybe I can get back some of what Trevor took from you. Plus, she might be able to help me."

Julia looked at him questioningly. "Oh, how's that?".

"With this vampire stuff. I have no idea what I don't know about this, um, change in me. Hopefully, Raven can help." He shrugged.

He tried to push his other thoughts from his mind - thoughts of Raven and his powerful attraction to her. He couldn't allow it to cloud his mind or distract him. He looked at his watch and realized that he had a few hours to kill until he would return to Trevor's house - to Raven.

He walked Julia to her apartment and then went to his own. He planned to use this time to send his resignation to his boss as there was no way he could work there any longer. It was just a job, after all. He shook his head.

Jacob watched from the trees as Ashton walked Julia to her apartment. Then he watched as he went on alone to his. Once Ashton walked around the corner to his apartment, Jacob emerged from the trees and made a beeline straight to Julia's.

Chapter 11

Expecting Ashton to be the one knocking, Julia didn't even bother to set her wineglass down as she strode over and opened the inside door.

"Oh!" she exclaimed.

She recognized the lanky teen from the complex but had no idea why he would be knocking on her door.

"Um, hi there." The young man clearly was very nervous. "My name is Jacob. I live here in the complex. I, uh, need to talk with you about something."

Julia didn't like how he kept fidgeting around while talking to her. His constantly shifting eyes offered her no comfort.

"OK?" Her voice rose as if she was asking him if things were OK.

"It's, uh, kinda private." He looked up at her and smiled uneasily.

"Well, it's late, and I don't know you." She pulled her inner door closer, getting ready to step back and close it.

"I need to talk with you about what happened the other day with the vampire." He blurted, trying to stop her from shutting the door.

Julia's heart jumped, and she froze. She felt a little dizzy, and her knees weakened.

"What do you mean?" She asked. Her voice trembled slightly. She offered a weak smile, hoping that charm would be the best course of action.

"I saw it. I saw the vampire guy burst into flames. I saw the big guy get attacked and hurt bad. You know, the kind of bad that ends in dying." As he spoke, he watched as she failed to control her reaction.

Her skin had turned white as a sheet, and her legs buckled a few times, but she used the door to stay on her feet.

"I, uh, I..." she struggled to swallow and then realized she still had her wineglass in her hand. Without thinking further, she downed the nearly full glass.

"Just a sec," she closed the door and returned in a few moments. She unlocked the security door and stood back to let Jacob in. Once he walked past her, she poked her head out and looked around. She had no idea what she was looking for but felt the need to check anyway.

Jacob was standing in the middle of her living room, awkwardly looking around. She recalled that not very long ago, Ashton had stood in her living room where Jacob did now. Ashton's presence demanded her attention, while Jacob's struggled to be acknowledged and was almost revolting. The comparison struck her and filled her with disdain for the nosy man-boy before her.

"Have a seat." She motioned to the couch and walked to the counter to refill the glass she had set next to the half-full bottle a few moments earlier.

Jacob sat down on the edge of the couch and looked up at her. His hands rested on his knees. Julia leaned against the counter.

"So," she said, trying to get Jacob started.

He looked at her, and she could tell that he was having a tough time.

"I got video of it." He mumbled, but she was able to understand what he had said.

"I saw what happened to that short guy and that Ashton guy. I also see that he don't have no bandages." As he spoke, he seemed to gain confidence. "So, I figure he is a vampire too."

"I don't know what you are talking about," she tried to deny it, but knew it was pointless.

Then she set her glass down. She walked to the dining room table and grabbed her phone. She unlocked it but didn't dial any number.

Jacob held up his hands, expecting her to call the police. "Hold on. Wait. I don't want to start any trouble. Chill, lady."

"Julia."

"What?" He wasn't quick on the uptake, Julia thought.

"My name is Julia. Call me Julia, not lady, OK?"

She raised her eyes as if to say, got it?

"Oh yeah."

He smiled at her sheepishly.

"Anyway, I shot the whole thing. No use denying what happened. I haven't seen him during the day since then either." He didn't mention that he was at work during the daytime. He wanted her to think he was around the complex.

Julia didn't know what to say. She decided to stay quiet and let him do the talking.

"I want in."

"In?" she asked.

"Yup. I want in."

"What do you mean?" she asked, her voice growing annoyed.

"I want to be a vampire, just like Ashton."

"You what?" she asked, unable to believe what he said.

"You heard me. I want to be a vampire. I've always wanted that." His face took on a more boyish appearance, lighting up at the thought. He wasn't looking at her when he spoke. He was looking into the past.

"Ever since I read Dracula when I was eleven. I just wanted to be a vampire."

He saw the alarm on Julia's face.

"Not a *bad* vampire. I want to be a *good* vampire."

"A good vampire?" she asked, her doubts about Ashton coming to the fore. "How can you be a good vampire? They live by sucking the blood of innocent people." She felt guilty after asking the question, but it was one she had asked herself more than a few times, desperately hoping for a good answer.

"By only feeding on volunteers or homeless people or criminals. Maybe even getting blood from a blood bank."

She realized that Jacob had given it thought.

"So, what do you want from me?"

He smiled as if he was waiting for her to ask that very question.

"I want you to talk to Ashton about it and convince him."

"I can't convince him of anything. We barely even know each other."

He studied her, thinking about his next move.

"Well, unless you guys want to be famous for all the wrong reasons, you need to figure something out."

As what he just said began to sink in, he reached into his pocket and pulled out his phone.

"What?" Julia asked, standing up and walking towards him so quickly that he stumbled back. "Are you threatening me?"

He moved his thumbs around his phone and handed it to her.

"I have this video saved in several places, including my attorney." He lied about the attorney, but she had no way of knowing.

He watched as Julia played the video. Her eyes grew wide, and she put her hand over her gaping mouth. When it was over, Julia looked at him with disgust and fear on her face. She wanted to ask him many questions but was too stunned to formulate them into anything coherent enough to vocalize.

"Give me your phone number so I can text you a link. Show that to Ashton. Let's see. It's Wednesday now. I'll give him to Friday night to make a decision. If he agrees, I'll take the video down from YouTube. If he doesn't, I'll start contacting some influencers I know. It won't take long for this to blow up and you guys to get hounded for answers. How will they react when he isn't available during daylight hours?"

He was right, and she knew it. She gave him the number, and he texted her a link to the video on YouTube. She turned to set her phone on the counter and glanced over her shoulder at him. He had been checking her out, and Julia shuddered at the realization. She set her phone down and turned to face him.

"Fine. I'll let Ashton know."

She crossed her arms over her chest.

Realizing that she had just dismissed him, he pushed his phone back into his pocket and walked to the door. He left without saying another word. Once he had left, she hurried to her phone and sent Ashton a message.

"Ashton, we have to talk. There's trouble." She sent that message and contemplated sending him the link to the video. She chose to wait.

Chapter 12

Ashton had just finished sending his resignation letter when his phone chimed, letting him know of a new text message from Julia. He called her right away. She explained Jacob's visit and his demand. Wanting to judge his reaction first, she waited to mention the video. She knew he had already been through too much and wished she didn't have to add to his worries. For long moments, the line was quiet, and Julia grew concerned that the call had dropped.

"Ashton?" she asked.

"I'm here." He whispered his reply. "I just don't know what to say."

"Well, there's more."

"He wants more than that?" Ashton's anger filled his voice.

"No, that's not what I mean. I'm going to send you a link. Watch it and call me back, OK?" He could hear her pull the phone away from her face, followed by her whispering to herself. A moment later, Ashton's phone vibrated.

"I got it. I'll call you right back, OK."

"Sure."

Ashton hung up and opened the link. When he saw the title of the video: "Vampires exist in Scottsdale of all places!" He cringed. He watched the video in horrified fascination. After seeing Trevor rip the chunk of flesh out of his neck, Ashton felt dizzy and disoriented. Without thinking, he put his hand to his neck. At the part where Julia stabbed Trevor in the back, Ashton smiled. He stared in amazement as the scene continued with him pushing Trevor off and into the sun. The sudden combustion of the monster disturbed him further. Something about that - about seeing the daylight's effect on Trevor - twisted him up inside. It served as a reminder of what he had become. He inspected the page and noticed it only had five views. The video had no comments either.

Ashton called Julia back.

"Well?"

"I don't know what to say."

"He gave you until Saturday to give him an answer."

"Who is this guy?" Ashton asked.

"His name is Jacob. He's tall, has long black greasy hair, and is skinny. Oh, he also has a fair amount of acne."

"Yeah, I know who he is. Maybe I'll talk to him. Maybe I can..." he trailed off, lost in thought. He didn't want to say that he was thinking about using his ability to compel him, but what choice did he have?

"Let's think about this. Maybe we can figure out a plan? You - we've - got until Saturday." He could hear the hope in her voice. He shrugged to himself.

He closed his eyes and rubbed them out of habit and then shook his head. He exhaled. "Fine, I'll get back to you. I'm heading over to Trevor's for a chat with Raven. If it's not too late when we finish, do you want me to call you?"

"Nah, I need to get up early for work, and I'm already late getting to bed."

"OK. Give me a call after you get home from work," Ashton said, his voice becoming flat.

She could tell he was worried and felt guilty for adding to his concerns.

"After sunset, you mean, right?" She laughed, hoping to ease the mounting tension.

"What? Oh, yeah, after that. See you then, Julia." He ended the call, and the screen switched back to the video.

"Fuck!" He jammed the lock button.

The pressure kept building up inside his head, and he knew that he was nearing his breaking point. As the unexpected issues were piling up, he fought to maintain at least a semblance of normalcy as his life continued to creep out of control. This loss of control scared him more than the implications of becoming a vampire. He had struggled to keep his life on track after the deaths of his mother and sister. After his mother had passed, he had to keep things together for his sister - he was all that she had. That became his mission and purpose. When she died years later, he fell into a deep depression. He knew he had failed his sister somehow. With the loss of his sister went his purpose in life and ultimately, he thought, his reason to live. After over a year of living life feeling nothing except despair, he decided he had had enough. He decided to end it.

That night he had a strange and exceptionally vivid dream. It started with his sister standing before a long brick wall. It was impossibly long, stretching from horizon to horizon, dividing a field of wildflowers. She stood in front of the wall. In her left hand, she held a basket. She would reach into the basket and retrieve a brick. Next, she placed the brick on the wall. As if by magic, the mortar appeared around the brick. She repeated the process.

Ashton came up to her.

"Why are you building a wall in the middle of this field?"

She continued to work. She either ignored the question, or she didn't hear it. Ashton reached out to shake her shoulder, but she surprised him by turning around with lightning speed.

"Don't!" she screamed at him.

When he tried to speak again, she dropped her basket and stomped the ground, causing everything to shake. A wave undulated along the wall, moving in and out instead of up and down.

"Don't! Don't! Don't!" She stomped harder after each utterance. Even the sky shook.

Without warning, everything went black. The sky, the wall, and the landscape - all of it vanished. Ashton's sister emerged from the darkness to stand before him. Not as the emaciated young lady who had passed away but as the vibrant young girl he had protected and taken everywhere when she was much younger. When she looked up at him, she smiled such a sweet and peaceful smile that he sobbed.

"Ashton, just don't!" She said in a sweet and lulling voice that soothed his troubled mind. He thought to ask her what she meant, but he knew.

"I can't stay, Ash. They won't let me. Tell me you won't, please! Ash?"

She slowly faded away before his very eyes. Only she could call him Ash. She made him promise he would only let her call him Ash.

Tears ran down his cheeks in swollen rivers. He felt like he needed to do something as she continued to fade away. He worried if he didn't figure it out, she would disappear forever.

"I won't. Sam, I won't," he called out to assure her.

Her name was Samantha, and he was the only one she would allow to call her Sam.

While she faded, before disappearing, she smiled at him and reached her hands out to him. He reached to take her tiny hands in his. As they touched, he jerked awake, screaming and covered in sweat. He went to the bathroom and splashed water on his face. When he looked into the mirror, he swore he saw a kiss disappear off his cheek. He ran his hands down his face, and when he looked again, the mark was gone.

Even though it happened several years ago, he still relies on that experience to assure himself he is moving forward in life - that he keep his promise to his little sister. He longs for his sister to visit him and tell him he still has a purpose. He needs that purpose - he needs a reason to live, now more than ever.

His thoughts shifted to Raven and how thinking of her somehow made him feel more at peace. It was as if she belonged in his thoughts. He stopped himself from thinking about what other feelings she stirred in him. He had to be wary of her. He didn't know why she showed up or what her intentions were.

He grabbed his phone and his keys.

"There's only one way to find out," he told himself as he left his apartment.

Chapter 13

Ignoring her request to let her know when he was on his way, Ashton drove there in silence. The rhythm of the road kept his focus and prevented his thoughts from drifting to the issues at hand. He was pulling into Trevor's driveway before he knew it. Everything seemed the same as when he and Julia were there a few hours ago. Yet, there was something surreal about being there again. As he walked to the door, his feeling of trepidation grew. He stopped a little more than ten feet from the door and considered getting back into his car and going back to his apartment. At that moment, the door opened, and Raven stepped out. Her black hair was wet and shiny. She stood barefoot with a large towel wrapped around her waist. The coral and navy blue cover-up she wore did little to hide her figure, yet it did add a touch of modesty and class to her appearance. Ashton found that he liked this about her. He realized that he was staring at her when she spoke, snapping him out of it.

"I'm glad that you came, Ashton." She spoke in even measured tones, no emotion present in her smooth voice. She didn't mention that he didn't call ahead or that she had caught him staring at her.

"I simply love the water and couldn't resist the temptation."

Ashton resumed his walk to the house. Raven turned and walked inside, allowing him a comfortable distance to follow her. In doing so, he noticed how toned her legs were and that she walked like a model, her svelte body swaying with each graceful step. Ashton closed the door behind him and followed Raven back through the foyer, the living room, and the kitchen. The French doors were wide open, and she walked through them to a set of patio furniture along the deck next to the pool. Raven took a seat on the edge of a chair next to an above-ground fire pit that radiated intense heat. She crossed her legs and reached for a half-empty glass of red wine. Ashton sat across from her with his elbows resting on his knees and hands clasped before him.

"Would you care for a drink?" She asked.

"No, no thanks, Raven." He replied, doing his best to make his voice steady and calm. He struggled to prevent his attraction to her from distracting him. Not only was it distracting, but it was also irritating. He felt like he was a 17-year-old sitting across from a supermodel.

She set her glass down, smiled, raised her eyes, and tilted her head to say, "very well then."

"So." He managed to say, feeling like a complete idiot.

She smiled at him patiently, somehow picking up on his discomfort.

"You have nothing to fear from me, Ashton." She tried to ease his evident apprehension.

"OK," he said.

Ashton thought, "wow, nothing like dazzling her with your elocution."

His ironic smile conveyed the wrong message to her.

"You don't believe me?" she asked, offended by what she considered his misperceived doubt.

"Uh, no. It's just, I mean I..."

He took a slow breath and ran his hands up and down his legs. He decided to be open and honest and expected the same in return.

"Listen, Raven, I believe you. I also want you to know that you have nothing to fear from me. It's just these dreams I've been getting ever since...."

He realized she might not even know what had happened. Then he thought of Jacob and his video. He took his phone out, opened the video, and handed her the phone.

"Ever since this." He lowered his head and waited. Ashton listened as the video played for a few seconds before it stopped without warning. He looked up at her.

"I've already seen this."

"Wait, Jacob already showed you this? You know him?" Anger crept into his voice. He didn't like being toyed with, even by a beautiful woman.

She noticed his growing displeasure and shifted in her seat.

"Of course not! I already told you I came here to find out what happened with Trevor. I found the video because I was searching for it. To be more precise, I searched for Trevor or anything to do with vampires in Arizona. That video needs to come down. He needs to be dealt with, as does Julia."

He wondered exactly how she planned to deal with them. Maybe she is a monster like those others he had seen do horrible things in his dreams. Yet, none of his dreams of her included anything that caused him alarm. As these changes were new to him, he decided to proceed with caution.

Part of him wanted to reject the notion, but the threatening nature of her statement brought out his protective side. He leveled an icy glare at her, causing her to start. His voice rumbled in his chest in warning, like a tremor before an avalanche.

"What do you mean?"

He paused, then added, "I won't let you hurt Julia or Jacob."

The thought of someone hurting Julia, especially after all she had endured, enraged him. Every muscle in his body tensed in anticipation of an attack.

His reply both stunned and confused Raven. She thought again about what she said. Then she realized what he must have been thinking. She held her hand up, horrified at the realization.

"No, you misunderstand. I didn't mean to imply harm would come to either of them. Julia and Jacob need to forget about this, and Jacob needs to destroy all copies of the video."

Her shock at his misunderstanding endeared her to him. His incorrect conclusion couldn't have upset her if she were a cold-hearted person. His tension eased but didn't disappear.

Raven took a modest drink of wine to wet her mouth. She could sense his trepidation and confusion. She wanted to calm him, but she knew she had to be very careful as the coven would see her actions at the next Blood Communion.

After the initial meeting with Ashton and Julia, Raven sent her preliminary findings, including the video's existence. While she expressed that the situation was in hand, she couldn't help but feel something more loomed around the corner. She had no logical reason for such thoughts, but that didn't stop them from happening.

"You mentioned dreams. Tell me about those." Her voice had resumed its cold, maybe even clinical tones.

"Well, ever since Trevor... since I became this way, I have these odd dreams or visions. They can't be dreams. Sometimes they happen while I am awake, but I don't know what to call them. I see through many perspectives at different points in the dreams. Sometimes, I think about something, and my mind jumps to it, like searching through a video. I even dreamed about you before I met you today."

He hoped she could explain the memories.

"So, you haven't fed since being turned then?" It wasn't a question.

"How do you know?" he asked, skeptical of her surety and confused about its implications.

"If you had, you would understand that these dreams, as you called them, are actually memories. We call them Blood Memories. When we consume blood, we receive memories from the vessel. With human blood, the more we consume, the more memories we receive. If we take all their blood, we get all of their memories. That is why it usually takes several visits to turn a human. They become lethargic and confused during the process. If the vampire decides not to turn them or kill them, their memories will return, but it will take a few days."

Ashton didn't allow her use of words like "consume" or "vessel" to obfuscate the truth. She was talking about feeding on humans.

"We don't need to consume blood very often to sustain ourselves." She sighed and added as an afterthought, "like humans, some of us indulge more than we need to."

"Why would you want to do that?"

He thought of how confusing it had been for him to have so many foreign memories in his mind.

"Like anything else - pleasure. Most people who overindulge don't do so because they dislike it. It can be like an addiction. It can be the same for us." She saw his eagerness to learn more and felt a little guilty when she continued, "I can't get into that right now, though."

Ashton decided to play along and get as much information as he could. He wondered why she wasn't more willing to share information with him.

"OK. You mentioned how things work with humans. How does it work with, say, animals or other vampires?" He scrutinized her, watching for anything that might indicate she was being deceptive.

"Well, with a vampire, it is different. For one, it takes much less blood to transmit memories. Another difference is that when a vampire gives blood to a human, the human can't immediately access the memories. That only happens after the transformation is complete. As for animals, I couldn't tell you. I've never consumed animal blood."

"What if you don't want to drink human blood?" He emphasized the word drink, assuring that he had no illusions about what they were discussing.

"You die, an excruciatingly horrible death. That won't happen. You will drink human blood. It is inevitable."

Ashton shook his head emphatically. "No, I won't do that!"

Her expression changed for a brief moment, showing her pity for him.

"She isn't an ice queen after all," he thought.

Chapter 14

Claud read and reread Raven's report. Everything seemed in order. Yet, he could not help but worry. Trevor's death was the least of his concerns now. What Trevor may have left behind was the source of his anxiety. Had he left anything that would reveal their plans? It was a risk Claud refused to take. He was sure that Raven would be able to handle those involved in the altercation, including the tall man who was most likely a vampire now. He liked the man's look and hoped that Raven would be able to bring him in. If not, it didn't matter.

He summoned his human assistant, Malcolm, by pressing a call button under his desk. In under one minute, the door to the office opened, and a tall, thin man of advanced years entered.

"Malcolm, I need you to arrange a trip to Scottsdale, Arizona for me," Claud explained.

"Yes, sir. Right away, sir." Malcolm stood straight and kept his eyes forward and averted from Claud's visage.

"While you're at it, please select a host family for me."

Malcolm stiffened slightly. "Yes, sir," he didn't like the task, and his posture betrayed his efforts to hide the fact.

Claud smirked.

"Is that all, sir?" Malcolm inquired, hoping to remove himself from Claud's presence.

"Yes, Malcolm. That is all."

Malcolm leaned forward into an abbreviated bow, stepped back, and turned to leave. As he opened the door to do just that, Claud's voice halted him. He didn't have time to turn around before Claud conveyed his last instruction.

"Oh, and Malcolm, make sure that I'll enjoy my stay. Otherwise, I might need to visit your daughter and her family. I haven't seen young master Johnathan in quite some time now. How I do miss the young man."

The threat rolled off of Claud's tongue with relish. While made to torment Malcolm and give Claud the type of pleasure he enjoyed, it made him think of Malcolm's daughter and her family. He might visit them, regardless.

Malcolm left the office to make the arrangements.

Minutes before lunchtime, Claud boarded a Gulfstream G550. He worked closely with engineers to customize the craft to provide maximum comfort and protection. He had two travel pods created to withstand catastrophic conditions. If a crash were to occur, recovery services would be alerted, and the GPS beacons within the pods would be activated. While traveling along usual flight corridors within the contiguous states, search and rescue would occur within two hours. When he traveled during daylight hours, he would remain within the travel pod while wearing a protective suit. The suit would allow him to survive daylight exposure long enough to find shelter in the unlikely event the pod were to be breached.

Once the plane landed in Scottsdale and taxied to the hangar, he unlocked and opened the travel pod. He changed from the protective suit into his business attire.

The limousine did not take Claud to an upscale, five-star resort like the Fairmont Scottsdale Princess or the Phoenician. Instead of those luxurious destinations, it arrived at a modest home in the upper-middle-class neighborhood west of Chaparral Park. It belonged to a wealthy family in their mid-thirties. A family of three, the Kellers were both focused on their careers and left little time for their son. As declared atheists, Claud could be sure the home was free of bothersome religious paraphernalia. They held no qualms in projecting their perceived superiority over the less fortunate. The wife worked tirelessly to grow her real estate business, doing whatever it took to keep it on the top. As is almost always the case, the son suffered the most in his lonely and isolated childhood. Most important to Claud, they were a very handsome family, and their closets were full of skeletons.

Claud rang the bell and smirked at the nasally and whiny voice from the security speaker next to the door.

The man scrutinized Claud on a small security monitor and asked, "may I help you?"

When he asked, the man's voice sounded apologetic.

"That must be Lance." Claud thought.

"Yes, my name is Claud. I have a 7:00 pm appointment with Mr. and Mrs. Keller and their son, Jeremy."

After a brief pause, the man responded.

"I'm sorry, Claud, there are no appointments scheduled this evening. Honey?" Lance had called out over his shoulder. When his wife Desiree answered, "Yes?" he asked her to come to the door. Claud heard the speaker cut off as Lance had released the talk button. He listened as the couple spoke furtively before the door opened. The handsome couple from his dossier now stood before him. Their eyes took in the limousine and Claud's attire. He purposefully checked the time, flashing his Rolex Cosmograph Daytona as he noticed their scrutiny of him.

"Seven o'clock, pm. That's the correct time, no?" He looked at them, expecting agreement. While he preferred an invitation over direct manipulation, he would use his power to gain entrance if needed.

"Yes, it is. Please, come in. We can get this sorted out. There must have been a mistake." They parted like the red sea for Moses and made way for Claud to enter their home. He smiled a broad and warm smile as he stepped into their house.

"They know not what they do," Claud thought, and his smile became genuine.

"Where's your wonderful son Jeremy?" he asked, allowing them to get ahead of him and guide him to a well-furnished living room.

"Oh, he's in the great room watching his Little Einstein videos before we put him to bed. He gets one hour of screen time after dinner and bath." His mother chimed in, sounding proud of herself.

"While we can't be sure, our theory is he still benefits from it at his age. After all, the sounds and the shapes still stimulate the same areas of his brain." She explained in a superior tone, caring little whether or not he accepted it.

She hurried on to add, "plus, we are very protective of him and what he watches. There is just so much violence in today's programming for children."

She leaned closer to him and added in a conspiratorial whisper.

"They try to slip liberal indoctrination into the shows. You can never be too careful when it comes to your kids."

Claud was going to love making friends with these people.

While Desiree spoke, Lance walked to a table and picked up an iPad. After a few gestures, he moved to where Claud and Desiree stood.

"I'm sorry, Claud, but I don't see any appointment scheduled for us, nor did we hear anything from your company. What was the name again?" Lance realized he hadn't asked before. He looked to Desiree, and she shook her head. This lapse concerned him, but Lance kept a welcoming smile and moved closer to his wife.

Claud reached into his suit pocket to retrieve what they assumed to be a business card. Instead, using the same motion as with a business card, he produced a condom. Desiree looked at Lance, embarrassed for Claud, thinking it was a mistake. Lance stepped between his wife and the stranger, putting his hand out to push Claud back.

Claud's smile became sinister.

"Lance, go take care of Jeremy and put him to bed. Your lovely wife and I need some privacy. I assume your bedroom offers the most privacy, yes?"

Lance was already walking to the back of the house towards the Great Room, Claud presumed.

"Yes, the bedroom," Lance replied as he disappeared through a double door leading further into the house.

Desiree stared after her husband in disbelief. She turned to Claud and prepared to scream.

"Hush!" he commanded, and she went silent. Eyes wide with panic, she turned to run. Claud grasped her bicep in his vice-like hand and squeezed. She tried to pull free and failed.

"Good. Join us once Jeremy is asleep, OK, friend?" he taunted. He whispered to Desiree, "now take me to your bedroom." He released her arm and could see the first hints of the bruise that would spread around her arm in a band. He liked that.

Nostrils flaring as she drew shallow breaths, she turned and walked down a hallway to the right of the foyer. Claud followed. He looked over her fit body and shoulder-length, jet-black hair. To Claud's dismay, her skin was untouched by the sun and shone milky white in the artificial lighting. He preferred a woman with sun-kissed skin. He made a mental note to mention this to Malcolm. Still, she bore a resemblance to *her*.

"I guess I'll have to settle for the next best thing," he thought.

His wicked smile revealed the twisted thoughts and plans filling his mind with evil intent.

She turned left at the end of the hallway and led Claud to the door at its end. She opened the door and stood at the threshold. Claud came up behind her and pressed himself into her. Putting a hand on her shoulder, he whispered into her ear.

"Well, what are you waiting for?"

She didn't reply. Claud nudged her forward with his groin. Still, she didn't budge.

"Go!" he commanded.

She stepped into the bedroom. Claud rubbed his hands together. His excitement throbbed in time with the beating of his heart.

"Take off all your clothes!"

Desiree obeyed.

Chapter 15

"Have you ever heard that humanity is just nine meals away from anarchy?" Raven asked.

"No," Ashton replied.

"A little over a hundred years ago, a remarkable man named Alfred Henry Lewis proposed that once people cannot eat for three days, they would become willing to commit crimes to feed themselves. The need to survive would outweigh their need to obey social laws. The longer they would go without food, the more desperate they would become and the worse crimes they would commit - only to survive."

"Makes sense to me." Ashton offered.

"As a vampire goes longer and longer without blood, their predatory nature starts to override their humanity. Senses magnify, making it easier to find prey. The body requires additional energy to support this, and the vampire's body consumes its blood to feed the process, leading to more rapid starvation. If they can't find blood, it leads to what we call "The Hunger". Once it takes over, someone like you would look like a concentration camp survivor in a few days. At that point, there are no traces of humanity left, and The Hunger becomes insatiable. A vampire in the grips of The Hunger can wipe out an entire village overnight."

Blood drained from her as a faraway look appeared in her eyes. She shuddered, sighed, and took another drink of wine. Like that, she was back to her frosty self.

Ashton felt uneasy. He couldn't imagine letting that happen to himself. He vowed to kill himself before it could. A walk into the sun and poof, problem solved. Part of him scoffed at being the shortest-lived immortal ever.

"So, how long does it take?"

He was going to ask, "How long do I have, doc?" but didn't feel comfortable enough to joke with the withdrawn Raven.

"It's not exact, but it usually starts within a few weeks. You might last another week without feeding before all of your humanity is gone. Then it gets more and more unlikely that you could recover. No one has ever made it that long on their own."

"On their own? Then how do you know it would happen at all?"

"You are very curious, aren't you?" She asked in her customary aloof tone.

"Weren't you?"

She chuckled. "Hardly. I was part of the crew that had to track down and kill Henri when it happened."

He stared at her, mouth agape. He considered asking her who Henri was but knew she would tell him if she wanted him to know. Plus, she had just commented on his questions.

Raven sighed.

"For now, I'll give you the condensed version of the story. If that's not good enough, it can wait for another time. Frankly, I don't care to think about this at all."

He asked, "will you be willing to tell me more later if you tell me the quick version now?"

"Sure, if the time is right." She answered as if she didn't care either way. She hoped it would never be right because it was a very unpleasant tale.

"OK, I'll settle for a quickie then." He regretted it as soon as he said it. Ashton wondered what he was thinking by making a joke like that, especially after deciding not to only seconds ago. He hung his head in shame. To his surprise, she laughed a heartfelt laugh, not a polite or a mocking one.

"Oh, that's funny. Thanks. I don't laugh that much lately."

She saw the relief in his eyes at her statement. Raven realized then that she enjoyed the man's company. Something about the mixture of intelligence, raw physical power, and his occasional boyish innocence tugged at her. Then came his attractiveness, his devastatingly good looks. She sighed to herself, pushed those thoughts away, and proceeded to tell the story.

"A long time ago, in a land far, far away, there was an evil king."

She paused, waiting for him to look up at her. When he did, he saw the playful smile on her face, and it warmed his blood in more ways than one. Before he could speak, she continued.

"During this king's reign, a terrible disease swept through his lands. Wild rumors abounded. Some blamed the Jews, others blamed God, and others blamed foreigners. Regardless of the cause, rulers had to protect their lands and fortunes. Some despots issued decrees to have foreigners arrested and imprisoned. They did this with zeal, and soon his dungeon became overcrowded with foreigners and natives alike. All were locked in close and squalid quarters. The disease, which we now call the Bubonic Plague, spread like wildfire among the prisoners. One prisoner was a French vampire named Henri. Normally, he could have fought off his captors and fled, but he had fed on a drugged prostitute who happened to be sick with the disease. By that time, we discovered that feeding on someone with the disease would weaken us temporarily. Unfortunately for Henri, he did not know this. The drugs she had taken and her infected blood put Henri into what seemed like a drunken stupor. He would have offered little resistance to the guards."

"We get high if the blood has drugs in it?" He asked without thinking about it.

"Yes, with certain drugs. With Opioids, for example, the effect is dangerous. We receive the drug and the endorphins."

She emptied her wineglass in one drink. Ashton stared at her the entire time. She set the glass back on the table and continued.

"At first, the guards would bring meager amounts of what barely passed as food to the prisoners and watched as they fought over the slop. By then, the disease had ravaged the entire town. Soon, there were no longer guards to bring food to the prisoners, and no one stepped in to do it. Those who were still alive had other, more important problems to deal with. Or so they thought."

"It took days for Henri's weakness to subside. When he recovered, he knew his predicament was dire. He needed blood to strengthen his body and to resist feeding on the sick prisoners, or he needed clean food to survive the physical starvation. Neither option was available to him. What little strength remained to him, he used to fend off the other prisoners as they succumbed to starvation."

"By the time the sickness released his body from its control, he was already starving physically. Once he reached the point where he could no longer reason, he began - like other prisoners in the dungeon - to consume the flesh of the dead. Once he did that, the weakness returned. Soon after, The Hunger took him. When he awoke, his blood lust was in complete control. His body had changed. In a frenzy, he drained every prisoner in the dungeon. We don't know why he didn't succumb to the weakness again. Maybe the people who were still alive were immune to the disease. Maybe it was something to do with his altered state. Either way, his feeding frenzy didn't weaken him - quite the opposite. He broke free from his gory tomb and emerged into the night. Then he set upon the castle first, and after devouring all there, the village was next. His only motivation was blood, and he killed indiscriminately. Men, women, children - no one was safe. As he fed, his power would grow, but at a terrible cost. It required more and more blood to sustain that level of power. By the time we arrived, his power only lasted for seconds after draining an adult male of all his blood."

"Jesus," Ashton whispered, imagining how terrible it must have been.

"Our coven wasn't too far from where it happened. Word somehow got out from one village that a blood-hungry beast was slaughtering everyone in its path and drinking the blood of the fallen. We knew Henri was in that area as we had sent him on a scouting mission to find a haven to house us as we fled persecution from the east. Our coven dispatched three of us to take care of it. Once we found where he was hiding during the day - back in that horrible dungeon that spawned him - we could put him down. It wasn't easy. Two of us almost died."

He sensed his mind focusing on the Blood Memories and caught a few glimpses of Raven facing a horrific-looking beast. He immediately pushed the thoughts from his mind. Raven noticed this and nodded in somber understanding.

"We learned a great deal from that situation. It is why most of us get our blood from known sources."

"Like blood banks or volunteers," Ashton stated, remembering what she had said earlier.

"Yes. That's right. Some of us never enjoyed feeding on humans by biting them. There is a narcotic effect that doing so has on both the vampire and the human. It's very addictive and can lead to a similar problem as starvation. Fortunately, it is temporary and easily reversed. Yet, it may be even more dangerous than the hunger."

She paused briefly, then added, "there seems to be a natural barrier to letting it get out of hand, but that doesn't mean it never has."

"What do you mean, natural barrier?" He asked, trying to understand. "Is it like overeating? Once you're full enough, you can't eat anymore?"

"Well, yes, it is quite like that. Gluttonous vampires need more and more blood to feel satisfied and become insatiable. However, if these vampires bleed themselves, they can continue to feed. One way to bleed yourself as a vampire is to open your veins and let humans drink your blood. So, you can imagine how this symbiotic relationship could get out of hand, can you not?"

Her tone seemed to have switched back to being cold. Ashton wondered if she wasn't detaching to protect herself instead. He thought he knew from what as well.

"Is that how you became a vampire? Were you in one of those symbiotic relationships?" Glimpses of her when she was being turned by a vampire named Claud flashed through his mind when he asked the question. They made him feel sick and he pushed them away.

"What?" she exclaimed, horrified that she had revealed this about herself. She jumped up from her seat and bumped into the table. Her wine glass fell and shattered on the ground beneath her. As she moved, a piece of the glass embedded into her foot, and she hissed in pain and sat back down, groping at her foot and the glass protruding from it. It was sticking out of the arch of her foot.

Ashton went to her, unconcerned with the broken glass on the ground between them. She was holding her foot out and hissing and gasping from the pain. He knelt and grabbed her heel in his hand. He had an uncontrollable need to help her. It reminded him of how he cared for his younger sister, but it was distinctively more pressing. If he didn't help her, he knew he would be a failure.

"Raven, let me get this for you, OK?" he said.

Her initial thought was to tell him no, that she would take care of it herself. She was unaccustomed to accepting help from others. She reached for the glass, but the movement pulled on her leg and then the tendon in her foot and brought blinding pain.

"OK," Raven said through clenched teeth, leaning back in her chair and resigning herself to accept his help. She gripped the arms of the chair.

Instead of doing something clever like saying he would pull it out on the count of three, he decided to grab it and yank it out as quickly as possible. He knew that it all came down to speed - the faster he could pull it out, the faster her pain would go away.

Focusing his mind on the path his hand would take and how far it would need to move, he coiled his hand and blocked everything else from his mind. Raven watched Ashton closely. She noticed the signs of what he was doing and wondered how well he would do. Concern that he would cause more damage made her doubt the decision. She considered changing her mind. Before she could protest, however, Ashton snatched the piece of glass from her foot with superhuman speed. Her wound began to heal, the pain quickly becoming a fading memory. Ashton gaped at the shard of glass in his hand with disbelief. He successfully used his enhanced speed. Closing his eyes, Ashton recalled the blurring movement of his hand as it reached out and pulled the offending protrusion from her foot. Before a single drop of blood fell to the ground, it was out, and he held a towel to the wound.

Raven could not help but feel a sense of pride in the accomplishment, no matter how minor it was. He had figured out how to do this entirely on his own.

Ashton could not help feeling something entirely different. As he looked at the towel in his hand and then the delicate foot he held, a surge of desire stirred within him. He noticed the bright red polish on her pedicured toenails and the exquisite golden chain that looped around her ankle, resting against her dark, silky skin. It had various charms attached to it, some of which appeared to be a bird in different stages of flight. They could be ravens. On their own volition, his eyes wandered along her shapely leg, which she extended before him in supplication. His heart began to pound and thud in his chest. He breathed deeply through his nose and smelled the subtle floral scent of the soap, or perhaps lotion she had applied to her skin mixed with chlorine from the pool. His eyes roamed further over her shapely perfection. The smooth skin of her calf reflected the shimmering light from the pool and fire pit, and her feminine curves enticed him further. Her firm thigh seemed to present itself as a reward for his efforts, asking him to take it in his hands. He anticipated the next spot his eyes would fall upon as they roamed further upward on her body, and his nostrils flared, fanning his desire like a wind-fueled wildfire.

Oh...and yes, it was wild. Ashton leaned forward, coming to rest in a squatting position. He licked his lips as the passion welled inside of him.

Raven was mesmerized. Her heart pounded, her breathing quickened, and her desire stirred. She stared as his cursory glance at her wounded foot became something much more dangerous and exciting. It was as if his eyes controlled invisible hands that caressed every inch of her body they passed over. She felt his presence on the back and sides of her calf as his eyes moved higher over her leg. The strong muscles of her thigh quivered at the gentle kisses his ethereal fingers traced along her warming flesh. She began to panic as his eyes crept closer and closer to her core. The pressure from his ghostly appendages grew, and she had to use every last ounce of her self-control to keep her legs from spreading for him. Fear mingled with desire flooded her blood.

Ashton would forever swear that as his eyes moved over her, he could feel the warmth of her silky-soft skin and the quivering muscles beneath it. He licked his lips in anticipation of the warm center his mind was about to touch. He sensed panic, maybe his, maybe hers, but he felt it, and it soured the experience.

Ashton snapped out of the trance-like state as if plucked from some alternate reality and rudely deposited where he was. He breathed, deep and rapid, as one does when woken unexpectedly, and released her foot.

Raven jolted back at the sudden and unexpected loss of the connection she had felt with Ashton. She pushed her arms behind her to catch herself if she fell.

Ashton made the incorrect conclusion that his leering at her body caused her to retreat, and he felt ashamed. His mind quickly recalled a similar experience when he had trespassed this way against Julia.

He turned and walked into the kitchen to get what he needed to clean up the mess. On his way back to the pool, he grabbed the bottle of wine and corkscrew that Raven left on the counter.

Chapter 16

By the time Lance returned, Desiree was standing in the middle of their bedroom, legs spread wide, arms held out to her sides, parallel with her shoulders. She resembled Leonardo da Vinci's Vitruvian Man, or Vitruvian Woman, as the case may be.

When Lance came into the room, Claud asked him what he had done. He said he had put Jeremy to bed and pointed to a baby monitor next to their bed. He explained he wanted to turn it on to keep an ear out for his son's safety.

Claud snickered. "No, tonight, little Jeremy will be a big boy. He can handle it just fine."

Lance and Desiree looked at each other with alarm.

Claud compelled Lance to tell him if he tried contacting the police while they waited for him. Claud's snicker turned into laughter as he watched Lance realize the opportunity he had just missed.

"It doesn't really matter, buddy."

Claud walked over to Lance, put his arm around the man's shoulders, and pulled him into a friendly embrace.

"This isn't my first rodeo."

He looked at Desiree, whose blank expression did little to hide her terror or shame.

"From what Mrs. Keller just told me, it isn't her first rodeo either, is it?"

Tears ran down her cheeks as she shook her head.

Claud walked over to Desiree and looked her up and down. Then he walked around her, inspecting every inch of her body as she stood rigid in the pose.

"Not one single tattoo! What a rare treat you are!" He patted her rump.

"As for you, Lance, please disrobe as well. It isn't fair that Desiree is the only one in her birthday suit."

Claud did not compel him to obey. He turned to the bed, presenting his back to Lance and Desiree. Claud removed his jacket and took extra care to set it neatly on the bed. He used his hands to smooth it out.

"This is my favorite road suit, you know. Christian Dior. A classic." He reached his hands down by his waist. Lance and Desiree couldn't see what he did, but they heard the belt buckle clink and then heard and saw the belt as Claud pulled it out of his pant loops. He held it up in his left hand and lay it on the bed next to the suit jacket.

Lance looked around the room for any weapon he could use. He chose a cross-section of a geode he had purchased years ago at a mineral show in a small town west of Phoenix named Quartzite. It wasn't worth much money, and he wasn't fond of it, so he grabbed it and looked at Desiree. She was doing her best to say "Yes, yes!" with her eyes. Lance reared his arm back and slammed the specimen into the back of Claud's head.

Claud didn't even flinch as a bright red line opened up on the back of his skull, trickled a few drops of blood, and then closed again. He laughed.

"To be honest, I didn't think you had it in you, old bean."

He said in a thick English accent as he turned to face the pair. Both wore expressions of shock. Lance stepped towards the door.

"Now hold on, old boy. Let me tell you what game is afoot."

Lance stopped.

"This is my favorite game. I love playing it with new friends. We are friends, aren't we?" He didn't wait for a response. "Here's how we play. I'll ask you some questions, and you answer me with the truth."

While saying this, he still hadn't turned around and went about rolling his sleeves up over his elbows. Then he turned around and walked towards them. His feet crunching on the broken rock sounded far too loud in the quiet room. He looked around and saw a silver mesh wastebasket and told Lance to hand it to him. Lance did so, and

Claud put the large pieces in the trash.

"It is a shame, though. It was the only decoration I didn't consider trash. Now, look at it." He shrugged as he continued to clean the mess.

"If you lie to me, Desiree will get punished. Do you understand?"

Lance nodded. Claud turned to Desiree, "get the vacuum and clean the rest of this up." He motioned around the floor where the stone had further shattered against the tile after it fell. She hurried out of the room.

Moments later, she returned with the vacuum and cleaned the floor. Lance stared at Claud with anger as he observed him ogling his wife's fit body. Claud noticed this and quietly chuckled.

When Desiree finished, Claud told her to put away the vacuum and return immediately. To save himself time and energy, he had already compelled her to obey his every command and do what he said and only what he said. She was to remain quiet unless he asked her a question.

Once Desiree returned, he told her to get on the bed on her hands and knees, pointing her backside towards them. Lance opened his mouth to object, but Claud hushed him.

"Sh, sh. It's OK, Lance. Just be honest with me, and everything will be fine, understand?" Claud struggled to contain his mounting excitement. Now was his favorite part of the game, but it was just one part of one game. He had many games planned for his time with his new friends.

"Now, Lance, have you ever cheated on your beautiful wife, Desiree?" he asked the now naked Lance, who stood with his hands over his privates.

"What? No!" Lance said in a loud voice.

"OK. So you haven't cheated on your wife. Good."

"Now, do you think your wife has cheated on you?" Claud asked, looking at Lance with questioning eyes.

"No. Not really. I mean, maybe. I don't know." He already sounded flabbergasted.

Claud thought, "this is going to be so much fun!"

He almost playfully smacked Desiree on her taut bottom again.

"Well, do you know if you think she has cheated on you?"

"OK, fine. Yes."

"Hear that, Desiree?" Claud chuckled at her.

"Yes," she whispered, tears and shame subduing her anger.

"Have you thought about cheating on Desiree?" Claud asked.

"No!" Lance replied, seemingly appalled at the idea.

"Commendable. See, I knew you are a good man, Lance, a good man." Claud patted Lance on the shoulder and gave him a little shake in a friendly fashion.

"Now, I have one more question for this part of the game, OK?" Claud asked, smiling in devilish anticipation.

"Why are you doing this? Who are you?" Lance asked, his voice cracking with tears. "We haven't done anything to you. Just leave us alone!" Lance begged, knowing it was useless.

"No, I am not ready to quit the game. Now, answer my next question, and then we will see what happens."

"Have you ever thought of killing your wife?"

"What? Are you mad? What kind of question is that?"

"One that requires an answer, Lance."

Claud walked to the bed next to where he had put his clothes. He picked up the belt, placed the tip against the top of the buckle, and let the leather belt sag. He grabbed both ends in his hands and pushed both ends toward each other. The stiff material separated, forming the shape of an opening mouth. When it spread apart to his satisfaction, he pulled his hands apart. His massive strength made the snapping sound that followed ring out like a gunshot.

"No," Lance shouted. "Now, can you please leave?"

Claud placed his hand on Lance's should again and squeezed. He used just enough strength to make Lance wince in pain and suck air through his teeth.

"Now, we find out how you did. Let's see. You said you haven't cheated on your wife, right?"

"Right." Lance spat the words.

"Now, tell me the truth. Have you ever cheated on your wife?"

"No!" Lance repeated.

"Such a good husband, huh, Desiree?"

She mumbled, "he's OK."

Lance's eyes snapped to her. He could only see her rear end on display.

"Next, you said that you think your wife has cheated on you."

"Right," Lance repeated, sounding dejected.

"And was that answer truthful?" Claud compelled him again.

"Yes," Lance answered, sounding impatient but could not hide the mounting panic in his voice.

"Excellent, excellent. Next, you said you have never thought about cheating, even with your suspicions."

"Right." Lance exhaled the word.

"Now, was that true, Lance?"

"Yes. That was true."

"See Desiree? See how good of a husband you have?"

"Yes," Desiree sobbed, and her shoulders shook as she did.

"Now, there's no way Lance would have ever even had the idea to think about hurting his precious wife, is there?" Claud asked no one.

"So, you said you have never thought of killing her, right?"

"Right!"

"Was that the truth?" Claud asked expectantly.

Lance struggled not to speak but stammered, "no!".

He looked at Desiree with sad eyes.

"It just crossed my mind, is all. It was after the fourth or fifth time I suspected you of cheating." He looked at his wife, who was still on all fours, head hanging low while she cried.

"Oh, Lance. You lied to me. You know what that means, don't you?"

"Please, don't hurt her. Hurt me."

Claud stared at him, dumbfounded at how Lance would martyr himself over this whore. While true that he had suspicions, Lance had no idea how much of a slut his wife was. Claud already knew. He had made her tell him everything while Lance was putting their son to sleep. It took almost the entire time.

"Me? No, I'm not punishing her, Lance. That's your job."

Claud smiled and turned to Lance, holding out the belt. Lance shook his head in refusal.

"Take the belt," Claud commanded. Lance grabbed it from Claud and held it in his other hand, trying to preserve his modesty.

"Now, you need to give her a good whack with the belt, Lance. If it is too soft, I'll do it." Claud waited for Lance to look at him. "You don't want me to do that, Lance. Trust me. Neither of you wants that."

"Please," Lance begged.

"Come on now," Claud ignored his pleas. He reached his hands out and grabbed hold of Lance by his shoulders. He moved him to the left and behind Desiree's exposed buttocks.

"There." Claud stepped back. He wasn't in the mood to directly participate in the night's activities. Not yet. He looked forward to joining later.

"Lance, maybe it would help you decide if you heard how much she cheated on you?" Claud asked in a compassionate voice.

"What?" Lance asked, not wanting to understand the implication.

"Maybe you would like to know how many times this week?" Claud put a friendly hand on Lance's shaking shoulders. "You know, she has been a very naughty wife."

They heard Desiree sobbing on the bed. She shook her head in desperation but did not speak.

"I know. I know." Claud exaggerated his pretend compassion. "How about we ask her to tell you who she had sex with on your wedding day? From what I understand, when you kissed the bride, you might have noticed a salty taste in her mouth."

"No!" Lance screamed and let the belt fly. It smacked across her backside. A long red welt blossomed across both of her cheeks. He pulled his arm back to strike again, but Claud caught his arm. He turned his head. Then they heard Jeremy's soft voice call out from his bedroom. "Mom? Dad?".

Claud smiled.

Chapter 17

When Ashton returned, Raven had busied herself by picking up the larger pieces of glass and setting them in a pile. He put the wine bottle on the table and realized that she no longer had a wineglass.

"I'll get a glass for you after I clean this up. Sorry, I didn't think about that before."

"No need - to apologize or get a glass. I can drink from the bottle."

Her statement helped to ease his discomfort. Even if he didn't believe that a lady of such refinement would drink straight from the bottle, he did appreciate the sentiment. He was wrong, though. She wiped her hands in the air, grabbed the bottle, and took a long drink. She sat it down loudly on the table, wiped her mouth with the back of her hand, and let out a long "ah!". She turned to him and smiled a playful and challenging smile, which he felt like no other.

"Who are you?" he asked without thinking.

She looked at him and cocked her head. "Sorry?"

He shook his head and replied. "Nothing, never mind." Then he went about finishing his task. After putting the broken glass into the recycling bin, he put the broom and dustpan away. This time, he stopped and took two wineglasses out to the patio. He sat them both down and filled hers first, then the rest of the bottle went into his glass. He picked his glass up and saluted her with it.

She looked puzzled while he promptly drank all of his wine.

Not wanting to return to the topic they previously discussed, he sat down and mentioned what he had noticed when grabbing at the glass.

"Raven, did you see me take the glass out of your foot? Did you see how fast my hand moved?" He had to fight the urge to remember his view of her body.

"Yes. That was very impressive. Have you been practicing?" Raven sounded almost friendly, not so detached as she seemed at first. She was present and no longer guarded.

"No, I just wanted to get it out of your foot. I didn't want you to be in pain."

"Oh?" His earnest tone pleased her greatly.

"Yeah, I didn't want to hurt you more by taking it out. I wanted it to be over as quickly as possible." He explained to her.

She looked at him, her composed face softened. In an instant, her expression returned to normal. He knew she felt good that he was concerned for her. Then he wondered why he concerned himself with her at all. He knew so little about her. Apart from what he had seen of her in his dreams, he knew very little. At the same time, he felt drawn to her, unlike anything he had experienced before.

"Do you mind if I ask you some questions? I am new to this, after all."

"Before we do, I need to explain some things to you. Then, if you have questions, we can discuss them when I finish."

"Fine." He stated, somewhat disappointed.

Raven explained why they had a coven at all. She explained the Blood Communion and how it makes sure that the vampires follow the rules and do not plot against one another. At that point, he interrupted her.

"So each vampire has about one year to do something before being discovered, right?"

"Sure, if you look at it that way. There are pros and cons to everything. For us, though, it has kept things in good order for a very long time. There isn't a need to act against one another. The main purpose of the coven and the Blood Communion is to prevent the spread of vampires. That is the biggest risk to us, especially in today's hyper-surveilled world."

That made sense to Ashton. He didn't like the long gap between meetings, but he also didn't have to worry about it. He wasn't part of their coven. Or was he, he wondered?

"Wait, are you here to make me join?" he asked.

Raven's response sounded rehearsed. So much that he was pretty sure she wanted him to understand that it was.

"You must be part of the communion and share your blood. Only then can we decide whether to accept you among us."

"And what if I refuse or I am not accepted?"

"Whenever a slot opens, the potential candidate presents themselves to the entire coven for a vote. Their blood is shared, and we judge the candidate. If rejected, the coven compels the candidate to forget about everything to do with vampires. The process also serves to assure us that the candidate is willing." Ashton saw another brief flash of emotion on her face when she said that last part.

The more he thought about his situation and these revelations, the angrier he got.

"I didn't ask for any of this. It's all bullshit."

He made a fist and clenched his teeth, his jaws flexing with effort.

"This has fucking ruined my life, and now you tell me I have to be judged by people I don't even know? What about you, Raven? Do you think I am worthy?" He delivered the last like a slap to her face. The words stung like one too.

"Like you, Ashton, I didn't ask for any of this either. I didn't ask to come here, and I shouldn't be the one here. I also didn't ask to be made into a vampire. So, yes, I know how you feel."

He felt like a total asshole. In the long silence that ensued, more memories of what Claud had done to her flitted through his mind. He also realized that it had happened before the coven existed. He stared at his feet while the Blood Memories battered him with what had been done to her.

She broke the silence, "for what it's worth, though, I think you are worthy and would be a fine addition to our coven."

Now he felt even worse. He knew he had many reasons to be upset and that a certain amount of understanding was due, but that didn't change that he knew better.

She reached out and placed her hand on his knee. "Are you OK?" she asked in a soft voice, so full of compassion it shocked him. She quickly withdrew her hand as she felt him tense up. He almost reached out for her hand to reconnect with her. He wanted to feel her touch again. His realization of this new blunder renewed his anger towards himself. He let out a long and disappointed sigh.

"Sorry. Man, I think I've said sorry today more than I have in years."

He grunted a laugh.

"I mean it, though."

He looked into her eyes, allowing his feelings to pour out of his into hers.

"I am very sorry for all of this and how I have been tonight. I wish we could have met under different circumstances. You might have at least found me more charming."

Raven just looked at him in silence. She had to be wary as well. Yet she could not sense any level of deceit coming from him. He seemed to be an open and honest person. Even if they were vampires, their humanity - who they were - remained intact. Then she thought of Claud and Trevor. It remained so for those who wanted it to, at least.

What he said next took her by surprise.

"You could drink my blood and see if I was lying to you, right?"

Just the thought of her mouth on his neck ignited a long-dormant fire within her. Her heart spread the embers of passion throughout her body, and soon, heat radiated from her. The idea of drinking his blood appealed to her on so many levels. He did not know what he had just proposed to her. She self-consciously crossed her legs and then put the towel on her lap.

"No," she whispered and added in a louder voice, "we can do that later, at the meeting. It won't be so, um, personal that way."

"What do you mean?" he asked, not understanding how being bitten wouldn't be personal.

"We use a device to share our blood. Being bitten is too, well, it's not something we do." She thought to add that they didn't do it to each other but didn't.

"What about compelling me to tell you? Would that work?"

"No. Only a vampire's sire, or dam, as the case may be, can compel a vampire."

She thought for a moment and explained further to avoid confusion.

"When a male vampire turns a human, he is that vampire's sire. If a woman does it, we call her the dam. There is a special bond between them. One that only exists between the creator and the creation."

"So the blood is the only way to know for sure?"

"Blood is life and truth," she repeated the ages-old mantra.

"Raven?"

He waited for her to look into his eyes before he continued.

"I won't lie to you. I can't explain it, but I know I can trust you, and I want you to trust me."

Ashton wanted to touch her, to create a connection to her so that he could feel her energy. He felt like he was drowning in the deep cold ocean and that she was the only thing that could save him.

"Is there any way to undo this? Can I go back to being human?"

She shook her head, frowning slightly. He figured as much and deflated. A look of intense sadness surfaced in her warm brown eyes and then vanished.

"What do we do now?" He asked her in a sad voice.

"I need to clean up Trevor's loose ends. We need to compel Julia and Jacob. We also need to get rid of the video. It seems you are friends with Julia, and I am sorry, but they both should forget about you and Trevor. It will make their lives, and yours, much simpler in the long run."

That worried Ashton.

"Do *they* know about me yet?" That was a question she hoped that he would not ask.

"Some members of the coven know of you, but not your identity. I will have to report everything before long, so it's just a matter of time before they do. Otherwise, they may draw the wrong conclusions."

"Oh, like you are hiding something? I understand." He shrugged and arched his brows, "do what you have to."

She nodded.

"In the meantime, I think we should stay in touch. We have much more to discuss."

"OK. Thanks, Raven."

As she started towards the front door, he called to her.

"Raven, I need to talk about Julia. While you're figuring out how to handle things with her, don't forget that Trevor took a great deal of money from her. That's why we were here earlier. There's a wall safe upstairs. I've seen it in the, uh, blood memories. She really should be paid back. After all, it's clear he didn't need the money. It was just part of his sick and twisted fun."

"I figured that you were here for something like that. I did find the safe, but I just haven't figured out the combination yet." She had stopped walking towards the front door and turned to face him.

"I know the combination."

He decided to show her that she could trust him. Her look communicated that she was uncertain why he would make that announcement.

She walked back to where he waited. Then, she grabbed a magnetic pen and paper set from the fridge and handed it to him. He took it and wrote down the combination.

"Three - six - two - four - three - six - pound sign - pound sign".

She looked at the numbers, and their meaning escaped her. She shot him a questioning glance.

"Thirty-six, twenty-four, thirty-six, pound, pound."

He laughed at the absurdity of a grown man, let alone a nearly two-hundred-year-old vampire using such puerile mnemonic devices. She turned her nose up at it in disgust.

"Trevor was always a lecherous, revolting pig."

Then she added, "Disgusting."

"No doubt." He agreed, chagrined over having laughed at it.

She made her way to the stairs and looked at him. "Coming?" she asked.

"No. I'll let you sort it out." He walked towards the door and put his hand on the knob. He didn't want to leave. He enjoyed her company, but he had to take some time to sort things out and imagined that she did as well. Still, he hoped that she would stop him and rush to him like characters from an old black and white movie and throw herself into his arms.

"OK then. Have a good night." She said and walked up the stairs to the bedroom where the safe was.

He shrugged, then got into his car and drove away.

Once she was in the bedroom, she let out a long breath that she had held in since Ashton moved to leave. His voice was deep and manly but not fake like those on the radio. When he spoke to her, her body listened. She didn't want him to leave. She wanted him to turn to her, pick her up, and carry her up the stairs. Instead, he left her alone with his trust and her desire.

Once she opened the safe and set aside the small fortune, she found a stack of journals. She took them out and leafed through them. She recognized Trevor's handwriting in all of them. The idea of reading his private thoughts held little appeal to her. The fact he stored them in a safe did interest her, however. Raven didn't recognize any of them. They were old and should have appeared in some blood memory. That bothered her - no, it worried her. She decided to have a look at them. On the first pages of the journal on top, she noticed a mention of Claud. What she read changed everything for her.

Chapter 18

"Lance, you sit next to your lovely wife. Desiree, you sit next to him. Tell him about every person you have had sex with since you were married. Lance, you stay quiet and listen. You should hear this. When you finish, sit still and wait for my return." He compelled the couple.

"I'm going to get little Jeremy to sleep. But first, I have some questions for him as well."

Claud left the room, hearing Desiree's soft, tear-filled voice speak the words that would break Lance and leave him forever a broken man.

After a moment, Claud found Jeremy's room. The dim light cast off by the night light muted the bright colors of the room. He paid little attention to the plethora of toys, stuffed animals, and figurines lining the shelves. The overstuffed toy box near the window was of no interest. Jeremy sat up in his bed, rubbing his eyes.

"Hi, Jeremy." Claud gave the little boy a tender smile.

"Did that loud noise wake you up?"

Claud leaned against the door frame of his room.

"Where's my mommy and daddy?" he asked, his eyes filling with tears.

Claud rolled his eyes but replied in the same tender voice. "They're in their room talking. They asked me to check on you. Are you OK?"

The boy waited a minute and shook his head.

"Why?" Claud asked.

"I'm scared."

"Oh, is that all?" Claud smiled. "Being scared is a good thing, you know."

"It is?" Jeremy pepped up at the thought, voice rising as he spoke.

"Sure it is. It keeps us safe. You wouldn't pet a mean-looking dog, would you?" Claud asked.

"No, sir!" Jeremy pulled his hands up to his chest, palm out in a protective gesture.

"Good. Why not?" He prodded.

"'Cause I don't wanna get bit," Jeremy whispered, eyes wide, shaking his head. Claud had to fight back a chuckle at the sincerity of the little boy.

"So, you are afraid of what the dog might do, right?"

Jeremy nodded emphatically.

"So, if you weren't afraid, you might stick your hand out, and the dog could bite it." Claud chomped his teeth together to emphasize his point.

"No! I wouldn't do that!" Jeremy shrank back, hiding his hands under his legs.

"See!" Claud clapped to reinforce the boy's reasoning, "Fear is good!"

Jeremy smiled. One of his lower teeth was missing, making his smile much cuter to see.

"So, is there a big, scary dog in your room?" Claud asked him, taking a few steps into his room and pretending to look around.

"No. Mom's allergic to dog hair," Jeremy said in a mock stern voice.

"So, what could scare you in this wonderful room?" Claud asked as he squatted next to Jeremy's bed and looked around from his vantage point.

"The dark!" Jeremy leaned forward to whisper in Claud's ear.

"Dark?" Claud asked in mock amazement. "It isn't dark in here! You have a night light on."

"It's dark enough," Jeremy countered.

"Dark enough for what?" Claud asked, having a good idea of what was coming next.

"Monsters," Jeremy said. He tried to act bravely for the strange man. He resisted the urge to cover his head with his blanket and hide from the dark.

"Oh." Claud sounded dejected.

"Huh?" Jeremy squeaked out.

"I said oh. I understand. Monsters are scary."

Jeremy's eyes grew wide. His face grew white with fear.

"D-d-don't you mean monsters aren't real, mister?" The anguish in his voice was real. His mother and father must have told him that monsters weren't real. Claud knew that wasn't the case.

"Whether they are real or not, you are afraid of them. You are afraid of monsters, right?"

None of this was helping Jeremy feel any better. He nodded to be polite.

"Now, I have a magic power. That is why I am here. Do you know what it is?" Claud asked, waiting for Jeremy to look at him.

"N-no." Jeremy sniffled.

"I can take away your fear of the dark, just like that!" He said and snapped his fingers. Jeremy's eyes blinked at the sound.

"For real?" Jeremy's tears stopped falling. Hope replaced his sorrow.

"Oh, yes. I can. Do you want me to?"

"Yes. Please do." Jeremy pushed himself back until his back rested against the wall.

"All you need to do is look at me and listen."

Jeremy wiped his eyes with his hand and looked at Claud. He stared at Claud with an innocent intensity that forced Claud to hide a smile.

Claud waved his hands around using grand and sweeping gestures. He made funny faces that made Jeremy giggle. Then he turned to the young boy and pointed his hands at him, wiggling his fingers as if he were casting a spell.

"Jeremy, young noble warrior, you are now granted magical powers by the council of toes." Jeremy giggled at this and wiggled his toes. Claud's eyes grew wide, and his head moved in tiny circles.

"The council of toes - the stinkiest toes on all the lands - the stinkiest toes to have ever touched the sand - bestow upon you immunity from the fear of the dark!"

Now, Claud compelled the young boy. "You are no longer afraid of the dark." He clapped his hands together and rubbed them up and down as if he was wiping away dirt.

"That's it?" Jeremy asked, looking around the room. He had expected a dazzling light show or some other grand sign that showed magic at work.

"No, there's one more thing." Claud smiled, about to compel Jeremy again. "You will be the perfect son. Whatever your parents ask you to do, you will do. You won't ever lie to them or ever hide something from them. OK?"

Jeremy nodded and smiled. "That's easy. I already do that." His smile faltered a little after saying that. Part of him knew that wasn't entirely true.

"Now, go to sleep, Jeremy."

The boy laid down and closed his eyes. In a matter of seconds, he was fast asleep. Claud pulled the night light out of the socket and returned to the master bedroom where Desiree and Lance were waiting for him. He knew that he had created a time bomb by programming little Jeremy in that way. The boy's honesty would create tremendous problems for them. He hoped they lived long enough to find out.

When he walked into the couple's room, he tossed the night light at them and closed the door behind himself. Lance caught it, and they both looked at Claud. They screamed.

"Now, which one of you wants to be first?" He asked as he set his shirt down and finished undressing.

Hours later, Claud had his laptop set up in their home office. It would be dawn soon, and he had some things to get done before he rested.

Few people in Scottsdale had basements because of the high cost to dig one in the rocky ground. The Keller family had one. Now, his new family would have him close at hand until he finished with them.

Chapter 19

The first part of Trevor's journal was a personal manifesto and contained ideas he and Claud had discussed with the coven many times throughout the years. This knowledge came to her via blood memories on many Blood Communions. Raven thought he had either given up on those ideas or had stopped discussing them with anyone. His ramblings amounted to vampires being the supreme beings on the planet. Not only were they the true apex predator, but their immortality also made them better suited to be rulers of the world. Generation after generation of human rule had yielded little except a poisoned planet and a neglected majority. Then, along came the industrial revolution and a type of progress exploded onto the world. The rate of change was amazing to witness. Even within a single generation of human life, substantial shifts occurred. The changes included a rapid increase in the destructive mining processes. The amounts of poisons dumped into the land, the air, and the water increased. The die-off of species occurred much faster as man encroached on an ever-expanding frontier. A minority of people spoke out in protest or tried to raise the alarm, but the industrial machine was unstoppable. For some, the standard of living improved drastically, the numbers of poor and forgotten swelled. Trevor proposed vampires take power to correct man's failed stewardship of the earth and its peoples. None believed that Trevor cared about either the planet or the people. They saw it for what it was - an attempt to seize power and bend the world to his will. However, the idea had merit, and others in the coven supported it. Even Raven had to agree that man's rise came at the cost of the planet. Trevor even conjectured that if their coven seized power and made their existence known, other vampires - if any existed - would come out of the shadows and join with them.

Raven already knew all of this. Over the centuries, they discussed the problem and potential solutions. The destruction of the environment continued and eventually sped up. Support was growing for some action, but they couldn't agree on what to do. Now that Raven thought of it, they hadn't discussed it since the 1970s. With the global warming scare, she had often expected it to come up, but it never had.

The next part of the journal changed everything for her. Trevor had developed a means to communicate without it showing in blood memories. If that wasn't bad enough, he had shared how to do this with Claud. Once she read the explanation, Raven couldn't believe that she hadn't thought of the idea herself. Then again, she wasn't a deceptive person, and she wasn't looking for a means to hide anything. Regardless, she felt stupid that she had missed it. It was the telegraph which Trevor and Claud used to destroy the sanctity of the Blood Communion.

Raven could remember the excitement over the invention and rapid adoption of the telegraph. Trevor and Claud urged everyone to learn about it and proclaimed it to be the way of the future. It also promised to be an excellent investment opportunity.

Almost overnight, countries began creating the infrastructure to support this rapid communication. The earlier forms of the devices didn't work well for Trevor's plans. Some of the transmitted characters used odd shapes and would be very difficult to discern without seeing them. The adaptation of the key-operated transmitter in the 1850s and the creation of the International Morse Code made Trevor's plan feasible.

The method was quite ingenious. Trevor used one transmitter to write a message, one letter at a time. When written to the tape, his assistant would cut and glue it onto a sheet of paper, then mail it to the recipient. The recipient's name was the first part of the message encoded by Trevor. He received incoming messages the same way. A letter would come in that had a message either written in customary languages or in the coded fashion. The assistant would use a separate transmitter attached to a custom-designed receiver to apply pressure to Trevor's wrist. Short pressure represented dots and sustained pressure for dashes. Learning the code was the most challenging part of the process, and doing so wasn't suspicious.

The new technology became trendy. Even high society took an interest in the novel entertainment it offered. The wealthy held telegram parties in their homes where their guests would sit in different rooms and send questions and answers between rooms to guess each others' identities. As with all new fads, it fell out of favor. The participants either returned to their lives or lost themselves in the next to come along. For Trevor and Claud, it became a tool for them to hide their communications and whatever sinister plans they created.

Raven read and reread all of this information and sat back in horror. Claud and Trevor had been deceiving the coven for over one hundred fifty years. No one in the coven would stand for it. It wasn't only a violation of trust - it violated the very reason for the coven's existence. Yet there was something much more ominous at play. She could feel it in her bones. A message from 1921, one of the few Trevor kept, confirmed her suspicions. The communication was a single statement that turned her blood to ice.

"I will discuss your suggestions with the others and get back to you."

She read the follow-up to that letter, which made her dizzy with dread. Claud communicated to Trevor if his experiment failed, Trevor would need to sacrifice his own life. Otherwise, the failure would expose the secret communication during the next Blood Communion. That alone would destroy the coven and might reveal those sympathetic to the cause.

"What suggestions, what test, and what cause? Most important - what others?" Raven spoke these words to herself in hushed tones.

The truth she discovered was now in her blood. Claud's involvement in anything nefarious would never surprise her, but who else might be part of it? She doubted Isa's or Tamjen's involvement in anything like this, whatever *this* was. It was unlikely for Gitlam or Zana to involve themselves. Even if Gitlam, out of some misguided philanthropic sense, would want to be involved, Zana would not permit it. Her devotion to the purpose of the coven was unwavering. For Gitlam to go against her wishes, he would be going against her.

She could see Marius liking the idea. Raven and he discussed how men held little regard for the damage and destruction they had done to the planet. Raven would have to assign Sasha to those who might favor a change. What concerned her the most was that she didn't know who to trust. Somehow, Raven had to find out. Until then, she must act normal and keep her thoughts to herself. She could only do so until the next Blood Communion.

She sighed and turned her attention to the things at hand. Raven could not put off her report any longer. As the video was on the internet, she needed to include it in the report. While anyone in the coven could hire a team to track the video to its location, Raven doubted anyone would. By volunteering to handle it, she should be able to buy some more time. After the revelations from the journals, Raven had some options. Even if she kept the discovery to herself, for now, it would come out at the next Blood Communion. Raven needed a plan. She decided to act as if she knew nothing about the deception until she had a better idea. One thing was for sure - she had to be very careful.

She omitted the journals from her report and her discovery of Trevor's and Claud's treachery. She explained that Trevor may have inadvertently created a vampire immediately before his death. She needed to interview and deal with at least two humans who witnessed the event. They didn't need to know her involvement with Ashton.

When she thought of Ashton, she realized he would get sucked into the issues with the coven, like it or not. She had to prepare him, and maybe he could become an ally. This thought made her smile.

Less than fifteen minutes after she sent her report, her phone rang. She looked at the id and cringed.

"Hello, Claud."

Chapter 20

The next night, Raven arrived at Ashton's apartment early in the evening. They had to discuss Julia. She couldn't tell how they felt about each other. It was clear they were protective of one another, and Raven could sense Julia's attraction to Ashton. Despite Julia's beauty, she suspected Ashton considered her more a friend than a romantic interest. Raven had seen no signs of his attraction to Julia, but Raven had seen signs that he was attracted to herself. Many times she had noticed his eyes run over her body. At Trevor's house, he had done so more than once. Hope and hunger shot through her. She couldn't deny his attraction to her, nor could she deny her attraction to him.

Unfortunately, more important things were at hand, and she pushed such thoughts from her mind.

"Ashton, we need to talk about Julia."

"Oh, what about her?" Ashton replied, only half listening as he made coffee for the two of them. He was still getting used to having his morning coffee after sunset. He had no way of knowing that Raven had skipped her usual first cup of the day to wait to share it with him.

"I mentioned last night that we need to make her and Jacob forget about this."

"Oh?" he replied as he filled first her cup and then his own with the piping hot brew. He waited for her to drink.

Unaccustomed to such gestures, Raven couldn't help but notice them. Much to her surprise, she liked them - a lot. With Ashton, they didn't come across as formality or simple courtesy. He did so for her, to give her pleasure. He enjoyed her enjoyment, and if he could add to it, he would. These thoughts drifted through her mind as she lifted her cup to her mouth. She noticed his hopeful stare as he waited for her reaction. She closed her eyes and took a slow, deep draft of the steaming black liquid.

The coffee was excellent.

She let out an involuntary hum of pleasure which made his smile broaden. She opened her eyes to see him staring into hers. His delight at seeing her enjoy the coffee somehow heightened the feeling she had when he looked at her. She set her cup down, her red lipstick standing out against the white porcelain of the mug. She had to steady herself to prevent a blush.

"Right, I was thinking about that too," Ashton said, coming back to the point. He set his cup down next to hers.

"I think it is the best thing to do, Ashton. They need to get on with their lives and leave all of this behind. You might not know how this knowledge can weigh upon the human psyche." Raven wished she didn't know either.

"That's true. I don't know." He admitted.

He took a step back from her. She didn't like that. She didn't like it when the distance between them grew. She realized she wanted him closer than she should admit. Raven put her hands around her mug, sliding her fingers through the handle on one side and interlocking them with her fingers on the other. The heat from the cup radiated into her hands. The idea of his warm hands on her body enticed her mind. She lifted the cup close to her face and blew across the steaming coffee, allowing the steam to warm her face and tickle her nose. When he spoke, she looked up at him. He had turned away from her and her realization of this stung.

"Was she driving him away? Was he choosing Julia?" she asked herself. She closed her eyes and shook her head. She told herself she needed to rein in these feelings. Her emotions were clouded and unsettling the inner peace she worked hard to maintain.

"I mean, I understand what you are saying. I also see how it might be best to forget it ever happened. Something doesn't sit well with me about doing that," Ashton said.

"She suffered through all of that and came through it stronger. To take that away from her doesn't seem fair."

He turned back to her with a questioning look on his face. His expression made her feel terrible, but she knew she was right. She set her cup down and met Ashton's gaze, allowing her pain to show as she explained.

"Think about all the terrible things she has gone through. Do you think she told you everything? I can imagine you wouldn't want to relive Trevor's memories by seeking them out in the blood, but they are there. Everything Trevor did to her should be in your blood. You can check and see for yourself if she told you everything or not. Who would want to admit to such treatment?" She watched as the memories came to his mind. He stumbled back and reached his hand out to grab the counter behind him to regain his balance.

Vile images of Trevor's treatment of Julia flooded his mind. He tried to push them away, but they kept coming in a deluge of disgust. Scenes of violence, domination, sex, and humiliation inundated his mind and soul. The barrage of evil pummeled his being in ways that wounded him to his core. He wondered if he would ever heal from the onslaught. He was not an innocent, but this level of sadism was more than his mind could comprehend. What bothered him the most was that part of him liked the wickedness. The perversion of this enraged him. He lifted clenched fists to his head and began thumping at his skull, hoping to pound the horrid thoughts out of existence. He didn't notice Raven come to him and gently grab his wrists. At first, her arms jerked along with his, causing her body to be pulled side to side as he continued his flagellation, hoping to rid himself of the evil inside.

"Shh, shh, Ashton, shh. It's not you."

As his arms slowed, tears of rage poured unchecked from the corners of his eyes. The self-pity and despair in his eyes cut Raven like a knife. She knew what she had just said caused him this pain. To make it worse for her, she said those things to make him relive those memories, knowing it would hurt him. She put her hands on his cheeks and pulled his head to hers, resting his burning forehead against hers as she wiped the tears away.

"I'm sorry. I am. But you must understand how Julia felt. If I could make you forget about what Trevor did, I would. Do you understand now why I want to help her forget these things? Do you?"

They stood together, Ashton's forehead pressed to hers. Her hands fell to his heaving chest. She sensed his power, vast and terrible, hidden behind his crumbling control. Like a warrior waiting for battle, his heart pounded to the rhythm of a million unseen war drums.

He pulled away from her, separating the connection she never wanted to end. He looked at her, his eyes clouded with confusion and rage as he struggled to understand what was happening to him.

"Then what is wrong with me? Why do I…" he opened and closed his fists, arms shaking with fury.

Raven worried he would hurt himself. She stepped back up to him and took his hands by his wrists. She felt the tension in his arms from his fists clenching and releasing. His muscles pulsed under his skin with the opening and closing of his hands. She gently pushed down on his arms to get his attention.

"Tell me, Ashton."

He wanted to tell her, but how could he admit that part of him liked what he saw when he relived those horrible memories? After all the abuse he had witnessed and endured as a child, the pain he had suffered over losing his mother and sister, how could he get some sick arousal from such horrible things?

"Don't be afraid, Ashton, please trust me." She implored him. She had seen his inner struggle before when this topic came up. The time she had first met him at Trevor's when he had pointed out that Trevor was a monster. She had witnessed Julia's reaction too.

Ashton realized he was afraid to tell her. He feared what Raven would think of him, that he might lose any chance of being something more to her. What could Ashton hope to ever be to her? She was so far out of his reach, in a completely different league altogether, that he couldn't help but chuckle at the idea of her wanting to be with him. He had noticed her looking at him, but what did that matter if she learned of his revolting thoughts?

He hated how his life had become unpredictable. Nothing was simple anymore. He wanted simple. And there was the answer - he needed to make things simple. Tell her what was bothering him, and she would hate him. That would make everything simple.

She must have sensed his decision or some change in him because she pressed him then.

"Ashton, please, let me help you through this."

He didn't pull away. He deflated against Raven and closed his eyes.

"When I see those memories... of what Trevor did... they disgust me. They anger me."

"I know, Ashton, I have seen them too. From him and Claud. I force myself to live those memories when they occur to be the witness for those women, hoping one day, they will receive the justice they deserve. And you, you and Julia, you two settled Trevor's accounts, didn't you? Those women got justice, finally." She let go of his left wrist and put her hand back on his cheek, and turned his head so that he would look into her compassionate eyes. She recoiled when she saw the raging war in his eyes.

"But something else happens when I see those things. Part of me..."

He ground his teeth and blinked. When he opened his eyes again, shame radiated in a torrent of humiliation.

"Part of me likes it!" He nearly yelled and shook his head in disbelief.

His heart broke to see her kind eyes flash with fear and disgust when he said those words. Then her eyes widened with understanding, and she smiled a kind and gentle smile.

He couldn't believe that she had smiled at him. Ashton tried to pull away, but she held him. He tried to close his eyes and hide that way, but her compassion wouldn't allow it. Their eyes had locked, and she knew that she was the only thing that could save him now.

"No. That's not what is happening, Ashton."

She had a caring look on her face as her eyes reached out for his soul.

"But it is!" He seethed his hatred of self at the admittance. "I don't know why either! After everything, I've had to deal with in my life! For fuck's sake, Raven, I died to stop that from happening to a woman I had never met before! And now, boom, some sick part of me likes it? I can't handle this."

"No, that's not it at all, Ashton. It is about Trevor, not you."

"But you told me that Blood Memories don't contain the thoughts or feelings. So, how do you explain that?" He felt like a kid who thought he had done something wrong, only to find out he hadn't. He hoped that was the case and Raven would tell him he was OK.

She continued to smile, and her eyes shone with promise as they penetrated deeper into his soul.

"No, it's not from the Blood Memories. It is from his blood, the blood that changed you. I had to deal with similar feelings from Claud."

She shook her head slightly from side to side, her smile growing.

"It happened so long ago that I forgot about it. Vampires don't get created often either, so it hasn't come up."

She noticed the alarm in his eyes and knew what concerned him. The same thing had troubled her.

"It doesn't last long! It's temporary!" She hurriedly assured him.

It took a minute for him to understand what she was saying.

"You mean I won't stay like this? Someday, when I experience these memories, part of me will no longer react like it is now?"

"You're right. It will pass." Her smile looked like it was about to split her face.

"Why are you smiling like that?" He asked, smiling despite everything. His eyes were red and glassy as if he was about to cry.

"You. That's why!" She stood on her tiptoes, kissed him on the cheek, and hugged him quickly. She quickly stepped back before he even thought to wrap his arms around her and pull her to him. She couldn't let that happen, not now at least.

Raven explained that the personality of the vampire transfers to the new one via the blood they share. When Claud made her, she struggled with similar feelings, but she refused to let it change her into being like him. As Ashton had, she rejected it. In time, memories of what he did to indulge himself no longer created unwanted feelings in her. Her usual response reasserted itself. When Claud sired Trevor, it was different. Trevor was already like Claud, maybe even worse than Claud. The transfer magnified his perversions and took his depravity to new lows. Now, think of what would happen if Trevor found yet another sick and twisted person to turn? She explained that transference was the chief reason the coven rotates who creates a vampire.

Of all the questions, the one he chose shocked her.

"Have you, you know, done that?"

"Done what?" She asked, confused by the question.

"Have you turned someone?"

She blinked and then shook her head. "No! I mean, I have had the opportunity, but I refused."

They stood in silence for a few minutes after that. Raven's thoughts distracted her while he looked at her, taking her in, absorbing her. Thinking of taking a part of her into himself triggered a hunger inside him. It was unlike anything he had ever experienced. Maybe her mentioning blood over and over caused it. Perhaps it was just time for it to happen. Either way, blood was on his mind, and not just any blood, Raven's blood. Then he noticed her scent. Her delicate feminine tones called to his masculine nature. He wondered if he could taste her in her blood as if she would have a distinct flavor. Ashton wanted to find out. He felt the hunger grow, and the thought of quenching it intoxicated him. He languidly closed and reopened his eyes, lounging in her radiant glory.

"Ashton?" Raven asked with a peculiar tone in her voice. "Are you OK?"

He focused on her face and her eyes, smiling as beautiful thoughts of sharing their blood flooded him with pleasure.

"Hmm?" He asked in reply, sounding drunken.

"Are you feeling OK?" A note of alarm in her voice acted like a bucket of cold water that woke him from the dream.

"What? Oh, yeah, I'm fine."

"What was that all about?" She asked, curious to understand what she had just seen.

"It was nothing. Just forget about it, OK?"

He needed to distract his mind from such thoughts. He stepped over to the fridge.

"Are you hungry? I could make you an omelet."

Before she replied, he started stacking ingredients next to the stove and then made one for her. She watched him in stunned silence as he did so. In under five minutes, he handed her a plate with a basic cheese omelet and two pieces of hot buttered toast. He set the plate down and caught her eyes. He saw the confusion in them. He flashed a quick smile and excused himself, saying he needed to change.

Although confused, she was hungry, and the omelet smelled quite good. By the time Ashton returned from changing into loose-fitting blue jeans and a tight tee-shirt, she had finished the last bite of her impromptu breakfast. She noticed that his demeanor had changed back to normal and let it drop, figuring he would tell her more if he wanted to.

"How was it?" He asked as he took her clean plate, rinsed it, and put it into the dishwasher.

"It was just what I needed, thanks."

He wanted to avoid any uncomfortable silences and jumped right back into the topic.

"So, I have been thinking about Julia and what you proposed."

When he said he had been thinking about Julia, she connected his love-drunk look to his feelings for Julia, and it made her jealous. She knew it was out of character to get jealous, but she and Ashton shared something. She wasn't sure what was between them, but it was more than a simple attraction. Not wanting her voice to betray her feelings, she raised her eyebrows to say, "And?"

"I think we should leave it up to her. If she wants to forget about that stuff, then we can help. If not, we need to respect that."

"OK," was all that Raven said.

Ashton noticed that something had changed with her, and he attributed it to his weird behavior, so he didn't press her for an explanation. He considered himself lucky if that turned out to be his only worry over it.

"Great. I texted Julia while I changed, and she said we could stop by. You ready?" He asked.

"Sure," she said.

She stood up and walked towards the door. Ashton hurried by her to open the door for her. The gesture annoyed her for some reason. She didn't understand why as she liked his gentlemanly behavior. Although she said nothing, she stiffened and walked through. Ashton noticed this. He wondered if she had guessed his thoughts. Perhaps she didn't want him to be close to her because of it? He pushed himself away from her, causing his inside door to knock into the wall behind it. As he locked his door, he shook his head and scolded himself. He needed to get a grip on his emotions.

Chapter 21

"Wow, Julia, you look great!" Ashton said in greeting, partly because it was true and partly because he wanted to make her feel better after all she had endured. It seemed to work. When she smiled at him, he could see it touched her eyes.

"Thanks!"

She looked from Ashton to Raven, and her smile faltered. She jerked back to Ashton for assurance, which he gave in a nod. When he had texted her about coming over with Raven, Julia admitted she was afraid. He told her he trusted Raven and that she could as well.

"Hello again, Julia," Raven said.

She remained outside the door after Ashton followed Julia to the living room. Julia looked back over her shoulder, expecting Raven to have followed. Then she realized that Raven needed an invitation.

"Oh, sorry. Please come in, Raven." Julia seemed to be chagrined by her faux pas.

"You really do look great in that suit." Raven offered as she entered the apartment and closed the doors behind her.

"I forgot about that." Julia nodded towards the door.

"It's fine, don't worry about it," Raven said as she looked around the apartment. Her eyes finally came to rest on the well-dressed woman before her. Raven rarely felt jealous or inadequate. Wearing black boots, blue jeans, a white tee-shirt, and a loose-fitting leather jacket did nothing to bolster her confidence. What puzzled her the most was why any of it mattered now. While she acknowledged her attraction to Ashton, she didn't understand the myriad emotions she was experiencing again after so many years of ignoring that part of herself. Her usual approach of just pushing the thoughts from her mind no longer worked, and it was becoming a distraction.

A wine glass was in front of the right-side seat of the sofa. A remote control lay on the table next to it. Raven assumed this was where Julia had been sitting. Ashton must have already noticed Julia's glass as he sat on the left end of the sofa, allowing plenty of space for Julia. Raven smiled slightly, liking that Ashton hadn't chosen to sit closer. Raven sat on the love seat, which was to the right of the sofa. It jutted out, forming an "L" between them and surrounding the coffee table.

"Would either of you like a glass of wine?" Julia asked from the kitchen.

"No, I'm good," Ashton answered.

"Sure, that sounds lovely," Raven replied. She noticed Ashton look at her with a trace of surprise on his face. She ignored it.

Julia handed Raven a full glass, filled her own, put the bottle on the table, and sat down. She sat closer to Ashton than Raven had expected, and Raven hid her annoyance by drinking her wine.

"The wine is quite pleasant, thank you, Julia, " Raven said in her soft and full voice.

"I'm glad you like it," Julia replied. She didn't look at Raven when she did. Instead, she shifted to face Ashton, turning her back to Raven.

"So, what do you want to talk about?" She asked Ashton, who looked at Raven before turning to Julia.

"We talked about this earlier this morning. I mean, earlier tonight."
He laughed nervously.

"Man, that's going to take some getting used to."

"I bet," Julia said.

"Anyway, we were wondering, well, let me start over. You know how we, you know, Raven and I..."

"You mean vampires?" Julia said, smiling at Ashton as he tried to avoid using the word.

"Uh, yes. You know how we can compel people, right?"

Julia nodded. She looked uncertainly at Raven.

"OK, good. We wondered if you would like us to help you forget about everything that's happened. You know, with Trevor and all of that."

The suggestion shocked Julia, and it showed. She must not have entertained the idea herself.

"Wow. I mean, I don't know." She fidgeted with her glass and shifted around in her seat.

Ashton continued to explain.

"We were wondered if having you forget about that stuff would make your life easier. It might be better than having memories come up randomly, you know, like post-traumatic stress."

Julia turned to Raven. "What would you do?"

"Well, I would be sure to think about it and not hurry a decision. Some things have happened to me I wish I could forget. I suppose that is true for most people."

Ashton wasn't sure what Raven was referring to, but the thought of anyone forcing her or hurting her spread anger throughout his body like a match would spread fire through a drought-plagued forest. He jumped up from his seat, scaring Julia enough to cause her to stifle a scream. The sudden movement shocked Raven as well.

"Is something wrong?" She saw the look in his eyes. Rage and compassion warred inside of him as he looked at her.

"No, sorry. I got a cramp in my leg." He lied as he bent slightly forward to rub his calf. He wondered if vampires even had muscle cramps. As he leaned forward, his long dark blond hair covered the side of his face. Still, Raven saw his jaw clench and unclench. The light caught his eye as he looked at her sideways to check if she was OK.

"Anyway," Raven slowly continued, "Ashton or I could help you forget about everything, even that vampires exist."

She let that hang in the air, wondering how long it would take Julia to realize the implications. Julia snapped her head to Ashton and covered her mouth. She didn't like the idea of forgetting about him, it seemed.

"I don't know." She said as she shook her head. She took a breath and slumped her shoulders.

"There's no rush, Julia," Ashton said, nodding his understanding. "It is just an idea. Think about it, if you don't mind."

"I will," Julia spoke in slow tones.

"I'll let you know if that's what I want to do."

She took a drink from her wineglass and set it on the table.

"Wow, what a day!" She chuckled softly and turned to Raven again.

"By the way, did Ashton tell you about this Jacob character?"

Raven nodded. "Yes, we also have to figure out what to do with him."

"You won't do what he wants, will you?" Julia asked. She laid her right hand on her chest in a protective gesture.

"We have to consider it, but there are rules about such things, which he might not like. You know how some people are. They want something so badly that they don't care about the consequences."

"To be honest, I have been thinking about it too," Julia admitted.

"Oh?" Raven was very shocked to hear this.

"Sure, who wouldn't?" Julia replied.

Raven could say that she didn't give it much thought and refused it on the spot. She had never been thankful for being turned. Even while these thoughts played across her mind, a faint idea teased at her from the recesses of her subconscious - could the time have finally come where she would think differently? Before Raven could dwell on that idea, Julia continued to share her thoughts.

"I mean, who wouldn't want to live forever and not grow old? I mean, look at you, Raven! How old are you anyway?"

Ashton perked up with interest.

Raven glared a warning at him.

"Hey, I didn't ask!" He laughed at this, waving his hands in front of him.

"But I've wondered the same thing."

"Oh, I've been around for a while."

Both the tone of her voice and her look informed them both the topic was closed for discussion.

"I would love to look as good as you for the rest of my life, ever how long it is." Julia teased.

Ashton knew enough to stay out of it.

"There are very few benefits of being like us, Julia. Unfortunately, there are many more downsides to it."

"Like having to drink blood." Julia shivered after saying this and added, "Yuck!"

Realization dawned on her, and she looked mortified by her lack of tact.

"Oh, my God! I'm so sorry! What I was thinking. I didn't mean to offend you, either of you," she said and turned to Ashton. She wanted to make sure he could see her sincerity. She stood up and put her hand on his arm.

Ashton shrugged, not knowing what to say either. She was right, after all.

"That was one of the biggest issues I had at first. Now though, we get sustenance in a less, shall we say, direct way?"

Julia didn't want to press for more, so she returned to her original topic.

"Well, after thinking of all that I know about being a vampire, I still can't honestly say that I wouldn't want to do it. I also can't say that I would want to. So, I guess I am in the undecided category."

Julia recalled what Raven had said about rules. "You said there are rules about doing that. What did you mean?" Julia asked.

"It's a complicated topic. Let's just say that we are not allowed to create a new vampire without consulting our coven."

"Coven? Isn't that what they call a group of witches?" Julia asked.

"Sure. It is also what we call ourselves." Raven answered.

Suddenly, Julia understood the implications of what Raven had said about permission. She spun from Ashton to face Raven. "What about Ashton? No one gave their permission for him. He didn't ask for it."

Her eyes went wide. "Wait, is that why you are here?"

"No. That isn't why I came here. I came to find out what happened to Trevor. He missed an important meeting, and this created concern for him." Raven didn't want to reveal much to Julia, at least not yet.

Ashton shot Raven a concerned look over Julia's shoulder. Raven didn't look at him but noticed it nonetheless. Raven was more worried about other questions Julia might have. She could see Julia's mind working, churning the information around, trying to put everything into a nice and neat bundle.

"Julia, you must understand, there are things I can't discuss. I may have already said too much. I came here for a purpose, and I have fulfilled part of that - I know what happened to Trevor. However, there were unexpected complications."

Julia looked at Ashton. She knew what Raven meant.

"I'm a complication, aren't I?" Julia asked.

Raven nodded.

"So is Jacob, but he is more a threat than a mere complication. He doesn't know what he is doing by making threats against us. Others will not be level-headed about that. They will demand drastic measures. I can refuse to be their instrument in that, but they will demand it, and unless I change his mind, someone will act."

Raven could tell that Julia understood what she was saying, so she hurried to finish her point.

"If I can deal with Jacob by making him forget, then I can say that I have handled the threat, and there is no additional action required. You aren't a threat to us."

"Which brings us back to Jacob," Ashton added.

"Right," Raven said while nodding.

"We need you to get in touch with him and set up a meeting between him and Ashton. I assume he doesn't know about me, so I should be able to bump into him after he has met with Ashton and take care of it then."

Julia asked, "you promise not to hurt him, right? I don't want to be a part of it if he's going to get hurt."

"There is no need for us to harm him." Raven tried to assuage Julia's concerns.

While Raven explained the plan to Julia, Ashton became restless, almost agitated. He was feeling very uncomfortable and confined in the apartment. He wanted to get outside, out into the night. Something beckoned him to come out into the night and take his place within the shadows. He wanted to go, to hunt. Time seemed to slow down for him. He could feel his heart beating in drawn-out compressions, each thud brought with it more power. He gripped his toes in his shoes, spread them wide, and dug into the padded surface. His muscles tensed in anticipation of action. As he turned to the door, he saw Julia. He didn't see her as the attractive woman, smartly dressed and talking to Raven. He saw her as sustenance. His mouth watered. His breath was slow and deep, drawing her scent to him. He fought against the urge to push Raven away and take Julia for his own. At that moment, he thought of Raven as competition for the prey. Thinking of her that way bothered him. Then, as if the desire changed to placate his objection, he considered sharing Julia with Raven. Erotic energy jolted throughout his body, flooding him with intense yearning. His hunger grew, and his pulse quickened in anticipation of the attack.

Raven, busy talking to Julia, had an unexpected urge to glance at Ashton. Maybe it was the change in his posture that alerted her. Perhaps she sensed the animal in him rising to the surface or his struggle for control. For whatever reason, he caught her attention. She did a double-take when she saw him. Her eyes grew wide in alarm at the hunger in his eyes. Her looked helped save Ashton from succumbing to the beast inside of him. He felt his human nature being sucked from the recesses of his consciousness and thrust into the forefront of his mind, restoring his control. He turned away from the women and walked to the bathroom down the hall.

Ashton didn't want to look at himself in the mirror, ashamed of the thoughts he was having. He just wanted to cleanse them from his mind. Ashton splashed handfuls of cold water over his face, focusing on the coolness as it covered his skin and drained away. He opened his hands and let the water drain into the sink. Then he put his hands on the counter on either side of the basin. The sound of water hissing as it escaped through the faucet soothed his racing mind. He watched drops of water fall from his nose and chin and then into the swirling torrent at the drain. He turned the water off, and the hissing stopped. Doing so abrupted the racing currents in his mind as well. He exhaled hard and saw his breath push the dripping water as it fell from his nose. He took a deep breath and released it slowly, purging the unwanted thoughts. After Ashton repeated that a few times, he stood up and grabbed a hand towel to dry his face. As he lifted it towards his face, he could smell Julia's scent on it and stopped, holding the towel to his face, breathing her scent. Ashton quickly put the towel back and used the inside of his shirt to dry his face. He steadied himself and went back to rejoin Raven and Julia.

When he got to the living room, the two women were already standing, and he could tell that it was time to go. Julia didn't notice the look Raven gave Ashton when he stepped into the living room. He nodded to assure her he was good, and she turned her attention to

Julia as they finished up.

"You ready?" Raven asked him.

"Uh, sure." He replied.

"I'll give Ashton a call once I've talked with Jacob."

Julia turned to him and smiled. Ashton was very thankful that she didn't seem to have noticed anything.

"I'll keep my phone handy."

He assured her, wanting to avoid the uneasy feeling in his gut.

They said their goodbyes and left. Raven said nothing as they walked back to Ashton's apartment. When they got to the stairs leading to his door, she told him she would be up in a minute. She needed to get something from her car.

He sat on his couch, hunched forward with his elbows on his knees, hands clasped in front of them. Nervously, he bounced his legs while he waited for Raven to return. As he sat there, burning off the nervous energy from the encounter, he thought about Raven and what she was in his life. Beyond being a vampire, and a sexy one at that, he didn't know what role she played. She kept a distance between the two of them. Was it a trust issue? Surely she must know he was nothing like Trevor or Claud. She was neither a mentor nor a teacher, not really. She acted friendly enough, but there was still something standing between them, keeping them apart and part of him yearned to be near her. He shook his head to prevent the thought from getting a footing in his mind. Already confused, he didn't need those thoughts to muddy the waters.

"What am I going to do?" he asked himself in a whisper.

A soft knock preceded Raven's entry into the apartment. She was carrying a leather satchel that reminded him of the one doctor's used in movies about 19th century England.

"You OK?" she asked in her soothing voice. Ashton wondered if she knew that hearing her soft and warm voice would always make him OK.

"Yeah. I'm good." He said, legs still bouncing nervously, although maybe not as fast.

"You don't look it." She pointed out.

After a few seconds, she added, "That was close back there." Raven nodded toward Julia's apartment.

He slowly shook his head. "I don't even know what happened. One second, I'm standing there, just being me. The next, I felt different. I wanted to get out of there and into the…"

"Night." Raven finished for him. He snapped his head in her direction and looked at her in shocked awe as he exclaimed, "Yes!".

She nodded in understanding. She knew Ashton had more to say, so she remained silent.

"Then, when I turned to leave, I saw Julia, but it wasn't me that saw her. It was something else, and it was taking over my thoughts. I wanted to…and then me and you…her…and…what is wrong with me?"

He looked at her, imploring her to fix him.

She didn't ask him to explain what he said as his words caused conflicting emotions to spark within her - some of which were emotions she was still trying to suppress. Raven walked over to the couch, sat next to him, and placed the bag on the coffee table. She faced Ashton. She put a hand on his shoulder. His rocking slowed and stopped, as did the nervous shaking of his legs. He huffed out a breath and sat still. After a few moments, he turned to face her. She offered a regretful smile.

"You need to feed, Ashton."

She expected him to refuse.

"I know. Well, I mean, I figured as much. But how can I do that to someone?"

He shook his head as if trying to shake the thought out of his mind.

"We used to use our charm and then simply bite them," she said.

Her tone was so matter-of-fact that he looked at her in shocked horror. She shrugged.

"What do you want me to say? That's what we did. It isn't unpleasant for them either."

He thought back to how he felt when Trevor drank his blood. A pleasant sensation had spread throughout his body. He started to relive the encounter and then stopped it.

"Regardless, we rarely feed that way anymore."

She reached for the bag and opened it. She pulled out a small clear plastic bag with what had to be blood in it. There were no markings on the bag.

"Now, we use these." She tossed it to him, knowing that he would catch it. She also knew that if she held it out for him to take, he might refuse to do so, and it would become awkward. He had to become accustomed to the idea of drinking blood. It was the only way to save him.

He caught the bag and almost threw it back at her. It felt odd in his hand. He turned it over, inspecting it, searching for some sign that he should get rid of it. None came. The longer he held it, the more it fascinated him. He realized he had someone's life in his hands - or at least a portion of it. He held it up to the light, and his hunger grew as he watched the dark red liquid glow.

She nodded.

"It's OK, Ashton."

"What do I do? Do I pour it into a glass?"

"No. We don't consume blood that way. We don't drink it. You must use your fangs."

The word - fangs - bothered him, yet part of him felt empowered by it. He had suspected he had fangs, and Raven just confirmed it. He had a new weapon and a means of survival.

"How economical, a two for one," he thought and grinned.

"Well, I um, I haven't been able to see my fangs, Raven."

He couldn't help but feel foolish. Reminding himself that he was new to all of it didn't help assuage his chagrin.

"You haven't bitten anything while intending to feed, then." Again, she showed no emotion in the discourse. She might as well have said that the night is dark.

"So, what then? I bite it, that's it?"

He looked back to the bag, running his thumb along a plastic seam that held it together.

"Yes, but be careful. Don't squeeze the bag with your hands when you do, or the blood might spray out. Just put your mouth on it."

She stopped to think and then asked, "Have you ever eaten a plum? A very ripe and juicy plum."

He had when he was young while visiting his grandparents in Ohio.

"Yes."

"Then think of it like that. You don't want all the juice to escape. So you put your mouth on the plum, seal it with your lips, and then use your teeth to pierce the skin. Once you bite, your fangs will extend, and you will reflexively suck through them."

He gently cupped the bag between his hands and lifted it to his mouth. Stopping when it was almost there, he looked at Raven. She nodded. He couldn't believe that he was about to do this, and part of him wanted to stop and give it back to her. But he knew he had to. After almost losing control at Julia's, he vowed never to become some out-of-control monster like Raven described. His heart began to pound. There was no going back, he knew. Ashton took a deep breath and gently put his mouth on the bag. The cool surface touched his lips. Ashton wondered why he didn't smell anything. He closed his eyes and tentatively bit down.

Chapter 22

Ashton's eyes flashed wide open at the sensation of his fangs descending from his upper jaw. The speed and force behind their eruption were completely unexpected, although he would admit that he didn't really know what to expect. As soon as they pierced the plastic barrier of the blood bag and came into contact with the blood, his mouth pulsed with a sucking motion that produced much saliva. An odd sucking sound accompanied the feeling of the room temperature blood flowing through his fangs and into his body. He swallowed involuntarily, but only saliva went down his throat. Like slowly turning the volume up on a radio, the taste of the blood began to register. It was unlike anything he had ever experienced. If life and vitality had a flavor, this was it. Euphoria spread throughout his body, and he had to struggle to keep his eyes open.

Ashton felt his heartbeat slow, and time seemed to crawl. Each second he fed, the euphoric sensation intensified and quickly became erotic. Soon Ashton was aware of an uncomfortable tightness in his pants but ignored it. All that mattered to him was the sweet nectar he consumed. An eternity passed before Ashton realized that the blood bag had collapsed into a squished ball of wrinkled plastic. It was empty. His fangs ascended into his upper jaw, detaching from the holes in the bag. He swallowed again, and this time he recognized the oddly flat and coppery taste of blood.

He realized his eyes were open and that he was staring at the empty blood bag in utter disappointment. His eyes shot to Raven as if to ask her why. Then, the tightness in his jeans caught his attention again, and he dropped his hands to his lap, still holding the empty bag, which Raven was reaching to take. That she might discover his excited state terrified him, and he tossed the bag to her.

"Here, it's empty." He blurted.

Then he moved back in his seat and turned to the side to hide his arousal.

She blushed in understanding.

"It's perfectly normal, Ashton."

"What is?" His voice slurred as he spoke, and he started to feel drowsy.

He tried acting ignorant to avoid discussing the sensitive topic. Raven would have none of it.

"Your reaction. It is perfectly normal."

He said nothing and avoided her eyes. The drunken feeling began to fade.

"So that you know, the entire experience is amplified when you feed on someone directly. Even more so if it is a vampire."

An image of Raven putting her mouth on the neck of a petite blond woman, who Ashton recognized from the Blood Memories as Isabeaux, flashed through his mind. The image did not help to ease his excited state.

He glanced at a blushing Raven. He realized that she must have had the same memory. She picked up the handbag and opened it.

"Well, now that you have fed, you won't be at risk of losing control."

She offered the encouragement with an embarrassed smile.

"Great." He said.

Raven put the empty bag into the handbag and snapped it closed.

"But why could I taste it when I was feeding? It wasn't going over my tongue, at least not until the end, and when it did, it tasted different than when I was feeding."

"I am not sure why, but maybe it is because the thing that makes us who we are releases some chemical into our blood when we feed, or because of our heightened senses, we can somehow smell it while we feed. "

"Where does it go? I didn't feel anything go into my stomach."

"It goes into our bloodstream, but not through our digestive system. When we become vampires, a new organ grows inside of us. Our fangs deliver the blood directly to it."

"Where is it?"

"Right here."

Raven put her hand over her heart.

"It completely surrounds our heart and seems to merge with it."

"I bet that is why stakes through the heart kill us," Ashton said.

"That's what I think too." She agreed.

Raven wanted to tell Ashton everything she had learned about vampirism, but her embarrassment from the flash of memory from her time with Isabeaux kept her quiet. Ashton wasn't looking directly into her eyes as he usually does when speaking to her. She knew he had seen the images, and for the first time, she cared what someone else thought of her.

For many moments, she sat still, absentmindedly fingering the leather flaps of the handbag, lost in thought. When she looked at Ashton, he was asleep. He seemed so calm and peaceful, almost boyishly innocent. She placed a hand lightly on his cheek. He shifted, then smiled and nuzzled his cheek into her hand. A soft groan of happiness, almost a purr, escaped him just before he stopped moving. The smile remained.

The swell of love she felt was so strong and pure that tears welled into her eyes and fell from her cheeks. She pulled her hand away and sat on the couch. She would let him rest for a while before they needed to leave and take care of Jacob.

Chapter 23

Jacob threw himself into his bed, landing on his pillow face-first. He screamed his frustration into his pillow and slammed his fist into his mattress. Everything pointed to one horrible conclusion - he had to die to become a vampire. Death was not an option for him. The idea of his blood draining from his body was something he could get behind. Yet, he had witnessed the process happen, and once he broke down what happened in the video, it matched what he found in his research. Drink, share, drain, die - that is how it happened. No grave dirt and no burial required.

He considered using sedatives and then having Ashton take care of the details. All Jacob needed to make sure of was that Ashton shared his blood. So, he would drink Ashton's blood, take the sleeping pills and wait. For now, it was his only acceptable option - until he could find a better one.

He heard the soft sound of his phone vibrating and looked at his computer desk. He grabbed the phone and saw he had a text message from Julia. He grew excited thinking about her. She was sexy and could be his first.

"Ashton needs to talk with you to explain some things. When and where?"

It relieved Jacob to have some questions that he could answer. He picked up his phone and sent his reply.

"Fashion Square mall food court, one hour from now."

He looked at his room and viewed the various anti-vampire devices he had gathered since this all began. He chose a few items to take with him, just in case.

Ashton parked in the parking structure of the mall about forty-five minutes later. He called Raven to let her know he was meeting Jacob. She would be ready if things went poorly with Jacob. She could intercept him after the meeting.

Ashton made his way into the mall. At first, the noises and the smells overwhelmed him. It was an immediate overload that he should have expected. He had grown up going to malls and enjoyed the sense of community he found there. Unfortunately, the community had morphed into people sharing space while staring at their phones.

Jacob was waiting at the food court. Ashton had to give credit to the kid for thinking of it. There should be plenty of people and many exits nearby. When he saw Jacob, he realized he was there for a different reason. He sat at a table near a pizza shop. A tray with crumpled-up napkins lay atop a greasy plate in front of him. Jacob stiffened and pushed himself up in his chair when he saw Ashton. He glanced at the bag next to him, and Ashton guessed he had a weapon, or perhaps weapons, in there. As Ashton got close to his table, the odor of garlic intensified. He squinted and tried breathing through his mouth, which only helped a little.

"Did he bathe in the stuff?" He wondered as he approached the guy. He must have noticed the way Ashton reacted as he smiled triumphantly.

Ashton pulled out a chair and sat down. He leaned as far away as he could from Jacob's miasma of garlic and covered his mouth with his hand.

"You're early." Jacob said.

Ashton didn't reply.

Jacob fidgeted as he expected Ashton to have said something. Ashton's calm and icy glare made Jacob uneasy.

"Julia told me what you want."

Jacob nodded.

"Sorry, I can't help you."

Jacob wasn't expecting that. He looked at Ashton in disbelief. He started to object, but Ashton cut him off.

"Even if I was willing, I am not sure exactly how to. But we are stuck at the part where I would need to be willing."

He shrugged and lifted his hand from his face. He spread it wide and then placed it back where it was.

Jacob shook his head.

"No, you have to. Or I'll..."

Ashton leaned forward so fast that Jacob nearly tipped over in his chair in reaction.

"Or you'll what? Post another video? Tell your mom?"

"I could call the police and say that you kidnapped a girl. Tell them that you took her up to your apartment. Anytime after daylight would work, right? They would show up in force. They might bring a SWAT team, too. Then, when they pull you out of the apartment, poof! Ashes to Ashes."

Jacob chuckled and corrected himself.

"Or Ashton to Ashes?"

"Well, shit!" Ashton thought.

He hadn't thought of that one. If that happened, it would put the video in a different light. He suspected that the feds would be interested if they got wind of it. They would start digging, and where would it take them? Julia, Raven, and all the others. Jacob did not know how dangerous of a game he was playing.

Now Jacob leaned forward.

The garlic odor intensified, and Ashton sat back, stifling a cough. His eyes teared up, and he waved his hand through the air in front of his face. Jacob almost apologized but caught himself. He liked how he felt just then, brave and powerful. The big man did not seem so big at the moment. Jacob knew he could feel bigger if he were willing to pay the price.

"What's it like?" Jacob asked.

"It's like an allergy or being super sensitive to it," Ashton answered. The question confused him.

"No, not that. What's it like being dead?"

Ashton's heart skipped a beat at the question. That was a subject he tried to ignore. He didn't feel dead. Sometimes he felt even more alive than ever. Maybe he never died at all. Maybe whatever turned him into a vampire finished before he died. He shrugged.

"I'm not dead. Sure, some things are different, but I feel alive."

"Yeah, but now you drink blood."

He whispered while he looked around to make sure no one overheard him.

"You were there, and you saw what happened. I'm on my own here. I'm trying to figure things out."

Ashton shook his head as he thought about how much had changed for him in such a short time.

"Basically, I'm fucked. I didn't plan for any of this, and I certainly never asked for it."

"Maybe, but you have forever to figure things out, don't you?"

Ashton laughed.

"Do I? How am I supposed to know that for sure? I don't have instructions or anything to help me figure this out. I looked things up too. Not everything is how the books describe it, but some are. You know as well as I do that even the stories don't agree on what is or is not bad for vampires. Like the garlic, you must have rubbed over your entire body. To me, it's just disgusting, but it's not stopping me from getting closer to you. I can hold my breath, you know."

Jacob sat back at this. He glanced at the bag next to him. Ashton raised his eyebrow as if daring him to do something. Instead, he pushed aside the desire for a battle that had sprung up inside him and explained further, hoping Jacob would not force his hand.

"What about the hottie?"

Ashton's eyes shot to Jacob's as he growled through clenched teeth, "What about her?"

He thought Jacob was referring to Raven. He wondered how Jacob knew of her.

"Had he been watching his apartment?" Ashton wondered.

These thoughts rekindled his desire for conflict, and he felt his body tense in anticipation.

"Easy, easy."

Jacob made a patting gesture in the air with his hands.

"I didn't know it was like that with you and Julia. I was wondering if she is, you know, like you."

Ashton smiled in relief. "No, she's not like me. She's like you, sort of."

"What do you mean, sort of?" Jacob asked, a smile spreading across his face.

"She's a normal person, but she wants to help me, not herself."

Jacob's smile faded into a hurt frown.

"You asked." Ashton pointed out, liking that the kid didn't like the news.

"Fair enough," Jacob muttered, then smiled as a new idea came to his mind.

"Is she, like, your thrall or Renfield or whatever you call them?"

"Friend. I call her my friend."

"So you haven't, you know... with her?" Jacob asked. His interest in Julia was pissing Ashton off.

"Done what? I told you, she's my friend - just my friend."

He was losing his patience with the kid.

"You know, drank her blood." Jacob tried and failed miserably to sound like Bela Lugosi.

Ashton laughed out loud, attracting the attention of a woman who was walking through the food court, looking for a table. When he noticed her, their eyes locked for a moment, and her demeanor changed. Ashton recognized that look and immediately thought of the woman at Walmart just a few days ago. He regretted the outburst. She began walking their way.

"Great!" He thought, "now I have to deal with this!"

Jacob stared at Ashton with a sort of perverse expectation. Ashton could see that Jacob wanted him to say yes because he had fantasized about such things.

"No. Of course not." Ashton scrunched his head down, allowing the collar of his jacket to hide part of his face. He snapped his head forward, making his hair hide his face from the woman. She slowed, seeming confused, and then sat at a table about fifteen feet from where he and Jacob sat. She got situated and then began eating. He looked back at Jacob and felt pity for the young man. While Ashton never wanted to be a vampire, he could understand why Jacob would. He realized that was why Jacob shouldn't become one. He would use his power to get whatever he wanted, never minding the consequences. It would corrupt him. Ashton decided then that he would never let Jacob become a vampire.

Ashton's phone buzzed in his pocket. He pulled it out to check. It was Raven, and she was in position. It took every ounce of his self-control not to look around for her. He put his phone back into his pocket.

"I have to go. I have things to do."

Ashton pushed his chair back.

"Wait!" Jacob blurted without thinking. He looked around with a smile, embarrassed by his outburst.

"Why?" Ashton asked in reply.

"You haven't given me what I want!" He whined, and this made Ashton's stomach churn in disgust.

"I already told you, even if I knew how to, I wouldn't do it."

"And I told you what I would do if you don't." Jacob wasn't brave, but he said what he did before he could think better of it.

Ashton stood up, put his hands on the table, and leaned forward. Not wanting to attract attention, he lowered his voice and replied to Jacob.

"I take that as a threat, Jacob."

Then he turned and walked away. He focused his attention on Jacob as he left the food court. He heard Jacob muttering to himself and was only able to make out the words, "He'll be sorry."

He took his phone out and texted Raven.

"You're on."

Chapter 24

Raven watched from her vantage point on the second floor. She glanced at Ashton as he left, her eyes taking in his body as he walked away, noticing his nice ass. She smiled to herself and returned her gaze to Jacob. He reminded her of Trevor, just a younger and much less experienced version. She could tell that he wasn't happy with how his meeting with Ashton had ended. Her phone buzzed just as Jacob reached for his bag. She prepared herself to act. She would jump over the railing to stop him if he attacked Ashton. He just grabbed the handles and stood up. She noticed he left his tray on the table and didn't bother to push in his chair. She shook her head at this.

As expected, he left the food court in the opposite direction of Ashton. He looked in the direction Ashton had taken and searched for him. Once he appeared satisfied, he quickened his pace and headed towards the exit. Raven hurried to get ahead of him while not attracting too much attention from the other people on the second level. She started walking down the stairs towards the exit just as Jacob turned the corner to head down the same wing of the mall to leave. As she neared the bottom of the stairs, she stumbled and fell, landing hard on her hands and knees. Her oversized glasses slid off her face and shattered on the tile floor as they skidded to a stop just before Jacob stepped on them.

She cried out and then whimpered in a pathetic voice, "Oh no! My glasses!"

She started patting around the floor for them. Her hands still held the handles of her bags, jerking them along as she groped around. She turned away from Jacob, still on her hands and knees, and patted the ground toward the stairs. He had a perfect view of her backside as she did this, and he liked what he saw. The position of her legs pulled the fabric of her skirt tight across her buttocks. Instinctively, he reached into his pocket for his cell phone to take a picture before thinking better of it.

"Miss?" he called to her as he stepped back and crouched to pick up the destroyed glasses.

"Uh, are you looking for these?"

When he held them up, he saw how thick they were and wondered if she was blind. He looked towards her as she turned, still patting the floor.

"I'm looking for my glasses, gosh darn it!"

She looked in his direction as she spoke. She didn't pinch up her face to see better. She let him get the full view of her lovely face before she did. He gaped at her.

"Did you find them?" she asked, crawling towards him and looking up hopefully.

She reached her hand out, about one foot to the right of the glasses he had held up. He moved his hand to hers, but she had swept it the other way. He grabbed her hand and put the glasses in it.

"Careful, they're broke. Sorry about that."

She put the broken glasses on her face. Even though she looked silly, Jacob was still captivated by her beauty.

"Oh, there you are. Thanks! They'll work well enough until I can get to my car. I always keep a spare in there because I can't drive without them."

As she prepared to get up, Jacob jumped up and stuck his hand in her face. "Allow me!"

"Oh, how sweet you are!" Raven exclaimed in a syrupy voice that made Jacob's soul shiver.

Once she got to her feet, she smiled.

"Thank you so much. I don't know what I would have done without you."

She opened her purse. Jacob thought she was going to offer him money. Instead, she pulled out a key fob and snapped it closed. Raven smiled at him again and walked towards the doors. She cried out and fell into Jacob, clutching at him to stay on her feet. He grabbed her and held her up. One of his hands slid under her arm as she reached to grab hold of him, landing on her firm breast. Her hip had somehow ended up against his crotch. The sensations were too much for him to contain, and his excitement grew. He pulled his hips back, and this caused her to stumble. She cried out in pain again. He pushed his leg against her, twisting so that it wasn't near his front.

"Ouch! My ankle!"

She lifted her foot to see that her heel had broken. She slid the shoe off and tried putting her weight on it. Then she tried stepping forward and winced. She sucked air in through her teeth and leaned into Jacob. Then she rested her head on his chest. Raven couldn't stand the strong garlic odor and realized that her eyes were watering from it and that it would help sell the deception. He might think she was crying from the pain.

Just like that, a beautiful woman was in Jacob's arms, her head resting on his chest, and one of his hands was resting on the side of her breast. When he started to pull it away, she bent her arm and trapped his hand. She looked up at him with teary eyes and smiled a pitiful and sincere smile.

"Thanks again for saving me."

She sniffled, closed her eyes, and put her cheek against his chest.

"You're so *big* and strong."

The way she said big excited him further. She wasn't that kind of girl he knew, but it still turned him on to hear her say it. She patted his chest and pulled away. He slid his hand from under her arm, and he could swear that just before it slid off her breast, she squeezed it with her arm to let him know she knew where it was.

"Oh, uh, you're welcome, miss."

He stammered the words as he adjusted himself. Then, he had an idea. He was beaming a triumphant smile when he asked, "Can I help you to your car?"

"Oh, no. You've done so much already. I need to sit down. I'll be fine in a bit."

She looked around and didn't see a place to sit. She frowned, and her watery eyes made it look like she was about to cry.

"Please, I would love to help! I don't mind, honest!" Raven had a slight twinge of guilt over tricking him. He sounded so innocent, but she knew better.

"Would you mind? I can give you some money to show you how much I appreciate you."

He smiled so big and nodded so hard that she knew he would do anything she asked. The guilt flared up again. This time, she reminded herself that what she was about to do was the best thing for him. All she needed to do was get him somewhere more private. She didn't want to be observed compelling him.

"Sure!"

He grabbed her bags and positioned himself so that she could lean on his right side and keep her weight off of her left foot as much as possible.

While slow going at first, she quickened her pace as they walked, and a little over five minutes later, they were standing next to a silver Honda Accord. Her modest car was clean and smelled good. Once she opened the trunk, Jacob set her bags inside it. She dug into her purse for some money. He opened her door for her. She tried to give him ten dollars, but he refused the money and told her over and over that it was his pleasure. He helped her get into the car and then said goodbye and that he hoped she would be OK.

As he turned to leave, she called out to him.

"By the way, what's your name? I want to know. Then I can give you proper credit for it in my journal."

He couldn't believe what she said. Here he was, helping one of the most beautiful women he had ever seen, and she wanted to write his name in her journal?

"Uh. Jacob, I mean, Jake Spence."

Although no one ever called him Jake, he thought it sounded more manly.

"OK, Jake Spence."

She smiled and then tilted her head and gave him a knowing look.

"Did you drive to the mall, Jake?" she asked him, knowing he did not.

"No, I took the bus."

He pointed to the bus stop. The last bus of the day pulled out. He almost cussed but kept his cool in front of the lady.

"Looks like I am walking now, though."

He smiled and turned to walk away again.

"Oh no, you're not, Jake Spence. Now, get in, and I'll drive you home."

Her smile was warm and inviting. A hopeful look filled her eyes with tender pleading. Jacob could not resist, but he tried to nonetheless. He was about to protest when he realized it was cold out and the walk would take him over half an hour. He walked around and got into the car, setting his bag between his feet.

Raven retrieved her glasses from the glove compartment and put them on. He didn't notice they were not prescription.

"Much better!"

She smiled and began pulling out of the parking spot. She asked him for directions. A few minutes later, they arrived at the complex.

"My apartment's at the back of the lot. You can drop me anywhere over there."

He pointed to the area she knew his mother's apartment to be. During the brief ride over, she had turned the heat on full blast and lowered her window to let air circulate the stench of garlic from the car. He seemed to understand what she was doing, and he shifted away from her and cracked open his window. He kept glancing at her as she drove. She explained why she was at the mall, but he didn't hear her. He was busy fantasizing about making her his first vampire slave once he convinced Ashton to turn him.

She pulled the car into a spot and turned off the engine. He almost didn't notice as he was staring at the shape of her breast as she turned the steering wheel and then at her hand as it rested on her thigh.

"Jacob."

Realizing that she must be able to see what he was doing, he blushed and looked at her. Her expression grew hard, not like the soft and kind expression of the woman he had just helped.

"You need to stay quiet and listen to me. Nod if you understand."

He nodded once.

"I will ask you some questions, and your will answer me truthfully."

He remained silent.

"Why were you at the mall today?"

She always asked a question that she knew the answer to whenever she had to do this. It confirmed the person was indeed under her power.

"I went there to meet a vampire and make him turn me into one so I could..." he began to explain in a flat and dreamy voice.

"OK, that's enough. Listen carefully. I'm going to tell you what you need to do."

He stopped talking and focused on her words.

Raven told him to take the video down and delete all copies. He needed to forget about vampires, about Ashton, and her. Jacob was to go on with his life the way it was before.

"Now, go to your apartment and get started. Oh, and for God's sake, take a shower!"

He got out of the car with his bag and walked away, forgetting everything about the pretty lady he helped in the mall. When he got to his room, the first thing he did was delete the video. He didn't look at the view count. Next, he cleaned his room of all the protective gear. Then he took a long shower but still smelled of garlic for days.

Chapter 25

Claud woke with a smile. He always smiled when he spent time with new friends and family, and the Kellers were no exception, especially the little tart, Desiree. She was a terrible person and had somehow managed to keep her depravity from Lance. What surprised him most was that she privately reveled in her evil nature. True, she wasn't as creative as Lance, but she was a piece of work. Aside from her many affairs, her petty and vindictive nature helped mold her into a supreme bitch. Lance, on the other hand, surprised Claud. He could be quite imaginative in devising ways to punish Desiree. Claud had to keep a close eye on him to assure Lance didn't accidentally kill or disfigure her. Oddly enough, little Jeremy proved to be a big disappointment to Claud. Unfortunately for the little fellow, he had a flavor Claud couldn't resist. His blood was the perfect dessert. Claud's smile faded as he stretched and sighed with exaggerated disappointment. He had work to do. The fun would have to wait.

Claud sat up in the bed and stepped his feet into his luxurious slippers. He stretched again and looked at the large cages Lance had purchased from the local pet store. They were large enough to store a medium-sized dog, like a German shepherd or a golden retriever. The current occupants were very cramped in the confined space. Claud walked over to Desiree's cage and smiled lovingly at his new pet. Yes, pets are part of the family, after all, he assured himself. He did love his new family so very much.

He reached down and slid the catch open, allowing the door to spring outward from where her heels and rump pressed against it.

She didn't move. Desiree had to fight with every ounce of her self-control not to budge until Claud told her to.

Claud smiled at how good she was being as he inspected the red squares on her rump from where the metal door of the cage had dug into her flesh. He liked that her perfect skin had a blemish, regardless of it being temporary. Before long, he would leave lasting reminders of their time together. Claud began to get excited, and his mind offered him ideas of how to use the squares for his entertainment. Maybe Lance could write the names of the men who had taken her from behind in them. No, he frowned, not enough boxes or room to fit the number required. Suddenly, a devious grin spread across his face as Claud recalled why his name now belonged in one of those boxes. He looked over at Lance, hoping to see his rump positioned in the same way to have the same rectangular decorations. He frowned as he realized that he was sitting on his feet and that no such patterns would exist.

Claud sighed again in disappointment and walked to the bathroom. As he entered the small accommodations, he turned his head slightly and called to Desiree.

"Come on, girl."

She crawled out of the cage, her back already scratched from the effort of getting in, received new scratches as she squeezed out. Claud saw the tiny red lines appear on her skin. He rubbed his belly and regretted that he had gorged himself on his meal and dessert before retiring that morning. Claud continued to stare at her as she withdrew herself, and in the process, he saw other areas of her body that had offered him much pleasure.

"Bring your water bowl. You've been a good girl, and daddy has something for you." He remarked in a sing-song voice.

He didn't like calling himself the owner of his pets. He preferred to consider himself their father. After all, he had to provide for them, care for them, and, most importantly, train them.

Desiree thought about running and considered plugging her ears to block his voice. She had no idea how he controlled her. When he told her to do something, sometimes she could resist, and other times she had to obey.

"Jeremy," she whispered to herself, and her spirit deflated.

Slowly, she stood and stretched, her body taking its time to release the cramps from the hours spent in the cage. When she saw Lance in his prison, a mixture of anger and sorrow filled her. Claud made her expose all of her lies and deceptions, but she refused to forgive Lance's one sin of thinking about killing her. She knew he would never do it and that his guilt over having the idea haunted him. None of that mattered. What mattered was that she didn't predict that he would think of doing such a thing. Now, he started to be very cruel over meaningless affairs.

The main reason she married the wimp is that he would inherit millions when his parents finally died. Although, she was beginning to wonder if that would ever happen. Having a kid was just insurance, and having more wasn't worth the risk to her body. If he ever grew a spine and wanted a divorce, she would be able to get more money with a kid. Having more kids wasn't worth the extra money to her.

As her eyes swept from her pathetic husband back to her feet, she saw the water dish and cringed. She remembered asking for something to drink last night and how the monster had shocked her by giving her spoiled milk from the fridge. When she refused, he made her drink just by using his words. He explained that a good mother would not have milk that expired two weeks ago in her fridge. He didn't let her explain that they never drink milk or that it was there from a house guest.

She clenched her fists even as she picked the bowl up. Then she joined Claud in the tiny bathroom and he shook his head at her, expressing his disappointment.

"That took far too long, my love."

Desiree's heart turned to ice as he smiled at her and held his free hand out towards the water bowl. He filled the bowl with warm water from the bath where she and Lance had bathed earlier in the day.

An hour and a half later, Desiree knocked at Jacob's apartment door, pressing her clothes with her hand out of habit while she waited.

"I got it, ma," a high-pitched male voice rang out.

A moment later, Desiree heard the clicks of the door's locks opening. The door swung inward, revealing a gangly young man in his late teens or early twenties. His jaw dropped upon seeing Desiree standing on the other side of his security door, wearing a smart business suit with a short black skirt, shiny black heels, and dark nylons. She had already strategically unbuttoned her blouse to show her ample cleavage. If her plunging neckline proved insufficient to draw his attention, the pearl necklace would and did. His eyes lingered over her breasts, far too long to disguise as innocent, and then up to her face. She flashed him a smile.

"Jacob Spence?" She asked, smiling broader and raising her eyebrows in hope.

"Uh, yeah, yes, I'm Jacob." He made no move to invite her into the apartment.

"You are? Whew, that's great! I've been trying to find you."

She opened the clutch hanging over her left shoulder and retrieved her phone. She unlocked the phone and then looked at Jacob as if she was comparing him to something on her phone.

Jacob couldn't speak. It was all he could do to stop staring at her body. When she talked again, his eyes shot up to hers, and she smiled a knowing smile at him that took him off guard. He blushed at the implication and shifted his stance behind the metal security screen.

"Oh, sorry," she said.

"I'm Desiree Keller from Five on Your Side. Can you please spare some time for me? It'll only take a few minutes."

Her pleading and hopeful look tugged at his heart. He had never seen such a beautiful woman in person, much less spoken with one. And here she was, begging him to spend time with her. Upon this reflection, he had a nagging sense that he had seen and spoken with a beautiful woman recently, but he chalked it up to a dream he must have had.

"Who is it?" An older woman's voice called from the dim recesses of the apartment.

"It's for me, ma."

He snapped back at her over his shoulder and then turned to Desiree.

"What's it about?" He asked, not caring in the least.

He had just realized that his phone was back on his desk. He wanted to get a picture of this woman for his collection.

"Well, it's about a video." In one of her hands, she held a jumble of keys, and in the other, she had her phone.

"Would you like to come in?"

"Well, it would be easier if you came down to my car. I'm not allowed to enter anyone's house on my own, and my cameraman wasn't available tonight. My driver is down there, waiting as he couldn't find a parking spot for the limo."

It was too much for him to dissect and expose the threat. Here was a beautiful woman - a journalist - wanting him to sit with her in a limo to talk about what? Then he remembered she mentioned a video.

"What video?" He asked.

"Well, it's one you recorded about a week ago. I think it happened here, in this complex, but I am not sure. I was hoping to ask you questions about it. Maybe you can clear some things up."

He had no idea what she meant. He hadn't posted any videos online for quite a while. Her expectant look, the slight pout of her eyes and lips, and her exposed gifts sealed the deal.

"Um, OK, one sec."

Before she could object, he pushed the door to and disappeared. A few seconds later, she heard him tell someone, presumably his mother, that he had something to do and would be back in a few minutes. His mother wanted him to take the trash down, and he told her he couldn't and that he would do it later. Desiree chuckled to herself when she listened as his mother made him promise to do it and not forget. He did as asked. A few seconds later, he came out of the apartment with his cell phone in hand. She turned and walked down the stairs, taking care as the surface was pebbled concrete and she was wearing stiletto heels. She rebuked herself for spending so much effort to make herself look so good. She could have had this man-boy eating out of her hand in no time, no matter what she wore.

Jacob followed her as she led the way. Once they had turned a corner, he could see the limousine waiting at the end of the sidewalk. The driver exited the car, opened the rearmost door, held it open, and waited. Desiree crouched and stepped into the luxurious vehicle. Jacob followed, and once he was completely inside, the door closed behind him.

It was very dark inside the limo, and Jacob's eyes took a few moments to adjust. The lovely Desiree had sat on the seat facing the one where Jacob sat. Next to her sat a man that gave Jacob the creeps.

"What's going on?" He asked, turning to Desiree.

Her look of disgust further confused him. She was busy buttoning up her blouse, which she could tell disappointed him.

"Fucking creep!"

The level of disgust and anger in her voice made Jacob cringe. He reached for the door handle. Just then, the car jerked into gear and pulled away. He heard the sound of the doors locking shortly after.

Claud's thunderous voice boomed out as he reached out and grabbed Desiree's face, yanking it to look at him.

"Don't you dare disrespect my guest! Do you hear me?"

Claud's transformation into the enraged man sitting before her scared her, and she instinctively nodded. He pushed her away with such force that she slid back and slammed her head into the security panel. She fell to the floor between the two seats, arms wide and legs splayed, heels in the air. Jacob looked to Claud and then back at Desiree as she scrambled to pull herself back into her seat.

Claud turned to Jacob and apologized.

"I'm sorry, Jacob. She is still learning her place. Please, forgive the insult so that we can discuss why you are here."

Jacob turned back to Desiree, who looked much less beautiful to him. His anger began to rise, quickly supplanting what little sympathy he felt for her. His face scrunched up in anger and disgust. Her words echoed in his mind.

"Fucking creep! Fucking creep! Fucking creep!"

Claud laughed.

"Oh Desiree, you've made another enemy."

She glared at Jacob, eyes boring into him like a laser drill. Usually, Jacob would have looked away, but he held her gaze and returned it with equal, if not greater, hatred.

Claud, sensing that Desiree was about to say or do something that would prolong the interview, compelled her to apologize and be quiet.

She did so.

"Now, be nice to our guest."

Claud smiled, trying to decide how nice she should be.

Jacob was not under any compulsion to hold his tongue. Years of looks of disgust, rejection, and outright laughter played in his mind, recalling the humiliation at the hands of women like her. They would tease boys like him to get what they wanted and then treat them like garbage.

"You fucking bitch!" Jacob screamed, spit flying from his mouth as he did.

"You fucking whore!" He added for good measure.

His chest heaved, and his fists clenched open and closed. He wanted to jump across the seat and attack.

"Oh, my! Does he have you pegged! Do you know each other?"

Claud was laughing as he watched Jacob's rage mount. Desiree smiled at Jacob. Doing so was the worst thing to calm Jacob. He thought she was laughing at him.

Claud had to intervene at that point.

"Jacob, sit back and be still. I will ask you some questions, and you will answer me honestly. Nod if you understand."

Jacob sat back in his seat and nodded.

"If you do a good job, I might let you have fun with her. Does that sound good, Jacob?"

He nodded again and smiled a wicked and devious smile.

Chapter 26

Julia immediately recognized the song as soon as it started to play.

"Oh my God, I love this song!" she shouted and cranked the volume up.

She was bouncing and swaying, waiting for the light to change. The light just changed to red when she pulled into the turn lane. She knew she had a few minutes before it would be her turn to go. She didn't let herself worry about what anyone else would think of her dancing in her car, singing at the top of her lungs. She felt great for the first time in a very long time. As she snapped her fingers and sang, she saw her reflection in her rearview mirror.

"Looking good, girl!"

She winked at herself and smiled. It was going to be a good day. No, it was going to be a great day!

Julia didn't see the car driving the wrong way in the oncoming lane, and she didn't hear the horns blasting to warn her. The left turn arrow changed to green, and she pulled away from the traffic.

Jacob's eyes locked onto the beige sedan that Julia drove. The smell of freshly spilled gasoline didn't even register. The empty can next to him, and the four full five-gallon cans in the trunk, were of no concern to him. Only the woman mattered. She had to die. A faint echo in his mind cried that he didn't want to die and shouldn't do what he was about to do.

He had timed everything perfectly. As Julia turned to merge onto the 202 West, his car slammed into hers at nearly seventy miles per hour. The impact was deafening. Julia never knew what happened. Before the fire engulfed him, Jacob felt joy for completing his task. Once he had finished it, so were Claud's commands, including the one to feel joyful while completing his mission. Then, nothing stopped the feeling of horror that the compulsion had suppressed. Nothing could stop the pain as the fire melted his flesh.

After the extraction of the bodies, the police investigation started. The driver of the stolen car had beaten and raped a wealthy real estate agent and took her car, along with a few hundred dollars of cash. The attack on the real estate agent happened only hours ago and in a different part of the valley. The rape victim, Desiree Keller, was already at the police station with her husband and had just undergone her medical examination. Once the story hit TV and radio, it didn't take long for a clerk at a nearby gas station to identify the car and driver as one who had come in earlier that morning to buy and fill several gas cans. The police quickly discovered that someone had reported the car stolen and that it belonged to the rape victim.

They still needed the identity of the male and hoped the images taken from the gas station's video would lead to a rapid identification. Then they could try to find a motive. Eventually, Jacob's mother's call to the police department to report her son as missing allowed the investigating officers to make the connection and ultimately identify Jacob as the body in the fire. His work had called to find out where he was as he didn't show up that day. His mother's growing concern was almost confirmed when she saw the news at lunch. Needing to be sure, she called to report him missing and mentioned that he may have been the young man in the car. She would later explain that she knew he was different, and he "did things" that weren't very nice. She had hoped that he would meet a young woman and settle down.

Usually, the officer who took the call would inform her that he hadn't been missing long enough to warrant a report, but her description of the boy led the officer to check his driver's license photo. As her description and the picture matched the surveillance video from the gas station, the officer reported it to her shift supervisor, who then got the ball rolling on making the official identification.

They would find a letter on Jacob's computer, which provided the motive for the attack. It explained he loved Julia and added that she had rejected him. Jacob concluded that the only way they could be together would be if they died together. Only then would she see how much he loved her, and she would finally love him. Then they could spend eternity together.

Investigators would also find the various pictures and videos of his other victims - the ones he had spied on through their windows. They didn't discover the video of Ashton or any other trace or mention of vampires. If the investigation had delved deeper into his recent activity, they could have found much more to investigate. They did not need to do any of that. The entire, albeit terrible, incident was wrapped up before dinner that evening in a neat bundle, just the way the police liked it.

Chapter 27

"She's dead. They're both dead."

Raven shot to her feet. "What? Who's dead?"

She grabbed her rental keys from the nightstand and stuck the room key into her back pocket. She held the phone between her shoulder and her ear and then pulled on her leather jacket, taking the phone back into her hand again as she shrugged the coat over that shoulder. Ashton still hadn't said another word. She heard him breathing and could sense his pain and his rage.

"I'll be right there."

She ended the call and hurried out of her room. During the short drive, she tried to figure out who he meant. Julia had to be the woman. The only other person both of them knew by name was Jacob.

She did not doubt that Claud was responsible.

"Claud, you son of a bitch!"

Her hands tightened on her steering wheel as her anger mounted. It was difficult for her to drive safely and not like a maniac to get to Ashton. She knew if Julia had died, it would be hard on him. A flash of jealousy shot through her, and she chastised herself.

"Hang on, I'm almost there," she said into the night and pressed down on the gas pedal. The engine made its best impression of a roar, and the car lurched forward.

Raven didn't knock when she got to his apartment. Instead, she walked in and hurried to Ashton. He sat at the dining room table, staring out the balcony door. He didn't look up at her or acknowledge her in any way. She walked over to him and stood by his side.

"Ashton?"

He didn't respond, just stared off into space.

She put her hand on his shoulder and gently squeezed. Then, she moved her hand to the center of his back, between his shoulders, and rubbed soft, soothing circles.

He let out a long and exasperated breath through his nose. He turned his head to look into her eyes. His eyes brimmed with tears and the anguish she saw in them stabbed at her heart.

"Tell me," she said in her soft and soothing voice.

She knelt next to him and put her hand on his cheek. In reply, he nodded to the kitchen. She turned her head to see a laptop on the counter, with a news article on its screen.

"Two Die In Fiery Crash." Read the headline.

Raven read that road rage was suspected in the crash as an unidentified male drove his car at high speed into the car of an unidentified female as she waited in traffic to get onto the Loop 202 freeway. Both cars instantly burst into flames upon impact.

"They didn't mention names. How do you know who it was?" She asked.

"When I woke up tonight, I tried calling Julia to find out if she had made her mind up, but she didn't answer, so I waited a while and tried again."

He looked at Raven with desperation on his face. She knew he wanted, more than anything, to be wrong. She could also tell that he knew he was right.

"Her phone went straight to voice mail, which only happens when it is off. She told me she never turns her phone off."

He took a deep breath and hunched forward in his seat. He clasped his hands together, rested his elbows on his legs, and rocked back and forth a few times as he continued to explain.

"I decided to go to her apartment. On the way there, I heard a woman crying and screaming."

He paused a moment as he relived the terrible scene. Two cops stood outside Jacob's apartment, holding the young man's mother up by her arms as she wailed over and over, "No! Not my baby, not my baby!"

He shook his head to chase the images from his mind.

"I knew. Somehow, I just knew that Julia was dead."

He shook his head again, still not wanting to admit what he knew was true.

"She didn't answer the door. I checked, and her car isn't in the lot. I waited for the cops to leave and tried asking them if Julia was involved in the accident, but they wouldn't say."

What he said made sense to Raven. She wondered if she should say anything to Ashton about her suspicions.

"I thought about making them tell me by compelling them. But I didn't know how it would work with two people. Not to mention that we were standing in the middle of the complex. Anyone could hear and see what I was doing."

He shrugged.

"I know she's gone, though."

Raven understood. She knew something too - that Claud made this happen. Still, she told herself, she needed proof so there could be no doubt.

She pulled out her phone and searched for the Scottsdale Medical Examiner's office, which led her to the Maricopa Forensic Center in downtown Phoenix. She pulled the address up on her phone and turned to Ashton. Even though she could tell he was in a bad state, she knew he was strong.

"How much can one man take?" she wondered as she tried to decide if she should tell him about her suspicions. She didn't want to leave him alone but wasn't sure if he should go with her.

"Ashton?" She asked.

This time he responded right away by immediately giving her his attention.

"I need to check on something and would like it if you came with me. Can you do that for me?"

He looked puzzled for a minute, and some of his normal personality showed as he smiled the charming smile she had come to love.

"Sure, Raven."

"You want me to drive, or are we walking?" he asked, patting his jean pockets for his keys.

"If you don't mind driving, I can navigate."

"OK, you want to go now?"

"Yep."

After a short trip along the 202 West and then the 10 West, they headed south on 7th Avenue into downtown Phoenix. They followed 7th to Washington and headed west. Soon after getting on Washington, Raven told Ashton to turn left onto 8th Avenue. They needed to find parking around Jefferson street and 8th Avenue. Ashton didn't know exactly where she was going, but he was familiar with this part of downtown Phoenix. Many roads, like Washington and Jefferson, are one-way in the area. They needed to pick the north and south street based on their destination, which Ashton still didn't know. He could see they were near many court buildings, police departments, and county offices.

As he approached Jefferson, he had to stop at a stop sign. Then he saw the reason they were there. Across Jefferson and on the left corner, he saw the Maricopa County Forensic Science Center building.

He looked around for a parking spot when he noticed something quite strange. A vast fenced-in area across 8th Avenue from the building contained hundreds of tents. With how much real estate was worth in this area, he found that hard to believe, but there it was.

They ended up parking next to a building just south of the Medical Examiner's office. When he pulled into the spot and turned off the engine, Raven turned to him and put her hand on his knee, hoping that the connection would help convince him that she had his best interests in mind.

"I want you to stay here and wait for me, OK?"

"No way. I'm coming with you. I know why you are here. If you find something, I want to know."

She thought about arguing with him and decided against it.

"I don't know if I'll find what I am looking for, Ashton. I've seen burnt - bodies in this condition before. It's hard to see. I'm not looking forward to doing this, and I didn't know Julia well. You two cared for each other."

She paused because the truth of it bothered her. She was jealous of their feelings for each other, but she didn't want to admit it.

At first, they had some trouble getting admitted to the building. The office closes at 4:00 pm every day, making it impossible for them to visit during business hours. It didn't matter as security informed them that the premises were not open to the public. Raven compelled them to take her and Ashton to the bodies of Jacob Spence and Julia Rhodes. The security guard issued visitor badges to them and escorted them to the storage area used by the Medical Examiner and his team.

"They're both on the table still, ma'am." The burly guard explained.

"OK. Thanks. Wait here." She told the guard.

"Why don't you wait here too, Ashton?" She asked, hoping he would agree. He shook his head and entered the room.

The odor of burnt flesh was unmistakable despite the large ventilation shafts suspended over the bodies.

It was easy to see which body was Julia's. She was much shorter than Jacob, and her breasts jutted against the sheet covering her body.

Ashton walked past the body of Jacob and stood near the head of Julia. He reached out his hand to pull the sheet back before Raven could stop him.

"Oh my God!" He gasped in horror at Julia's burned and disfigured body.

One side of her seemed normal, and the other was blistered and melted flesh. Someone had removed her clothes. However, at random intervals, pieces of fabric stuck to her body after being fused to it by the heat. It was her mouth that forced Ashton to look away. It hung open in a scream, frozen in terror and agony from the fire that melted the left side of her face. Her cheek looked like melted cheese, clinging together by tendrils of dried yellow fat. He could see her teeth and blackened gums and tongue. He covered his mouth to stop from retching. Raven gently pulled him away and took him to a large sink on the other side of the bay.

"Wait here," she said.

Her firm tone made it clear it wasn't a request. She turned the cold faucet on and pulled a few hand towels from a nearby dispenser, and dampened them in the water. She handed them to Ashton.

"Dab these on your face. It will help."

He did as she said.

Raven returned to the bodies. She touched Julia's unmarred cheek gently and whispered to her.

"I'm so sorry, Julia."

She covered Julia with the sheet.

She turned to where Jacob's body lay. She pulled his sheet back and noticed his body was in far worse shape. It was charred and completely covered in blisters. Tiny black flakes stuck to parts of the sheet as she lifted it off his body. All hair and nails had burned off. She avoided the eyes as she did not want to see them. She didn't see any traces of fabric as she had seen on Julia. But that wasn't why she wanted to see his remains. She pulled the sheet down below his waist. She examined the skin above his right hip joint below the stomach. Although the damage to the skin was extensive in that area, her suspicions were confirmed. After finding a scalpal, she used it to lift flakey, charred pieces of skin to reveal two puncture marks right in Claud's favorite spot, above the femoral artery over the hip joint. It was hidden in a crease and slightly masked by burned flesh, but it was there. If she hadn't been looking for it, she wouldn't have noticed it. Claud had gotten to Jacob and drank his blood to learn the truth. She carefully pushed the ruined skin back into place, hiding all traces of her examination.

"Shit!" she hissed and covered his body with the sheet.

"What?" Ashton asked, from where he leaned with his rump against the stainless steel basin.

He was wiping his hands with the moistened paper towels. He tossed them into the garbage can and pushed himself away from the sink.

"It's what I thought. Let's go."

She nodded towards the door. The guard escorted them back to the entrance. Raven instructed him to remove all traces of their having been there and forget about the incident.

One of the many things Raven liked about Ashton is that he wasn't pushy. He knew she heard him ask her what she found. Although she hadn't answered his question yet, Ashton hadn't asked her again. He remained silent as they made their way back to his apartment, allowing her to think. As they got near his apartment, he interrupted the silence.

"I haven't eaten yet, and I don't have much to offer at my place. Do you want to grab a bite to eat? I'm surprised I'm hungry after, you know, that, but I am feeling famished."

For a few moments, Raven said nothing, apparently lost in thought.

"Oh, yeah, I need to eat too. Can we grab something and go back to your place? We need to talk about this."

They went through a drive-thru Mexican restaurant for their food. When they pulled into a drive-thru liquor store, Raven laughed.

"Doesn't that seem odd to you?"

"What?"

"A drive-thru for alcohol."

"Never thought of it that way, but I guess so. I know one thing, when it is a hundred and ten degrees out, and you've had a long day, would you rather get out of your air-conditioned car or go through a drive-thru?"

She nodded.

"Makes sense."

"Wait, do you have drive-thru gun stores here?"

"Nope," he said with a drawl.

"That's good," she said.

"You have to go to Texas for that," he finished in the same voice and made a spitting sound.

"You're kidding, right?"

"No, ma'am. They have a one-stop-shop - paperwork, guns, and ammo."

She couldn't believe it.

"The drive-thru liquor store is on the other side of the street."

He pushed up an imaginary cowboy hat with his finger and nodded.

They both laughed for a few seconds before Ashton fell back into his sadness.

During their meal, Ashton shied away from getting into the topic. They ate mostly in silence, with the occasional "would you like some of this?" or "Can you pass me that?" interruptions.

He cleaned up after their meal, grabbed two fresh beers from the fridge, and sat on his couch. When Raven walked back into the living room from the bathroom, he held a beer out for her. She reached out and grabbed the bottle to take it. He didn't let go of the bottle, and she looked at him questioningly.

"Tell me," he used her words, ones she had spoken only a short while earlier, hoping that she would share her discovery with him. It worked.

She stared into his deep blue eyes, wishing he had never become involved in any of this. She wanted to kiss him, take away his pain and give him what little love remained in her heart. She wished to hold him and protect him from the evil she called Claud. Instead, she just told him.

"Claud did this. He made Jacob kill Julia and himself."

She expected an explosion of rage or maybe yelling, but she did expect some reaction. Nothing. Not even a blink.

"I found puncture wounds," her free hand went to the spot Claud had used on both her and Jacob, "right here. He's the only one who uses that spot to feed. He also likes having others take care of his dirty work."

Still, his impassive facade remained. He didn't realize that memories of Claud doing such things didn't come to mind.

"I'm sorry, Ashton. I am so very sorry." She whispered as her own emotions made her voice tremble.

"I'm going to kill that mother fucker," he said in such a matter-of-fact tone, the meaning of what he said didn't register with her at first.

Not until he saw understanding in her eyes did he let go of the bottle. She slowly took it and walked to her seat. In the back of Raven's mind, she had been holding onto the hope that things could get back to normal, except with Ashton being part of the coven in place of Trevor. Until then, she hadn't said or done anything against the coven. She knew that was about to change.

She looked at Ashton, who had kept his gaze fixed on her.

The longing in his eyes that she had become accustomed to had vanished. So had the compassion and tenderness she suddenly wanted to see. She realized with a shudder that he was devoid of emotion for the first time she had known him. For a horrifying moment, she wondered if they were gone forever. Understanding dawned on her making her feel like she had known him for a thousand years. He was ready to do anything to reach his goal or die trying. She sighed in reluctant acceptance.

"No, Ashton. We are going to kill that mother fucker."

As if choreographed, they smiled at the same time.

"There's more you need to know," she said and turned to face him.

Raven explained her discoveries in Trevor's journal and the caution she had to employ while figuring out what she should do. He understood why she didn't tell him right away and assured her he was not upset over it. Although she explained the meaning of the deception at length, she knew it was only an academic understanding that he gleaned. The cut of the lies went deep and forever altered her belief in trust. She wondered if she could ever trust anyone again.

Her eyes welled with tears as she stared out of the window, looking at the lights of the distant valley. For the first time in hundreds of years, she could not rely on anything she knew as truth. She had no idea who she could trust and who would be honest with her. Then, Ashton put his warm hand on her shoulder and gently squeezed. She could feel the heat emanating from his hand, and in a moment of despair and weakness, she tilted her head and rested her cheek against the back of his hand.

"Oh Raven," his voice was soft and deep and resonated in his chest. So much was conveyed in those two words. She turned to face him, deftly taking the hand on her shoulder into hers. Looking up at him with tear-glazed eyes, she sniffled and smiled shyly. A solitary tear escaped her eye and traced its way down her cheek, fading into nothingness as it surrendered its mass while carrying her despair in a rivulet of pain.

He said nothing, but his eyes told her everything. She could trust this man. He would not deceive her, and she knew she would never deceive him. For long moments, they stared into each other's eyes. Sharing emotions and promises words could never communicate.

Outside, a child screamed in delight, "Mommy!" Sounds of bare feet slapping against concrete followed as the kid ran towards his mother. These sounds broke the spell between Ashton and Raven and pulled them back to the present. She turned to look out the window and watched as the little boy ran and jumped into the arms of a professional-looking woman who was most likely getting home late from work. The broad smile on the woman's face, her outstretched arms, and the boy's glee as he jumped to hug his mother struck Raven like a blow. Ashton didn't see the pain in Raven's eyes as she watched a dream that would never come true for her play out before her eyes. Her hatred for Claud flared and reminded her that they needed a plan.

"I have an idea," Raven said as she stepped away from the window and Ashton. She walked to the kitchen and sat at one of the stools.

Ashton was a little surprised at the suddenness and the deliberate way she stalked off from the moment they had just shared. He hoped he hadn't overstepped but wasn't willing to say anything. Although he didn't want to risk whatever was between them by making a pass on her, he had decided that he would not hide his feelings either.

"OK, let's hear it then."

Ashton walked over to the kitchen and leaned against the stove, and faced Raven, his arms crossed over his chest. He raised his left eyebrow and looked intensely at her.

"Alright," Raven began, feeling a bit put off by the change in his demeanor. He's just getting down to business, she assured herself.

"Claud is a lot of things - he's vile, paranoid, cunning, and much else, but he's not stupid."

She sounded like she was thinking aloud more than talking to Ashton, so he absorbed what she said and waited.

"He's also arrogant and can be surprisingly predictable. All we need is a plan that he will think of on his own and get him to suggest it to me."

She began to drum her fingers on the countertop, her fingernails slightly clicking in a steady rhythm Ashton, oddly enough, found pleasant. She twisted her lips and furrowed her brow in concentration. Then, she started chewing on her bottom lip as she lost herself in thought.

Ashton chuckled to himself, his folded arms bouncing on his chest. After a few seconds, she looked up at him and saw his grin.

"What?" she asked, blushing for some reason.

"Nothing." He replied, his smile growing slightly.

She looked intensely at him.

"Ashton, what is it?"

"Nothing."

She closed her eyes briefly, opened them, rolled them up, and shook her head. She was getting mad, and not getting a straight answer made her angrier.

"Ashton!"

Her tone made it clear she knew it was something, and he better not say otherwise again. She stopped drumming her fingertips on the counter to emphasize the warning.

"It's just your expression, a minute ago, when you were thinking about something. You were really thinking about whatever it was."

"Oh?"

"Yeah, like I said, it was nothing."

She tilted her head a bit and looked at him. He looked back, and his expression did not hide that he had more to say but wasn't about to do so. Her feelings of betrayal crept back into her mind. She exhaled, and disappointment and hurt flashed across her face. Seeing this, he decided to tell her.

"It's just..."

She looked back at him expectantly.

"Well, I mean, you were lost in thought. You looked so..."

"What?" She sounded a bit angry with him. That caused him to doubt whether or not he should say it.

He shrugged.

"Cute. You looked so cute."

He didn't look away from her. She seemed puzzled - like she didn't understand what he had said. After a few moments, her eyes flashed wide, and her entire demeanor changed in the blink of an eye. She took on a more serious air and stiffened. He expected her to harrumph or do something to express her resentment.

The perceived rejection bothered him, but he decided to keep it to himself.

"See, I told you it was nothing." He offered in a flat voice which was quite unusual for him to use. She was accustomed to the warmth in his voice and noticed its absence. Its absence irritated her further.

"We don't have time for this."

She spoke in cool and harsh tones. Even as she did, she wondered why she was doing so. Ashton cringed at what she said and how she said it.

"Sorry. I told you it was nothing. Maybe next time, you will take my word for it."

"But it wasn't nothing, was it?" She almost seethed at him. He was shocked.

"Hey, Raven, take it easy, OK?"

He held his hands up and patted them down in the air before her like he was trying to tamp down her anger.

His response didn't calm her in the least. It infuriated her. She had been trying too hard to ignore her feelings for him, to ignore his constant leering at her, and now, after what had just happened to Julia and Jacob, he actually made a pass at her and not even a good one at that. In her mind, she yelled, "cute? You think I am CUTE?"

She slammed her palm down on the counter. The force of the blow caused the glasses in the drain to clank against each other. Ashton was dumbfounded.

"Raven, what is..." he started to say before she straightened and held her hand up, cutting him off.

"Don't. Just don't."

She walked to the front door and paused to pick up her purse.

"I need to cool down. I'll call you when I do."

Her tone made it clear for him not to bother calling her or saying anything to her. After snatching her purse from the table, she walked out the door and disappeared into the night. A moment later, he heard the faint sound of her starting the car and driving away. He stood there with his jaw nearly touching his chest.

"What the fuck just happened?" He asked no one and received no answer.

Chapter 28

Raven was furious with herself. For so long, she had stayed in complete control of her emotions. In the few days since getting involved with Ashton, her grip over her emotions had begun to slip. She recalled the many times that Isa had warned her that if she constantly suppressed her desires, one of two things would happen. She would either lose control or go mad. Images of her surrendering to her lust years ago flooded through her mind. Isa had persuaded her to loosen up and enjoy her immortality for once. She had done so passionately. The same desire was again building up inside her but with an alarming difference. Before, when she had surrendered to the pleasure of the flesh, her passion was only for such indulgences. This time, she longed for more. She wanted a connection with someone. The need to belong to someone who willingly gave themselves to her was tangible. She yearned to love and be loved.

After she had driven half of the way to Trevor's, she pulled her car to the side of the road. The constant ticking of the turn signal soothed her racing mind. She opened her purse and withdrew her phone. She opened the call log on her phone, where almost every entry on the screen was for Ashton. She paused with her thumb over his name.

What would she say to him? What could she say that would explain her reaction without revealing her deeper feelings for him? She shook her head and put the phone back into her purse.

"I need a swim," she said.

She could always find solace in the water.

Raven walked into the uninviting house and made her way straight to the pool in the backyard. She took her clothes off and neatly stacked them on the seat of the chair she had sat in when Ashton pulled the glass from her foot. Thinking of him, Raven felt ashamed and excited at the same time. A warm and gentle breeze caressed her body as she walked along the poolside to the diving board. The light from the pool reflected against the stucco on the house and the wall surrounding the yard. The light shined over the shrubs and citrus trees tucked away on the sides of the property. While it was a pleasant view, she thought it lacked the warmth of her quaint home and the lake. She stepped up to the diving board and walked to the edge. She bounced once and dove into the water. Her body effortlessly sliced through the water, and in a few seconds, she surfaced at the far end near the fire pit and chairs, where the steps led out of the pool. She pushed herself off the wall, and once her momentum waned, she reached her arms out wide and then let her legs drift apart. Floating on her back, she looked up into the moonless night and the stars shining down on her. Even during such a peaceful and pleasant moment, her mind couldn't rest. She knew she had wronged Ashton, and she needed to make amends to him. Part of her resisted the idea, wanting to keep the walls up around her, needing to keep her safe from being hurt - again.

Suddenly she turned and dove towards the deep end. The water irritated her eyes when she opened them to look around her watery surroundings. The stark emptiness of the pool urged her to close her eyes, which she did. Immediately, she saw an image of Ashton looking at her, with hurt and confusion in his so blue eyes. She reached out her hands to caress his face and even pursed her lips into a gentle kiss. Coming to her senses, she waved her hands in front of her floating body to dissipate the ghostly image which only existed in her mind. She pushed off of the bottom of the pool and shot to the surface. Then she heard her phone ringing. She looked towards the table and saw the faint glow from her phone as it illuminated the clothes next to it.

"Ashton!" she guessed aloud and swam to the far end of the pool in a flash, causing waves to slosh around the sides of the pool, and hurried to her phone.

Water ran down her hair and over her body as she picked the phone up and held it to her ear, completely disregarding how wet she was.

"Hello?" she answered in a bright and energetic voice as she used her other hand to push her hair back out of her eyes. She scanned the area for a towel but didn't find one. Instead, she grabbed her shirt and started to dry her face when the voice on the phone turned her blood cold.

"Raven? I am glad you are doing well!" Claud's enthusiastic voice grated her. She held her phone out in disgust.

She blew the last few drops of water from her lips and walked towards the house to find a towel. Even though she knew Claud couldn't see her, she covered herself with her shirt. The act of modesty surprised her. In the back of her mind, she knew it was because of Ashton. Her feelings about him were growing stronger. She rolled her eyes and shook her head but couldn't stop the smile that played across her face.

An idea flashed into her mind as to how she could set Claud up. She focused on it instead of anything about Ashton.

"Oh, sorry, I was just now getting out of the pool. Trevor's house isn't so bad. Especially now that he isn't in it."

"Raven," he said with fake scorn, "it's too soon for that."

Raven found the beach towels in the hall towards the bathroom. She wrapped one around her body, tucking it under her arms. Raven put her phone on speaker and set it on the counter. She looked in the mirror and recalled that Ashton had said she looked cute when she bit her lip. Smiling at herself, Raven repeated the gesture and realized he was right. She did look cute - in a playful and sexy way.

Her hair had always dried quickly, even when it was long, so she didn't need to wrap it up in a towel. She dried her hair one side at a time, keeping an ear out for Claud's voice. He hadn't said anything for a few moments, and she hoped the call was disconnected. After hanging the lightly dampened towel on a hook behind the door, she picked up her phone and walked back to her clothes by the pool.

"We have a problem here." She said.

"I know. That's why you are there," Claud replied sardonically.

"No, it's more than just Trevor. I was just about to send you and Marius an email explaining it. But seeing as you called, I'll tell you and send it later."

"OK," He agreed, but she could hear the trepidation in his voice.

"I have confirmed a new vampire here. Our suspicions were right."

"OK?" he stretched the word into a question, letting her know he expected more.

"The video I sent you is no longer on the web. The woman in the video and the man who shot it are both dead."

"Go on."

Was that fear in his voice?

"Ashton - the man in the video - got to them and must have figured out how to compel Jacob into killing himself and this Julia person."

Raven felt a twinge of sadness for Julia but had to push it away. She had to steady herself for the gamble she was about to take.

"I thought it was odd that they should both die like that when I couldn't find any ties between the two of them, other than they lived in the same apartment complex. So, I checked the bodies at the medical examiner's office and found..."

"What?" Claud's voice betrayed his fear. It was just another confirmation of his complicity.

"Fang marks."

Silence on the phone.

She waited, one second, five seconds, ten seconds, and then continued.

"I found the punctures under his skin. Someone fed on him."

"No!" Claud exclaimed.

His voice was a mixture of confusion, surprise, and relief.

"No!" He repeated, outrage now the only emotion in his voice.

Raven's shocked him further with what she said next.

"I am going to need help with him."

A long pause ensued, and Raven suspected her gamble had failed. Her mind raced for anything she could use to salvage the situation.

"You," Claud said in a voice dripping with sarcasm, "need help?" He laughed and added, "I never thought I would see the day."

"And I never thought you would expect me to take down a six and a half foot, muscular, male vampire by myself! You know how much stronger males of our species are than females." She replied in indignant tones.

It never seemed fair to her that the natural strength differences between male and female humans became magnified in vampires. She did find comfort in knowing that a female vampire is stronger than any human - male or female.

Claud said nothing.

"Well, maybe Marius can come and help," Raven said, hoping to provoke some reaction.

"Perhaps Gitlam would help if you and Marius are too busy."

She heard his sharp intake of breath followed by the sound of a hand covering the phone. She could hear the muffled sounds of his voice, but she couldn't make out what he was saying. Then, the distinct sound of a hand uncovering the phone signaled he had more to say.

"I just checked my calendar, and I should be able to get there tomorrow, just after sunset."

Raven's face lit up with a triumphant smile. She composed herself before speaking to keep her excitement out of her voice.

"OK. I'll send you the details of where I am staying. I don't want to stay here - at Trevor's house - any longer."

"Fine."

She could tell that he was about to hang up, so she hurriedly added.

"I've been through everything here, except for the safe in his bedroom. I think that I'll rip it out of the wall and take it with me. I should be able to find a way to get into it. It must be new because I didn't see it in the Blood Memories from last year's gathering."

"It must be. But leave it in place. We don't know what Trevor may have done to it."

"What?" She was shocked at his weak reasoning.

"You must have forgotten that Trevor was very fond of booby traps. Who knows what he might have done."

"Good point," she agreed, "I'll leave it then."

The line went dead, but her plan was coming to life. She thought of Ashton and her uncharacteristic behavior. She had to do something to repair the damage she had caused. She shrugged and looked at her glistening, naked body in the mirror. A knowing smile spread across her face.

"What's a girl vampire to do?"

Chapter 29

He tried to stay busy and keep his mind from whatever had just happened with Raven. The more he thought of it, the less sense it made. Yes, Ashton knew that his comment was silly, maybe even a little insensitive under the circumstances, but her reaction was over the top. He didn't deserve that, regardless of how long they knew each other.

He looked around his apartment for something else to do. Everything was clean and organized.

"I know!" he exclaimed and jumped up from the couch and grabbed his duffel bag.

Less than ten minutes later, he walked through the doors of his gym. After changing into his workout clothes, he skipped the free weight area and found the machines. Even at the late hour, a few people were in the gym. As Ashton walked by the mirrored wall next to the free weight section, he was silently thankful that vampires cast reflections in modern mirrors. He wondered if silver mirrors would just show his clothes walking by as if he were the invisible man. That idea had him thinking about what it would be like to be invisible. He laughed to himself as he came to the chest area.

"OK, just start with your normal weight." He told himself.

He slipped the pin down to the two hundred and twenty-five pounds slot and braced himself for the effort. He pushed the handles outward using his normal force, which was a mistake. The stack of weights shot up and slammed against the top of the machine and then fell, jerking the cable tight. The wire snapped taught as the stack of weights fell, jolting into his arms as he absorbed the shock.

"Holy shit!" he said and glanced around the room. A woman wearing leggings that were much too tight glared at him in the mirror.

"Sorry. Sorry. It, uh, slipped." He offered a weak smile, and the woman returned to what she was doing.

Ashton dropped the pin near the bottom of the stack, sliding in under three hundred and twenty-five pounds, and prepared to start again. He moved his arms slowly and made a face that looked like he was using maximum effort. Ashton even grunted while completing the last reps and let the stack drop back into place on the last rep. He glanced at the woman still working on her legs and no longer interested in Ashton.

His mind raced with the discovery of how strong he had become. When lifting regularly, six reps at three hundred and twenty-five pounds would have been difficult, maybe even impossible, for him to complete. This time, it was nothing to him. He put the pin under the last weight in the stack. Four hundred pounds of weight slid up and down the metal guide bars as Ashton completed another set of ten. Not even a drop of sweat had formed on his forehead. He looked at his arms and didn't see the usual web of veins he saw when he lifted.

He moved around the gym, checking the strength of each of his muscle groups. Ashton yearned to see how much he could lift, but he knew he shouldn't do that. Not in a public gym. As he walked out, passing by the free weight section, he glanced over at the dumbbells. The one hundred pound dumbbells seemed to taunt him.

"Fuck it," he whispered to himself and walked to the far corner where the heavy dumbbells sat on their thrones. Then he saw the heaviest dumbbell, a one hundred and fifty-pounder, was on the floor next to the last bench in the row. He sat on the bench next to it. Then he leaned forward, drug the dumbbell over to him, and wrapped his hand around the cold metal handle. He checked to see if anyone was looking at him. His heart began to pound with excitement as he wondered if he succeeded, would it be a world record?

He lifted the weight slowly, amazed at how little effort he used. While it was not as easy as the machines he had used earlier, neither was it strenuous. He slowly curled the weight fifteen times, switched arms, and did another fifteen reps. By the time he had completed five sets, the effort to finish the last of the reps was significantly harder than when he had started. When he stood up, he saw how engorged his muscles had become. Cords of veins stuck out above his tight skin.

"Fuck yeah!" he whispered to himself and inspected his arms, flexing them and turning slightly from side to side. He felt a little self-conscious about it, but he was very impressed with the look.

He walked to the locker room and stuffed the clothes he wore to the gym into the bag. He felt great, better than he had in a long time, maybe ever. As he walked out and to his car, he made another vow to spend more time at the gym.

Ashton tried to put all thoughts of Raven from his mind as he drove home to his lonely apartment. Despite his effort, he thought about calling her and was glad he had left his phone at home.

"What the fuck happened? What the fuck did I do?" he wondered.

He took a turn a little too fast, causing his tires to squeak in protest. Instead of slowing down, he slammed his foot down, and his car shot forward like a steel fist of rage into the soft underbelly of the night. His better nature warned him to stop, but he ignored it. The thrum of the nearly four hundred horsepower engine and the force pushing him back into his seat as it exploded forward excited him. He smiled a wicked smile when he realized that doing the wrong thing also excited him. For far too long, he always did the right thing. He had denied himself many pleasures, yet his life ended up in the shit show he was living in now.

"But not anymore!"

He narrowed his eyes, lifted his foot, and slammed it down on the gas pedal, forcing the engine to spew power into the rear wheels. He surrendered his thoughts to the tasks of calculating breaking time, incoming trajectories of oncoming cars, determining if his car could fit between whatever obstacles in time. It felt like a video game, except the stakes were much higher. One fuck up, and he could be dead, well, not dead, but hurt. That he could hurt or even kill someone else concerned him much more.

"Fuck 'em, fuck 'em all!" He yelled.

He slammed the brakes and cut the wheel to the right. The tires screeched and slid as his car struggled to make the turn. Once lined up, he punched the gas again, and smoke billowed from around his rear wheels as his car lurched forward. Further ahead and on the right was the turn for his complex. He didn't want to deal with any of those nosy bastards, and driving like a maniac through the complex would get them into the lot as fast as an ice cream truck would a bunch of fat people. So, he slowed down. His heart pounded in his chest. His muscles were tight and pumped from the gym. The feeling of power coursing through his veins was nearly impossible to contain. He wanted to smash something or someone.

Thoughts of what he would like to do to Raven came unbidden. Fueled by the pure energy raging in his body, his desire poured into his manhood, causing it to grow and throb in his sweatpants.

"Well, shit!"

Ashton pulled into his parking spot and shut off the engine. He heard tinging sounds from the engine and felt his heartbeat in the veins on his neck. His fully engorged and throbbing member pulsed against the tent in his sweatpants.

The absurdity struck him, and he fell into a fit of laughter lasting for minutes. He sat in his car, laughing and slapping his hand on the steering wheel. Just as he thought he was ready to get out, he looked down at his erection and burst into laughter again.

"Oh, man. Holy shit!" he gasped as the laughing fit ended, "I needed that!"

He ran his hand down his face and stopped as it covered his mouth. He looked around to see if anyone was out there. To his relief, no one was there. His hand had pulled the skin of his cheeks and eyes down, and he saw how silly he looked in the mirror. For a split second, he thought he would start laughing again. But he managed to overcome the urge. Giving the situation no further thought, he grabbed his duffel bag and walked to his apartment, strategically positioning it to hide his excitement.

Chapter 30

Raven knew she had to apologize to Ashton. What she wanted to figure out now was how she would do it. She picked up her phone and called him. He didn't answer. She wondered if he hadn't heard the phone or if he had rejected her call. She wouldn't blame him if he didn't, she had been a bitch to him, and she knew it. Her thumb touched the message button, and she began to tap out a message, but she stopped and deleted it.

"No. I need to stand before Ashton, admit my mistake and ask for forgiveness. He needs to see that I am sorry for acting crazy like that."

She walked up the stairs and entered the bedroom she was using. Not wanting to use the same room Trevor had used, she chose a guest room on the opposite end of the floor. She put the clothes into the top compartment of her suitcase with the rest of the clothes she already wore. Next, she walked to the dresser, where she had unpacked her clean clothes. The reflection of her full and bare breasts in the mirror caught her eye. Her nipples were hard from the coolness of the air. She ran her hands down her breasts and slid them underneath, cupping them. As her palms contacted her nipples, electric pulses flashed into her body. She closed her eyes. She turned from side to side as she lifted her breasts and inspected them in her reflection.

"Not bad for an old lady," she teased herself.

The image of Ashton coming from the shadows behind her and firmly cupping her breasts teased her in a different way. She imagined his warm hands closing around her and squeezing hard as he kissed her neck. She tilted her head, exposing her neck, and closed her eyes as the fantasy took her deeper into her desire. She could almost feel his hard and warm body pressing against her back. Heat spread through her as her cheeks flushed. At that moment, she made a decision.

She put on a pair of black lacy panties followed by cutoff shorts. Still topless, she leaned over the foot of the bed and found her tan leather sandals. Her firm breasts swayed back and forth from the motion of her body. She slid her feet into the network of straps that would wrap up her calves. After arranging the straps, she fastened them. Then she stood up and looked in the mirror, lifting her right foot behind her legs slightly and resting its toes gently on the floor to show her toned legs. The shortness of the shorts accentuated the length of her legs. The tan color of the sandals blended perfectly with her skin. Next, she slid into a white tank top that was tight across her chest. Her jutting nipples pushed against its cottony confines. She walked to the dresser, looked into the mirror, and applied a red lipstick she had bought earlier that year and had only used at the makeup counter in Macy's. The color was called Ruby Woo, and she remembered how sexy and full her lips looked in it. After brushing her hair a few times to free it of tangles, it fell into the silky, shiny bob expertly sculpted to follow her jawline, accentuating her angular features. She didn't put on any other makeup or use perfume. After brushing her teeth, she grabbed her clutch and keys and drove to Ashton's house.

"We need to either do this or put the possibility behind us," she said as she locked the door.

She turned and walked to her car like a fashion model down a runway, oozing sexiness. The exaggerated sway of her hips, confidence of her stride, and devilish grin on her face were enough to stop any man - or woman - in their tracks. Raven had it, and she knew how to use it.

When Raven arrived at Ashton's apartment complex, the second-guessing and doubts began. She withdrew her phone from her purse and called him again.

"If he answers, I'll go home," she bargained with herself, hoping that he wouldn't. He didn't, so she got out of her car and walked to his door. She knocked, but he didn't answer. That was not something she had considered. In her mind, Ashton would open the door and see her. At first, Raven imagined that he would take her in his arms and kiss her. But she knew he would probably blush and then stumble over his words. She expected to need to make the first move, although how she dressed was the first move. Instead, only silence greeted her. She tried the phone again and heard it ringing from inside his apartment.

"Is he ignoring me?" She asked herself, anger welling up inside at the possibility.

Then she wondered if he might be hurt. What if Claud had already visited him? What if he is dead?

Fighting her panic, Raven put her phone into her bag and retrieved the thin black leather bi-fold that held her lock picking tools. Then she crouched down and put her head close to the doorknob to hear and see better.

She inserted the tension wrench into the keyhole and gently turned it left and right. There was more give to the left, so she knew that was the way to turn the wrench once she set the pins. While keeping tension on the wrench, she slid the rake tool into the keyhole above the tension wrench and pushed it back until it hit the bottom of the tumbler. She pulled it slowly forward, keeping pressure on the wrench, allowing the ridges of the tool to push whichever pins matched their position into place. She felt two of the five pins set into place. Next, she withdrew the rake tool and held it between her teeth, and retrieved the saw tool from her kit. She carefully inserted it into the hole. She slowly pulled it forward while keeping upward pressure on the tip by slightly pulling up on the handle. The space between the tension wrench and the saw tool formed a "V" as she lifted. She felt it contact the bottom surface of the last pin. As she slid it forward, the tip snagged on the one in front of it. The rake had set it, and the next pin was still down. She relaxed the upward pressure on the saw tool, keeping the top of the "L" shape in contact with the unset pin. As she slid the tool down its inner edge, she gently pulled forward on it, feeling it scrape along the back surface until it hit the base and moved forward slightly. Once she felt the give, she stopped pulling forward on the tool and gently pulled up instead, lifting the pin it rested on. She felt and heard the pin click into place. Raven turned the tension wrench to the left while keeping the last pin in place, unlocking the lock. She replaced the tools into the bi-fold, dropped them back into her purse, snapped it closed, and entered the apartment.

She scanned the apartment and could find no trace that anything unusual had happened.

"Ashton?" She called out.

There was no answer. The apartment felt as empty as it was silent.

"Why did you leave your phone here?" The only response was more silence.

Ashton's scent was heavy in the air. Knowing it was his plucked at her desire. With eyes closed, she breathed in slowly. After a few long moments of standing still and inhaling his manly essence, she opened her eyes and seemed to realize for the first time that she was alone in his apartment. The idea of snooping through his belongings did not appeal to her. She wanted to look at the many photos he had hung on the walls or around his apartment. The pictures in the hallway were a time line of his life, arranged chronologically, starting with his baby photos at the beginning of the hallway and ending with his most recent images just before his bedroom door.

Various scenes of his childhood bliss brought a warm feeling to her soul. He always had a broad smile when anyone took his picture. She assumed his mother took the photos as she was absent in most of them. His sister, on the other hand, was in most of them. One of the picture frames was poster-sized and had little windows where he had placed various pictures. From the first slot to the last were pictures of Ashton with his sister. The first was her and him when she must have been a newborn, and the last was of her in a hospital bed as a teenage girl, a warm smile on her pallid face, Ashton standing next to her, wearing a stoic smile. Tears welled up in her eyes, and she hugged herself, hoping she could find any comfort at the sad moment. Raven desperately wanted Ashton to be there and to hold her. Then she imagined hugging Ashton and telling him how sorry she was for the pain he had endured in his short life. Raven knew what loss was and how it felt. She had to say goodbye to her family, just as Ashton had. Composing herself, she continued down the hall and looked at the remaining few pictures.

Then it hit her. She walked back to the beginning of the hall and looked at Ashton's eyes and his smile. Love and happiness seemed to shine out of his eyes. He smiled in each picture until the next one after the mural. He still smiled, but it never touched his eyes, and the smile itself seemed forced. The last image was the worst. He hadn't even made an effort to smile. He was on stage, receiving his college degree, which hung below the photo. He was nearly devoid of emotion in that photo. She remembered how he looked when she saw him just a few hours earlier. He had that same look in his eyes.

The last item hung on the wall of the hallway was his diploma. "Maybe he hadn't gotten around to hanging more," Raven whispered.

"Or maybe he had no plans to."

"And where is your father? There isn't one picture of your father."

She looked back to the image of his college graduation. Guilt slammed into her. She realized what her behavior must have done to Ashton. He had told her how much of a difficult time he was having adjusting to becoming a vampire. She ran to the bathroom and retched. She rinsed the foul taste from her mouth and brushed her teeth, not caring who had used the toothbrush before her.

She walked into the dining room, pulled out a chair, and sat down. She began to feel dirty for coming to Ashton with such intentions. She saw her keys and bag on the table and was ready to leave when the door flew open.

Ashton stood in the doorway. He seemed more massive than ever. His silhouette nearly blocked the door completely. His chest heaved, and his arms lifted with each breath. He closed his eyes and breathed in. A groan escaped his mouth as he moved toward her.

Chapter 31

He saw a shadow dance across the blinds in his living room as he approached his apartment. Ashton slowed his pace and lightened his step. He crept up the stairs and placed his hand on the knob of the security door. While holding his breath, Ashton slowly turned the knob and carefully pulled it open. Then he grasped the knob of the apartment door, splayed fingers wrapping around it one at a time.

He crouched and prepared to spring. In a blurring movement, he pushed in the door and jumped inside. The security door snapped shut behind him while he looked around the apartment. As his eyes landed on Raven, her scent filled his nostrils. His blood boiled in response. He closed his eyes and breathed deep. A soft moan escaped his mouth as her scent entered his body and stoked the fires of his passion.

A silent giant, Ashton wanted to wrap himself around the woman sitting before him, enfolding her in his power while he devoured her body.

She wiped her eyes and stood up. Raven seemed embarrassed and uncertain. She had never seen such an expression on his face. His entire demeanor seemed different, and she suddenly feared him while wanting him more than ever.

"Ashton, I'm so sorry. I thought something happened to you," her voice trembled as she spoke. She didn't know if her need or fear caused it to happen.

He stared at her with hooded eyes running up and down her body, drinking in every inch of her. He wanted that image burned into his mind for all eternity. He knew she had dressed this way for him, and knowing this fed his desire. She wore no bra. That much was clear from the jutting peaks that topped her heavy breasts.

Seeing the effect it had on him, Raven blushed.

His passion strained and throbbed against his gray sweats in a jerking need for her attention. He dropped his bag and closed the inner door with his foot. He stepped forward.

For some reason, Raven was not afraid of the man, no - the vampire, who stood before her. Power emanated from his body in waves of fervid need. Every aspect of her femininity was on fire for him. Of its own accord, her hand raised and spread open wide, coming to rest on her heaving chest.

He took another step towards her. Her pulse quickened further.

Raven could tell that something was different about him. She noticed the bulging veins in his arms, and the size of his chest muscles had never seemed so massive.

"Neither has that," she thought as her eyes took in his caged manhood.

She licked her lips and stepped back towards the kitchen counter.

Another step. Ashton pulled his shirt off with lightning speed and came to stand before her like a warrior and a conqueror. The dull ache between her legs pulsated with searing heat.

Ashton closed his eyes and tilted his head, slowly moving it in circles through the air as he drew her musk to him.

"Mm." He licked his lips and took another step toward her.

The counter met her back as she tried to move away from him. She could retreat no further. She spread her feet apart. Cool air flitted over the heat between her thighs and did little to soothe her burning desire.

He grabbed her face, roughly cupping it in his hands. He guided her head upwards, allowing their eyes to meet again. He put his mouth over hers. Her mouth opened to accept his probing tongue. Once inside her mouth, it slowly caressed hers. Her knees weakened as her heart threatened to explode in her chest. Then his mouth sealed over hers, and he sucked her tongue into his mouth, licking it and caressing it with his powerful lips.

Her hands found his broad and powerful shoulders, and he forced a knee between her legs, nudging them to open wider. She ran her hands down his shoulders and over his bulging arms. Heat radiated from every inch of him, and she felt power coursing under his skin. Then he pushed his hips against her. His massive erection pressed along her stomach at an angle towards her chest. She felt it throb against her as he pulled his mouth from hers and kissed her chin, along her cheek, and then her neck. Already beating at what she thought was its fastest, her heart rate doubled as two fears hit her at once.

Is he going to bite me? Where will all of that go?

Both fears sent her sexual hunger into a frenzy.

"Look at me!" Ashton commanded with a soft and firm whisper. Even though he could not compel her, obedience was her only choice.

When her eyes locked onto his, she saw his pain and his need mixed with certainty as he slowly spoke, each word creating waves of carnal need inside her.

"I want you. Do you want me?" His eyes were alight with his promise and seemed to glow in the dim light of the apartment.

She bit her lip and nodded.

He unfastened her shorts and unzipped them. They fell to the floor. A seductive grin spread across his face when he saw her sheer, black lace panties. He knelt before her and slowly pulled the panties down over her hips. He kissed her legs as he slid the panties down their long silkiness. One leg at a time, she stepped out of her panties. He saw her well-trimmed mound, and his grin deepened into deep hunger. Then he rose and slid his hands under her shirt and up her body until they came to her breasts. He squeezed hard and slid his thumbs over her engorged nipples. She moaned and rocked her head back in pleasure.

Raven lifted her leg and hooked it over his hip. She used it to pull him into her. Her hands greedily groped at the front of his pants. There was no need for any exploration for her to find his throbbing member. Her hands fell against its massive length as he ground his hips into her.

He put one of his hands on the side of her face. She whimpered in submission - something she had never done before in her years on the planet. An animal growl escaped him in understanding, and he kissed her in acceptance. His tongue danced with hers as their passion grew.

Raven pushed his pants down around his ass. She pulled forward on the elastic of his sweats and underwear to free him. Released from its confinement, it thudded against her tight stomach and shot pleasure into her core. She felt herself contract in expectation.

When she looked down at his manhood, it took her breath away.

She reached down to guide him into her waiting depths.

"No!" Ashton commanded in a breathy whisper, "look at me!"

She put her hands on his chest and dug her nails into his rippling muscles. A fire raged in his eyes as hers met his. Ashton put his hands under her ass and lifted her, guiding her hungry opening to the tip of his throbbing flesh. He stopped there, the head of his manhood sliding between her folds, greatly exciting her clit as he rubbed against it. Each contact of his flesh against her sex sent jolts of pleasure throughout her body. She thought she was already going to have an orgasm. Never had this been so good.

"God, Raven, I can feel how hot you are."

She moaned and kissed him. Then she sucked his tongue into her mouth and wished it was something else, something bigger, something unyielding.

He reached down and slid his fingers along her slit. Two fingers entered her tight passage.

"You are so wet."

He lifted his fingers and put them in his mouth, then moaned as he sucked her juices off of them.

"And oh, so sweet." His velvety voice dripped with satisfaction and desire for more.

He then put his fingers into her mouth, and she sucked on them, again wishing it was his throbbing hardness.

"Yes," she exhaled in erotic bliss, "for you, Ashton."

As he slid his fingers out of her mouth, she chased them with her tongue. He pushed his hips closer to her. They could feel her opening spread as the head of his thick cock sank into her waiting depths. She clutched at his mountainous chest, bracing herself for the feeling of fullness that engulfed her.

He panted and rested his forehead against hers.

"Do you want me?" He asked.

"Oh, God, yes." She moaned in answer.

Her need blossomed, and she thrust her hips to him in the hopes of taking him inside of her - every glorious inch of his hard length. He pulled back to stop her, and she nearly screamed.

"Ashton!" She panted and pulled at his hips. Her need demanded release.

Her warm brown eyes stared into the endlessly deep blue of his. Both of them moaned as he slammed his cock into her. Never had she stretched and filled like this. She bit her lip hard, attempting to distract herself from the exquisite pain that erupted throughout her center. He buried himself inside her. All of him was inside her. She couldn't believe all of it had fit in her, and she felt delightfully ashamed.

He slowly pulled out and showed her all of him - from base to tip. It jerked up, and he pushed slightly forward. His thick flesh landed along her slit, and the bottom of its head felt hot and hard on her clit. He thrust forward, pushing the length of his shaft over her pulsating pleasure, drawing her nearer to her first orgasm. She gasped and moaned louder when he withdrew in the same fashion and pressed himself back to her opening.

He slammed into her, and Raven cried out in bliss. Even her delightful outburst was not enough to cover the sound of his body slapping into hers. Again and again, he withdrew and pounded into her. Only when she closed her eyes in pleasure was she not able to see his manhood disappearing into her.

He grabbed her hips and pushed her back into the counter. Her other leg had already locked around his hips. He guided it back, holding it against her body from under her knee. Her foot bounced in the air between them as every powerful thrust bore into her.

"You are so fucking sexy, Raven." He almost purred at her as he quickened his pace. She was on the verge of release before he spoke. His powerful, deep, and resonating voice, telling her how much he wanted her, pushed her over the edge.

Raven had had orgasms before, and to be quite honest, she had been with many different men - and a few women - in her long life. Never had an orgasm shaken her body so hard. She ground herself into him, wanting to fuse with him in ecstasy.

Faster and harder, he drove himself into her, soon surpassing what any mortal would ever be able to achieve. Raven abandoned herself to his onslaught, riding him as hard as he rode her, meeting him thrust for thrust and losing herself in the ocean of bliss that welled inside of her being. Each time he sank into her convulsing passage, he extracted louder and deeper moans of pleasure from further and further inside her.

When he came, he didn't stiffen and stop. Instead, he continued to piston into Raven's exploding and hugging depths.

"Oh, fuck!" He yelled in a mixture of a grunt and a cry.

Raven put her hands on his hips and pulled him into her. Each time she felt his explosions, she squeezed him with both of her hands, wanting every last drop of his hot passion inside of her.

When his orgasm was over, she threw her arms around his shoulders and clasped them behind his neck. He released her leg, and she wrapped them around him as well. He turned and carried her to the couch. Then he sat with her on top of him, still buried in her. As he sat, she pulled her legs to either side of him and leaned back, holding his head in her hands, pulling him to her breasts. They were both panting and covered in sweat. She pulled back, and they looked into each other's eyes.

Then, they burst into laughter, giving a different release to another kind of tension that existed between them.

Chapter 32

Claud ended the call and set his phone down on the desk. Raven's discovery unsettled him. Thinking back to his brief interview with the boy - Jacob was his name - Claud hadn't seen bite marks on his neck, but he also hadn't looked closely. He wore a hoodie and had long hair, and Claud supposed it could have hidden a bite mark. Claud knew that some vampire had compelled the kid recently. He considered it might have been Raven but couldn't think of why she would do such a thing. She would be exposed at the next Blood Communion if she did, as she didn't know how to hide those memories from her blood. Try as he might, he could not think of a reason for Raven to deceive him. Even if he believed what he decided were her fake attempts to convince him that she hated him, she would still need some excuse to act against him.

Claud shifted in the luxurious leather chair, clasped his hands behind his head, and put his feet on the desk. He closed his eyes to contemplate the news. After running every scenario through his mind, Claud kept coming back to the same conclusion - Raven had nothing to gain and everything to lose by taking direct action against him. Her request for help with the new vampire didn't alarm him. If she hadn't requested aid, it would have created more suspicion. While Raven was faster than any human, she was no match for a male vampire. The differences in strength and speed between male and female humans became magnified after becoming a vampire. Female vampires were much weaker when compared to male vampires than they would be if both were human. Even if that were not true, Claud wouldn't be concerned with Raven attacking him. If she did, he could compel her to stop as he was her sire, after all. He cringed at the thought of using that power over her. Compulsion is the most humiliating action a vampire could take against another and is why the coven only allowed a sire or dam to use that power over their progeny in self-defense situations. Attempts to cover up after were pointless. Their blood would reveal the truth.

He smiled a knowing and wicked smile. Claud knew better - he knew how to hide memories and actions. The only problem with him compelling Raven is that she wouldn't forget. Compulsion could not cleanse memories from the blood of a vampire. If he had to use that power over her, he would kill her and remove the memories from his blood, the way he and only a few others knew how. He and the others who knew already agreed that keeping the secret was paramount - nothing or no one was more important than that.

"Needs must, when the devil drives," he whispered to himself and sighed in mock sadness.

He stood and pressed his clothes with his hands. After brushing imaginary lint from his shoulders, he walked out of the office and to his new family. As he passed the young boy, Jeremy, who was busy turning the kitchen walls into a horrid mural of playground slaughter, Claud leaned over and tousled his hair.

"You're doing a fine job, young master Jeremy," he crooned in fake adoration.

"Oh! Thank you, Papa Claud! I am ever so happy that you like it!" He beamed and swept his hand around the kitchen and dining room to indicate his work. Paint, markers, colored pencils, and clay adorned the walls, revealing the inner creativity that Claud had worked hard to find. Kitchen knives, screwdrivers, or nails stuck into the wall, piercing the eyes or hearts of the crude drawings that represented Jeremy's enemies. Violence was last on Claud's mind when working with Jeremy, but sure enough, once he discovered the boy's inner desire to inflict pain, he helped Jeremy realize it. Now, in fledgling blossom, the creative evil inside of the lonely boy bloomed into glimpses of what lay ahead. Jeremy turned back to his work, and Claud walked down the hallway to the bedroom and the rest of his new family.

Mr. And Mrs. Keller were on their hands and knees before either side of the foot of the bed like macabre sentries. They both perked up and smiled at him when he entered the room. Claud could, and would, reprimand them for their half-hearted attempt to appease him, but he had more urgent matters to discuss first.

"Tell me about your neighbors," he said and began to undress.

Both Lance and Desiree spoke simultaneously, trying to win Claud's favor and, hopefully, a reprieve from his cruel ministrations. After carefully laying his dress shirt along the bed, he stepped back and held a hand up to silence them.

"Too bad, Desiree, Lance wins."

He turned to Lance and smiled.

"Would you like to go first?"

Claud knew the answer. Lance shook his head a few times.

"What's that? I can't hear you?" Claud asked, his voice dripping with fake concern.

"No, she can go first." Lance jerked his head towards Desiree, who was glaring at him, her eyes filled with a fierce hatred.

"Fuck you." She muttered through clenched teeth.

"Tut-tut, Desiree. Turn about is fair play, isn't it?"

She shook her head in defiance of the truth.

Claud turned to Lance.

"So, which of your neighbors has a basement?"

As Lance answered his question, Claud took Desiree's wrist and pulled her to her feet. Next, he guided her to the bed, where she climbed up and waited on all fours. He looked down at Lance, who was doing his best to make sure he answered all of Claud's questions.

"Excellent. Can you get one of the neighbors over here tonight?"

Lance nodded vigorously and looked at Claud expectantly.

"He was such a good listener! It is good to have him in my family." Claud thought.

Then he said, "you should go now. It's getting late, and let's face it, you won't be in any shape for guests later."

Lance grew pale and swallowed hard. Desiree trembled on the bed. Her damaged flesh stood out like a neon sign against the unmarred pale white of the surrounding skin. Claud became excited and smiled. Lance scrambled to his feet and grabbed clothes to put on. Desiree began to whimper and plead. Claud took the belt from his pile of clothes and put his hand on her shaking bottom. He rubbed his cold hand over her rump and patted it as if she was a dog or a horse.

Just as Lance was about to leave the office, Claud called out.

"Oh, Lance. Be a good boy and do hurry. Make up whatever story you think will get them here and hurry back. Don't try anything that you know will upset me."

Claud turned back to Desiree. The evil smirk on his face forced a whimper out of her mouth.

"As for you," he began, raising the belt overhead.

A sound, like a gunshot, rang out as Lance closed the door. A smile spread across his smug face when Lance heard the muffled scream that followed.

He walked across the street to the Hessian family's house.

Chapter 33

Raven's eyes shot open, and panic overtook her. A glance at her wrist assured her that she had not slept too long. There was still enough time to talk with Ashton and get back to the hotel. She felt Ashton's warm and solid body under hers, and she had to use all of her willpower to push herself off of him instead of nuzzling him. Raven walked to her clothes on the floor. In his soft and deep voice, Ashton called out to her.

"Hey, where you going?"

"Getting dressed."

She continued and grabbed her panties and shirt and then her shorts. Memories from earlier washed over her, stirring her desire all over again. She forced them away and fought to calm her mind.

Raven quickly slid her panties on and pulled her shirt over her head. She put her shorts on, and he watched as they slid up her long, silky legs. As she zipped and fastened them, the sounds of Ashton getting off the couch pulled her attention back to him, which she regretted instantly. He stood and stretched. His muscular body grew taught from the effort. Before she could stop herself, her eyes ran down his body. When they took in his manhood, her body responded with a deep hunger. He let out a long sigh and walked toward her with a loving and passionate smile until he looked into her eyes.

"What's wrong?" He asked her, concern filling his voice. Then he too hurried to get dressed.

"Did I do something wrong?"

He pulled on his sweats and turned back to Raven.

"No, no. It was wonderful. There's something we need to talk about."

"Already?" He teased and stepped towards her. His intentions were clear. '

"Ashton, listen, this is important. I have to leave soon and get back to my room at the hotel."

A look of puzzlement clouded his face. He tilted his head slightly as if trying to understand.

"I spoke with Claud last night, and I told him that you killed Julia and Jacob."

The words hit him like a back kick to the stomach.

"You what?" He raised his voice in disbelief at the end.

"While I talked with him last night, I suddenly had an idea, and I went with it. It should work, but you need to hear me out. My plan is still risky, and you need to understand why it might not work."

Something about the look on her face told him how much she was understating the risk.

"I won't let anything happen to you, Raven."

"I know you won't, and thanks, but it's not that simple."

"Claud is my sire, Ashton. He can compel me."

Ashton stared at her in stunned silence. Why hadn't he thought of that? Anger began to build up inside of him at the thought of Claud compelling her to do anything.

"I don't think he will because the Coven forbids it. But if he does, I won't be able to resist. The only time it is permitted is in self-defense. He could make me hurt you, Ashton."

He could tell that the idea of being forced to betray him was painful to her, which served to piss him off even further.

"Then I'll kill him by myself."

"Ashton, he is much too powerful. He is ancient."

He thought of his encounter with Trevor. While it wasn't exactly a fight, he knew that Trevor wouldn't stand a chance against him now.

"Well, if Trevor hadn't compelled me, I don't think he would have been able to take me."

"Not so close to dawn, he couldn't." She agreed, and that gave him an idea.

One of the things they agreed upon was that Ashton would not try to contact her in the next few days as she would more likely than not be spending most of her time with Claud. Ashton wanted to ask her a question before she left.

"Well, as I won't be able to talk with you anytime soon, I want to ask a favor."

She raised her eyes in anticipation.

"Will you let me cook dinner for you when this is all over with? I mean, when this business with Claud is done I want to have a date with you."

Raven couldn't help but smile.

"Sure, that would be nice."

"Anything you would or wouldn't like?"

"I'll leave it up to you."

She stepped up to him , put her hand on his chest, stood on her tip toes, and kissed his cheek. Then she stepped back and headed towards the door.

Ashton walked Raven to her car. Once she got in, she rolled the window down and started the engine. He wanted to kiss her and mention their time together, but he knew Raven had to go. She seemed very tired. Her eyes looked sunken, and her cheeks gaunt. She put the car in reverse, and he stood back as she pulled out of the parking spot. Then she drove off into the fading night as it gave way to twilight. Raven felt excited and nervous. She glanced into the rearview mirror and saw Ashton standing in the middle of the parking lot, watching her as she drove away. The gesture brought a smile to her face that stayed there until she reached her hotel.

Chapter 34

Claud arrived at her hotel shortly after sunset. Raven was in the lobby waiting for him. He arrived in a hired limousine, which pleased her as it would be much easier for Ashton to follow without being detected. She even considered thanking him for picking that option. Claud emerged from the luxurious depths and walked straight to her. She stood there waiting, arms across her chest. As he approached, both of her hands, hidden behind her arms, tightened into fists. His lustful gaze made her skin crawl. Only her coolheadedness prevented Claud from knowing just how deep her loathing of him went. With one last look at her figure, he greeted her.

"Raven, it's good to see you."

He smiled warmly at her as if they were old friends. The fake endearment disgusted her further.

"I have a table for us," Raven said.

She turned and walked to the restaurant.

The knowledge that he was still ogling her turned her stomach, yet she maintained her composure and led him to their table, far to the rear of the otherwise empty dining room.

"We'll have privacy here," she explained.

She waited for him to seat himself. Having him sit first would allow her to sit opposite him, putting maximum distance between them. He was trying to find a way to prevent this as he worked to choose a spot. Before the pause would become awkward, he shrugged and sat where she guessed that he would, with his back to the wall so that he could keep an eye on the room around him, vigilant as always for some overdue reckoning waiting to come his way. She sat down across from him and produced a stylish attaché case. From it, she removed a tablet and a manila folder with a thin stack of papers inside. When Claud glanced at the items, she tapped the fingernail of her index finger on the bundle.

"Have you discussed recent events with Marius or Gitlam?" She asked pointedly.

"No, I haven't, nor do I need to." Claud demurred in a dismissive tone, but she could still hear his annoyance.

"I see."

"Do you?" He asked as if he were talking to a child.

She glared at him. She wanted to tell him just how much she could see.

"As you pointed out in one of our earlier conversations, this is my problem. Then, I chose to make it your problem, and now, I am making it our problem."

Raven wanted to reach across the table and smack the smug condescension off his face. He must have noticed a change in her demeanor and guessed her reaction.

"Come now, Raven. Let's don't make a scene."

The wry smile highlighted his vulpine visage, and she had to struggle to contain herself.

"Your time is coming," she spoke the words in her mind to stem the rising tide of anger within her.

She took a cleansing breath, exhaled slowly, took a drink of her wine, and looked back to Claud, who acted as if none of the interchanges had happened. She sighed.

"So, I have found everything I can about this man."

She pulled a page with several printed images of Ashton from the folder and set it on the table. In the top center of the page was his driver's license photo.

"He is pretty much the model citizen. No police record, no bankruptcies, always pays his taxes—"

"He volunteers at the animal shelter," Claud interrupted and made a show of stifling a yawn.

"Well, not at an animal shelter, but he did volunteer at a children's hospital for a short while after his sister died."

That wasn't true, but she liked the surprise she saw on Claud's face. He must have been looking into Ashton as well.

"It was an informal program he went through when trying to cope with his grief over the loss of his sister. One of his coworkers told me about it, and I confirmed it with a nurse who still works there."

While she was hurrying to come up with a fake name for the coworker, in case Claud asked, she watched Claud pull an invisible piece of lint from his maroon dress shirt and drop it in the air, fingers twitching to make sure it didn't stick on them.

Raven continued, "he lives alone, is not involved with social media, doesn't appear to be in a relationship, and takes good care of himself. He eats well and is a member of a nearby gym."

"What do I care about his exercise habits?" Claud sneered.

Raven knew he felt challenged by Ashton's austere lifestyle, which stood in stark contrast to his.

Raven gave him a look that asked, "Are you an idiot?"

"Well, until recently, he goes to the gym every other day at 7:00 pm, rain or shine."

He thought for a moment.

"What do you mean, until recently?"

"Seeing as you ask, until four days ago. Ashton was due in then but never showed. The girls at the counter were pretty unhappy that he didn't make it in. If he does turn up, they promised to call me. I haven't heard from them yet, so I assume he hasn't turned up there."

Claud seemed disinterested.

Raven added, "I bet those young beauties are losing sleep over it."

She knew vanity was a great way to get Claud angry and off-balance. Despite his average-at-best looks, he had convinced himself that he was God's gift to women. He refuses to attribute his effect on women to his vampirism or his liberal use of compulsion. When Raven saw his brows knit together, she knew her ploy had worked. She waited for him to find some way to turn it into an insult. She didn't need to wait long.

"What difference does it make? He's obviously gay."

She chuckled and agreed, "must be. For a man to be that sexy and live like a monk."

He shot her a glare, and she responded with a questioning look.

"Hey, I agree with you." She lied and never felt so good in doing so.

A long pause ensued. Raven made a show of looking through her papers. She prepared to rattle off his credit score, income, and outstanding debts when Claud spoke in his dry and controlled voice.

"So, we know where he lives. Let's go pay him a visit."

She looked at her watch and then at Claud.

"It's almost seven. Should we go to the gym first, just in case?"

She didn't bother hiding her smile as it was clear to them what she was doing. Claud glared at her, then glanced around the dining room. He was about to suggest they have dinner when a family, including a toddler and a crying baby, came out of the elevator and made their way to the hostess.

"Let's go check his apartment," Claud said.

Chapter 35

Ashton sat in his car, the engine softly idling as he listened to some guy named Wolf talk about the Arizona Cardinals football team. The voice was engaging, like a mix between Jesse Ventura and Macho Man Savage, wrestlers from the 80s his sister had made him watch. The mixture of sad and happy feelings washed over him, and Ashton felt like laughing and crying. Instead, he kept staring at the entrance and agonizing over Raven being in there with Claud. The limo driver got out of his car and lit up a cigarette, also keeping an eye on the entrance, presumably to be able to hurry over to pick up his fare.

Like a bolt of lightning from a clear blue sky, an idea hit Ashton. He looked around his console and the glove box before finding a white pen with a blue cap. He quickly disassembled to pen and held the white tube between his fingers like a cigarette. Then, he turned off his car and walked over to the driver.

When he was just a few feet from the limo, the driver turned to look at Ashton as he approached. The man gave him a wary look which Ashton ignored and then cupped the white tube in his hand and pretended it was a cigarette.

"You got a light?" he asked, "I left mine at the bar."

The guy shrugged and dug his lighter out from his pocket and handed it to Ashton, who just held it in his hand. When he didn't use it or say thanks, the guy looked at Ashton's face.

"Where did you pick him up from?" Ashton asked, compelling the driver to answer.

"Who?"

"Claud, the guy you drove here. Where did you pick him up from?" Ashton repeated.

The driver gave him the address and, once questioned further, told him how long Claud was in town and any other places he drove them. Ashton returned his lighter and compelled the man to forget about the questions and Ashton himself.

A few moments later, Ashton drove to the Keller home. He kept his phone plugged into a USB port and showing Raven's location. When he parked in front of the house a few minutes later, she was still in the hotel when Ashton unplugged his phone and walked up the steps to the Keller home. As he neared the house, he noticed a face pressed against the screen in a window that must have been to a basement as it was very close to the ground. Although he couldn't make out the finer details of the face, he could tell that it belonged to a young boy.

"Hello!" Ashton smiled and waved to the little boy.

"Hi!" The boy replied, clearly excited to see anyone.

Ashton had to be careful as he didn't want the boy to run off and call the police. He tried to imagine being that young again and decide how to approach him.

"Are you the lookout?" Ashton asked. The boy's expression appeared to show he was confused by the question. Ashton considered compelling him from where he stood on the sidewalk, but he wasn't sure if it would work, and he also wanted to get out of the brightly lit walkway and to the shadows by the boy before he tried.

"No, I'm Jeremy." The boy answered as best he could.

"Jeremy?" Ashton asked and squatted down to be closer to his eye level. "That's a cool name. Are you playing a game? I thought that maybe you were a lookout on a pirate ship."

The boy's eyes rolled in exasperation.

"No! That's dumb. A lookout would be at the top, up in the crow's nest."

Ashton was impressed with the kid's knowledge.

"I'm in the observation lounge of the Nautilus II."

Ashton smiled and looked over his shoulders, then back at the boy, giving him a fearful look.

"Are there any monsters coming?"

As Jeremy thought about this, Ashton took the opportunity to skulk closer to the window and into the shadows. While doing so, he strained to hear anything that would indicate his detection. When he turned to Jeremy, he saw the conflicted look on his face. This troubled Ashton.

"Mother and Father told me there aren't any monsters...but Papa Claud told me they are real and that my parents were just trying to protect me."

The mention of Claud confirmed he was at the right place, but he wanted to be sure.

"Did you meet Papa Claud recently, like in the past few days?" Ashton asked. He had continued to move near the window. He was kneeling in the gravel border around the house and nearly concealed in the shadows. His face was just inches from Jeremy's, separated only by the thin screen.

"Yes! Papa Claud came here to, um, elevate or escalate me. I don't remember which. But, he spends most of his time with Mother and Father in their bedroom. He says that they need the most help and tells me to be good for now. So, that's what I am doing. I am being a good boy and looking out for monsters."

Jeremy's face grew pale, and he pulled back from the screen.

"You're not a monster, are you?" He gasped, fear cracking his young voice.

Ashton realized he didn't know how to answer that. Despite all of the things that had happened to him, the revelations about how certain religious items affected him, how he could barely tolerate sunlight, and his need for blood, he didn't feel like a monster. Then he thought about what he was about to do to this innocent boy.

"Well?" Jeremy asked again, withdrawing further into the basement.

"Oh, no, I'm not a monster, which is what a monster would say. So, I was thinking about how I can prove it to you."

"You're right!" Jeremy said and pushed his face against the screen again. "That's what I was thinking too!" His happiness at having his thoughts confirmed outweighed his caution.

Ashton made a silent prayer, one of the very few times he ever did such a thing, and asked for forgiveness for what he was about to do.

"Jeremy, I need you to listen to what I say."

Using his ability to compel a child made him sick to his stomach.

After extracting an invitation to the home and making sure that Jeremy would remember nothing of the encounter, Ashton hurried back to his car and drove away. After he pulled out of the subdivision, he pulled over and vomited on the side of the road. He had made the mistake of asking Jeremy to tell him what Claud had been doing.

Once his disgust had settled, it turned into rage. He pulled his phone out and brought up Raven's location. His heart jumped into overdrive at what he saw. She was not only at his apartment complex - she was inside his apartment!

Chapter 36

Claud invited Raven to ride with him to Ashton's apartment. She reluctantly accepted the offer as it would allow her to keep an eye on him. The chauffeur held the door open for them, with Raven entering the cabin first. Before Claud entered, he asked his driver if anything had happened. After receiving an answer to the negative, Claud climbed in and sat opposite Raven, facing her and the rearview window. Raven cursed herself for the oversight. If Ashton followed them, Claud could see it first hand. If she noticed him staring out of the rear window, she might have to use her body to attract his attention. Raven wouldn't let him touch her - that would be too much - but flashing some skin in his direction might be enough to distract him. Then she remembered purposefully wearing slacks to avoid his unwanted attention.

"I'll think of something," she assured herself.

Much to her gratitude, the relatively short ride to Ashton's apartment complex was uneventful and mostly filled with Claud offering her a drink or sharing his grim musings about the state of the world. She tuned him out and placatingly offered agreements to his assertions while hoping Ashton would remain undetected.

To Raven's surprise, the limousine came to rest at the exact entrance Ashton would have used when he walked from his parking spot to his apartment. The driver opened her door first, which was on the same side of the street as the sidewalk. She stepped out and glanced at Ashton's spot, which was empty. She watched the entrance to the complex for any cars, but none came.

"Where are you, Ashton?" she asked herself.

Once Claud stepped out of the car, he turned to Raven, giving her the lead. She walked to Ashton's apartment and knocked. No one answered. She retrieved her lock-picking tools from her purse and began to unlock the doors. Thinking of the last time she broke into his apartment, Raven forced the pleasant memories of what happened between them from her mind. It was not the time, nor was it the place and certainly was not the right company to revel in those delicious memories.

It only took Raven a few minutes to pick the locks and open the doors. Claud looked at her expectantly.

"Ladies first."

"Thanks," she whispered and pushed past him.

As expected, the apartment was empty. The coppery notes of blood mingled with the acrid odor of garlic were very unexpected by Raven.

"Do you smell that?" Claud asked.

She nodded. While the odors were overpowering and distracting, she could not help the memories that flooded her mind with images of her and Ashton being together in that very room less than twenty-four hours ago. The memories brought with them a deep and sensual stirring of heat. Claud waved his hand in a futile effort to dissipate the foul stench.

"Disgusting!" He exclaimed, sounding like a posh English bureaucrat who realized he had stepped in dog shit.

Raven covered her mouth with her arm making her voice sound muffled.

"He's not here."

Claud walked over to the kitchen area, following the smell of blood. He opened the garbage can lid and pulled out a white container. He lifted the lid and showed Raven the whitish beef livers inside.

"All of the blood is gone," Claud explained and put the lid back on the container and returned it to the garbage. Then he walked to the fridge and saw the other container on the bottom shelf in the back.

"Looks like he is using cow's blood," Claud mentioned more to himself than Raven.

This alarmed Raven.

"Why would he drink cow's blood if he was supposed to have fed on Jacob?" She didn't realize she spoke the words until Claud snapped around to face her.

"What?" He asked.

"I was wondering," she said slowly, "why he would use cow's blood if he had fed on Jacob. Jacob was the kid that killed himself and Julia."

"That's a good question."

He looked at her suspiciously. She had to think of something before he went too far with his doubts.

She looked around quickly. The apartment was clean. The only thing that seemed untidy was the smell of garlic and liver.

"Maybe he hasn't been here for a few days. He might have even drank that blood before he encountered Jacob."

Although she knew the answer, she asked Claud, "What else is in the fridge?"

"Just some eggs, a little butter, and the other carton of that." He pointed to the garbage can.

She made a production of thinking about the discovery as if she were trying to piece together an elaborate puzzle.

"I bet you are right, he must have used the cow's blood before he got to Jacob and is keeping the other container as a backup, but I have no idea about the garlic."

Claud hoped to keep her suspicions on Ashton.

Raven pointed to the sink. "I bet the smell is coming from there. He probably tried using the garbage disposal on something in his fridge and didn't expect the stench."

As Claud walked out of the kitchen, Raven had to back up to let him leave the confined space.

"Let's look around," he said and walked towards the end of the hallway to Ashton's bedroom.

Raven made an effort to look around, starting in the living room and tracing her steps from last night.

"Wow," she thought, "was it just last night?" It seemed like a lifetime ago when she had entered his home without permission, and they had been together.

She made her way to the small bedroom he used as an office and heard Claud opening drawers. A few minutes later, Claud came to the office where Raven was. She opened the drawers and busied herself by rifling through them. One drawer contained files, and the other seemed to serve as a to-do file for incoming mail. Inside, she found a few opened envelopes and a letter opener. Claud stepped out of the office and looked at the pictures hanging on the wall. A shudder crept up her spine at the thought of Claud seeing Ashton's precious memories. After a few more moments, she opened the closet. He had converted it to a storage area for office supplies. A wooden storage unit contained many cubicles filled with paper reams, pens, whiteout, and ink cartridges. Raven could tell that Ashton had built it, and she ran her hand over its polished surface and smiled.

She left the office and announced what she had found that would be useful to them.

"Nothing in here or the living room."

Claud responded in kind.

"That's what I found in the bedroom."

He sounded disappointed.

"The man must be the most boring man on the planet."

Raven had a feeling where Claud's head was.

"Why? Because he doesn't have a dirty magazine collection or weird sexual devices?" she asked, taunting Claud with her insight.

"Exactly!" He exclaimed, sounding triumphant, "no girlfriend, no porn, no anything! What does he do for fun, watch paint dry?"

Raven thought, "I would be happy to watch paint dry with Ashton, thank you very much."

She had to admit, that wouldn't be her first choice of how to pass the time with him. She didn't want to think about what her first choice would be. With a shrug and a sigh, she asked Claud what they should do now.

"Why don't you visit the neighbors and ask them to contact you if he turns up. I'll go and wait in the car. I could use another drink."

While she didn't want to let him out of sight, she would enjoy not being in his company. He had a way of wearing on her, and she had spent more time with him recently than she had in centuries. Other than the Blood Communion, she never saw him in person, and that's how she liked it. She secretly hoped soon she would never have to see him again.

As Claud walked towards the car, Raven hoped Ashton hadn't shown up. He probably knew where she was and would hopefully conclude that Claud was with her. She hoped that he would continue to be so clever at following them.

She turned to the apartment door of Ashton's neighbor. She knocked, and a silver-haired man answered the door. After a few minutes, she gave him a card and asked that he call her if Ashton showed up. She didn't use her persuasive ability on him as she didn't care if he called or not. All that concerned her was telling Claud someone was watching out for Ashton. She walked to the car to join Claud.

When she climbed into the waiting limo, after thanking the chauffeur, she was pleased to find Claud sitting in the back seat, facing the front of the car. Once inside, she sat facing Claud and, thereby, the rear end of the limo.

Without a word from Claud, the car pulled away from the curb and left the complex. Raven asked Claud, "Where are we going now?"

"I have some personal matters to address this evening, Raven. Maybe we could grab a bite and then call it a night."

"If it is all the same to you, I would appreciate getting dropped at my hotel."

She smiled her customary smile he correctly interpreted as "Go fuck yourself." She did have to keep up her normal behavior, she assured herself.

"While nothing would make me happier, there are some things we need to discuss, so I think we should dine together and discuss them."

She rolled her eyes but nodded.

"Let's get it over with."

They dined at an upscale steakhouse in old town Scottsdale. Besides the excellent food, it served as more of a sports museum than a fine dining experience. Framed autographed jerseys, pictures, and other memorabilia filled the walls.

It didn't take long for Raven to realize that the young and attractive patrons were what lured Claud to the place. While he did hide his perverse appraisal of the crowd well, Raven knew what he was doing. Claud was ranking the men and women. She found solace in knowing that he was her ride and that he wouldn't send her off on her own and allow her to interrogate the driver.

Over what turned out to be an excellent meal, Claud gave her a set of instructions that would keep her busy. While she would not be able to do much of it due to the time, she would need to coordinate with Malcolm, his long-time servant. After their meal, Claud reluctantly traveled with Raven to her hotel. He would have preferred the company of some of the couples at the bar, but Raven convinced him that even he had to make sacrifices.

"Keep your phone handy, Raven, just in case I think of something," he said in a haughty tone which she ignored.

Claud watched Raven walk into the hotel. His eyes latched hungrily on her hips as they swayed ever so slightly as she moved.

"What a waste," he sighed in disappointment and tilted his head so the driver would hear.

"To the Keller house driver, posthaste."

Chapter 37

As soon as Ashton saw the limousine pull into the hotel parking lot, he pulled out of the lot across from it and headed to the address he got from the driver earlier in the evening. He wanted to wait and maybe catch a glimpse of Raven, but he had more important plans - plans that could resolve the Claud problem permanently. Ashton looked at the stakes he fashioned from a chair in the bulk garbage at some house he passed, wanting nothing more than to bury one into Claud's heart.

He parked along a street close to the Keller's house, where he had seen a large olive tree during his earlier visit. He would use that as a hiding spot, and it would give him a good view of the front and rear entrances of the home.

The plan went very well, for all of two minutes. As planned, Ashton turned off one street before their home and hurried to hide in the tree. He didn't count on the dog that started barking, nor did he consider that Claud wasn't going to the Keller's home. The limo stopped a few doors before the Keller's and on the opposite side of the street. Claud exited the car and walked straight into the wrong house. The limo pulled away, and a dumbfounded Ashton stared at the door Claud had just entered.

"Shit!" He mumbled to himself and caused the dog to begin frantic barking.

After a few moments of the unrelenting barking, Ashton heard the sound of a patio door opening and then heard someone call the dog inside.

"Come in, Princess."

Princess was having none of it.

"I don't know what her problem is."

The sound of the man's voice changed, and Ashton imagined him turning his head and speaking to someone inside the house.

"I don't have shoes on! There could be a scorpion!"

The man whined to whoever was inside. Ashton understood. He had been stung before, and it wasn't fun.

Ashton barely heard a woman's shrill and grating voice tell the man to "put your damned shoes on then."

The door slid closed. Less than a minute later, the door opened again, and this time, the outside light turned on. The man walked over to the frantic dog. The beam from a flashlight lit up the dog's eyes and then the dog itself as the man stepped out from the back of the house to the side and into Ashton's view. He wore polka dot boxers, black tube socks, sandals, and a white tank top. He was partly bald on the top of his head and was very pale. Ashton felt sympathy for the guy but had to stifle a laugh over his attire.

"What's the matter, girl?" he asked the dog.

Princess reminded him of the mutt that played a dog named Benji on an old TV show his sister had found and had loved. Ashton did not feel love for this dog, though, far from it.

The man grabbed her collar and began pulling her towards the patio.

"Come on, Princess. We don't want another noise complaint."

Princess writhed to free herself and kept barking. The man was losing his patience.

"If we get another complaint, you'll be visiting the pound."

That was a big mistake. In the midst of it all, the woman must have made her way to the open patio door because as soon as the man mentioned the pound, she went off on him.

"Oh, no, she's not! How dare you! If anyone around here needs to go, it's you!"

Apparently, this wasn't the first time he dealt with her wrath over the dog because he stayed quiet and pretended not to hear her. Ashton knew her type, and he knew the poor man just had to let her vent until she ran out of steam. Once inside, the closing patio door cut off her further high-toned wailing over the terrible treatment of her "precious little Princess" by the "no good man."

All the while, Ashton remained as still as possible in the olive tree next to their house. He didn't know which he was more thankful for, not being able to hear the dog bark or the woman's bitching. His phone buzzed in his pants pocket. While he did plan ahead and put his phone on silent, he didn't anticipate needing to look at his phone while twenty feet up in a tree on a residential busy side street in the middle of the night.

After some consideration, he took his jacket off and draped it over his front, and created a tent under it. Then, he took his phone from his pocket, pressed the button, and nearly dropped the phone when the bright screen lit up. He squinted his eyes to shield them from the glare and hurriedly opened the brightness setting and cranked it to its lowest. He let out an audible sigh once he completed the task. A distant memory of reading a book late at night while under his covers with a flashlight crept into his mind and caused him to smile fondly at the recollection.

He nearly screamed in frustration after realizing the vibration was from a work meeting reminder. He smiled, knowing he would never have to sit through another pointless meeting again. Just like the last time this reminder popped up, he didn't want to take the time to delete the appointment from his calendar, so he just cleared the notification. He made himself a promise to take care of it soon. However, he did take the time to check Raven's location, which was still at her hotel. He quickly turned the phone off and put the jacket back on, and continued his vigil of watching both houses. It would be hours before dawn, so he did his best to make himself comfortable.

While it seemed to be a simple enough task to watch a couple of houses, Ashton soon realized it was more like a form of torture. After what he thought was an hour, which was closer to fifteen minutes, he developed an appreciation for cops on a stakeout and wished he had a partner. He would have loved a coffee and a donut right about then.

Ashton learned a different lesson soon enough. He discovered what fed the perversion of peeping toms and night prowlers the world over - people will do anything if they think no one can see them. Almost all of the homes in the valley had at least seven-foot-tall privacy fences made out of cinder blocks bordering their property. These fences prevented line of sight views into the homes of their neighbors. As multi-level homes were uncommon due to the heat, people were less concerned with closing their windows and curtains to rooms on the back of their houses.

Even without using his enhanced hearing, Ashton would pick up occasional pieces of conversations drifting out of windows. Most related to mundane tasks like chores or preparing for the next day. As the night wore on, in the house behind the Keller's home and directly behind the one with Princess and the tree he was in, Ashton noticed lights turned off in one room, then turned on in the previously dark room. Once illuminated, it was clear to Ashton that it was a bedroom. The next thing that became clear was that the couple who lived there was getting ready for bed. The woman walked into another room and turned on a light. The frosted glass obscured the view and made it clear to Ashton that the room was a bathroom. Moments later, he could hear the faint hiss of a shower running, followed by the woman asking the man if he was coming or not. Before Ashton could turn away, the man took off his shirt and shorts and threw them on the top of a hamper. He rushed to the bathroom and joined her.

Realizing he had been looking at that house for too long, he turned his attention to the others and observed more of nothing. He shook his head and exhaled through his nose. It was going to be a long night indeed. The sound of the shower faded to background noise, and Ashton forgot about the couple until the shower shut off and the absence of the sound caught his attention. Then, he heard laughing, followed by a woman crying for the man to stop.

Ashton looked into the room.

The man reached his hands out and tickled the woman as they walked backward into the bedroom. She hit him ineffectively with a towel. Ashton tried not to pay attention to the naked couple, but the woman had massive breasts, the kind you see on the cover of magazines dedicated to big-breasted women.

"You better be careful, buddy. She could smother you with those." He whispered to himself and chuckled.

His merriment turned into disbelief when she did just that. Well, that's how it looked to Ashton, anyway.

In his retreat, the man tripped and fell backward onto the bed. The woman kept moving toward him, which caused her to fall forward, but she was able to get her knees on the top of the bed and ended up straddling him. She grabbed his wrists and pinned them down against the bed, over his head. Then, she turned her head to the side, and Ashton could see her playful smile and barely heard her say, "you're in for it now, mister," before she smashed her fleshy mounds into his face. She tucked her elbows in on her sides, which prevented her breasts from spreading outward.

The man made a good show of writhing around and pushing her off. Then, the entire mood shifted when the woman released his hands and arched her back, removing the obstructions from the man's face. His hands found her mounds, and the woman sighed in pleasure as his mouth covered one of her nipples.

Ashton's eyes grew wide when he realized he was peeping on the couple. His face flushed, and he nearly fell out of the tree as he shifted his body in the hope of blocking the view. Unfortunately, it didn't work, and he could still see the room from the corner of his eye. For long minutes he stared at the Keller home. Despite his efforts, he noticed the couple had moved further into the bed and began more advanced activities, the motion of which kept drawing his attention. After catching unwanted glimpses of the pair and their sensual actions, he pulled his coat off and draped it over his left side, blocking his view completely.

"There!" He triumphed quietly to himself, "problem solved."

Then came the moans, followed by the smacking of lips and asses, followed by talking. It became evident that the woman enjoyed a little naughty repartee which made Ashton squirm. While he had nothing against it, hearing it while not being involved in the action - or even interested in it - created a completely unexpected problem for him. Ashton wanted to laugh. Soon, it became his need to laugh. He made those sounds unique to trying to stifle a laugh that sounded like stopping a sneeze. He hoped no one had heard him. Silently laughing eased the growing tension and allowed him to try controlled breathing. It all seemed fine until the woman spoke in a commanding and surprisingly loud voice.

"You want mama to feed the wittle baby?"

The man made a smacking sound with his mouth. That pushed Ashton over the edge, and he belted out laughter.

Ashton wrapped his coat around his head and bit down on the lining while simultaneously burying his face in his jacket. Tiny pinholes of light lit up his closed eyes from the pressure.

"Who's out there?"

Ashton froze, then started to chuckle again. He kept telling himself to stop laughing, but he couldn't.

"Why didn't you at least close the window?" the woman whisper-yelled at the man.

A moment later, Ashton heard the window slide shut. He started to pull the coat from his head but decided to check his phone for the time instead.

"You have to be fucking kidding me!"

Only 30 minutes had passed. Ashton checked Raven's location, which was still the hotel, and then turned his attention to the houses and resigned himself to the long night ahead.

At one point, Ashton noticed a golf course not too far off in the distance, maybe a mile, maybe closer. Thoughts of the golf course triggered memories from when he and some friends had found an entrance to a large concrete tunnel on the side of the golf course nearest to his location.

Heavy iron gates guarded the entrance into the tunnel. He and his friends managed to lift the gates and make their way inside. They discovered a network of concrete tunnels. While exploring them, they found graffiti and areas where some homeless people were hiding from the heat. The homeless ran them off, and they never went back into the tunnels after the encounter. Over the years, he and his friends would occasionally hear stories about the tunnels and things people found in them or bodies pulled from them. He realized he could use them for emergency shelter if something went wrong here. Until then, his trunk had been his only option.

As the distant horizon started to lighten in the east, the door to the house across the street - the one Claud had entered - opened, and a figure emerged. It appeared to be a man, and he made a beeline to the Keller home. His movement was cautious and determined, and moments later, he entered the house.

Something about how the man moved caused Ashton to remember Raven explaining that ancient vampires such as Claud weakened as dawn approached.

He jumped down from the tree and ran to the rear of the Keller house. He pulled one of the homemade stakes from his coat, where he had pushed them through the fabric on the inside pocket. He forced open the patio door and stepped inside.

He could see the entrance and saw the man standing there, leaning against the inside of the front door as if exhausted. Ashton's anger spread, and he shot toward the man with lightning speed. The man cried out. Something about his voice made Ashton look closer at his face. It was all wrong.

Ashton grabbed the front of the man's suit, which he could tell now didn't fit. He pulled his right arm behind his body, preparing to pierce the man's chest with the stake. The man raised his arms and folded them, trying to shield himself from the imminent attack.

"Mr. Hessian, what are you doing here?" came the voice of Jeremy from behind and to the left of Ashton.

Then Ashton heard something that froze his blood. It was the sound of the slide of a gun wracked.

"Snick-snack."

Ashton spun to his right and tried to pull the imposter to cover. The man fell to the floor without injury, but not Ashton. The explosion of the pistol firing was deafening, and the white-hot pain that slammed into Ashton's side blinded him. Too late, he realized he had fallen into a trap.

"Shoot him! Shoot him!"

The shrill voice of a tall, thin woman Ashton could see standing behind the man holding a gun in his shaking hands. Ashton's panic heightened his senses, and everything seemed to slow. He could see the woman screaming, but her yells sounded muffled and distorted.

He watched the man mouth the words, "I am! I am!"

His finger jerked back and pulled his shot high. The bullet punched a webbed hole through the frosted glass privacy panel next to their door. Ashton launched himself toward the man with the gun and shoulder blocked him into the screaming woman. Then, he raced out of the house and towards the golf course. The car wasn't an option.

Seconds later, Claud entered through the front door and looked pointedly at the broken glass. He saw the man he had dressed in his suit on the ground, and then he saw Desiree pushing Lance off of her.

"Can't you do anything right, you fucking loser!" She shouted at him while pushing his shoulder forward. His arm moved forward and then sprung back, hitting her in her chest.

Claud, momentarily forgetting about Ashton, watched with bated breath as Lance looked at the gun in his hand and turned his head slightly to see Desiree behind him.

Lance whirled on her and smashed the gun's barrel into her face. Her scream abruptly cut off as he pushed the muzzle into her mouth, driving her backward and pinning her head to the ground. His face was red with rage. The veins on his forehead and neck bulged out. When he spoke to her, spittle flew from his mouth. His crazed eyes flared wide and wild.

"Shut your fucking mouth, you stupid fucking whore. Shut the fuck up for once in your miserable, worthless life."

Although in terrible pain from the smashed lip, chipped tooth, and cuts on the roof of her mouth from the gun sight, she didn't cry or whimper. Her life flashed before her eyes, and she voided her bowels and wet herself. It was the end for her, and she knew it.

"And to think that I wasted so much of my life on an unfaithful piece of shit like you."

Claud was enthralled and overcome with the expectation of the mild Lance finally breaking and doing something to redeem himself and punish the vile woman he had married.

Then came a tiny and fear-filled voice, soft and wavering, "Daddy? Don't hurt mommy, please, daddy."

Claud hushed him, and Jeremy recoiled behind a nearby chair.

Lance shook his head and pulled the gun from Desiree's mouth, a mouth she had used on many, many men since their marriage. The thought of her whoring was almost enough to make him put the gun back into her mouth and pull the trigger, but a sniffling sound from Jeremy's hiding place saved her and probably Lance as well. He pulled the gun out and stood over her. He toggled the safety and walked off to the bedroom.

Claud shook his head in disappointment. Not only had Lance failed him, but Claud had also failed to pursue the fledgling vampire. He supposed it wasn't a failure as the vampire had left before Claud arrived, preventing pursuit. Then Claud noticed the growing light filling the house from the back patio, which faced east. He hurried to the basement and called the people to him for their instructions.

Then Claud, his strength nearly depleted from the recently risen sun, found his refuge in the dark basement and rested.

Chapter 38

Even with the searing pain in his side, Ashton made it to the gates that led to the tunnel system with a few minutes to spare. He needed the extra time as a surprise awaited him. The gate was now chained and locked. Bars extended over the top of the entrance, forming a cage. He considered his options - he could try to bend the bars, snap the chain or break the padlock. He chose the chain option. He found a section of the chain that he could grip with both hands. It wrapped between the door of the gate and the bars next to and below the door. He pulled apart on the chain for several seconds and stopped with a gasp. The sky grew much lighter, and it was getting harder for him to bear the brightness.

He focused his mind, like he had done when using his compulsion power, and took a deep breath. Again, he pulled on the chains. Once he felt that he was at the limit of his human strength, he willed his body to provide more power to his muscles. He felt the chain begin to stretch and redoubled his effort of pulling and using his willpower.

The snap that he heard when the chain broke was surprisingly disappointing. It had a hollow ting which he didn't expect. He hurriedly unwrapped the chain and pushed the gate up. After stepping through, he again wrapped the chain around it and did his best to make it look as it had. Then, he found the link that had snapped and used his enhanced strength to push it together again. If someone was inspecting the chain closely, they could tell something had happened, but otherwise, it looked fine.

Ashton made his way into the darkness of the tunnels and thought to use his phone as a flashlight but was surprised with how well he could see. He needed to find a safe spot to inspect his wound. The tunnels seemed much smaller than when Ashton was in high school. Back then, he could walk at a crouch through them, but now he needed to crawl. Thankfully, there was no water collected on the bottom of the curved pipe, but there was still a fair amount of gravel and pieces of glass. As long as he kept his hands and knees wide and high up on the sides of the concrete pipe, he wouldn't have to worry about getting hurt.

He laughed at the thought of not getting hurt. It was too late for that. Once at the juncture of two tunnels, he turned around for a look. The light at the beginning of the tunnel seemed like a distant pinhole.

He remembered if he kept traveling the tunnel he entered through, it would eventually reach a cistern. The pipe that intersected with the one he was on slowly rose and ended at drains. The angle out was steeper than the one towards the cistern, but the juncture was lower on the cistern side than the side that ran to the exit. Water got channeled to the cistern. Once filled, the excess ran out of the tunnels. The cistern allowed the golf course to collect rain during the monsoon season and use it for landscaping needs.

After making sure the area was clear of any dangerous debris, he took his coat off and sat on that. Then he lifted his shirt and looked at the gunshot wound. To his amazement, the injury had healed. Then he realized it hadn't been hurting at all during the last few minutes when he made his way to the juncture. He poked and pinched the skin around where the bullet had hit him. When he pulled the skin from his side towards his stomach more, he could see two small pink circles separated by a few inches. Putting his finger on the one closer to his back, he let his skin go, and it snapped back to position. The holes lined up to form a line, which he concluded where it entered and exited his body.

"Well, fuck me," he said in disbelief and let his shirt fall back into place. When it did, he saw the small bloodstains on the front and back of his shirt corresponding to the fading wounds on his side. He checked his jacket and did see a small hole in the lining with some blood on it, but there was no hole in the jacket leather, nor could he find a bullet. He rolled the jacket up into a makeshift pillow and stretched out, angling his feet across the bottom of the tunnel and towards the entrance while propping his head against the curved intersection of the tunnels behind him.

It didn't take long for him to slip into a deep sleep.

As soon as he saw her, Ashton knew he was dreaming. His sister was sitting on her bedroom floor setting up a game of Monopoly. It had been so long since he had dreamed of her he didn't object to the choice of games. He had hated playing Monopoly with just the two of them because it took forever. Now and again, they would be able to convince their mother to play, but it was usually just her and him. He was able to keep the times they had played to only once or twice a year. More than once since her death, Ashton had wished more than anything to be able to play one more game with his sister, even if it was Monopoly.

Everything was ready to go, except they had to choose their tokens for the board. Sam always chose the dog, which she called Toto, and wanted him to call her Dorothy during the game. He didn't mind indulging her, especially when he saw how much she enjoyed the pretense. She took something from the box behind her, turned back around, and hovered her hand over the "Go" space. She dropped the metallic terrier and smiled. Again she reached behind herself and soon pulled her hand forward again, keeping it cupped to hide her selection. She hovered it over the "Go" space again.

"I know which one you picked, Sam." He teased her as she always chose the race car for him.

"Really?" She answered him in a skeptical voice.

"The race car, Sam, you always pick the race car." He taunted her back.

"Right!" She exclaimed, and then her face contorted into uncertainty. Then she added, "sort of," and dropped a red car with a blue peg and two pink pegs onto the spot. It was from the game of life, and Ashton looked up to her, equally confused. One pink peg was next to the blue peg, and the other was in the back, a space behind the two pegs in front. Ashton assumed that the one in the back was Sam.

"Who is that?" He asked, pointing to the pink one in front.

"Her." She replied.

"Her who?" he asked.

"The one you met, the bird lady." She replied in an uncharacteristically cryptic fashion.

"Raven? Do you mean Raven?" Ashton asked, a feeling of joy filling him at the idea.

"Yes, her! She is so pretty, Ash. Have you kissed her yet?" Sam asked as she picked up the dice and started shaking them in her hand.

"Well, uh, maybe once or twice." He suddenly felt very embarrassed, which Sam had a way of doing to him. He thanked God that no one was around, or she might start teasing him about it. She surprised him further by what she said next.

"That's good, Ash. She is special, very, very, very special."

His smile beamed as he agreed, "yes, she sure is."

"But you have to protect her, Ash. She is in danger." The somber tone of her voice was very unusual. She turned her head as if listening to whispers in the wind.

"I know," she whispered in reply to someone Ashton could not hear. She took his hand in hers, wrapping two small hands around it. Tears ran down her cheek, and she pulled his hand to hers and kissed it.

"You have to be brave, Ash - very brave. Bad things are coming, and only you and her can stop them."

Suddenly, they were in the yard outside her old room, standing side-by-side and holding hands.

"You have to go home, Ash. It's safe for you there."

"What do you mean, Sam? What danger, what bad things. Is it Claud? What?"

She shook her head and held her hand up, then turned her head in that peculiar way again. She shook her head furtively and squeezed his hand tighter than she ever had.

"No! He can do it. He is strong and good."

Another pause.

Her voice slowly took on an imploring, almost begging tone.

"I know he is different than before, but he is still a good person and much stronger too!"

After yet another lengthy pause, she nodded and smiled slightly.

"OK, Ash, you have to go now. Wake up! Wake up!"

She disappeared from the dreamscape, and her voice echoed and faded away. It seemed to cause Ashton's head to shake back and forth. Suddenly he woke. He swore he heard her words echoing throughout the tunnels.

"Go home! Wake up!"

Ashton checked his phone, and he had only about 10 minutes before the sun would set. He crawled to the edge of the tunnel and tentatively emerged from the darkness. The pressure of the sun's light hit him hard, and the brightness bore into his eyes. To his relief, his skin wasn't burning, and he didn't feel pain other than the light that seemed to stab his brain.

He squinted and fought with the chain. After it popped apart as before sunrise, he crawled under the gate and went to his car. Using his enhanced speed appealed to him, but he didn't want to risk it in the fading sunlight, just in case his vampiric energy was running out. He felt weak and realized he would need blood - and that meant Raven.

Ashton jumped into his car and drove home. Only a few minutes remained before the sunset and before Claud would be free to hunt him again. On the way, he called the hotel and asked for her room.

Chapter 39

The front desk put Ashton's call through to the room number he provided. He was glad they didn't ask for a name as he didn't know if Raven had a last name. The receptionist explained to Ashton how he could dial the number directly in the future and put the call through.

"Come on, come on, answer."

He knew she or her phone was there because her location hadn't changed.

When her phone rang, Raven had only been awake for a few minutes. She had a terrible time getting to sleep without knowing if Ashton was OK. As she turned to pick up the room phone, she grabbed her phone from the nightstand.

"Hello," she said into the room phone and unlocked her cell to see that she had no missed calls or text messages.

"Yes. Hello, I am calling from the concierge to check that all of your amenities have met your expectations."

She recognized his soft and deep voice as soon as he spoke, even though he did so in an exaggerated professional tone. For a moment, she didn't know what to think. Alarmed, she lowered her voice even despite being alone.

"Ashton? What are you doing? I told you not to call!"

Her cell phone vibrated to indicate a new text message. She ignored it.

"I *might* have fucked up a little last night, but I have a plan."

She panicked.

"What do you mean, you *might* have fucked up a little? You either did, or you didn't."

He took a deep breath.

"I'm sure your buddy Claud will explain everything. Can you leave some of that blood for me at the front desk? I need some, and I don't want to get it on my own."

"OK."

He could hear the alarm in her voice and was thankful that she didn't press for answers.

"Thanks, Raven. Listen, I have a plan, but I need your help to make it work."

She didn't say anything, so he just rattled it off.

"The main thing I need is for you to stall as long as possible and get to my house as close just before dawn."

"Your house?" Raven asked. She sounded confused.

"Yeah. My mother left it to us when she died. After Sam died, I couldn't stand living there, but I couldn't sell it either."

"I understand," Raven said.

"I need time to prepare, at least eight or ten hours. I'm not sure how long it will take as a vampire."

"What do you mean?"

"I have to make some changes in the basement to prepare for Claud. Normally it would take me about 12 hours to do everything. But now, I'm not so sure. If I use my enhanced speed and strength, it should be quicker. "

"Oh, OK."

The vibrating sound of another text message arriving on Raven's phone was loud enough that Ashton heard it. He hurriedly finished his instructions.

"Once you get there, separate from Claud and check the hamper in the bathroom on the first floor. I'll leave some stuff there for you."

"I need you to stall him as long as possible, without making him suspicious, and then come to my apartment. I'll leave a smudge on a photo of my old house. You can pretend to discover it on your own. Then, search my desk, and you can find the address of my old home there. Oh, the key will be under the mat!"

Her phone vibrated again and then rang. It lit up with Claud's name on the caller id. She saw the missed texts and knew she had to take the call.

"I have to go."

"Can you do that and leave the blood? I really need it after last night."

"OK. Sure, but I have to go."

He hung up, and Raven answered her phone.

"What?" She let her frustration of not being able to ask Ashton any questions come out in her voice. Her mind was going in a thousand directions.

"Why didn't you answer my texts or call me. like I told you to?" Claud asked in an accusatory tone.

"You didn't give me time too. I was indisposed."

"Doing what?"

"None of your business, Claud. Now, what do you want?"

"He found me, Raven. How in the hell did he do that?" Claud's voice was ice, absolute zero. Fear stiffened her spine, and she could almost feel the temperature in the room drop.

"I...uh...I have no idea, Claud. What happened?"

"Somehow, he figured out where I was staying. He attacked just before dawn."

The anger in his voice was palpable. Raven needed to calm him down before they met face to face, or he might compel her.

"You're OK, though, right? I mean, you sound OK."

"He didn't get to me, but he caused one hell of a scene. It took most of the day to get the cops out of the house."

"House? What house? Where are you?"

She realized then that she didn't know where he was staying, and that was why he hadn't started the conversation by accusing her outright.

There was a long pause, and Claud told her that he was staying with some friends. They both knew that was a lie. Claud knew he hadn't told Raven where he was staying, and he knew no one had followed him from her hotel. The driver would have noticed and told him.

"Have you been to Trevor's? He may have followed you from there."

"No."

"If he is hunting or following me, he might have seen you when you came to the hotel, or maybe he saw me asking questions at his apartment complex."

While she spoke to Claud, she put the bag with the blood packs by the door to her room. She would need to run that down to the front desk. She slipped into some sweats and an old pair of sneakers. When she left the room, the door closed loudly, and Claud asked her what the noise was.

"My door - I am going down to the receptionist now. I will get the security team to show me the surveillance video from yesterday and work my way backward. They should have footage dating from before I even arrived. If he followed either of us to or from here, I should be able to find it."

A loud electronic ding signaled the arrival of the elevator seconds after she pushed the call button.

"I am getting in the elevator. If the call drops, I'll call you back, OK?"

"Don't bother. I should be there in a few minutes."

Claud's voice was still laden with distrust.

Raven's heart jumped into overdrive. She ended the call and stepped into the elevator. Immediately, she pressed the lobby button and then repeatedly pushed the button to close the doors. She knew it wouldn't help, just like she knew willing it to get there without stopping at other floors made no difference. Luck was on her side, and within a few seconds, she exited the elevator and approached the desk, where a young man she had seen a few times waited. When he saw Raven, he smiled and straightened up.

"Hello, how may I help you?" he asked.

She immediately turned on her compulsion, set the bag on the counter, pushed it towards him, and read his name tag.

"Thad, I need you to put this in the office and wait for a man named Ashton to pick this up. He will be here later this evening. Tell no one and if anyone asks you, tell them you are taking care of it for a customer. Do you understand?"

"Yes, I understand."

He took the bag and placed it in the office. He closed the door and quickly came back.

"I need to see your security videos for the last few days."

He nodded and walked around the counter. Next, he led Raven down a hallway and through a door marked for employees only. Once through the door, he led her to the end of the hallway and took a left. The security office was also clearly marked and only five feet from the turn.

Raven turned to face Thad.

"Soon, a man is going to come here looking for me. His name is Claud."

She thought about asking him to stall Claud but decided against it as that might make him suspicious.

"When he shows up, lead him here right away. OK, Thad?"

He nodded and then knocked on the door. The door opened, and a stout, middle-aged woman scarcely five feet tall asked in a raspy voice that must have been the product of years of smoking.

"Yeah, what do you want?"

"I need you to help me review videos of the last several days," Raven explained.

The security guard ignored Thad and looked her over.

"You ain't no cop, and you don't work here. I'm busy."

She pushed the door to close it.

Raven held her hand out to stop the door. Thad started to speak, but she silenced him with a glance.

"I'll take care of it from here, Thad. Go back to the front desk."

"Who do you think you are, lady?" The woman puffed her chest and bumped into Raven, who almost laughed.

"Be quiet and show me the videos," Raven commanded.

The woman turned back into the office and obeyed. It didn't take long for her to learn the controls and take over the search. Raven could work much faster than the security guard.

She hadn't seen Ashton inside the hotel that night, so she focused on the exterior. In just a few minutes, she saw Claud's arrival at the hotel and watched as the limo pulled away from the entrance and parked near the end of the front parking lot. Soon after, Ashton got out of his car and walked to the limo. He spoke to the driver briefly, returned to his car, and left.

"That sneaky bastard!" Raven whispered and then turned back to the fuming security guard.

"I need you to email this segment to me, from here," she clicked on the spot when Ashton exited his car, "to here," and then on the one when he got back in and drove away. The woman took over, quickly created a video clip, and attached it to the email. Next, she clicked on the field for the email address and looked at Raven expectantly. Raven typed her email address but did not click send. She continued her search back through time for other signs Ashton had been to the hotel. While Raven doubted finding anything involving Ashton, finding another car like his could be helpful. She would know when or if she saw it.

The camera in the lobby caught her attention as Claud entered. She sent the email and watched Claud's interchange with Thad at the front desk. Then she watched the pair move from camera to camera as they approached and then knocked on the security door. The security guard opened the door.

"Well, have you found anything?" Claud asked.

"Yes. Our guy was here alright."

She played the clip for Claud. As Ashton walked to the limo in the video, Claud clenched his fists so tightly that Raven could hear his skin creak. Even before Ashton began to speak to the driver, Claud was already cussing.

"That son of a whore! He got to my driver! *My* driver! Shit!"

Raven focused her attention on the other files from other dates.

"What are you doing now?" Claud asked, still cursing under his breath and seething with anger.

"I'm trying to figure out how he knew to come here in the first place. I am looking for him or his car in any other videos. There's another computer over there if you want to help."

She looked up at the monitors that showed live views of the cameras and counted them.

"Looks like there are sixteen external cameras, is that right?" She looked at the security guard, who nodded in agreement.

"It's going to take a while to go through all days for all cameras since I got here."

"For fuck's sake. How long do you think?"

"Several hours, at least. Do you agree?" she asked the guard, who nodded again.

Claud groaned.

"You have anything better to do?" Raven asked him.

"Anything would be better than this." He replied in a desperate voice.

"I can have her check the videos and send me anything she finds. We can go to Trevor's and check out the safe."

Claud thought a bit and agreed.

"I think I might know his combination. If not, we can at least search the place again."

"Fine."

Raven wrote down her number and explained to the guard that she wanted the time that any car matching Ashton's came into the parking lot or drove by the hotel, especially around the times she entered the lobby. Raven jotted down her best guess of the days and times she had come to the hotel.

"Start around these, and then, if you don't find anything, search the rest."

The guard nodded again and glared at her. Raven knew if looks could kill, she'd be dead.

As Claud and Raven waited for the limo to pull up, she made it clear to Claud that the issue was not the driver's fault and made Claud promise not to do or say anything to him about it. Reluctantly, Claud agreed.

At Trevor's house, Claud proved he did indeed know the combination to the safe. She wanted to ask how he knew it, because the Blood Memories didn't include it but decided to keep silent on the subject. Raven watched him closely as he opened it. She knew it was mostly empty. All valuables which were easily convertible to cash were gone, as were the journals. All that remained were some stocks and other financial papers. Disappointment flashed on his face.

"What?" She asked.

"Nothing. I expected, uh, more than this."

He held up the small stack of papers.

"I wonder if the other one got here first." Raven posited, still watching Claud's reactions closely.

After she spoke, he dropped his hands to his sides. Claud had been sifting through the stack. Each of his hands held papers. He seemed to think about it and sighed, shoulders sagging. Then he put them back into the safe and closed it.

"We should look around the house again."

"What are we looking for?"

Raven was curious because he would not want her to discover the journals.

While Claud was thinking about his answer, her phone rang. The shrill sound of the ringer caused Claud to glare at her. Raven, ignoring him, answered the phone.

"Hello. Yes. Mmhm. Yes. When was that?"

Raven looked at her phone quickly to check the time.

"Did he say where he was going?"

"Do you know where it is? OK. Thanks for letting me know."

She hung her phone up and smiled at Claud.

"Well?" Claud asked, his voice harsh with impatience.

"That was his neighbor. He just left his apartment."

Claud recalled the conversation.

"Where did he go?"

"To his childhood home."

"Do you know where it is?"

"Somewhere in northern Scottsdale."

"That's it? You don't know where?"

"No, but I bet we can find out at his apartment."

Claud didn't want to go back to Ashton's apartment.

"Ashton told them that he would be gone for a few days and to please sign for any packages that might come. We need to find out where his childhood home is. I didn't find anything online or in public records, so our best bet is to look for something there."

Claud debated whether or not to spend more time searching Trevor's house. He knew that Trevor had journals that contained communications between them. Claud had his own set of journals with similar information. His journals included documents from other members of the coven. Still, if one of the others, like Raven, found the journals, it would be disastrous. If Raven had already located them, she revealed nothing, and he doubted if she would have been able to keep the discovery to herself. Reluctantly, he admitted he needed to search the apartment again.

"Let's go to the apartment."

He brusquely pushed past her and headed to the limo.

During the ride over, Raven received a text from whom she assumed was the security guard at the hotel. It contained a date and time from a few evenings ago and was not long after she had returned to the hotel after compelling Jacob and discussing plans with Ashton. The message also included a very grainy photo of the side view of a black Chrysler 300C as it passed the hotel.

"The security guard just sent me a picture of what could have been his car passing the hotel a few nights ago, shortly after I arrived."

He held his hand out, and she put it in his palm without hesitation. She knew he could look at her phone all he wanted, and he would find nothing.

Claud looked at the phone briefly and then looked back at her.

"So he followed you then."

She shrugged.

"Apparently so, and he must be good at it because I never saw anyone following me, and I looked."

Claud shook his head.

"Who the fuck is this guy?"

Raven picked the locks, and they were inside Ashton's apartment. The first thing they noticed was the smell. The mixture of blood and garlic was nearly gone. Normal senses wouldn't have detected the faint traces, but their enhanced sense of smell did.

"Thank God for small miracles," Claud said.

"No kidding." Raven agreed.

Besides the smell, Raven couldn't find anything different about the apartment. Still, she walked along the hallway towards the bathroom, glancing at the photos.

"Where are you going?" Claud asked as he stopped in the doorway to the office.

"I have to use the restroom. Can you start looking for us?"

"Fine. Just hurry up."

Raven, keeping to her usual response to that sort of treatment from Claud, replied angrily.

"I'll take as long as I need, and I think I need a little bit longer now."

Claud clenched his fists. He knew how stupid it was to hurry her and should've expected the attitude he received in answer. He sat in the chair and started rifling through Ashton's desk. Before leaving the bathroom, Raven put a towel up to her face in the hope of finding his scent. She breathed in the aroma of his body soap and faint traces of him. The thought of the towel running over his tight body excited her. With a soft moan, she put the towel back on the rack.

Raven walked down the hallway while looking at the photos hanging in the hall. She searched for the clue Ashton mentioned he would leave. She noticed a picture of Ashton with his mother and his sister standing in front of what she assumed was their childhood home. Raven didn't recall seeing the picture before. Upon closer inspection, she noticed two distinct fingerprints. One print was on the house behind them. Another was over the face of his mother. It was the only picture she had seen of his mother, and she was sure it was not there before.

Gently, she placed two of her delicate fingers over the prints Ashton had left while thinking of her. She felt connected with him and thought of his tender yet powerful touch. Raven felt emotions stir within her heart. Inexplicably she nearly cried in response, not knowing if it was pain or pleasure that tried to draw tears from her.

When she made it to the small office, Claud had stacks of papers spread out across the desk and on the floor.

"You find anything?" She asked.

"No! I am double-checking everything now."

Claud sounded frustrated.

She spotted an old Rolodex on the edge of his desk, next to his phone. Like the picture of his mother, she knew that wasn't there before. Claud continued to rifle the papers, and Raven continued to mull over the clues - a picture with his family home and mother tagged with a fingerprint and an old Rolodex.

"This is pointless. Check the computer."

He threw the papers in his hand onto the floor and pointed to the monitor. Raven looked for a computer but did not see one. A few USB cables for a mouse and keyboard, a network cable, and an HDMI cable formed a rectangular border where a laptop must have been.

"He must have been using a laptop," Raven announced, and Claud looked up.

"Now that I think about it, I'm sure there was a laptop on the desk right there," she pointed to where the cables converged.

"Shit!" Claud cursed.

He pounded his fist onto the desk, causing the monitor to shake and the keyboard tray and keyboard to bounce.

"Now, what the fuck are we going to do?" he asked.

"Hand me that," Raven pointed to the Rolodex.

He handed it to her.

"While I check in here, can you clean this up?" She waved her hands over the papers on the floor.

"What the fuck do I care if it is neat. I'm going to kill the mother fucker when I find him."

She shook her head.

"If we leave it like this and he shows up, he'll know we've been in here. You want to tip him off that we are hunting him?"

Claud rolled his eyes.

"Fine."

Raven flipped through the Rolodex, looking at each entry for people with the last name of Steele or one with the word mom or mother on it. She found a card for his mother in the M's section under mom but kept flipping to kill more time. Raven's phone beeped, signaling another message had arrived. After setting the Rolodex on the desk, she looked at her phone.

The message contained several photos - one picture was of a car that looked like his and then another of him walking into the lobby. Each image had a date and timestamp overlayed in its corners. Her heart skipped a beat, and she worried it might stop altogether. They had been taken over an hour ago when she and Claud were at Trevor's house. She panicked. If the security guard included a photo of him picking something up at the desk, she would be screwed.

"What is it?" The concern in Claud's voice told her that he saw her fear.

She took a moment and calmed herself. Then she handed Claud the phone.

"Holy shit!" He gasped.

For a long moment, they remained unmoving and stared at each other.

"What took her so long?" He asked.

Raven held her hand out for the phone. Once she had it, she typed the question and sent it to the security guard. Nearly five minutes passed before she got a reply.

"She was on lunch break and had to review the footage when her break ended. That took time, and she has other responsibilities."

She added, "there's nothing we can do about that, but what should we do now?"

"We have to find out where his old house is." Claud seethed.

"Then we can kill that little shit," he added.

"Uh, he's not so little, Claud. We have to be careful."

He shot up and put his face within inches of hers. His hot breath had a fetid odor, and Raven pulled back slightly.

"I am ancient Raven, especially compared to a mere baby like him. I am going to enjoy every last drop of his blood. Just fucking find out where he is already!"

He stood there, his chest heaving with rage. Raven had no idea that her words would have caused such a reaction. After taking a step back, with his head and eyes tracking her movement like an animal tracking prey, she reached out for the Rolodex and made sure it showed Ashton's mother's card. It did, and she handed it to him.

"Christ! Claud, I'm not your enemy here."

She tried to assuage his anger and suspicion.

He continued to glare at her, and Raven grew concerned. If he attacked, she would have no time to make it out of the room. Glancing around the room, she could not see a weapon or a way out. If he compelled her or took her blood, Ashton would be lost.

Claud saw the look of fear on her face.

"For fuck's sake, Raven, I'm not going to attack you!"

"If you saw yourself, you wouldn't be so sure, Claud."

He ripped the card out of the Rolodex and headed for the door. Raven thought about mentioning the mess he was leaving behind, but he had already made his position on that clear. She followed Claud out of the room and out of the apartment.

Chapter 40

When they pulled up to the house, they noticed Ashton's car parked in the driveway. Raven liked that car for him as it suited him well. Both were big, powerful, fast, and well maintained. She knew Ashton could handle curves well, but she wasn't sure about the car.

"He's in there. We need to go." She zipped up her leather jacket and looked at Claud. He was fidgeting with his stake, using his thumb as a pivot while twirling the stake in circles around it.

He flicked it, and it spun around his thumb.

Raven checked her watch, "we have about 45 minutes before dawn, and that's plenty of time."

She looked at Claud. He seemed lost in thought as he continued to fidget.

He flicked it again, and again it spun around his thumb.

Raven pulled her bag from the back seat and set it on the driver's seat. She opened the bag and pulled out a solid silver Ka-Bar knife. After snapping the sheath over the right side of her belt, she withdrew the blade. Its wooden handle allowed her, or any vampire, to wield the knife. She glanced at Claud as she reached back into the bag for the stake sheath. It held three stakes made of fire-treated oak, sharpened with silver tips. Claud still hadn't budged. She snapped the stakes onto the belt on her left hip and stood up. Claud's inaction frustrated her.

"Hey, Claud, where are you?" She watched him as he stared off into space with a blank look.

"Claud!" She called to him again.

"I've never had to fight a vampire. It's different from fighting a human. They are easy to kill. They're slow, weak, and fragile."

He turned to look at her. She couldn't believe the transformation that he had undergone. All of his airs of superiority had gone, and he stood before her, pathetic and weak.

"Like the coward that I knew he was," she thought.

"This doesn't have to be a battle. He knows nothing about our society or our rules. I bet he is confused more than anything else. Without training, he can't order the Blood Memories properly and won't be able to make sense of things. He'll only see fragments of the memories."

A small change flitted across his face as he considered her words.

"He isn't even responsible for Trevor's death."

Claud looked at her, confused by what she had said.

"From the video, it seems like an accident that he received the blood. He wasn't the one who killed Trevor. This Julia woman did. Maybe we should talk with him. Can you imagine what it would be like to become a vampire with no idea what's happening?" she asked him and realized she might seem too sympathetic.

"Yet, he killed those two, Julia and Jacob. Why would he do that?" He asked.

His face clouded with anger, and he glared at her.

"He also attacked me," he added as his eyes narrowed on her.

His anger changed to suspicion.

"Are you trying to protect him, Raven?"

She was stunned by the question and didn't answer before Claud walked towards the rear of the home. He grabbed the handle and turned to Raven with a wry smile.

"Wait here. I'll be back soon."

He turned the handle and found it locked. His snicker fell to a frown, and he prepared to use his strength to force the lock.

Raven pulled his hand away from the handle. He turned to face her. He was about to say something when she put her finger up to her lips and pointed to the lock.

"Are you trying to let him know we're here?" she whispered.

Raven reached into the inner pocket of her leather jacket and pulled out a set of lock-picking tools. She busied herself with picking the lock and occasionally cursed under her breath from apparent frustration. She could sense Claud becoming impatient and turned to him.

"This is a complex lock, Claud. I'll get it, but it will take a few minutes. This way, he won't hear us coming."

She turned her attention back to the lock and worked on it again. In reality, she could have already unlocked it but wanted to burn more time. She was already starting to feel the effects of the approaching dawn and knew Claud must be feeling them harder.

Wiping sweat from her brow, she rested against the door and took a deep breath.

Growing impatient, Claud bent over and whispered in her ear.

"We have little time before dawn."

She looked up at him, her expression asking if he wanted to do it.

He glared at her in response.

She continued the ruse until she heard Claud exhale sharply, signaling he was out of patience.

"Finally!" She whispered and opened the door.

She tucked her tools away and smiled up at Claud.

Claud didn't even wait for her to rise. He entered the house. Raven rose to her feet as Claud brushed past her. Raven began to follow, but he looked at her and shook his head. Then Claud closed the door. She heard the faint sound of the door locking, followed by the muted strain of metal as he used his immense strength to crush the handle into place. While Raven could hear the sound, Claud blocked it inside the house with his body, making it unlikely that the sound would carry to Ashton's ears.

He pointed to his eyes with two fingers and then to her. She shrugged and pointed to her wrist and then the sky. He smiled a wicked smile and turned his back on her, disappearing into the darkness. As she feared, Claud acted alone and not according to their plan. Raven panicked.

One of many skills a vampire has is the ability to move in silence, most likely because of its predatory nature. Claud's skill in stealth is exceptional, a gift he credited to his years of prowling through the homes he robbed, both before and after becoming a vampire. Once shrouded in the darkness, he paused and expanded his mind into the night. His senses heightened as he fused with the darkness. With each passing second, his mind and senses continued to reach further. Air flowed like a great river through his nostrils. It ran down the back of his throat and over his tongue. In moments, he found a trail to follow. It led directly to the door to the left, just up ahead. He was positive it went downstairs, into a basement. He crept to the door, making no more noise than an insect. He closed his eyes and breathed slowly and deeply, swaying around its edges, pulling all traces of the scent to his palate. He could tell that his prey had passed that threshold very recently. The trail was strong with sweat, and he could pick up the faintest traces of blood.

"He has fed." Claud thought, alarmed by the implications. He sniffed the air again, focusing more intently on the deep and alluring coppery notes of blood.

"No, that isn't a fresh scent...a day or maybe two..." again, he tested the air.

"Not sooner than two days," he thought.

This discovery eased his trepidation somewhat. His enemy was not fully blooded, and the gunshot wound he had sustained at the Keller home would have used more than a small amount of energy to heal. He slowly opened the door to the basement and descended into the darkness that lay ahead.

Raven raced to the front door and retrieved the key under the welcome mat. She looked to the sky and saw the growing twilight, separating the deep darkness of night from the first rays of dawn. Raven had to be in the house before the day broke. She had to find a safe place in a bathroom, closet, or bedroom - anywhere the sun could not touch her.

Claud effortlessly glided down the steps to the landing below. He stepped into the partially finished basement. As Claud moved forward, the darkness folded around him like a blanket. He followed the trail like a bloodhound. Claud looked around while walking on the carpeted floor towards the far wall, where the scent trailed off to the left and probably into another room. He cautiously stepped further into the room. To the right, he could see evidence of construction. A tarp, covered with a fine layer of sawdust, lay under two sawhorses. Several cut pieces of plywood leaned against the wall. He slowly approached the work area and noticed a sheet of plywood on the sawhorses had a shape drawn on it - an old-time coffin. He smiled.

"Don't worry. I'll finish it for you," he teased in his mind.

He looked at the door to the left of the work area. Other materials leaned against the wall, including what looked to be a section of a small I-beam.

As Claud approached the door, he noticed sunlight trickling in through some of the small rectangular windows along the tops of the walls. He saw that someone, probably Ashton, had blackened the glass, but the edges still let light through. He also noticed a growing sense of foreboding grow as he approached the door.

As his apprehension grew, so too did the urge to kill. The emotions warred in his mind, with caution giving way to his desire to inflict pain, misery, and permanent death on the new vampire. He rushed forward and yanked the door open, not registering that it was unusual for an interior door to open outwards or that it was reinforced steel.

Ashton watched everything that Claud had done since he entered the house. He sat at the desk, waiting for Claud to make his way into the small office that one of them would use for refuge. The other would use it as his final resting place. The laptop's screen lit up Ashton's face and shoulders. As Claud entered the room, his eyes locked onto Ashton's.

"Come in, Claud, and please close the door. I haven't finished sun proofing the basement yet. We wouldn't want to get a sunburn, would we?"

Claud could feel pressure from the sun in the room behind him, even if it was only coming through in tiny slits on either side of the small windows. He reached back and closed the door. The only light in this room was from the laptop.

Claud grinned in anticipation of the kill. His predatory nature had taken over. Even though the feeling of foreboding was much stronger now, he ignored it. Instead, he quickly evaluated the room and the man before him for any weapons or other threats.

Raven was moving towards the bathroom on the first floor when she heard Claud open the door below. She hurried to the room and removed her leather coat and shoes. Next, Raven found and opened the hamper that held her gear. Then she stepped into padded coveralls. The potent smell of UV-resistant spray filled her nostrils.

She grimaced from the strong chemical odor. After zipping up the coveralls, she stepped into the black leather combat boots and cinched up and tied the laces. She then put the welding mask on and flipped up the rectangular protective cover. Next, she pulled the hood over the helmet. The hood helped protect her skin and hold the bulky helmet in place. Ignoring the uncomfortable heat from the heavy clothes and the sweat that poured down her body because of it, she hurried towards the stairs to the basement.

"So, you are the father of the monster I killed?" Ashton taunted Claud. He wanted to buy the time Raven needed to get into position. Ashton put his hands on the desk and pushed himself to his feet. When he rose to his full height, he curled his hands into fists, stretched his arms behind his waist, and pulled them forward, shrugging his shoulders to prepare for battle. This action charged his body with power. It thrummed from him in waves. Claud felt this, and so did Raven as she walked towards the basement stairs. Claud stepped away. Raven smiled. Ashton worried Claud would try to flee.

Claud considered escape, but he realized that sunrise would be over at any moment and that he would not have time to escape the house and find another sanctuary. The realization hardened his resolve, and he stepped forward instead of back.

"I see you have fed, and quite a lot, too. It was clever to leave those clothes out like that. The blood on them is a few days old. He looked around the room. First, he smelled, then spotted the empty blood bags on the floor in the corner, poking out from under a heavy blanket. Claud admired this creativity and realized that it could come in handy someday. Then he remembered he had no hold on Ashton. A sinking feeling replaced his initial jubilation.

"Too bad that we didn't meet before you ran into Trevor. We could have accomplished much together, you and I." He slowly shifted his weight, preparing for an attack and hoping that his words would distract Ashton.

"I am going to enjoy killing you, Claud. The things you and Trevor have done. You are vile. You're like a disease, and I am the cure."

Claud laughed. "You have no idea." He summoned his power into his legs and launched himself at Ashton, bellowing a ferocious cry of rage as he did.

Ashton was fast but not fast enough to fend off Claud's charge.

Claud dropped his shoulder at the last moment, landing it squarely into Ashton's solar plexus, snapping the sternum from the rib cage. Ashton's scream of agony got stifled by his inability to breathe. He fought to catch his breath and rolled to his side, pushing himself to his feet to face Claud, who was already thrusting the stake at Ashton.

The pain of the broken sternum was nothing compared to the blinding pain of the wooden stake as it sank through Ashton's shoulder and into the wall behind him. With lightning speed, Claud grabbed another stake. He pierced it through Ashton's other shoulder, embedding it into the wall behind him. Again Ashton screamed in agony. This time, the powerful wail echoed after he slipped into darkness.

"Oh no you don't," Claud smacked Ashton's face until Ashton stirred. His head lolled from side to side, and the blood continued to pour down twin rivers from the holes on either side of his body.

"You thought you could defeat me?" Claud sneered at Ashton as he held his face in his hand, applying pressure on his cheeks. Ashton thought his skin would rip on his teeth as Claud pressed his fingers towards each other in a macabre pinch. He shoved Ashton's head back, denting the wall behind him. He pulled the last stake from his belt and put it up to Ashton's heart, pushing it into where the silvertip hissed as it sank into Ashton's flesh. Blood and tissue bubbled against it, eventually fusing to the silver. The spike stayed in place after Claud let go of it, held up by the gruesome connection. Claud didn't need a hammer. He could force the wooden shaft into Ashton's heart with little effort. A flick of the wrist or a slight push would be enough.

"You know you are lucky, right?" Claud asked.

"Oh?" Ashton managed.

He could feel his sternum healing as it was being attached back together with his rib cage. The wounds around the spikes closed, and the bleeding stopped. The stake in his chest felt like someone had poured molten lead into his body. He heard and smelled the flesh as it sizzled against the silver. Once the tissue fused to the silver, the pain radiated throughout his body, making him nauseous and lightheaded.

"What?" Claud asked as he lifted Ashton's head, turning it side to side, admiring the man's rugged and refined looks. It is a shame that he had to destroy him. They could have had so much fun together, or at least Claud could have.

"You said that I," Ashton coughed hard and swallowed, "I had no idea. How could you have done anything viler than what you and half-pint did at that orphanage?"

"Half-pint?" Claud wondered aloud and then realized he was talking about Trevor. "Oh, I see. Yes, Trevor had a bit of a Napoleon complex, didn't he? You did ruin things for him, or rather the woman, Maria, or something like that. What was her name?"

"Her name was Julia, you putrid puss bag." He held his head up and glared into Claud's eyes, letting his rage burn like the sun.

"Right, Julia. Too bad she had to die along with that greasy loser. The real tragedy is that neither of them suited my needs."

Ashton couldn't contain his anger at hearing Claud speak her name. Thoughts of what Claud and Trevor had done at the orphanage sprang to his mind.

"I know, you prefer children, you disgusting maggot." Ashton had no idea if it was true but felt like he had to keep Claud interested in punishing him. He had to keep Claud distracted.

Claud backhanded Ashton so hard that he felt his jaw pop out of its socket, and then the pain of its being pulled back into place by his tendons amped the pain up.

"I heard she burned to death in that car. I can't imagine what that must feel like." Claud taunted Ashton. He could see Ashton's reaction, and he delighted in it.

"Oh, that toad, what was his name...." Claud tapped his chin thoughtfully and glanced at Ashton for the answer.

"Jacob."

"Yes, Jacob. I told him to drive his car into Julia fast enough to kill them. I made him believe that the faster he went, the more pleasure he would experience. He was going fast enough to explode both cars on impact! What a trooper he was!" Claud let the words roll from his mouth, dripping with fake exuberance, "I am so proud of him."

Ashton felt the muscles strengthen around the silver-tipped stake hanging from his body. He tightened his abdomen and pushed, trying to force it out. It moved a little, but the pain made him gasp and cease his effort.

"Hurts, does it?" Claud smiled. "Good, good. You should thank me."

Ashton's phone vibrated, and his sunrise alarm's tinny tune played. Claud looked at the phone. Just then, the monitor showed a figure approaching the door to the room. The movement caught Claud's attention.

"Who is that?"

He couldn't recognize her in the clothes she was wearing. Claud turned to the door, reaching for the handle.

"Now!" Ashton screamed as he clenched his muscles as hard as he could. As he hoped, when the muscles tightened around the tip of the stake, it shot out like pinching a seed between his fingers. The stake fell to the ground. The sound of wood clanking against the concrete floor caught Claud's attention. He turned back to face Ashton and saw the stake roll across the floor. Ashton reached his hand into his pocket and pulled out a small jewelry box. It was the one Julia had kept her grandmother's crucifix in. Pain lanced his shoulder while his body rocked against the other stake that held him to the wall.

"What?" Claud froze with indecision - go for the stake, go for Ashton or go for the door.

A loud scraping sound of metal on concrete, then metal on wood, came from the other side of the door. Claud turned the handle and pushed on the door, but it didn't budge. Ashton saw Raven had braced the door with the I-beam. If Claud had paid close enough attention, he would have understood the modifications. He would have known why he changed the door from the hollow panel that opened inward to a steel-reinforced solid door that opened outward. Once braced by the I-beam, it should be able to withstand Claud's attempts to break it open long enough for Ashton to finish him off. Claud tried slamming himself into the door, but it didn't budge. He tried punching through the paneling on either side of the door. Ashton had filled the empty spaces with reinforced concrete. It needed more time to cure and set completely, but it was strong enough to withstand the onslaught. Claud cried out in pain and frustration, holding his shattered hand to his mouth.

He turned to Ashton, his fear-stricken face silently questioning Ashton.

Ashton was flicking open the jewelry box when Claud reached out for Raven with his mind and commanded her to come to his aid.

Raven had braced the door, and she turned to remove the

sunscreens from the windows. She flipped the protective filter down and ripped off the first screen. Even with the welding helmet, the light that flooded the basement was blindingly bright. She stumbled away from the window and pivoted to her right, slamming her back against the wall. After taking a few deep breaths, she walked to the next window. She ripped its screen out and rolled towards the last window in the basement when Claud's mind grabbed hers in its vice-like grip.

"HELP ME!" his voice screamed into her mind, its loudness as deafening as the sunlight was blinding. She stiffened and walked towards the door as all other thoughts vanished from her mind. If he could focus and concentrate on her, he would be able to see through Raven's eyes and control her accordingly. In the current situation, he could only beckon her. The events prevented him from both focusing on her and watching Ashton. He called her to him, just through the door. Raven reached her hands out to take hold of the brace.

Claud turned towards the door, but the laptop caught his attention. The screen looked like a solid white rectangle with no discernible detail. He watched as a washed-out form stepped through the white haze and approached the door. Suddenly, Claud understood. Raven was the person in the strange clothes. She was working with this Ashton interloper!

"Traitor!" Claud screamed.

Raven placed her hands on the I-beam, which blockaded the door. Claud realized that if Raven managed to open the door, the light would kill him. Claud turned to Ashton in disgust, knowing the fledgling vampire would be able to outlast him in sunlight and survive.

Ashton had to open the jewelry box without touching the crucifix. If he came into contact with it, their plan would fail. Claud would kill them both. He just needed to get free from the wall.

Raven lifted the beam and dropped it on the floor. They could all feel the thud as it slammed into the concrete. She reached out for the handle.

"Stop!" Claud screamed in his mind and aloud. Caught off guard, Ashton quit pushing the lid off of the box with his thumb. Raven froze in place as well, becoming a statue.

Claud looked like a trapped animal, rapidly glancing from the door to Ashton. Then something happened that gripped Ashton in fear. Claud smiled.

"She fell for you? An insignificant infant? I knew she wasn't worth my effort. After everything I gave her, she chose you!" Claud's face screwed into a rictus of repulsion. Spittle flew from his mouth as he spoke. His rage at what he considered a betrayal stripped away any last grain of decency he possessed.

"You want to see what happens when an ancient vampire embraces the sun? You want to see that? Look at your precious screen and witness what happens to those who dare stand against me!"

Raven had tried with every ounce of her will to dislodge Claud's control over her but nothing could overcome the bond between her sire and herself. She watched her hands fall away from the door and move to her helmet.

Ashton grew desperate. He flopped from side to side, his shoulders pulling against the stakes, and then he pushed against the stakes pinning him to the wall. His flesh tore, and he heard a ripping sound as his body slid along the stakes embedded into the wall.

Raven panicked and screamed as her hands reached for the latch that secured the visor to the welder's helmet. Her thumbs rocked up the latches and then slowly lifted on the protective filter.

Claud stared at the screen as Raven's muffled screams filled the room.

Ashton pushed his shoulders forward and his back up the wall. He put both feet against the wall for leverage. The pain intensified as his weight became supported only by the stakes. His strength was fading. It took all of his will and the power of his blood to stay conscious through the pain. Raven's screams energized him, and he called upon every last ounce of his energy, every shred of anything he had within him. His shoulders fell forward, finally freed from the makeshift anchors. He fell with a slurp and a pop, like pulling a foot out of the mud. He pushed with his legs, launching himself like a fleshy torpedo into Claud's side. The jewelry box fell from his hand as he reached to lock his arms around Claud like a football tackle.

When Ashton slammed into him, Claud's concentration broke along with his connection to Raven. He had to focus on this new threat and couldn't do both.

Ashton and Claud crashed into the door. Unfortunately for Ashton, much of the impact was to the top of his head, causing him to release his hold on Claud.

Raven, liberated from the icy grip of Claud's will, refastened her visor and reached for the door just before Claud and Ashton hit it. The powerful impact made her falter for a moment.

Claud collected himself and moved clear of Ashton. His hatred fueled his decisions, and he kicked Ashton in the side of his head, spinning his body around almost 180 degrees as it slid across the floor.

Ashton opened his eyes to see the jewelry box inches from his face grow blurry and refocus several times. He reached his hand out to take hold of it.

Raven grabbed the doorknob and turned it to open the door.

Claud raised his foot in the air to stomp Ashton's head into the concrete.

Ashton took hold of the jewelry box and turned from his side to his back. He felt the air blow by as Claud's foot smashed into the concrete floor where his head had been a split second earlier, rippling the concrete in a circular web.

Raven opened the door.

The sun had risen high enough that its rays penetrated the windows of the small room.

Ashton grabbed the lid with his other hand and pulled it off.

Claud tried to focus his mind on Raven to command her to close the door when light from the crucifix flooded the small room. He became frantic with terror as the warm light from the box washed over him. His visage became a rictus of unspeakable dread, all traces of rational thought gone as if washed away by a tsunami of fear.

"Raven, get down now! Get down!" Ashton yelled, holding the box towards Claud.

She dropped to the floor and covered her head with her gloved hands, hoping this would finally be the end of Claud and his vile existence.

As Claud backed away, his right hand crossed into the path of the sunlight that shone through one of the far windows. His skin hissed, and he yanked his hand away from the unforgiving light. Claud held his hands up to shield himself from the warm energy radiating from the crucifix Ashton held up before him. His heel caught on something and fell backward onto the ground, landing near Raven. When he realized it was Raven, his rage exploded. Claud knew he was about to die and decided he wasn't going alone. He reached for Raven's hood on her coverall and pulled it down.

Ashton realized Claud's intentions, and he moved forward, desperate to help Raven. The scintillating sun almost blinded him. He stumbled toward the pair. Raven had turned to fend Claud off from getting a hold of her helmet. During the struggle, parts of Claud's body touched the sun's beams, forcing him to withdraw further into the living room and closer to the wall now on Ashton's left. During his forward movement, Ashton had turned the crucifix so that it didn't face forward, and Claud's panic eased. Then he changed his tactic.

Claud reared his arm back and punched Raven on the lower side of her back over her kidney. Even through her helmet, Raven's shriek was deafening. Over and over again, Claud unloaded his brutality onto Raven's body until she stopped moving. With great effort, Claud rose to his feet. The multiple burns had taken their toll, and Claud wavered, swaying back and forth as he looked around the room for something to use as a weapon. His eyes came to rest on the metal I-beam that lay on the floor near the wall. Claud bent over and ignored the searing flesh as he reached through the sunlight and grabbed the I-beam. Once his hand closed around it, he pulled it towards himself.

Claud looked at Ashton and grinned. His fangs showed, and his wicked soul seemed to shine in his eyes in anticipation of the misery he was about to inflict, not just on Raven but Ashton as well. Claud gripped the I-beam in both hands and pulled his arms back like a batter readying his swing. Claud looked at Ashton, wanting to make sure he saw the pleasure in his eyes before destroying her.

"She will always be mine, you insignificant flea."

He hissed at Ashton and swung.

Ashton dove at Claud. The box fell from his hand and landed under the desk. Claud was already too far into the swing for Ashton to prevent it. His only hope now was to shield Raven from the blow. Nothing else mattered to him.

The I-beam did not smash into Raven's motionless body. Instead, it crashed into the side of Ashton's head. The sickening hollow metallic thud barely made a sound. Neither did the crunching of Ashton's skull nor the smashing of the cartilage in his ear. Ashton felt the disfigurement vibrate through his skull and to the bone behind the ear as it wrought his handsome face into one of hideous disfigurement. His cheekbone caved in, elongating his nose and upper jaw until a loud snap deafened him as the bones splintered under the force of the blow. He felt nothing except relief that he had protected Raven. The shock to his overloaded body spared him the deluge of intense pain. Ashton's eyesight blurred, and the room fell out of focus. He was only aware of the body he had slumped over. He felt some movement in that body, and his soul sighed in relief to know she still lived.

Claud closed his eyes and focused on the euphoric feeling from the carnage he had rendered. He let forth an evil laugh that dripped with cruel mirth and proclaimed his victory. Ashton was still conscious and heard this sound through his working ear. He felt the pressure of the I-beam lift off of the side of his head as Claud hefted it for his next blow.

Ashton tried to turn his head and lift his arms, but nothing happened. He was incapable of movement.

"She was mine! You turned her against me! Don't worry. She'll be joining you in hell soon enough."

Ashton could feel time slow as he waited for the coming blow to end his existence. He desperately wanted to see Raven's beautiful face smiling at him one more time before it did. He closed his eyes and thought of her, of the night that she lay in his arms, smiling up at him with unabashed love in her eyes - love for him. It had all felt so perfect, so right. He focused on that solitary perfect moment and vowed to hold onto it until darkness claimed him. Finding strength in the memory, he called upon his entire being to give him the ability to speak.

"Raven, I'm sorry," was all he managed to say before the blow hit him, followed by another and then another. He felt his shin breaking into tiny tooth-sized fragments. Then his knees. By the time Claud had turned his attention to his thighs, Ashton knew no more. The merciful embrace of darkness wrapped its protective arms around him and drew him down into the deep recesses of unconsciousness.

Raven heard and felt the thudding impact of metal slamming into flesh and bones snap as they broke. Slowly, she came to her senses and assessed the situation. Claud was pulverizing Ashton, one inch at a time. She remembered the three stakes on her hip and realized they must have broken when Claud hit her with the metal beam.

"My knife!" she remembered.

Slowly, she tucked her hand under her chin and found the zipper. Silently, she propped herself up on her elbow enough to allow her hand to reach down to the knife sheathed on her hip.

Claud noticed her movement as an afterthought, thinking she was weakly trying to get to her feet. He thought about kicking her but instead decided to use his words to torture her.

"You chose this pathetic excuse of a vampire over me? I made you! You owe everything to me, including your life."

He trailed off, and then she heard another whack followed by the explosive sound of Ashton's femur crack like kindling. Ashton did not scream or make any sound at all. In the corner of her eye, she saw his body rock from the impact and then lie still. She couldn't tell if he was breathing or not.

"Hold on, Ashton, please hold on."

"This is how you repay me, by betraying me with him?" he spat on her back. The thickness of her clothing was not enough to prevent her from feeling its stomach-turning impact.

She grasped the knife and freed it from the sheath, slowly pulling it up the inside of her coveralls toward the bottom of the unzipped zipper. A moment later, it was free, and she gathered her strength and readied herself to lunge. Claud saw none of this.

"I can't take all day with this, as much as I would like to." Claud breathed laboriously. "Do you think if I smash his head and rip it off of his neck, he would die?"

Raven said nothing, imagining her strike, tensing her muscles and shifting her weight onto the tips of her feet, lifting her knees slightly.

"Well, we are about to find out." He shuffled forward and stood over Ashton, his feet on either side of the battered, motionless body. Again, he pulled the I-beam behind his head and prepared to swing it down onto Ashton's unmoving head.

Raven unleashed her rage into the lightning-fast strike. After rocking onto the balls of her feet, she sprang up and turned towards Claud. Her left arm was nearly straight as she twisted her wrist to align the knife's point to her target. She used all of her power and momentum to plunge the blade into Claud's neck. The razor-sharp tip sunk into his flesh and slid between the vertebrae. Its serrated edge sawed through the cartilage, tendons, and finally, the brain stem. Smoke wafted, and flesh sizzled from the wound as the silver contacted his vile flesh.

Claud dropped the I-beam behind him, his face frozen in surprise at the mortal wound he had just received. His knees gave way as his nerves were severed. Raven kept his body supported by the flat of the knife and the strength in her arm. She looked Claud in the eyes, all of her hatred and rage coming to the fore.

"You took everything and gave me nothing. Nothing but misery."

She grabbed his hair with her free hand and pulled the knife out with a rapid jerk, slicing his neck in half.

He remained hanging by the left side of his neck. Blood spurted out, showering them both in its dark red mist. Some blood sprayed into the sun, instantly vaporing with a hiss into tendrils of red steam - mortal fireworks as Claud shed his immortal coil.

While holding his head by a handful of hair, she quickly turned the knife over, allowing the cutting edge to face the gaping wound and the remaining flesh that held Claud's head to his body. He couldn't speak, but his eyes found hers. The fear and despair that swirled in his soulless pools gave her grim satisfaction. She rested the cutting edge on his flesh, producing another hissing sound.

"You took everything that I loved. Through all of these years, I survived only for this moment, when I could send you to hell where you belong."

Before she severed his head from his shoulders, Claud smiled. Then she completed the gruesome task and sliced through what remained of his neck. Her hand and his head jerked up after being freed from the weight of his body as it fell to the floor. She had lived through the French Revolution and witnessed several beheadings. It was how she learned that after decapitation, a person's consciousness lingered for several seconds.

She looked at the room and picked her spot. She avoided stepping into the direct beam of sunlight as she approached the one she chose with Claud's severed head hanging in her hand, its mouth opening and closing like a fish out of water. Her welding mask prevented the light from blinding her until she reached her desired spot when she pushed it up to expose her face. She lifted Claud's head to hers, face to face with the horrid remnant of her mortal enemy.

"This is just a taste of what awaits you in hell, Claud!"

She slowly extended her arm, raising his head into contact with the sun one agonizing inch at a time. She heard the sizzle and smelled the sickly fragrance of burning flesh. His mouth moved, but no sound came out. His eyes flashed around frantically, hoping to find a solution to the impossible problem of his mortality. When she felt the first touch of his mind to hers, she thrust his head fully into the light where it burst into flames, turned into a glowing cinder, and then fell to the floor in streams of ash. His body crumbled to ash, lining his clothes with their powdery traces.

Claud was dead.

Raven stood in the fading darkness, her body shaking. She felt a strange sensation of pressure receding from inside of her head. It was as if tendril-like fingers were sliding out of her brain, releasing their hold. Something in her fought against this exodus. Realizing this, Raven pushed the tendrils out with her mind. After seconds of struggle, the grip broke, and she was free. The sudden release caught her by surprise, and Raven nearly stumbled into the same rays of light that had just eradicated Claud. She braced herself and smiled. Already, she felt Claud's stain leaving her. For the first time in over eight hundred years, Raven was free from Claud.

Then, she remembered Ashton.

She turned to Ashton and gently hooked her arms under his shoulders. She dragged him into the small room where he had waited for Claud's arrival. She closed the door and pulled him to the wall. She sat between him and the wall and positioned her legs on either side of his waist. She rested him against her and covered them with the padded blankets. She rested one hand on his crushed cheek, kissed his forehead, and whispered to him.

"You'll be fine, Ashton. You'll be fine."

She pulled the blanket the rest of the way over them and passed out.

Chapter 41

Raven held Ashton close to her under the heavy blanket throughout the day while she remained in a deep slumber. Ashton drifted in and out of sleep, waking in fits and starts. His body used the blood he had consumed to start repairing the damage caused by Claud's vicious attack, but his body already craved more. He was in immense pain, and it seemed to him that he could feel every fracture and bruise. From what Raven had explained, Ashton would not need surgery or casts, just rest and blood. A few times when he woke, he looked at Raven's peaceful and beautiful face and nestled into her arms, which had not released him once. She was more than his savior - she was his salvation. He belonged to her in ways he had never thought possible, as she did to him.

Ashton had wanted to be the one to destroy Claud, and he felt more than a little embarrassed that Raven had done so. It was true that Ashton had done his part and that Raven wouldn't have been able to handle Claud by herself, but he had wanted to be the triumphant hero and stand before her, victorious after a glorious battle. He shook his head, wondering from where such thoughts came.

On what he considered the bright side of things, his body healed at an extraordinary rate. His face healed first and was back to normal before sunset that day. Most of the damage he received was to his legs. He was bedridden until his legs healed.

As he wasn't going anywhere and Raven seemed unwilling to leave him alone, he took the opportunity to tell her how the plan came together. Once he had explained the generalities of getting the items he needed and heading to his old home to prepare, she had a few questions for him.

"How did you get that small metal beam?" she asked.

"That was just dumb luck. I stopped at a repair shop that does welding to get your gear and saw it in a scrap pile. One of the guys cut the angles on it so you or I could brace the door. I considered putting it across the door, but I worried about the door and wall coming down if Claud hit it hard enough from behind. By bracing it between the floor and the center of the door, I knew it would be much stronger and harder to force open. Then, I filled the sides of the frame with concrete and rebar. If that failed to stop him, it would have at least slowed him down."

"Pretty clever."

She smiled and pressed her hand on his shoulder.

"Well, it was important, and I thought about it the entire time I was in those tunnels."

She looked at him, uncertain what he meant. He then realized he hadn't told her much about what happened to him after his failed attempt on Claud. He took the time to do so. When he explained his attack on Claud, Raven couldn't help her anger.

"That was foolish, Ashton. You weren't supposed to do anything. You could have gotten hurt, or ..."

He could see the pain in her eyes as they welled with tears at the thought of what might have happened.

"Never mind any of that. I'm fine."

He smiled at her and pushed himself up further in his bed, and patted a spot next to him. She was not sure whether to stay mad at him or cry. She sat down, and he took her hand in his. She loved the warmth and softness of his touch and closed her eyes, letting it soothe her racing mind.

"I am sorry, Raven. I didn't want to let him get away. I also didn't want you to be involved."

"You mean you didn't want me to get hurt, don't you?" She asked in a soft but defiant voice, still entranced by the connection that happened every time their bodies touched.

"No. I mean, yes. I didn't want you to get hurt then and I don't want you to now. I didn't want Claud to get away either, especially if I could have destroyed him."

She looked down at their entwined fingers and rubbed her thumb over the top of his hand, tracing the veins. Lifting their hands to her lips, she gently kissed his hand and rubbed it against her cheek. She looked at him with tear-filled eyes.

"But look at you, Ashton. Look at what he did to you."

He made a pretense of looking at his body and smiled at her.

"It's nothing. It's a flesh wound." He said in an odd English accent.

A moment later, she laughed and sniffled.

"Are you kidding me? You are going to quote Monty Python in this situation?"

She smacked him playfully on his chest and let him know that he was, in fact, terrible.

"Ouch!" He cried out in mock pain, making her laugh some more.

He reached his hand and put it on the side of her face, then rubbed her cheek with his thumb. When she looked into his eyes, they clouded with emotion.

"I know we've just met, but there is a connection between us, Raven. You mean something...no...you mean a lot to me. No matter what happens, I want you to understand that. When we were together the other night," he began, but Raven cut him off.

"You mean a lot to me too, Ashton, and I agree, there is a connection between us. I feel it whenever we touch, and not only like we did the other night."

She began to blush and closed her eyes. The warmth emanating from Ashton's hands soothed her. His soft and gentle touch didn't stop her heart from pounding or fear from welling up inside her. Raven knew she feared taking another chance on love, on completely surrendering herself to it.

They sat there for several minutes in silence until Raven got up.

"I have to deal with the Coven, Ashton."

"OK."

He gestured to his legs.

"I'm not going anywhere."

"Neither am I."

She smiled at him.

Raven spent much of the day planning how to break the news of

Claud's death, the existence of a new vampire, and the discovery of the deception perpetrated by Trevor and Claud with at least the knowledge, if not the involvement of others in the Coven. If they were, they had to have been for quite some time.

Her first idea was to request an emergency meeting with all members of the Coven present. She could then inform them of Claud's death, confirm Trevor's death, and reveal Ashton. Once she had the opportunity to judge their reactions, she might glean who else was involved.

That, she soon found out, would not work for Beatrice, Tamjen, and Isa. The soonest they would be able to return from their overseas residences was nearly two weeks away. She went with the option of meeting with some in-person while including the others via video. Raven requested a few days longer to wrap up all of her activities in Scottsdale before joining those who would attend in person at Gitlam and Zana's estate. She had three days to get there.

Isa reached out to her immediately. Raven explained to her that she wouldn't discuss anything until the meeting. Even Tamjen called and, in his fumbling way, tried to get her to reveal something. Again she refused. When finished with her calls and emails for the day, Raven ordered takeout Chinese food for the two of them and picked it up.

She considered using serving dishes and plates with the meal but opted to share it out-of-the-box style with him instead. After their dinner, Ashton showed her how much he had healed. His legs were still horribly bruised, but the swelling was nearly gone, and they looked like legs again and not the battered tube of flesh that they had resembled. Looking at his wounds took a toll on her, especially the bruises that clearly showed the squared outline of the beam Claud had used to pulverize his legs.

He noticed her cringing at the sight of his legs and covered them with his blanket. It took her a few seconds to look away. She sighed and stood up. Ashton wanted to cheer her up and get her into a better mood.

"You know, we have tonight and two other nights before we need to be there. I'm going to be pretty useless tonight, and we will need to travel the day after tomorrow, but tomorrow night, I get to cook dinner for you. We have a date, remember?"

"Of course, I remember. Do you honestly think I would forget?"

Despite his excitement over having a date, he yawned. Raven told him to rest as she needed to take care of her business and clean up after Claud. It would probably take most of the night to wrap things up. Then she realized that her car was still at the hotel and the limo was long gone.

"Ashton?" she asked with a playfully pleading tone in her voice.

"What?" he replied sleepily.

"I have a favor to ask you."

"Sure, whatever it is, Raven."

"Can I borrow your car?" she asked hopefully.

Silence.

"Ashton?"

"My keys are in my pants pocket." His voice was less dreamy and a bit concerned.

She remembered taking his boots, socks, and pants off of him once the sun had set. She ended up cutting the pants off due to the swelling in his legs. Before throwing them into the garbage, she went through his pockets. She had put his wallet and keys on the nightstand next to her bed.

"I'll take care of it, I promise."

"You better," he teased and then fell into a dreamless sleep.

Chapter 42

Raven sat at her dressing table, brushing her hair and thinking of the night ahead and her date with Ashton. It was almost surreal that they would be having their first date after the night of passion they had shared just a few nights ago. She spent more time with him in the past week than she had with anyone for almost three hundred years. They endured a lifetime's worth of pain and drama in that short time. He even helped her take revenge against Claud.

There was something unique about the man - a mere infant compared to her hundreds of years on this world. She had to admit he was handsome and would prove to be a powerful vampire, but her attraction to him was on a completely different level. He was compassionate and empathetic, while at the same time, he remained firm in his resolve and steady in his course - even in the face of such reality-shattering events that had altered his existence forever. While contending with and adapting his life to meet these challenges, he managed to comport himself with the equanimity of a noble-born. He had hinted at some tragedy in his past. Raven understood tragedy and never pressed him on it. His various acts of kindness were not unnoticed by Raven, nor was the respect he showed her and others like Julia. She could imagine him as the head of a great family or even a kingdom. Then it hit her. She knew what elevated Ashton so highly in her estimations. He reminded her of her father. The love of her family remained the center of absolute truth that she held closest to her heart. After her father had died, she had imagined his ethereal hands reaching out from the underworld to protect her and guard the warm glow of love she held deep inside of her being. The sense of security allowed the love inside of her to grow and radiate. It guided her as a young woman and still did so. Being with Ashton gave her that same sense of protection and feeling of being loved.

In all of her years living in a world that seemed to be in constant moral decline, she rarely encountered anyone with so warm a heart and had never found a man who enticed her womanhood with such absolute entirety. Everything about him appealed to her. She wanted him - no, she needed him. He had touched her in ways she was still trying to understand. But could she afford to let him in and give love another chance? She laughed, something she rarely did, especially at herself. She knew that whether or not she wanted to, her heart decided to give love another try.

Everything she had known - her place in the coven, the coven itself, the Blood Communion - was gone. Her part in the death of Claud and his treachery would soon be exposed. She did not know what their reactions would be. Still, she did not know with whom Claud and Trevor had communicated and how they would react when it was exposed.

"Enough of that!" She admonished herself.

"I need to get ready for my date."

At 8:00 precisely, Raven knocked on Ashton's door, carrying one bottle of white and another bottle of red wine.

"Just a moment." She heard Ashton call from within his apartment, followed a few seconds later by the metallic grind of the deadbolt retracting into the door.

If he lived forever, he would never forget that moment, the first time he had seen Raven dressed to the nines. He knew that she was beautiful and had a nice figure, but the woman who now stood before him was nothing less than a goddess.

He stared into her deep, warm, brown eyes. Whatever composure he may have been able to call upon vanished. He was lost in her, lost to her. The connection he felt to her was visceral and primal. As undeniable and immutable as matter itself. He half-expected to hear angels sing and light from heaven to fall upon her, illuminating her in their holy glory. When she smiled at him, nothing compared to her magnificent radiance. Everything magnified the intensity of his feelings, and her beauty became almost frightful to him. He felt vulnerable and exposed. Ashton knew then that there was nothing he could refuse her, nothing he would not give to her or sacrifice for her.

"Ashton?" she asked.

He didn't notice the pleading tone of her voice. She felt the intensity of his eyes and knew he had just surrendered to her. Her knees weakened, and she trembled.

"Yes, Raven," he replied, not breaking the intense gaze they shared.

Before she lost herself in the cobalt oceans that were his eyes, pulling her into his depths with a siren's promise of eternal bliss, she rescued herself with pragmatism.

"May I come in?" she held up the bottles of wine and gently waved them by the necks.

Just like that, the moment was over, the spell broken. Ashton staggered when whatever mystical force tethering his soul to hers snapped.

"Yes, yes, please, let me take those."

He grabbed the bottles and stood off to the side, allowing her to pass before closing the door. He thought about locking it but decided against it, not wanting to give her any reason to feel trapped.

A delicate yet powerfully alluring fragrance wafted to his nose as she passed.

"That is a lovely perfume you are wearing, Raven."

He didn't see her face flush with color.

"Thank you, but I never wear perfumes or scents."

He realized that he was smelling pure and unadulterated Raven, which pleased him greatly. Then he wondered if he had a unique scent and whether or not it pleased her.

He turned to look at her and then could see that she was blushing.

"I'll just put this," he held up the red wine, "in the fridge."

He set the bottle of white wine on the counter across from the stove. A large skillet was simmering on one of the burners, and a smaller skillet, with a glass cover, sat adjacent to it on an unlit burner.

"It smells wonderful. What is it?"

Raven followed Ashton, but instead of walking with him to the kitchen, she sat in one of the chairs next to the counter island that separated it from the living room and dining room.

"Well, I wanted to make it special for you and decided that I wanted to share a family recipe with you. It's chicken with sun-dried tomatoes."

"Sounds lovely."

"I've never made it for anyone besides my family, just in case you wondered."

She had briefly wondered if it was part of a routine he had created for getting women into bed but dismissed the idea almost as soon as she had it. Nevertheless, hearing his assurance made her feel jubilant.

"I'm honored."

His back was still to her, but she thought she had a good view. He stretched to reach a cupboard over the refrigerator. As he opened the door and retrieved two wine glasses, she couldn't help but notice how the shirt pulled tightly across his back or how his muscles flexed with his motion. She also took note of his firm buttocks and his thick, powerful thighs. Memories of their first time together teased her with promises of what was to come.

He closed the cabinet door and turned to her, setting one glass in front of her and another nearer him. He pulled open a drawer and rummaged through it.

"I know it's in here."

He continued to rummage, and Raven inadvertently looked at what he was doing and realized her view centered around the front of his waist. He wore black slacks with the white dress shirt tucked neatly into them. Around his waist was a very stylish black belt with a polished black buckle. She wondered if it was from a stone, like hematite.

"It would be fitting as he did have the body of a warrior," she thought.

His sleeves were rolled up to his elbows, showing his veined arms. As he moved his hands, the muscles on his forearms rippled. Raven glanced up to see if his eyes were on her, but his attention remained focused on his tasks. With his head bowed, his blond locks fell over his eyes, hiding them from her glances. Her eyes wandered down his chest like she imagined her hand would, slowly seeking the sculpted outlines of his dense muscles. Down the abs, each rise and dip became a promise of what would come next to her hungry fingers. A sensual tug stirred her desire when her eyes wandered over his belt to the fabric that hid his zipper.

"Aha! Got it! I knew it was in there."

His exclamation startled her, and she bounced slightly in her seat.

He held up a corkscrew triumphantly before her, proving he had indeed located the utensil. She jerked her eyes up to meet his and hoped that he didn't notice where they were moments ago as the image of his bulge danced through her mind. He did not show that he had seen her hungry gaze. To keep the mood from growing awkward, he made a production out of opening the wine bottle.

A slight popping sound signaled the task was complete. He considered offering it to her for inspection but decided against doing so as he didn't want to seem too formal.

"Thanks for picking up the wine, Raven."

She liked how he said her name often when they talked and supposed that he knew as much, which made her like it all the more.

He poured wine into her glass, filling it about one-third of the way, and repeated the process with his.

"You are welcome, Ashton. I hope you like it."

She also liked saying his name. Her mouth felt good as she said it, with the first part soft and elongated and the last syllable hard as it rolled off the tip of her tongue, somehow making her eyebrows lift. She unconsciously licked her lips.

Ashton swirled his glass and set the bottle down.

"I would like to offer a toast, if that is OK with you, Raven."

His eyes were locked on hers, hopeful and sincere.

"Of course, please do."

She slightly nodded her head to him and raised her glass in anticipation.

He held his glass out to her.

"To life's unexpected journeys and the gifts they may bring."

He nodded his head towards her and raised his eyebrows, silently telling her she was one of the gifts.

They touched glasses, the delicate crystal slightly clinking as they did so. They drank, and Ashton stood staring at her again, glass still held up, a knowing smile on his face. She smiled in return and felt such strong feelings of attraction and acceptance that her eyes were in danger of watering. She blinked it away.

A timer beeped on the stove. Ashton set his glass down and smiled expectantly.

"I hope you are hungry."

"Yes, I'll be right back."

Raven hurried to the bathroom to compose herself while Ashton set the table. When she returned, Ashton stood behind her chair. She reached for the chair to pull it out, and Ashton lightly put a restraining hand over hers. The touch was electric.

"Please, may I?"

She hoped he was going to kiss her and that he was asking permission. When he nodded his head towards her chair, she realized his intentions.

"Don't be silly. I can do it."

"I know, but I invited you, and I would like to do this for you, but only if you allow it."

His sincere smile and the earnestness in his eyes convinced her to let him get her chair. Usually, she would have considered this an old-fashioned and unnecessary gesture. But she knew he wanted to do something for her and wasn't suggesting she couldn't or shouldn't do it. She dropped her hand, and then he pulled her chair out and pushed it in as she sat.

"Thanks, Raven. I know it is out of style, and I don't feel obligated to do so. I want you to know that I respect and honor you. As we are in private, I didn't think it would make you feel uncomfortable to permit me such a small pleasure to do you the courtesy."

He said this as he walked around the table to take his seat across from her. After Ashton sat in his chair, he rubbed his hands together to show his anticipation of their feast. He turned to her with such genuine pleasure that she couldn't help but beam at him. She noticed a lively twinkle in his eyes and that he was thoroughly enjoying himself. No one had ever looked at her like this or been so happy to do something for her. She knew that if they were in the middle of a crowded room, he would only see her. It made sense to her as she admitted that she would only see him.

He reached for her plate, pausing for her to grant permission.

She smiled and said, "yes, please."

He lifted her plate and explained the food to her as he placed the portions on her plate.

"This is a light medley of zucchini and summer squash. I peeled them as I have found that doing so reduces the bitterness. While it does make the dish look a little bland, I sprinkled a little fresh parsley on the top to give it a little color."

She noticed how proud he was of his efforts. This massive man was nothing more than a schoolboy at that moment, innocent and hopeful.

"Now, this is my specialty. My mother taught me to make this years ago."

He positioned her plate next to a long rectangular serving dish that seemed very old, perhaps even antique. A corner of it had a small chip, and she noticed a crack in the corner that ran from the bottom of the chip. He served both of them very generous portions of the steaming and aromatic food.

"I eventually added my variation by adding thinly sliced mushrooms to the onions before deglazing the pan. It adds a certain something to the dish that makes it more complete. I don't know how to explain it."

After he served himself, he offered fresh bread, which she accepted. He put a piece on his plate and then covered the bread with a light blue and white checkered hand towel.

He looked at her expectantly, and she wondered what to do. He must have picked up on her incertitude.

"Please, you first. I hope I haven't lost my touch. I haven't cooked like this for a long time. Maybe since before my sister went to the hospital."

At that moment, Raven decided she would love it, even if it turned out to be the worst she had ever eaten.

"Please try the veg first. I want you to try the main dish last."

She looked at him with undisguised amusement. She couldn't believe the feelings that were awakening within herself. She tried the medley and loved the savory with the slight hint of bitterness from the parsley.

"Mm, that is yummy."

She couldn't believe that she had just used the word yummy. What was happening to her?

She took a sip of wine and had a brief pang of guilt that she didn't offer a toast to thank him for the meal. Her mind whispered, "you can thank him later." She almost choked on the sip of wine.

"Are you OK, Raven?"

He started to get up to go to her.

She held her hand up.

"I'm sorry. It just went down wrong. It is a lovely dish."

She smiled at him. He smiled at her. She doubted he had stopped smiling since they sat down, maybe even since she arrived. She was wrong on both accounts. He had been smiling since he started to prepare their dinner.

She turned her attention to the main course. A cream sauce covered the chicken cutlets, the sun-dried tomatoes, and the mushrooms. She couldn't see the onions he had mentioned but knew they were there. She used her knife to cut a small piece of the chicken, which she realized could have been done with her fork alone as it was so tender. She took bits of the tomatoes and mushrooms, then scooped up some more of the sauce.

Raven decided to torment Ashton for a few moments. She felt his gaze upon her and knew how much he wanted her to like the meal. She lifted the fork to her mouth, sniffed it slightly, swirled it in tiny circles under her nose, and blew on it gently. Ashton was mesmerized by her slow and deliberate movements. She glanced at him, expecting he would be impatient with her stalling. Instead, she had enthralled him with the sultriness of her actions. He licked his lips and looked into her eyes. Then, she slowly put the fork into her mouth and closed her lips around it. She slid the utensil slowly out of her mouth, closing her full red lips around the tines as she did. Languidly, she closed her eyes and turned her head slightly from side to side. While chewing, more delicious flavors passed over her palate.

"Oh, Ashton," she crooned, "this is delicious."

She looked at him with respect and admiration. Then her eyes grew wide in realization as a peculiar taste caught her attention.

"Is that garlic? Oh my God! I haven't tasted garlic since..." her words trailed off in utter amazement.

"I know. I remember your telling me that was one of the things you missed. So, I've been trying to figure out how to make it work."

"Is it some synthetic garlic flavoring?" She pondered.

"Nope. It is 100% fresh organic garlic. Just not very much of it." He teased, knowing she wanted to know all of the details.

She recalled the overpowering scent of garlic she and Claud had noticed when they entered his apartment the other night.

"He must have spent a lot of time trying," she thought.

"Tell me!" she playfully whined.

"Madame! A magician never reveals his tricks!" his French accent was terrible - no, it was worse than that. She burst into laughter as he screwed his face into an indignant expression and began to twiddle an imaginary mustache.

He followed that with, "I used my little gray cells!"

He tapped his temple knowingly and then dabbed his mouth foppishly with a napkin.

Her laughter was deep and heartfelt. It was music to Ashton's ears.

"Stop! Stop!" she managed between outbursts. Tears ran down her cheeks, and she wondered about its effect on her makeup.

"If madame wishes...." he continued, adding fuel to her out-of-control laughter.

Abruptly, she rose from the table and practically ran to the bathroom.

A moment later, Ashton knocked on the door.

"Raven, are you OK in there?"

"Yes. I need a moment."

She looked at herself in the mirror. Mascara ran down her cheeks in black runnels, looking like black tear stains. She couldn't stop smiling at how utterly silly she looked. It took her a few minutes to fix her makeup. Once finished, she straightened and looked at herself in the mirror. She ran her hands down her sides, and they came to rest over the bottom of her belly. She turned from side to side, not realizing what she was thinking about until it was too late. The long-buried thought pushed its way to the surface of her mind. It brought with it the sharpest agony she had ever experienced. Since her acceptance of not being able to have children, she buried all thoughts of it. She trained herself not to see pregnant women or women with their babies. She immediately forced the idea from her mind, finished her toilette, and returned to the table.

Ashton immediately picked up on her subdued mood. He was astute enough not to mention anything or force the issue, and they finished the meal in relative silence, with Raven complimenting him a few more times before its conclusion.

After the meal ended, he offered coffee which she refused. She ate more than usual and was feeling quite full. He didn't mention the strawberry shortcake he had waiting in the fridge.

Ashton set about clearing the table and refused to allow Raven to help. He asked her to put some music on and told her he would finish soon.

Ashton was buying time, hoping to figure out a way to get things back on track. He could tell that she was having a great time, and he had never seen her smile or laugh so much. What had gone wrong, though? He couldn't figure it out. He washed and dried his hands and walked up to Raven in the living room. She was looking through his music, trying to find something appropriate to put on, something that matched her mood. Unfortunately, she didn't know what it was.

Ashton stood next to her. His feelings and desires were building into a crescendo that threatened to burst forth at any moment. Since first seeing her that night, he struggled against losing control. He didn't have expectations of her, but he wanted her. He didn't want her to think he took her for granted since they had already been intimate.

She pulled a CD from the rack and turned to face him.

"What do you think about this?"

She couldn't finish by showing it to him as Ashton pulled her to him and kissed her. She put her hands on his chest and gently pushed him back. He looked confused at the perceived rejection when Raven held up the CD and tossed it onto a magazine on the coffee table. Then she turned back into his embrace and put her hand back on his chest. The firmness of his body and the warmth of his skin radiating through his shirt intoxicated her with desire. His lips closed on her mouth, and she surrendered to her need for his kisses. His soft, luscious mouth opened and closed first around her upper lip and then her bottom lip. Her hands began to roam over his barreled chest, which rippled as he moved his hands over her back. His hands were like furnaces, emanating heat into her wherever he touched her. They caressed her and pulled her closer to him. His left hand moved along the curve of her back to her shoulder, and his right hand slid up over the curve of her hip, fingertips teasing her rump as his wrist brushed against the side of her heaving breast. Their tongues met between their mouths, sliding over each others' lips and dancing in circles. Then he pulled her tighter to him. She gasped and drew his tongue into her mouth, sucking it and caressing it with her own. She could hear the desire in his breath, and she felt his need against her, growing and throbbing. She wanted to take him and be taken, to give and receive.

He withdrew his mouth from their kiss, and she moaned in disappointment until his mouth found her neck. He kissed his way up from the base of her neck to behind her ear. Each time his mouth lifted, he would drag his lips against her skin and place them back, sucking her flesh with raw passion. His hunger grew for her flesh, her sex, and her blood. It felt like he needed to fulfill his purpose. As he kissed her ear, hot breath brought shivers to her body. He teased her earlobe with his teeth and his tongue.

He thought of telling her that he wanted her, loved her, and needed her. He surprised himself with what he said.

"You are mine, Raven."

"Yes," was her only verbal response, but her body changed at that utterance. Her heat spread, as did her hunger - her need to have Ashton inside her was undeniable and inescapable.

His mouth covered hers and their tongues entwined as their bodies would soon.

He pulled his mouth away again and looked at her. Her hair was down over her eyes, but nothing could hide the burning passion blazing inside those brown pools of love. She bit her lip as each second he wasn't kissing her felt like a thousand years of loneliness. She put her hands behind his neck, feeling his curls tangle in her fingers. She closed her fingers over his curls and tried to pull his mouth back to hers. Instead, he dipped down and lifted her into his arms. His right arm was holding her under her knees, and his left arm was around her back, his hand spread out to support her shoulder. He carried her to the bedroom.

By the time they were at the door to the bedroom, Raven had switched her position. He no longer carried her like a blushing bride. She had her legs locked around his waist, and her hands ran through his hair as they held his head. As Ashton fumbled with the door and finally pushed it open, Raven straightened her back and pulled his head to her chest. He could feel her turgid nipples straining against her lacy bodice and silky gown.

He took a few strides to his bed while pulling his arms from his sleeves as Raven pushed his shirt back and over his broad shoulders. With a shrug, it fell on the floor behind them. He ran his hands down over her bottom and followed the curves of her powerful legs. When his fingers touched the hem of her dress, he grasped it and began lifting it over her shapely and firm ass. As it peeled over her breasts, their weight fell against his chest and sent ripples of desire throughout his body. When he lifted it over her head, she shook her head free, her straight hair bouncing slightly with the movement. Their eyes met, mirroring passion, desire, and hunger. She tentatively thrust her mouth forward, leading with her chin, opening it hungrily. As Ashton moved to meet it, she pulled back, using her forehead to keep him at bay. Again and again, she repeated this dance, and again and again, he grunted with disappointment when she did so. She put her finger on his mouth and hushed him. He kissed her finger and pulled it into his mouth, circling the tip with his tongue and sucking on it with rabid pressure.

She pushed away from him and landed on the edge of the bed. She wore a black lace negligee, silk stockings, and polished black patent leather high heels. Ashton lifted his undershirt over his head, and her fingers expertly unbuckled his belt. She unfastened his slacks and pulled them and his light blue boxers down to his feet. His manhood sprung free from the confines of his boxers. It brushed her cheek, and fire throbbed between her legs as her body remembered what it did to her. She wanted to take him into her mouth, taste his passionate flesh and feel its throbbing, pulsating glory.

"Oh my God..." he moaned in ecstasy as her hot, wet tongue danced and flicked off the head of his engorged member. She pushed her head and mouth forward, taking more of him in. She rocked her head back, his length slowly coming out from between her lips. She looked up at him, sucking and licking with a passion she had never experienced. A slow moan - sensual and exciting - broke the silence in the room. Over and over, she bobbed her head while exploring him with her tongue. She held his throbbing flesh in one hand and moved her tongue over the jerking shaft. When she moved to take him back into her mouth, he gently pushed back on her shoulder with one hand while caressing her face with his other. She knew what he expected of her and lay back on the bed.

He rose to kiss her mouth while his hand roamed her body.

"My turn to taste you, my sweet Raven."

His hand glided over her breasts and sensitive nipples and then slid down her flat stomach to the thin patch of dark hair between her legs. On their own, her legs spread, and he began to slide his body down hers. He didn't rush or neglect her with his mouth. Down her right breast, he kissed and sucked on her skin. When his lips met the top of her lacy bodice, he clenched it between his teeth and pulled it down to expose her firm, heavy breast. He kissed along the curve of her breast, tasting and breathing in her essence. When he touched the halo surrounding her nipple with the tip of his tongue, she arched her back and released a soulful and lustful hiss. His warm breath flowed over her olive skin, which seemed to glow in the soft moonlight that filled the room. He kissed her breast all around her nipple, careful not to brush against it. He moved his right hand to cover her other fleshy mound, squeezing hard and pushing it against her chest. Her writhing grew as he freed her other breast from the bodice. On one breast, his hand mirrored what his mouth did on the other. Where his lips touched her left breast, his finger rubbed her right. Closer and closer, his mouth and tongue moved toward her nipples. Her heart pounded faster, and she pulled at him, becoming more desperate to have him find her treasure. With his right hand, he cupped her breast from the bottom and squeezed it as he lowered his mouth around the dark circle surrounding her firm nipple. He sucked, pulling the nipple up as he slowly placed his tongue underneath it at its base. Her hands clasped the back of his head and demanded more of his ministrations. He rolled his thumb up the other nipple while slowly sliding his tongue up the one in his mouth. She squeezed his head, opened her hands, grasped more of his hair, and pulled him harder to her. She was groaning with pleasure and lost in bliss. He quickened the pace of his tongue, sucking and flicking around her nipple, pulling it into his mouth while he lifted his head, allowing it slowly to escape into the cool air between their bodies. As it popped out of his mouth, she cried out, an unintelligible sound that communicated despair on a primal level. Instead of returning his mouth to her nipple, he kissed his way down her taut stomach as it rose and fell with her passionate breathing. Her taste and the smell of her skin, of her, were intoxicating. Her warm, soft and supple skin belied the compact muscles he knew were underneath. As he kissed his way further down, he lifted his left hand and grasped the breast he had just abandoned on his way to other erotic frontiers. Soon, he felt the soft lace fringe of her panties as his chin ran over them. The fabric slid down, then snapped back to its original position, guarding the hot sweet dripping treat between her shifting legs. He could smell her desire but refused to hurry. He lightly kissed the border of her panties and then drifted down further with his eager kisses.

Raven was overwhelmed with pleasure and nearly frantic as her patience wore thin as she waited for Ashton's teasing kisses to reach her molten core. She wanted to scream with anticipation but refused to succumb. Raven ran her hands down his neck to his broad shoulders. She moved her hands, occasionally stopping to squeeze them in response to waves of ecstasy that crashed into her body.

He lifted his head and looked at her. Sensing his attention, she pulled her shoulders from the bed and looked at him. He drank in her beauty and smiled a drugged smile as he drifted further into the ocean of pleasure that pulled him to her. Keeping his eyes on hers, he lowered his mouth to the sweet crown of her burning lust. The contact was electric, and Raven threw her head back and grasped the edge of the bed, pulling the sheets in fistfuls. He gently grunted in pleasure as her body responded to his kiss. Ashton's lips drifted lower and lower. He stopped when he could feel the heat radiating from her entrance in sweet waves of need. He kissed all around the wet fabric between his lips and her. Slowly, he pulled his right hand down from her breast, allowing it to follow every contour of her lithe body. She lifted her back in anticipation of his removing the only barrier that remained between them, but his hand continued to slide down. As it reached the top of her left leg, he slid his index finger under the lace of her panties and gently lifted it as he followed the curve of the fabric down towards her center. As he moved his hand lower and lower, his mouth moved higher and higher, returning to its perch as his finger slid into her.

She squeezed her legs around him, locking her heels around his shoulders. Her hands slid behind his head as she drew him to her. Pleasure poured into her body from his hand on her breasts as he tugged her nipple and gently twisted it between his thumb and fingers, from his mouth and his other hand as his finger entered and exited her with excruciating slowness. He slid his left hand up her breast as he began to kiss his way back up her body. As he reached her mouth with his, their tongues touched. His right hand left her heat, and he shifted his body up, forcing her legs to part wide to accommodate his massive frame. He switched to his right hand and slid his left hand back to her panties, and pulled them aside, allowing him to push into her hot passage. He grunted, and she moaned. Her hands dropped to his buttocks and squeezed as she pushed herself up to meet his thrusts.

She had never felt such pleasure, and she was sure that no matter how long she lived, she would never find another man that would give her such wonderful and mind-bending delight.

He pushed himself up enough that he could look into her eyes. At first, she turned her head to the side and closed her eyes.

"Is she offering me her neck?" he thought.

He kissed her neck, her cheek, and then her mouth. He continued to thrust into her with long, slow, purposeful movements of his hips. Each time he sank into her, she responded with sighs and moans. His pleasure intensified, and he knew he was approaching release. He pulled his face away from her mouth and looked at her beauty. Her eyes were swimming in the pleasure they shared, impassioned by feelings neither had spoken. He sensed that she was also nearing climax. He stared into her eyes as he quickened his pace. She raised her arms to clench her hands around his back, placing her hands around his broad shoulders. She lifted herself to him, frantically kissing him on his mouth. She tilted her chin down and watched him sink into her, fascinated and further aroused by what she saw.

This sight sent her to the brink. Ashton must have sensed this as his rhythm seemed to have doubled. With reckless abandon, he bore into her, no longer concerned about being tender or sensual. His rutting became urgent and wild.

When he felt the deep pulsing tugs inside her, he thrust into her and exploded, filling her with his manhood and seed. She dug her nails into his shoulders as she arched her back and pulled him into her, desperate for him to fill her. Seconds stretched into eternity as their simultaneous release crashed into and washed over their bodies and souls in wave after wave of ecstasy. Once spent, he lay on top of her and kissed her deeply.

He cupped her cheek in her hand and noticed that she had tears trickling from the corners of her eyes. At first, he was alarmed that he had hurt her somehow and began to pull away from her. Then, she put her hand on his cheek.

"Shh, it's OK, I'm fine...better than fine."

Her sad smile offered little comfort.

"Then why are you crying?" he asked her, clearly upset by this unexpected event. He brushed her tears away with his thumb, and then he moved his hand to the other side of her face and brushed those away with the back of his forefinger.

She half laughed, half sobbed, "because I'm silly."

She looked at him, hoping that he wouldn't pursue it further.

"Hey, come on, Raven, don't do that. You know I care for you very much."

She smiled despite herself. She did know, and she felt the same. As if reading her mind, Ashton lightly poked his finger on the tip of her nose with each word.

"I bet you like me too, don't you?"

She rolled her eyes at this.

"Because I can't stop thinking about you. Since before I met you, I was captivated by you and your beauty."

She seemed confused until she realized he must be referring to blood memories.

"Even then, I felt a sort of familiarity or a sense that I knew you - like we knew each other. But when I met you, I was blown away, love at first sight if you want to call it that."

He shrugged, "I know it sounds corny, but it's true."

She grabbed his finger and kissed the tip of it. Then she pulled his mouth to hers and kissed him softly.

"I like corny. There's nothing wrong with corny." She kissed him again, and he knew she wanted to get up.

He slid to the side and let her use one of his hands to pull herself to her feet. She turned to face him, and he was once again stunned by her beauty. Even with her hair all messed up, and maybe because of it, she was not just beautiful - she was sexy, unlike any woman he had ever seen. She caught him staring at her and blushed.

He continued to stare and then smiled a guilty smile.

"What?" she asked.

"You!" he replied, offering nothing more.

"What about me?" she asked, stepping one leg over his so that both of his legs were between hers. Then she put her hands on her hips and teasingly glared down at him.

He put his hands behind his head and tilted it to the side. He pushed his lips out in a fake frown and shrugged.

"Ashton!" she warned.

"You really want to know?"

"Yes! Tell me," she sounded alarmed as if she was thinking the worst.

"You," he said as he looked her up and down, resting his eyes on hers, "are the most beautiful woman I have ever seen."

Her face softened, and she smiled at the compliment. Then, she ran her eyes over him.

"You aren't so bad yourself, you know."

She climbed on top of him. She felt him grow hard against her. He reached out to grab hold of her, but she locked her fingers around his and fell forward, pushing his hands over his head against the bed. Her body pressed against his. She playfully kissed him, dodging his mouth as he tried to kiss hers.

"Hey! No fair!" he said while pretending to try to lift his arms. Within a few minutes, their playful taunts led to more serious activities. They spent the remainder of that night making love and exploring each other's passions.

Chapter 43

Raven entered the driveway to Gitlam's estate but didn't pull up to the gate. She stopped the car and stared ahead. Ashton wondered if she was staring at memories and saying goodbye to a happier time when she would enter the grounds and see some old friends. He was partly right, as those thoughts did cross her mind. She was filled with apprehension and relief. She was happy that she was now free of Claud and would never deal with Trevor again. But some nagging corner in her mind told her that something else would change and that it would not be for the better.

She leaned forward and almost turned the car around when the gate slowly opened to welcome her and Ashton. She slowly lifted her foot off the brake pedal and pressed it onto the gas pedal. The care crept forward along the long, twisting driveway. Fog crept in out of the woods and onto the blacktop, making it shine with dampness. The stillness in the air, the mounting trepidation, and the general sense of the unknown acted in concert upon Raven's calm demeanor, and she trembled.

Ashton saw her sitting on the edge of the seat, wide-eyed and almost frantic. When she trembled, he reached out and put his hand on her leg, feeling the smooth fabric of her stockings pressed coolly against her skin. He squeezed gently.

"If you want to turn around and leave, I am with you. If you want to go through with this, I am with you also. Just let me do something, OK?"

She didn't look at him, but he felt her tension ease, and she no longer trembled. The heat from his hand spread a calm warmth throughout her body and eased her racing mind. He took one hand from the steering wheel and grabbed his. Their fingers entwined, then she lifted his hand to her lips, kissed it softly, and then nuzzled her cheek against it. She squeezed his hand and let it go.

Moments later, they stood in front of the massive oaken doors that led into the sprawling mansion. Granite columns framed the door and were expertly carved into figures of a man and woman, each supporting another slab of granite that spanned the top of the door.

"You ready?" she asked Ashton.

"I was born ready," he replied.

Then, they heard the scream.

Epilogue

Her eyes shot open and absolute darkness greeted her. Regardless of which direction she looked, the black scene before her did not change. She lifted her hands to check her face, but they crashed into a hard surface above where she lay before she could straighten them at the elbow. The woman wondered why she was lying down. Instinctively, she began patting around her and discovered she was inside of something made of metal. The metal felt very cold to the touch.

"Hello?" she called out, trying to remain calm.

"Hello?" she repeated uncertainly.

She listened for a response, but none came. The only sound she could hear was a faint humming sound.

The woman lay still and wondered where she was and how she got there. She tried to remember what had happened to her. Suddenly her mind filled with sights and sounds foreign to her. Then, she saw herself through someone else's eyes, through Trevor's eyes.

"No!" she whimpered and thrashed about in a wild panic.

Fragmented images of her sitting in traffic, listening to music, and driving played in her mind's eye. Then, completely disjointed snippets of an impossibly loud sound followed by airbags exploding and glass flying revealed to her what had happened. The next thing she remembered was opening her eyes a few moments ago.

"Oh, God, no!" Julia cried, and her frenzy grew. Kicking and thrashing at the metallic tomb she found herself in for what seemed like hours but was only minutes, her desperate flailing continued, with no results other than exhaustion. There the hysterical woman lay, chest heaving and mind racing. Despite the utter darkness, she looked around, trying to find something that would help her escape.

"Calm down. Just breath," She urged herself " and think!"

Her eyes grew wide, and she managed to cover her mouth in horror as she realized where she was. She was in one of those things in the morgue where they put dead people. Then, her heart stopped pounding as she slowly placed her hand on her chest, searching for those terrible scars she had seen on countless TV shows. She had heard them called Y-Incisions, and never had they been as terrifying as just then. The long sigh she let escape calmed her as not finding the ghastly evidence of an autopsy did.

She carefully maneuvered her arms above her head and reached back into the darkness. Her palms hit the end of the chamber where she lay. Next, she pushed her feet towards the other end, where she thought the door was. The tray she lay on also slid towards the door until she heard a slight thud when it made contact. She gathered her strength and pushed. Besides a louder thud, nothing happened. Over and over, she tried to force the door open and failed.

Then, she heard faint voices speaking in hushed tones.

"I told you, I heard it," a gravelly man's voice whispered.

"So?" A woman replied, fear evident in her voice.

"So, we have to check it out. You know the procedure. We have to investigate all unexplained occurrences."

"You check it out, and I will keep an eye on the hallway." The woman's voice was hopeful at the suggestion.

"Ever hear anything like this before?" The man asked, obviously trying to stall, a trace of his Mexican accent making itself known.

"No, never," she replied.

Julia stayed motionless, not knowing if she wanted them to help or not.

"It stopped," the man said, "let's just go back to the station."

"OK," the woman agreed.

The sounds of sneakers squeaking on the floor jarred Julia into action. She couldn't get out, and the only chance she had was about to leave. She banged on the door and screamed.

"Let me out! Help! Please!"

A few moments later, a door opened, and light flooded her dark tomb, temporarily blinding Julia. Only by squinting could she make out the people who had freed her from her appalling prison.

"Thank you! Thank you so much!" Julia sobbed, "I couldn't get out of there. I didn't know what was going on!"

The short, overweight lady stared at her in shock. She seemed to be middle-aged. Next to her, and closest to Julia's head, stood the man, a concerned look on his face. He appeared to be middle-aged as well.

"It's OK. It's OK," he said, looking frantically around the room. "Someone made a mistake. You aren't..." he trailed off, not wanting to say what he was thinking.

Julia pulled herself up to a sitting position, and the tray she lay on slid forward further and startled the lady into a short scream. Julia felt the sheet that covered her body slide off and realized she was naked. She hid her nakedness as best she could with her arms.

"Can you please get me something to wear? Where are my clothes?" Julia looked around. Instead of finding her clothes, she saw the various tools, containers, and other equipment used to process the dead.

The man put his arm around her shoulders and gently took her arm.

"Come on, let's get you down from there." He took a paternal tone with her, and it did comfort her. Once she had made it to her feet, he took the sheet and draped it around her shoulders and body. It was long enough to provide her with a sense of modesty. She looked down her front and made sure nothing showed. It was then that she noticed the toe tag. Balancing on one foot, she bent her leg and lifted the foot with the toe tag to her hand that wasn't clutching the sheet closed. She pulled at it to get it off of her toe. Eventually, the thin twine snapped, and she looked at the tag. It had her name in the box labeled "Name of Deceased." If that wasn't bad enough, the cause of death nearly made her faint.

"Combined effects of traumatic and thermal injuries."

She looked for a mirror and didn't see one. Looking over her body and even opening the sheet and inspecting her front, she didn't see any injuries. There were some pink blotches of skin here and there, but she assumed it was from being on the tray.

She gasped in understanding.

"What time is it?" she asked the stunned employees.

She looked and saw that the woman had a watch on her wrist. Julia shook her by her shoulders and repeated the question. The woman still didn't answer, so Julia grabbed and turned her wrist so that she could read the time - "03:15".

"AM or PM?" she asked.

"Uh, AM, we are the graveyard shift." The man slightly cringed when he said the word graveyard.

"I need clothes. Where are my things?"

The man walked to a terminal and entered data into the screens. A few moments later, he turned around to face Julia.

"It says here that you have no personal effects. Your clothing was unrecoverable due to fire damage, and you didn't have any jewelry on your body. I mean on your person."

"Shit!" Julia cursed. "I need clothes!"

She began to pace around the small medical bay.

"Don't they have scrubs or whatever they are? You know, for the medical staff?"

"Yeah! Hold on." The man walked towards the door, alarming Julia.

"Where are you going?" Julia asked in a trembling voice.

"To get you some scrubs, they are just down the hall. It'll only take a minute."

"Please, hurry!" Julia begged.

He quickly returned with a few plastic wrapped pouches that contained booties, pants, and a shirt, all a dark green color. Julia thanked the man and got dressed. He turned away while she did. The woman stared at her body in disbelief.

"They said you was burnt...burnt to a crisp."

Julia registered what she was saying. She ignored it, not wanting to try to find a believable explanation.

Once dressed, Julia said she needed a ride. After some debate, the man offered to take her where she wanted to go. Julia had to try to cover her tracks and gave her best effort to compel the woman to forget all that had happened to her tonight. Once the man dropped her off at the apartment complex, she gave him similar instructions, including that he had to return to work and then forget everything.

She had to force her way into her apartment as her keys were probably still in her car which must be in the junkyard by now. So was her phone. She changed into her own clothes and then went to Ashton's apartment. He didn't answer the door. She thought about breaking in but didn't want to cause alarm when he returned. She cursed herself for not bringing paper and a pen to write him a letter. In the end, she decided to try him again the next night. She was growing more tired by the moment and went back to her apartment for a rest.

As Julia slipped into her first slumber as a vampire, Raven and Ashton were headed to Gitlam's estate. It would take days for Julia to realize that she was on her own.

www.ingramcontent.com/pod-product-compliance
Lightning Source LLC
Chambersburg PA
CBHW070224260626
47160CB00002B/681